THE
KAISER'S
WEB

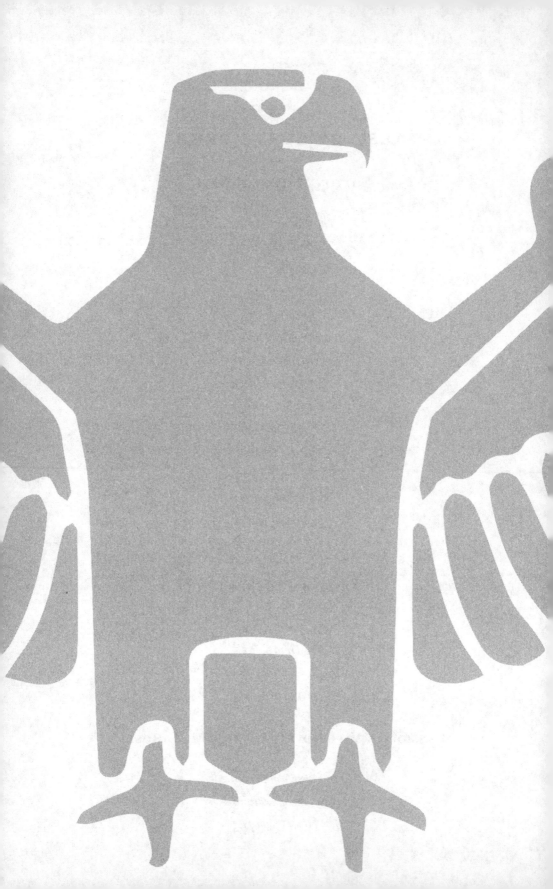

THE
KAISER'S
WEB

STEVE
BERRY

MINOTAUR
BOOKS
NEW YORK

First published in the United States by Minotaur Books, an imprint of St. Martin's Publishing Group

THE KAISER'S WEB. Copyright © 2021 by Steve Berry. All rights reserved. Printed in the United States of America. For information, address St. Martin's Publishing Group, 120 Broadway, New York, NY 10271.

www.minotaurbooks.com

Library of Congress Cataloging-in-Publication Data

Names: Berry, Steve, 1955– author.
Title: The kaiser's web / Steve Berry.
Description: First edition. | New York : Minotaur Books, 2021. |
    Series: Cotton Malone ; 16 |
Identifiers: LCCN 2020040135 | ISBN 9781250140340 (hardcover) |
    ISBN 9781250797988 (international, sold outside the U.S., subject to rights
    availability) | ISBN 9781250140357 (ebook)
Subjects: LCSH: Malone, Cotton (Fictitious character)—Fiction. | Political
    fiction. | GSAFD: Suspense fiction. | Spy stories. | LCGFT: Novels.
Classification: LCC PS3602.E764 K35 2021 | DDC 813/.6—dc23
LC record available at https://lccn.loc.gov/2020040135

Our books may be purchased in bulk for promotional, educational, or business use. Please contact your local bookseller or the Macmillan Corporate and Premium Sales Department at 1-800-221-7945, extension 5442, or by email at MacmillanSpecialMarkets@macmillan.com.

First Edition: 2021

10 9 8 7 6 5 4 3 2 1

For Kelley Ragland,
A world-class editor and an even better person

ACKNOWLEDGMENTS

Again, my sincere thanks to Don Weisberg, Macmillan's chief executive officer, Sally Richardson who serves as chairman of St. Martin's Publishing, Jen Enderlin who captains St. Martin's, and my publisher at Minotaur, Andrew Martin. Also, a huge debt of gratitude continues for Hector DeJean in Publicity; Jeff Dodes and everyone in Marketing and Sales, especially Paul Hochman and Danielle Prielipp; Anne Marie Tallberg, the sage of all things paperback; David Rotstein, who produced the cover; and Mary Beth Roche and her innovative folks in Audio.

A huge bow, as always, goes to Simon Lipskar, my agent and friend.

Also a big thank-you to Madeline Houpt, who makes things happen for me at Minotaur. Then there's Meryl Moss and her extraordinary publicity team (especially Deb Zipf), along with Jessica Johns and Esther Garver who continue to keep Steve Berry Enterprises running smoothly.

As always, to my wife, Elizabeth, who remains the most special of all.

For the past seven years Kelley Ragland has been my editor. When I moved from Random House to Macmillan in 2014 I came with a lot of anxiety. Thirteen years with one house, one editor, one team had settled me into a comfortable routine. I was worried that things would not be the same.

And I was right, they were not.

Instead they were even better.

And it all started with Kelley.

She's a lovely lady with a warm heart, gentle manner, and infectious smile. She never raises her voice or gets angry. Never a foul word or a derogatory comment.

But she has opinions.

And when she offers those, I follow that advice. After seven years I've come to know what others before me already knew. She's smart, savvy, and first-class all the way.

So this one's for you, Kelley.

Thank you.

For everything.

The masses have little time to think.
And how incredible is the willingness
of modern man to believe.

—ADOLF HITLER

THE
KAISER'S
WEB

PROLOGUE

Danny Daniels liked the freedom of not being president of the United States. Make no mistake, he'd loved being president. And for eight years he'd performed the job to the best of his ability. But he really cherished his life as it was now. Able to move about. Go where he wanted. When he wanted.

He'd refused any after-office Secret Service protection, which was his right, spinning it by saying he wanted to save taxpayers the money. But the truth was he liked not having babysitters. If somebody wanted to hurt him, then have at it. He was anything but helpless, and ex-presidents had never been much of a threat to anyone.

Sure, he was recognized.

It went with the territory.

Whenever it happened, as his mother taught him, he was gracious and accommodating. But here, deep in southern Bavaria, on a rainy, late-spring Saturday morning, the chances of that happening were slim. And besides, he'd been out of office for six months. Practically an eternity in politics. Now he was the junior senator from the great state of Tennessee. Here to help a friend.

Why?

Because that's what friends did for one another.

He'd easily located the police station in Partenkirchen. The mountain town intertwined with Garmisch so closely that it was difficult to tell where one municipality ended and the other began. The granite edifice sat within sight of the old Olympic ice stadium built, he knew, in 1936 when Germany last had hosted the Winter Games. Beyond, in the distance, evergreen Alpine slopes, laced with ski runs, no longer carried much snow.

He'd come to speak with a woman being held on direct orders from the chancellor of Germany. Her birth name was Hanna Cress. Yesterday, a Europol inquiry revealed that she was a Belarusian citizen with no criminal history. They'd also been able to learn from online records that she owned an apartment in an upscale Minsk building, drove a C-Class Mercedes, and had traveled out of Belarus fourteen times in the past year, all with no obvious means of employment.

Apparently no one had schooled her in the art of discretion.

Something big was happening.

He could feel it.

Important enough that his old friend, the German chancellor herself, had personally asked for his assistance.

Which he'd liked. It was good to be needed.

He found Hanna Cress in a small interrogation room adorned with no windows, bright lights, and a gritty tile floor. She was sitting at a table nursing a cigarette, the air thick with blue smoke that burned his eyes. He'd come into the room alone and closed the door, requesting that no one either observe or record the conversation, per the instructions of the chancellor.

"Why am I being held?" she said matter-of-factly in good English.

"Somebody thought this would be a great place for you and me to get acquainted." He wasn't going to let her get the better of him.

She exhaled another cloud of smoke. "Why send American president to talk to me? This doesn't concern you."

He shrugged and sat, laying a manila envelope on the table.

So much for not being recognized.

"I'm not president anymore. Just a guy."

She laughed. "Like saying gold just a metal."

Good point.

"I came to Germany to deliver envelope," she said, pointing. "Not be arrested. Now an American president wants to talk?"

"Looks like it's your special day. I'm here helping out a friend. Marie Eisenhuth."

"The revered chancellor of Germany. *Oma* herself."

He smiled at the nickname. Grandmother. Of the nation. A reference surely to both her age and the long time Eisenhuth had served as chancellor. No term limits existed in Germany. You stayed as long as the people wanted you. He actually liked that system.

She savored another deep drag of her cigarette, then stubbed out the butt in an ashtray. "You came to talk. We talk. Then maybe you let me go."

This woman had appeared yesterday in Garmisch for a rendezvous that had been arranged through a series of emails to the chancellor's office from a man named Gerhard Schüb. The idea had been to facilitate a transfer of documents from Schüb, with Cress as the messenger. Which happened. Hence, the envelope. Then Cress had been taken into custody. Why? Good question, one that his old friend the chancellor had not fully answered. But who was he to argue with methodology. He was just glad to be in the mix.

"Who is Gerhard Schüb?" he asked.

She smiled, and the expression accented a bruise on the right side of her face. The stain marred what were otherwise striking features. Her skin was a milky white, and the features of her mouth and nose made her attractive in a stark kind of way, though her blue eyes were misty and distant.

"He is man trying to help," she said.

Not an answer. "I'll ask again. Who is Gerhard Schüb?"

"A man who knows great deal." She motioned to the envelope. "And he is sharing some of what he knows."

"Why doesn't he come forward himself?"

"He does not want to be found. Not even for *Oma*." She paused. "Or ex-presidents. He send me." She stared at him hard. "You don't understand any of this, do you?"

Through the insult he caught the unspoken message.

There is more here than you know.

"There are people and things, from past, that still have meaning today," she said. "Great meaning, in fact. As German chancellor will find out—if she pursues this matter. Tell *Oma* to be diligent."

"Toward what?"

"Victory."

An odd answer, but he let it pass. He lifted the envelope. "Inside here is a sheet with numbers on it. They look like GPS coordinates. Are they?"

She nodded. "It is a place, I am told, you need to visit."

"Why?"

She shrugged. "How would I know? I just messenger."

"You didn't bother to mention any of this yesterday."

"Never got chance. Before arrested and hit in face."

Which explained the bruise.

"I read the other papers in the envelope," he said. "They talk of things that have been over for a long time. World War Two. Hitler. Nazis."

She laughed, short and shallow. "Amazing how history can have meaning. Pay attention, Ex-President, you might learn things."

He could see she was going to be difficult.

But he specialized in difficult. "Is Gerhard Schüb my instructor?"

"Herr Schüb is only trying to help."

"To what end?"

She smiled. "To find truth. What else?"

She reached for the pack of cigarettes. He decided another smoke might loosen her tongue so he allowed her the privilege. She quickly lit up, and two deep drags seemed to relax her.

He needed to know more.

Especially about the origins of the documents in the envelope.

Her eyes changed first. A forlorn, pensive gaze replaced by sudden fear, then pain, then desperation. The muscles in her face tightened and contorted in a look that signaled agony. Her fingers released their grip on the cigarette. Hands reached for her throat. Her tongue sprang from her mouth and she gagged, trying to suck air. Spittle foamed, then seeped from her lips.

He came to his feet and tried to help. She grabbed his jacket with both hands, her eyes wide with terror.

"Kai . . . ser."

She strangled one last breath, then her head fell to one side as the muscles in her neck surrendered. Her grip relaxed and she slumped over in the chair. On the waft of her last exhale came a tinge of bitter almond.

A smell he recognized.

Cyanide.

He stared at the pack of cigarettes on the table, the butt still burning on the floor.

What the hell?

And what did she mean by—

Kaiser.

THREE
DAYS
LATER

CHAPTER ONE

REPUBLIC OF BELARUS
TUESDAY, JUNE 11
8:50 A.M.

COTTON MALONE KNEW THE SIGNS OF TROUBLE. HE SHOULD, since he lived in that perilous state more often than not. Take today. It started off innocent enough with breakfast at the superb Beijing Hotel. A touch of the Orient in a former Soviet bloc nation. First class all the way, as it should be, since he had company on this journey.

"I hate planes," Cassiopeia Vitt said.

He smiled. "Tell me something I don't know."

They were five thousand feet in the air, headed southwest toward Poland. Below stretched miles of unpopulated forest, the towns few and far between. They'd come east as a favor to former president Danny Daniels, who'd appeared in Copenhagen two days ago with a problem. The chancellor of Germany was looking for someone named Gerhard Schüb. A Belarusian woman named Hanna Cress had appeared in Bavaria with some incredible information, then had been murdered, but not before uttering one word.

Kaiser.

"Do you think the two of you could take a quick trip to Minsk and see if you can learn more about her and/or Gerhard Schüb?" Daniels had asked.

So they'd chartered a plane and flown from Denmark yesterday morning, making inquiries all day.

Which had attracted attention.

"Do you think we can get out of this country in one piece?" she asked.

"I'd say it's about fifty–fifty."

"I don't like those odds."

He grinned. "We've made it this far."

They'd barely escaped the hotel after the *militsiya* arrived in search of them. Then they'd made it to the airport just ahead of their pursuers only to find that the plane they'd arrived in yesterday had been confiscated. So he did what any enterprising bookseller who'd once served as an intelligence officer for the United States Justice Department would do, and stole another.

"I really hate planes," she said again. "Especially ones I can barely move around in."

Their choice of rides had been limited, and he'd settled for a GA8 Airvan. Australian made. Single engine, strut-based wing, all metal, with an odd, asymmetrical shape. *A bit squared-off and boxy* would be a more accurate description. Designed for rough airstrips and bush landings. He'd flown one a few years ago and liked it. On this model the eight rear seats were gone, making for a somewhat roomy cabin behind them. Advertisements painted to the fuselage confirmed that this was a skydiving plane, and it had been easy to hot-wire the engine to life.

He watched as she studied the ground out the windows.

"It's not that bad," he said.

"That's all relative."

She was gorgeous. The Latin–Arab gene mix definitely produced some exceptionally attractive women. Add in being smart and savvy with the courage of a lioness, and what was not to love. Little rattled her save for she loathed the cold, and where he hated enclosed spaces she detested heights. Unfortunately, neither of them seemed to be able to avoid either.

"Do you know where we are?" she asked.

"I'd say north of Brest, which sits right on the Polish border. I was hoping to catch a glimpse of the town, off to the south."

He'd dead reckoned their course, keeping the morning sun behind them and following the dash compass on a southwest heading. Too far north and they'd end up in Lithuania, which could continue their troubles. Poland was where they wanted to be, safe back in the EU. The

Belarus State Security Committee remained the closest thing to the old Soviet KGB that still existed. It had even kept the same shorthand name, along with the rep as a major human rights violator. Torture, executions, beatings, you name it, those guys were guilty. So he preferred not to experience any of their methods firsthand.

He kept a light grip on the yoke, which sprang up from the floor rather than sticking out of the control panel. He had excellent visibility through the forward and side windows. The sky ahead loomed clear, the ground below a sea of dense trees. A road ran in a dark, winding path among them with an occasional farmhouse here and there.

He loved flying.

A plane was, to him, like a being unto itself. Flying was once supposed to have been his career. But things changed. Which, considering his life, seemed like an understatement.

He made a quick scan of the controls. Airspeed, eighty knots. Fuel, forty-five gallons. Electrical, all good. Controls, responsive.

Below, to the south, he caught sight of Brest in the distance.

Perfect.

"There's our marker," he said. "The border's not far."

They'd made good time on the 120 miles from Minsk. Once inside Poland he'd find a commercial airport to land where they could make their way out of the country on the first available flight. Far too risky to keep using this stolen ride.

He backed off the throttle, slowed their speed, and adjusted the flaps, allowing the Airvan to drop to a thousand feet. He intended on crossing at low altitude, under the radar.

"Here we go," he said.

He kept the trim stable, the two-bladed propellers' timbre never varying. The engine seemed to be working with no complaints. A few knocks rippled across the wings from the low-level air, but nothing alarming.

Then he saw it.

A flash.

Among the trees.

Followed by a projectile emerging from the canopy, heading straight for them.

He yanked the yoke and banked in a tight, pinpoint maneuver that angled the wings nearly perpendicular to the ground. Luckily, the Airvan had game and could handle the turn, but their slow speed worked against them and they began to fall.

The projectile exploded above them.

"An RPG," he said, working the yoke and forcing the throttle forward, increasing speed. "Apparently we haven't been forgotten."

He leveled off the trim and prepared to climb.

To hell with under the radar. They were being attacked.

"Incoming," Cassiopeia yelled, her attention out the windshield.

"Where?"

"Two. Both sides."

Great.

He maxed out the throttle and angled the flaps for a steep climb.

Two explosions occurred. One was far off, causing no damage, but the other left a smoldering hole in one wing.

The engine sputtered.

He reached for the fuel mixture and shut down the left wing tanks, hoping that would keep air out of the line. They were still gaining altitude, but the engine began to struggle for life.

"That's not good," Cassiopeia said.

"No, it's not."

He fought the lumps and bumps, the yoke bucking between his legs. "I know you don't want to hear this. But we're going down."

CHAPTER TWO

Cassiopeia did not want to hear that.

Not in the least.

The plane continued to buck. Nothing about this scenario seemed good. Her gaze darted to the altimeter, and she noted that they were approaching a thousand meters.

"Why are we going up?" she asked.

Cotton was fighting the plane's controls, which seemed to resist his every command. "Beats the hell out of down. Unstrap and go back and see if there are any parachutes."

She stared at him with disbelief, but knew better than to argue. He was doing the best he could to keep them in the air, and for that she was grateful. She released the buckle and slipped out of the shoulder straps.

The plane lurched hard.

She grabbed the back of her seat, then stumbled into the rear compartment. Benches lined either side of the open space. Other than those, nothing else was there.

"It's empty," she called out.

"Look inside the benches," Cotton said.

She lunged for the right side of the plane and dropped to her knees. She grabbed the bench and lifted the long cushion, which was hinged.

Inside lay one parachute. She freed it from the compartment, then shifted to the other side and opened the bench. Empty.

Only one parachute?

Come on.

COTTON KEPT FIGHTING.

Roll and pitch seemed responsive, but it took effort to maneuver. He had to be careful to avoid a stall. He retracted the flaps, which increased speed. Planes were judged on what they carried, where they could go, and how fast they got there. Under the circumstances, this one was doing great.

The RPG had damaged the wing and control surfaces. Fuel was spilling out from the carnage, draining part of the half-full tanks they'd had at takeoff. The engine continued to struggle, the prop not so much biting as gumming the air. The yoke had gone loose between his legs, which meant he'd probably cracked the cowl flaps on the climb. But he managed to level off with positive trim at just over four thousand feet.

All along they'd continued southwest.

No more projectiles had come from the ground, which he hoped meant they'd crossed into Poland. But that was impossible to know, as nothing but trees stretched below.

The control stick wrenched from his hand and the plane stopped flying. The gauges went crazy. Pressure and oil indicators dropped to zero. The plane bucked like a bull.

"There's only one chute," Cassiopeia called out.

"Put it on."

"Excuse me?"

"Put the damn thing on."

CASSIOPEIA HAD NEVER TOUCHED A PARACHUTE BEFORE, MUCH less donned one. The last thing on earth she'd ever anticipated doing in her life was leaping from a plane.

The floor beneath her vibrated like an earthquake. The engine was trying to keep them up, but gravity was fighting hard to send them down. She slipped her arms through the shoulder harness, brought the remaining strap up between her legs, and clicked the metal buckles into place.

"Open the side door," he called out. "Hurry. I can't hold this thing up much longer."

She reached for the latch and slid the panel on its rails, locking it into place. A roar of warm air rushed inside. Below, the ground raced by, a really long way away.

"We have to jump," Cotton said over the noise.

Had she heard right?

"There's no choice. I can't land this thing, and it's not going to stay in the air any longer."

"I can't jump."

"Yes, you can."

No, she couldn't. Bad enough she was inside this plane. That had taken all she had. But to jump out? Into open sky?

Cotton released his harness and rolled out of the chair. The plane, now pilotless, pitched forward, then back. He staggered over and wrapped his arms around her, connecting his hands between the chute and her spine.

They faced each other.

Close.

He wiggled them both to the door.

"Cotton—"

"Put your hand on the D-ring," he said to her. "Count to five, then pull it."

Her eyes signaled the terror coursing through her.

"Like you told me once, when I panicked," he said. "It's just you and me here, and I got you."

He kissed her.

And they fell from the plane.

COTTON HAD JUMPED BEFORE, BUT NEVER IN TANDEM CLINGING to another person without a harness, with no goggles, and at such a low altitude.

Once free of the cabin they immediately began spinning. A jet of burning air whipped away his voice and deafened his ears. A sour dryness scraped his throat and washed his eyes. He felt like he was inside a tumble dryer. But he had to keep his wits and hope that Cassiopeia did the same and remembered to count to five, then pull the rip cord. No way he could do it for her, as it was taking every ounce of strength he had to keep his hands locked around her body.

Their spinning lessened and he spotted the Airvan as it plunged downward. They needed to be as far away from that disaster as possible, which did not appear to be a problem.

Suddenly his head whipped back and they were both tugged hard as Cassiopeia apparently made it to five. He saw the chute emerge from the pack, its lines going taut as the canopy caught air. They were both wrenched upward, then they settled, slowly dropping downward in a now quiet morning.

"You okay?" he asked in her ear.

She nodded.

"I'm going to need you to reach up and work the lines and steer us," he said.

"Tell me what to do."

He was impressed with how she was holding up. This had to be the worst nightmare for someone with acrophobia.

"Pull hard with your left arm."

She followed his instruction, which banked their descent in a steeper approach. He was angling for a clearing he'd spotted, free of trees. Hitting the ground there seemed far preferable to being raked by limbs.

"More," he said.

She complied.

But they weren't moving far enough toward the target.

And they were running out of air.

He decided to try it himself and released his grip from behind her, quickly grabbing one set of lines, then the other, using his full weight to shift the canopy and alter their trajectory.

Only a few seconds remained in their descent.

He was holding on for dear life, his body twisting with their every movement, only ten fingers between him and plunging to his death. Cassiopeia recognized the threat and wrapped her arms around his waist and held tight.

He appreciated the gesture.

And kept working the lines.

They cleared the trees.

"When we hit, fold your knees," he said. "Don't fight the impact. Just let it happen."

The ground came up fast.

"Let go of me," he yelled.

She did.

And they pounded the ground.

She was pulled with the canopy. He fell away from her, landing on his right side, then rolling across the rocky earth.

He stopped.

And exhaled, settling his jangled nerves.

Nothing seemed broken.

Amazing that his nearly fifty-year-old body could still take a hit.

Cassiopeia lay on the ground, the canopy settling beyond her.

In the distance he heard an explosion.

The Airvan.

Crashing.

CHAPTER THREE

CASSIOPEIA BREATHED HARD, TRYING NOT TO HYPERVENTILATE. She'd done a lot of dangerous things involving fire, water, explosives, guns, and knives. But nothing—absolutely nothing—compared with what had just happened. Heights had always been a problem for her, but one she'd managed to control and contain. Of course, never had she faced falling through the sky, thousands of meters in the air with someone else clinging to her, one parachute between them.

"Are you okay?" Cotton asked as he ran over.

"No. I'm not okay." Her voice rose. "I just jumped out of a damn airplane. What part of that do you not see as insane?" Her breathing refused to calm. "That was way beyond anything I ever want to experience." Reality kept assaulting her brain. She was talking fast. "I jumped out of a plane. No. I was pulled out of a plane."

He knelt down in front of her. "At least I kissed you."

"Really? That makes it all better?"

He cupped her cheeks with both hands. "I get it."

Three words. That said it all.

She stared into his green eyes.

And remembered what had happened beneath Washington, DC, when the roles were reversed and he'd panicked, facing his worst fear.

What had she said to him? *It's just you and me here, and I got you.* Exactly what he'd told her.

He was right.

He did get it.

She fought through her panic and touched his hand. "I know you do."

"There was no time to debate the point. We had to go before the plane lost its trim. If it started spinning, we never would have been able to jump." He looked around at the morning sky, then out at the open field and trees. "I only hope we're over the border."

As did she.

He helped her up and released the buckles, allowing the empty pack to clump to the ground. The white canopy lay folded onto itself a few meters away.

She hugged him, breathing in his scent.

He held her tight.

She'd known a lot of men, a few who became quite close, but no one compared to Harold Earl "Cotton" Malone. He was tall and full through the chest. His wavy hair, cut neat and trim, seemed to always carry the burnished tint of aged stone. He was a forthright individual with strong tastes and even stronger convictions. But a crease of amusement liked to linger on his lips, which suggested a devilish side, one she knew to be exciting. He came from solid stock. His mother was a native Georgian from the southern United States, his father a career military man, an Annapolis graduate, who rose to the rank of commander before being lost at sea when his submarine sank. Cotton had followed in his father's footsteps, attending the Naval Academy, then flight school and fighter pilot training.

But he never finished.

Halfway through he abruptly sought reassignment to the Judge Advocate General's corps and was admitted to Georgetown University Law Center, earning a law degree. After graduation he served as a navy lawyer.

Then another shift.

To the U.S. Justice Department and a special unit known as the Magellan Billet, headed by a woman he had nothing but the greatest respect for, Stephanie Nelle. There he remained for a dozen years, until retiring out early, divorcing his wife, moving to Denmark, and buying on old-book shop.

Quite a change.

But this man knew what he wanted.

And how to get it.

They'd not been overly impressed with each other when they first met a few years ago in France. But now they were in love. A couple. There'd been ups and downs, but they'd weathered the storms. She trusted no one more than him, the past few minutes proof positive of that.

They released their hold on each other.

"That crashed plane is going to bring a lot of attention," he said. "I suggest we get some distance from it."

She agreed. "And you should make a call."

COTTON REACHED INTO HIS POCKET AND FOUND HIS CELL PHONE. Magellan Billet issue. Specially designed for encoded transmissions with an enhanced GPS satellite locater. Though he was no longer an active agent, Stephanie Nelle had allowed him to keep it. Probably so that she could more easily locate him when she needed a favor.

Which was quite often.

But maybe not anymore.

After what happened in Poland last week he doubted the Americans would be calling anytime soon. He and the current president, Warner Fox, did not see eye to eye. Better the two of them not mix. Which was in no danger of happening after Fox's assertion that he was now persona non grata. No more work would come his way from Washington.

But what had Doris Day sung? *Que sera sera.*

Yep. Crap happens.

Hopefully, though, other foreign intelligence agencies would still hire him from time to time, so things may not be a total loss.

He tried the phone but there was no service. So he grabbed the pack from the ground and began to gather up the chute, intending to ditch both in the trees. There had to be a highway or road nearby. A farmhouse. Village. Something. Once there, hopefully, his phone or someone else's would work. But if he had to be stranded in the woods, then at least he was with the one person he'd most want to be with. He'd been married a long time to his first wife. They'd shared a lot of joy and pain. Even a child. His son, Gary. When they divorced he honestly never thought love would come his way again. Then Cassiopeia appeared. Literally. In the night.

Shooting at him.

He smiled. Quite an ostentatious beginning.

One thing led to another, then another, and now they were a team.

In more ways than one.

Together they grabbed up the chute and headed for the trees. In the distance he heard a low-level bass thump cutting across the quiet morning.

He knew the sound.

Chopper blades.

He tried to decide on the direction and settled for west.

"It's getting louder," Cassiopeia said.

"Coming this way."

They hustled forward and took refuge in the trees, stashing the parachute in the underbrush. The steady throb of rotor blades echoed until an NH90 roared into view above the treetops bearing NATO insignia.

Confirmation.

They'd made it all the way into Poland.

The heavy rhythmic beating of the helicopter swept low over the trees and landed in the middle of the clearing. Its side door opened and a man emerged, dressed casually in jeans and a dark-blue jacket, wearing boots. He was tall, broad shouldered, with a thick mop of white hair. He marched across the clearing, headed their way, walking with the stature of a man in charge.

Which he'd been.

"Danny Daniels," Cassiopeia muttered.

CHAPTER FOUR

COTTON EMERGED FROM THE TREES WITH CASSIOPEIA. IT WAS good to see Danny, who always had known how to make an entrance. The only thing missing were the chords from "Hail to the Chief." The big man strode right up to them and gave Cassiopeia a hug, which she returned. They'd always had a special bond. Nothing romantic, more a father–daughter thing. She admired him, and the feeling seemed mutual.

"Everybody okay?" Danny asked. "You two have had quite the morning."

"How did you find us?" Cotton asked.

"I pinged your phone. I was waiting at our base in Grafenwöhr."

He knew about the military installation near the German–Polish border, home to the largest multinational training ground in Europe.

"You've been all over the chatter this morning," Danny said. "NATO listening stations picked up your theft of a plane and the unauthorized flight, monitoring the transmissions. The Belarusians were waiting to shoot you down."

"You could have warned us," Cotton said.

"You know the drill. We can't let them know that we know what they're doing. Was all that related to what I asked you to do?"

He nodded. "That's a yes."

Danny chuckled. "It seems there's a lot more here than meets the eye. Thankfully, the good folks at the base offered me a ride to come see what happened to you."

"We appreciate your attention."

Danny was looking around. "Where's the other parachute?"

"There wasn't one," Cassiopeia said. "We share everything, except toothbrushes and ice cream cones."

Danny shook his head. "What was that like?"

"Horrible," she said. "But necessary, under the circumstances."

The older man smiled. "That's an optimistic way of putting it."

"Have you ever had the pleasure?" she asked.

"Once. A long time ago. In the army. I decided then and there not to ever jump out of a plane again."

"I'm with you."

Cotton was allowing his old friend the luxury of building up to what he wanted. He sensed that the problem remained serious.

"Did you find out *anything* about Hanna Cress?" Danny asked.

"Bits and pieces. We needed another day or so. I was trying not to draw attention, which obviously didn't work out."

Danny shook his head. "We have a mess. Three days ago I watched Cress die, poisoned by a cigarette laced with cyanide inside a police interrogation room. We now know the cigarettes were supplied by the duty officer, who says another inspector, supposedly from Berlin, provided them when the woman requested smokes. Nobody, though, seems to know anything about that other inspector. Who, what, where, when? Nothing. He looked and acted official. Now he's gone."

"No cameras?" Cotton asked.

"Plenty of them. But not a single shot of the guy's face. He was careful."

"Which signifies a pro."

Danny nodded. "Exactly."

The helicopter waited out in the clearing, its blades still turning at low speed, churning up the tall brush.

"By the way," Danny said, "President Czajkowski sends you greetings from Warsaw. I had to call in a favor with him to get permission for this incursion into Polish airspace. Oddly, once he knew you were involved, he said I could do whatever I wanted. No questions asked. Care to explain that one?"

Cotton smiled. "You're not the only one with favors owed."

"I want to hear more about that. But at the moment the clock is ticking, and I still need your help."

Danny Daniels was one of the smartest people Cotton had ever known. He'd been elected president of the United States twice in overwhelming victories. They had a long history, accentuated by Danny's close relationship with the Magellan Billet and Stephanie Nelle. That had been all business at first. Now Danny and Stephanie were an item, Danny divorced from his wife and openly seeing Stephanie.

The Magellan Billet was all Stephanie's creation. A special unit within the Justice Department composed of twelve agents, most with military or legal backgrounds, who worked exclusively at her direction on some of the most sensitive assignments at Justice. It had been Daniels' go-to agency for trouble resolution. But not so much with the new president, Warner Fox. In fact, the Billet's days were probably numbered.

"How is Stephanie?" he asked Daniels.

"Still suspended from her job, but not actually fired. She made it perfectly clear that she did not want my help and I was to stay out of her fight with the White House. Nothing. *Nada.* God knows, it's been hard. But that's what I'm doing."

Last week, while Cotton had acquired some future capital in the president of Poland's eye, Stephanie had incurred the wrath of the president of the United States, earning a promise to be fired.

"Fox is letting her twist in the wind," Danny said. "It's his style. To her credit, she's handling it okay. Thankfully, she's civil service, so she gets a hearing. It'll be closed door and classified, but still a hearing. That'll take time. There's nothing I can do about any of it, but watch."

"Yet here you are in the woods of eastern Poland," Cassiopeia said. "With a NATO chopper at your disposal."

Daniels chuckled. "It's good to be me."

"We came into this blind," Cotton said, "thinking it was a quick meet and greet to gather some intel. It's obviously more than that. Maybe you should open our eyes."

"There's an election coming in Germany. Did you know that?"

They both shook their heads.

"National parliamentary voting is about to begin. Once done, the newly chosen Bundestag will meet and choose a German chancellor. To win that post, a candidate must achieve a majority of all the elected members in the legislature. Not just his or her party. All of them. The Germans have a name for it. *Kanzlermehrheit.* Chancellor's majority."

"Sounds like a tough job to get," Cotton said.

"It is, considering the number of political parties in Germany. About forty at last count. Even worse, the votes for chancellor in the Bundestag are by secret ballot. So nobody knows how anyone else votes. That allows a great deal of shifting alliances."

Unlike in Congress, where the vote for Speaker of the House was public, with each member having to openly declare their support or opposition.

"And here's the rub," Daniels said. "It's the German president who proposes a nominee for chancellor. That's usually the person who heads the party that gets the most seats from the election. But if that person can't get a chancellor's majority, then the Bundestag elects its own candidate. If it isn't able to do that, then things really get messy. Luckily, all of the chancellors since 1949 have achieved a majority on the first vote, so they've never gotten beyond that scenario."

"Until now?" Cotton asked.

Danny nodded. "It's shaping up to be a mess. It's Ringling Brothers all over again. A virtual three-ring circus come to town, which could take a bad bounce in many different directions. Then six months from now it gets worse. That's when elections to the European Parliament will be held. A once-in-five-years event when member states choose their national representatives. And there are big problems taking shape there. How Germany goes now could well be how the European Union goes then."

Cotton was beginning to appreciate the gravity of the situation.

"The German chancellor also has enormous power," Danny said. "He or she chooses all the cabinet ministers. The entire German government is shaped by whoever holds that position. Currently the chancellor is Marie Eisenhuth. A friend to the U.S. Also a decent person who tries to do the best she can for her country. But there's a second candidate, one who is trying to take her job."

"And he's the problem?" Cassiopeia asked.

"Front and center."

"What's his name?"

"Theodor Pohl."

CHAPTER FIVE

Cologne, Germany
11:00 a.m.

Theodor Pohl realized there was a problem. Not with the rally, which was progressing smoothly. The crowd seemed enthusiastic, just the right blend of cheers and applause. Perfect for the cameras that perpetually followed him and that were, at the moment, focused on the dais where he stood.

His message was the same at every stop.

Germany for Germans.

The liberal immigration and naturalization policies forced on the nation by the Allies after World War II must stop. No more appeasing the world for things that happened nearly a century ago. No more Germany ruled by Germans for non-Germans. His condensed platform tag had been carefully chosen. *The new, unified Fatherland was born from strife, but is powered by might.*

Nothing militaristic, though.

He was always careful to tinge his rhetoric. His message was simply that a strong economy bore a strong nation. But not with euros. Again, that was something forced by a fixated need to be overly accommodating. The mark was the currency of Germany. Always had been, always would be. Which fit the main slogan his high-priced consultants had devised.

Zurück in die zukunft.

Back to the future.

And the words seemed to resonate, drawing more and more people to his rallies. Today's crowd was particularly inspiring. He especially liked one of the signs that had become common at his gatherings.

WIR SIND DAS VOLK.

We are the people.

He stood in the shadow of Cologne's twin-spire Gothic cathedral, its towering exterior studded with an almost overpowering array of stone filigree. It rested near the railroad station amid a sea of commerce, only the passing crowds and a rumble of traffic disturbing its serenity. At least twenty thousand people filled the square surrounding the ancient church. Purists pronounced the spot the heart and soul of Cologne.

And he was not about to contradict them.

"Look behind me," he shouted into the microphone, "at this monument to what man can accomplish with both mind and body. Such a commanding pile of masonry. Its size reflects nothing but sheer power." He hesitated a moment for effect. "This is the soul of Cologne."

The crowd cheered their approval with an enthusiasm he'd grown accustomed to hearing.

Still, though, there was a problem.

He sensed it in the gaze of a man who stood off alone, near the entrance to one of the shops that ringed the cathedral square. He'd noticed him the instant he took to the stage, since he knew that Josef Engle was not a man given to concern. Yet something told him his associate was bothered. Maybe it was the way he stood, or his extra lack of attention to the rally.

Hard to say for sure.

Yet there was something.

At the moment, though, he could not be worried about that and returned his attention to the people who'd taken time from their day to come and listen to his message.

"I seek the chancellorship of this nation, my party seeks control of the Bundestag, because we have a vision for Germany that I believe you share. There is no longer a need for any of us to feel shame at the folly of another generation. We have atoned for the sins of the last Reich. Those men are dead and gone. Dust in their graves. There will be no

Fourth Reich. Such thoughts are nonsense." He paused an instant for effect. "For three-quarters of a century this nation has been forced to accept anyone and everyone that the countries of the world care to cast off. This indignity must stop."

He knew that statement would strike a chord. A hundred thousand Turkish immigrants lived in and around Cologne, and their presence was not popular. The Allies after World War II forced a clause in the German constitution that compelled free immigration with little to no control. His theme was simple. Pluralism threatened the German soul. He screamed the words he'd echoed throughout the land.

"Ausländer raus."

Foreigners out.

The people roared their approval.

He again noticed Engle, still standing near the shop entrance. His acolyte came from the old East Germany, heavy with the callousness all too common in the former communists. His last name meant "angel," but the man was anything but. Engle had also risen above the social barriers unification had quietly imposed on those from the former East Germany. He carried himself with the vigor of a man in his mid-fifties, adding the sophistication of a perpetual tan and a Vandyke beard dusted with streaks of silver-gray. A disarming look, like that of a country gentleman.

Pohl focused again on the crowd.

"American influence is also destroying our rich German heritage. We have American food, television, movies, books, you name it. Our young people feast upon those foreign influences, and can't remember a time when things German were thought important. They know only that a war occurred, horrible things happened, and we must pay the price for all of those errors."

The people erupted again.

"Make no mistake. I advocate nothing associated with the former Thousand-Year Reich. I abhor every single one of its policies. Everything it did was evil. I do not endorse violence in any manner to achieve a political end. Not now. Not ever. I ask only that Germany be allowed to exist in a form that is supported by a majority of Germans."

His gaze raked the faces, watching the anticipation that his words seemed to generate. Time to finish. He pointed, his gesture falling upon the audience equally. "Back to the future, my friends. That is my goal. I ask that you also make it yours."

Applause erupted.

The television cameras caught it all. He raised his arms to embrace the cheers. His eyes sought and found Engle, and through his held gaze he let it be known that they needed to speak. His minion headed toward a limousine parked just beyond the square.

He left the podium and headed for the same limousine, climbing inside.

Engle smiled. "Hanna Cress is dead."

That woman appearing on the scene had been unexpected. Not part of the plan. So it had required decisive action.

"You handled it?"

Engle nodded.

"Then what's wrong?"

"The Americans have entered the picture."

That was troubling. "Tell me more."

He listened to Engle describe how ex-president, now U.S. senator Danny Daniels had appeared in Partenkirchen, questioning Hanna Cress, there when she died.

There could only be one source for that complication.

Marie Eisenhuth.

CHAPTER SIX

CHANCELLOR MARIE EISENHUTH STARED OUT THE HELICOPTER'S window. Before landing she'd asked to be flown over the area, about sixty-five kilometers north of Bayreuth, so she could see the abomination for herself.

Below rose the stunted peaks of the Harz Mountains. The central German slopes were thick with blue fir and furrowed by valleys where villages nestled against deep lakes and gentle rivers. She knew the PR hype. The land of fairies, a kingdom of magic where children could be transformed by witches into princes and princesses, a place where myth dominated. She could still hear her father telling her about the fountain in Goslar. Knock three times on its lowest basin at midnight and the devil would appear.

She always smiled when she thought of her father. His death, nearly fifty years ago, still hurt.

The chopper banked right.

The site lay just ahead.

Amid a pine forest on the slopes of one of the older mountains, an odd spectacle had been spotted last autumn. Long ago, about fifty larch trees had been purposefully planted so that the seedlings formed a gigantic swastika. With the approach of fall the brilliant yellows and oranges of the dormant larches had stood in stark contrast with the evergreen pines, allowing the obscene symbol to blazon across the landscape. A pilot had spied the memorial and reported it to authorities, everyone amazed that the trees had not been noticed before. The best explanation was that they'd never all gone dormant simultaneously when someone high enough in the air could see. A decision had finally been made to ax them, and Marie realized a good photo opportunity when she heard one. So a campaign stop had been arranged that should garner her a respectable amount of national media coverage.

She stared down at the trees, most of which had already been cleared, the outline of the swastika still there in the open space. A few of the other trees were also to be felled to forever distort the image. A long time had passed since the demise of National Socialism, but remnants of Nazism stubbornly remained. The spectacle below was one of the more benign compared with the ethnic hatred and indiscriminate violence against foreigners that was sadly on the rise again.

She signaled to land, and the helicopter touched down.

She stepped out.

No cadre of aides nipped at her heels. Just her, come to confront the past. A contingent of reporters crowded around. Many of the faces she recognized, regulars to her press detail.

"Quite an odd scene," a female correspondent from Frankfurt said.

"A forgotten memorial to a horrible mistake." When it came to the past, she was always careful. "But we must remember Hitler was able to rise not from an abundance of Nazis, but rather because there were simply too few democrats."

Her usual theme.

Government was the responsibility of the people.

A prudent tactic, considering that her opponent was trying to entangle her in a moral debate over ethnic responsibility. But she'd not served as chancellor for the past sixteen years by nibbling on that kind of bait.

She moved away, and the press followed in her wake.

The woods around her belonged to a variety of national corporations. Some of the area was managed forest, most was land bought long ago for pfennigs. The tree memorial had apparently been planted by a contingent of the Hitler Youth, which once used the Harz region as an outdoor retreat. One of many wilderness camps where young men were indoctrinated with National Socialism through a hypnotic combination of sports, music, and comradery.

She made her way into the grove of evergreens.

Ahead rose a magnificent larch, the last of the offending trees.

It seemed a shame to destroy its beauty. But like Nazism, which stained the hearts and minds of Germany's best, the trees were a blight on everything beautiful that surrounded them.

And not for themselves individually.

But rather for what they collectively represented. Something she'd once heard came to mind. *One Nazi meant nothing, forty were a nuisance, forty thousand nearly ruled Europe.*

Her gaze drifted to the forest floor. No undergrowth littered the ground. Again, the symbolism was evident. Nothing had seemed able to flourish in the shade of Hitler, either.

She faced the cameras. "I have something to say."

Reporters huddled around her.

"My opponent likes to cry, *Back to the future.* True, he doesn't actively embrace the past or advocate any of its policies. All he does is remind us of it at every opportunity. He likes to constantly reassert German nationalism. He says that our identity only lies within our borders. On that I strongly disagree."

She was taking a calculated risk with that denunciation. But as her political consultants had repeatedly advised, Pohl's campaign depended on Germany's aging population. Most of his supporters were sixty and over. Pohl himself was nearing seventy, and she was nearly seventy-five. The press had politely dubbed their contest for control *a battle of experience.* Just a nice way of saying they were old. Interestingly, though, her base came mainly from the young, women, and the college educated. Another basic difference between them: She was Catholic, he was Protestant—and religion meant something to the German voter.

"Are you saying Pohl is too far right?" one of the reporters asked.

"I'm saying he's too certain as to what afflicts this country. He believes immigration is the root of our problems, that unification has destroyed the economy." She threw the press a smile. "Diversity is good. For everyone."

She caught sight of loggers heading toward the larch, chain saws in hand.

She turned her attention back to the press. "We have problems. That's not in question. Our political parties are losing strength. Unions are fading. Church membership is on the decline. We are the second largest exporter in the world, but possess the highest labor costs of any industrialized nation. Pessimism has become a malady, crippling our desire. My opponent does nothing to soothe any of these afflictions. Instead he uses them, content for the nation to be angry and confused."

She noticed loggers taking up a position before the tree. They were looking her way, apparently waiting for her to finish.

"*Keine Experimente*. No experiments. That is my theme. *Back to the future* is nothing but a blueprint for more problems. My vision is forward."

She motioned to the loggers.

Chain saws roared to life and blades bit into trunks.

She imagined the scene eighty years ago when eager-eyed youths planted the seedlings with an almost religious care, paying homage to a man they regarded as a god, respecting an ideal none of them understood.

Cameras recorded the action as the aging tree was attacked.

One of the saws bucked as wood caught the chain. The logger yanked the blade free and resumed his assault. She smiled at the tough old tree and thought again about Theodor Pohl's subtle message of hate.

And hoped the German people were equally as resilient.

CHAPTER SEVEN

COTTON SAT IN THE CHOPPER'S REAR COMPARTMENT WITH Cassiopeia and Danny Daniels. They were flying across Poland toward Germany. Each wore a headset on a closed-circuit loop so no one else could hear their conversation.

"Theodor Pohl has served six terms in the Bundestag," Danny said. "He's from the German state of Hesse. He owns a large estate there named Löwenberg."

Cotton silently made the translation. Lion's mount.

"Supposedly he's an ardent anti-communist. I have my doubts, though. He was not deemed a viable candidate for the chancellorship until three years ago, when his party rose to control nearly a quarter of the Bundestag."

"And whoever has that much of a say in the national assembly is a man to be reckoned with," Cotton added.

Danny nodded. "He has the voice of a demagogue, the face of a prophet, and his words resonate. He's a populist. Pure and simple, playing off xenophobic fears. He exploits the new right while keeping his distance from the fanatical elements. Immigration is a sensitive subject in Germany, but he likes to aggravate that open nerve. No pro-Nazi stance, or anything like that. Just a simple nationalistic theme."

Which made sense.

Cotton knew that German law banned any political party that advocated violence. No Hitler salutes or swastikas. Nothing that even implied the former Third Reich. But that didn't mean those ideas did not linger.

An old saying came to mind.

Clever be the tongue that can speak without talking.

"The new right is growing everywhere across Europe," Danny said. "Even in your adopted country."

Cotton was acquainted with Denmark's politics, which involved some of the toughest anti-immigration laws in Europe. Its cradle-to-grave welfare system was one of the best, so conservatives there had an easy time preaching isolationism. It was now next to impossible to seek asylum, obtain residence permits, or receive welfare payments. His own residency permit remained stamped temporary, subject to immediate revocation.

"Like I told you," Danny said, "after the German elections, the EU parliamentary elections are next. That's a Continent-wide vote. There's a real fear that the new right could take over the EU Parliament. It's been working in that direction for several years now. They realize they can't get rid of the EU, though they would love that. It's too entrenched. Nor can they individually opt out, country by country. God knows England proved that a folly. So they've decided to fundamentally change things from within. To do that, though, they need votes in the EU Parliament. And they're working on getting those."

Cotton had taken the time over the past few years to become familiar with the EU. It had been an experiment from the start. Twenty-seven countries thrown together by the Treaty of Rome in 1957, bound so tight with a common currency, free trade, and open borders that war among them would no longer be an option. The whole point had been to dissuade nationalism. In the last round of EU elections five years ago, only about 40 percent of voters had turned out. Not good. Unfortunately, many of the more centrist parties across Europe lacked the youth, vigor, and energy to compete with the excitement of the new right. And whoever controlled at least a third of the EU Parliament's seats could block vital appointments, overrule policies, and push hardliners for key positions, influencing myriad things including trade and immigration. It didn't help that Western European nations stayed at odds with the EU's newest members—all in the east, former Soviet satellite countries—which were luring jobs and industry from the west with cheap labor and low taxes.

A new east-versus-west battle.

Which the west was losing.

"Theodor Pohl is good at harnessing anger," Danny said. "He casts himself as a *macher.* Man of action. And, unfortunately, that's what he is. He can get things done. Marie Eisenhuth is more a *seher.* A visionary."

"Aren't you the bilingual one," Cassiopeia taunted.

"I do have my moments. But four things make Pohl dangerous. He's smart. No fool. Decisive. And most important, he can explain himself with an eloquence that others easily agree with. His nationalistic ideas are becoming widely accepted across Germany. His party could garner a solid number of seats in the Bundestag."

The chopper kept heading west, the ride smooth in the afternoon air. Even Cassiopeia didn't seem bothered by the flight. They'd learned that the Airvan had crashed into the woods with no one injured on the ground.

"Each European country seems to have their own charismatic new-right personality," Danny said. "Their own Theodor Pohl, fueling the flames of ultra-conservatism and exciting fears. The German system makes the problem even more acute. With so many political parties, it's doubtful anyone will achieve a majority. So a coalition will rule. Pohl has forged alliances with the Christian Democrats and the Free Democrats, enough to allow him to become chancellor. But to do that he, and his party, must outpoll Marie Eisenhuth and her party in the coming elections. His political partners are waiting to see how the people vote before finalizing their alliance. They want to shift right, but they also want to be sure it's the way to go."

"I assume Eisenhuth has a similar dilemma," Cassiopeia said. "If she prevails the other parties fall in behind her?"

"Precisely."

"So what does this have to do with us?" Cotton asked.

"The election is too close to call. It's a little over sixty days from now. Three weeks ago Chancellor Eisenhuth received an email." Danny hesitated. "Then two more emails after that. All supposedly from a man named Gerhard Schüb. What he was saying attracted the chancellor's attention, so a meet was arranged for last Friday where a packet of documents was hand-delivered to the chancellor's representative. The courier was Hanna Cress, the woman who was arrested, then murdered. And then there's another rub to this itch. We've actually had contact with a Gerhard Schüb before. Through Jonathan Wyatt."

That name Cotton knew.

A former American intelligence operative. Never a friend. For a while even an enemy. But eventually they came face-to-face on an island in Canada and settled their differences.

"Right before all that unpleasantness a few years ago with my assassination attempt in New York," Danny said, "Wyatt had a confrontation in Chile with a man named Gerhard Schüb. He filed a report on what happened. When Chancellor Eisenhuth talked to me about her problem, she asked if we knew anything about Schüb. I made inquiries through Stephanie and she told me about Chile. Supposedly, according to Wyatt, Schüb killed himself there."

"Wyatt is a loose cannon," Cotton said. "Always has been. Are you saying he lied in his report?"

Danny shook his head. "More like he got played. We think he was tricked into believing Schüb was dead. I have his report with me." Danny glanced at his watch. "We're about half an hour out. Before we land I need you both to read it and something else, part of what was delivered last Friday by Hanna Cress."

Danny reached beneath his jacket and removed a few sheets of paper, which he handed over.

Together, they read.

CHAPTER EIGHT

APRIL 30, 1945. THE FÜHRER'S MOOD HAS PROGRESSIVELY WORSENED SINCE yesterday when the generals informed him that Berlin was lost and a counteroffensive from the 11th Panzer Army, which he thought would save the Reich, had not been initiated. He became incensed on learning that Himmler was negotiating independently with the Allies for peace. That action made him suspect everything related to the SS, including the cyanide capsules supplied for the bunker.

"They are fakes," Hitler screamed. "The chicken farmer Himmler wants me taken alive so the Russians can display me like a zoo animal."

He fingered one of the capsules and declared it nothing more than a sedative.

"Malignancy is rife," he lamented.

To be sure of the poison, during the late morning he retreated to the surface and watched as a capsule was administered to his favorite Alsatian. The dog died quickly, and the act seemed to satisfy him. The Führer then descended back into the bunker and presented his two personal secretaries with a poison capsule each, commenting that he wished he could have provided a better parting gift. They thanked him for his kindness and he praised their service, wishing his generals would have been as loyal.

Earlier, near 2:00 A.M., they were all summoned to the bunker, officers, women, and men. Hitler appeared with Bormann. His eyes carried the same hazy glaze of late, a lock of hair plastered to his sweaty forehead, and he shuffled in what appeared to be a painful stoop. Dandruff flecked his shoulders thick as dust. The right side of his body trembled uncontrollably. The German people would be amazed to see the weakened condition of their Supreme Leader. We were assembled in a line and the Führer proceeded to shake each of our hands. Saliva drooled from his mouth. Bormann watched in silence. I heard Hitler mutter as he departed, "Alles in ordnung." All is in order.

We all sensed that the end was near. This man who by sheer force of personality had so completely dominated a nation was about to end his life. There was so much relief that we hurried to ground level and held a dance in the canteen of the Chancellery. High officers who days before would not have acknowledged we existed shook our hands and talked openly. Everyone realized that postwar Germany was going to be greatly different. A realignment would occur not only in people, but in social order. All at the dance seemed to grasp that reality, and I watched with great amusement as egos crumbled.

By noon the news was not good. Russian troops had partly occupied the Chancellery. The Tiergarten had been taken. The Potsdamer Platz and Weidendammer Bridge were lost. Hitler accepted the information without emotion. At 2:00 P.M. he took lunch with his secretaries and cook. His wife, Eva, who normally ate with Hitler, was not there. Their marriage was little more than a day old and her absence from Hitler's side was something to be noted. Such an odd wedding. The din of battle leaking in from aboveground. The cold gray concrete walls. A humid, moldy aroma that stained everything with a stench of confinement. Each declared that they were of pure Aryan descent and free of hereditary disease. Goebbels and Bormann served as official witnesses. The bride and groom barely smiled as vows were exchanged. An odd sort of fulfillment amid overwhelming failure.

After lunch, Hitler and his wife appeared together and we were all summoned again. Another farewell occurred with little emotion, then the Führer and Eva Braun returned to their private quarters. All were dismissed save for a few. Within minutes a single gunshot was heard.

Cotton looked up from the pages.

The helicopter kept churning westward.

"This is nothing new. I've read similar accounts before. Eva Braun bit down on a cyanide capsule and Hitler shot himself. Their bodies were taken up to ground level and burned, then buried. The Russians found the corpses, but told no one and took the remains back to Moscow. Stalin wanted the Allies to believe Hitler was still alive. His way of keeping everybody off guard and justifying his occupying Eastern Europe. All of the details came to light in the 1990s, after the fall of the Soviet Union when its archives were opened." He held up the sheets. "But this seems like firsthand information. Where did it come from?"

Danny shrugged. "Moscow. From those old Soviet archives. Historians have long thought there was a Soviet spy in the Führerbunker. Even Hitler believed it."

He knew the tale of *das Leck*. The leak. Many names had been attached to the label, similar to speculation over who could have been Deep Throat during Watergate. That mystery had been solved. But *das Leck* remained unknown.

"Keep reading," Danny said.

Bormann was the first into the room after the shot. A smell of cyanide smarted the eyes and forced a retreat for a few moments while the air cleared. Hitler lay sprawled on the left side of the couch, a bullet hole the size of a silver mark in his skull. Eva Braun lay on the right side of the sofa. A vase filled with tulips and white narcissi had fallen over from an adjacent table, spilling water on her blue dress, staining her thighs. There was no sign of blood upon her, but the remains of a glass ampule dotted her lips. A woolen blanket was produced and Hitler's body wrapped inside. The Führer's valet, Linge, and Dr. Stumpfegger carried the body up to ground level. Bormann wrapped Eva Braun's remains in a blanket. He shouldered the corpse and carried her from the room. One of the guards called to him and he halted in the passageway. There was a brief discussion and Bormann laid the body in an adjacent anteroom. He dealt with the guard, then

returned and passed Eva Braun's corpse to Kempka, who in turn passed
her to Günsche, who then gave her to an SS officer who carried the body up
to the Chancellery garden.

The two corpses were laid side by side and petrol poured over them.
Russian guns boomed in the distance and someone mentioned that Ivan
was less than two hundred meters away, near the Stadtmitte U-Bahn sta-
tion. A bomb exploded and drove the mourners into the shelter of a nearby
porch. Bormann, Burgdorf, Goebbels, Günsche, Linge, and Kempka were
all there. I watched from the doorway leading into the bunker. Günsche
dipped a rag into petrol, lit it, then tossed the burning fuse onto the bodies.
Sheets of flames erupted. Everyone stood at attention, saluted, then with-
drew. I was the last to retreat. Before closing the door I stood for a moment
and watched the flames. One thought kept racing across my mind. A detail
that I willed myself never to forget. When they laid out Eva Braun's corpse,
her blue dress was no longer wet.

"I've never heard this before," Cassiopeia said. "I've read Trevor-Roper's *Last Days of Hitler* and other definitive narratives. But no one ever mentioned anything like this regarding Eva Braun."

"The German experts agree with you," Danny said. "This is new information, supposedly from a Soviet spy who was there. You're reading an English translation from the original Soviet report. Hanna Cress delivered an envelope full of document images, each bearing the Soviet seal and stamp. But here's the really fascinating part. Those documents were delivered last Friday. But a summary of the same information, written by Jonathan Wyatt, appears in his report, filed in DC, on what happened in Chile a few years ago. Nearly identical information, leading us to believe he may have read this exact account, too. Supposedly told to him by a man named Gerhard Schüb."

Cotton connected the dots and gestured with the pages. "You think Schüb was *das Leck*? He wrote this?"

Danny shrugged. "We're not sure what to think. All we know is that this firsthand account has now appeared two times, on two different continents, and the common denominator is a man named Gerhard Schüb."

He had to admit. That was way too much of a coincidence.

"Chancellor Eisenhuth asked me to talk with Hanna Cress on her behalf and find out what I could. She wanted this kept close and didn't want to use her people. I tried to question Cress, but she told me little. Only what I told you before. But before she died, she mentioned one word. *Kaiser.* Needless to say, this has all grown way above my skill grade, so I decided to bring in the experts."

Which explained why Danny had appeared in Copenhagen on Sunday, and then here today.

"You think Eva Braun survived the bunker?" Cotton asked. "That she somehow escaped?"

"Why the hell not," Danny said. "Nobody has a clue what happened in that bunker. The people who were there all contradicted one another with their statements after the war. There are no forensics to prove a thing. No bodies. No nothing. The Soviets totally contaminated whatever evidence may have been there. And think about it. Braun returned to Berlin on April 15, 1945. Hitler had sent her south to the Alps for safety. It was always assumed she returned out of love and loyalty. It was actually one of the all-time dumb-ass moves. The Russian army was closing in and the city was on the verge of capture. So she walked right back into the hornet's nest? To a nearly certain death or imprisonment? Out of love and loyalty for Hitler?"

He had to admit, it sounded implausible. Still. "What aren't you telling us?"

"I know this is going to sound crazy, but part of the information Hanna Cress delivered says Eva Braun may have been pregnant. Supposedly, she came back to legitimize her child through a lawful marriage to Hitler."

"That is crazy," Cassiopeia said.

"Maybe so, but the information Cress delivered says that Braun and Bormann were ordered to leave the bunker. Their task was to ensure that Hitler's child survived."

"Why didn't Hitler leave himself?" Cotton asked.

Danny shrugged. "I have no idea. Nor is any explanation offered in the materials that were delivered."

"Was that child born?" Cassiopeia asked.

"We don't know. The information we have is silent on that. But there is this."

Danny removed a folded piece of paper from his pocket and handed it over. Cotton opened it.

He and Cassiopeia studied the information.

"That's Theodor Pohl's birth certificate," Danny said. "He was supposedly born in Hesse on December 23, 1952, to Wilfrid and Cornelia Pohl. Yesterday some experts quietly analyzed the records. There are discrepancies. Possible forgeries. He may not have been born there."

"How old is Pohl?" Cassiopeia asked.

"His bio says sixty-nine."

"So we're not talking about Theodor Pohl being Hitler's child," she said.

Danny shook his head. "Not at all. But with the information we have, he might be Martin Bormann's son, born almost a decade after the war."

Cotton now saw the implications. "That'll win an election for Eisenhuth and her party."

Danny nodded. "Exactly. Now you know why she's so interested."

"I get it," Cotton said. "But it's a bit far-fetched."

"Maybe not, again considering what happened in Chile a few years ago. Jonathan Wyatt seems to have had quite an experience. His report describes a mansion filled with Nazi trinkets, two coffins beneath the house that supposedly held Braun and Bormann, the deaths of Gerhard Schüb and another American agent, Christopher Combs, and a hoard of Nazi gold. Stacked five feet high on six pallets, according to him. Stephanie says the information was hard to ignore, so a team was sent to investigate and they found the house exactly where Wyatt said. It was supposedly owned by Schüb's brother. Not true. It was owned by an elderly couple who live in Ecuador. It had also recently burned to the ground. Not a speck of anything left but ash. Nothing Wyatt reported was there."

"I remember Chris Combs," Cotton said. "CIA deputy director. He disappeared."

"And has not been found to this day," Danny said. "According to Wyatt, Combs was killed by Gerhard Schüb."

"Wyatt is a bull in a china shop," Cotton said. "But he's not a liar."

"That's what Stephanie said, too. Hence another reason why I'm here. From our standpoint, all of this was forgotten. An anomaly that really didn't matter. Now we're not so sure. There could be more to this."

Bormann. Braun. What really happened in the Führerbunker at the end of the war? Hitler's child? Bormann's son? Cotton had to admit, it was all quite tempting.

"England is gone from the EU," Danny said. "The far left has sent Greece into economic chaos. In Hungary a neo-Nazi party has pushed the government to an extreme. The greatest mass arrival of immigrants since World War Two has strained the resources of nearly every EU country. Sweden, Italy, Hungary, and Austria have all drifted to the right. Greece, Ireland, Portugal, and Spain are nearly bankrupt. Couple all that with near-zero economic growth for the past ten years, and the fact that Russia is becoming stronger by the day, and the European Union is a powder keg waiting to explode."

None of which sounded good.

"Germany is the strongest economy and the most populated country in Europe. How it goes is how the EU will go. But recent opinion polls indicate that a quarter of German voters are unsure and the rest are split between Eisenhuth and Pohl. It's a skintight race."

"So anything could tip the scale," Cotton said.

"You got that right. Anything. Even unsubstantiated rumor, however far-fetched. We can't allow Theodor Pohl to claim the Chancellery."

"Why isn't Washington on this?"

"They are," Danny said. "But Fox managed to make an enemy of Marie Eisenhuth really quick. He's even hinted publicly at support for Pohl. It's another reason why I need your help. We have to ensure that Eisenhuth wins. And, full disclosure, there's no money here to pay for your time. This is a freebie. A favor to me. I'll owe you both."

Cotton liked being owed favors.

"There's more to tell you," Danny said. "But to know that you have to get off the pot or crap. It's your call."

He glanced at Cassiopeia, who shrugged in that cute way of hers that said, *I'm good if you are.*

The chopper bucked a bit, as if agreeing, too.

"We're in," he said.

CHAPTER NINE

THIS IS MY RECOLLECTION OF A VISIT WITH MARTIN BORMANN IN THE SUMMER of 1955. The occasion of our meeting was to celebrate the birthday of his son. The boy was three, and we enjoyed cake and beer during a party with neighbors. Bormann asked me about Nuremberg and the war trials, which had long since ended. He was amused at the notice the Allies ran in the newspapers notifying him of his conviction in absentia. A death warrant still existed, but he is not the least bit concerned. As to Gerda, his first wife, he lamented about her death but not with the sadness of a man longing for his lost love, more in the tone of a fugitive disappointed at failure. He was aware of her death from cancer in March 1946. Her conversion to Catholicism was particularly repugnant to him, as was her consignment of their children to a Catholic priest. He wondered about his children but realized they, like everyone else, believed him dead. His focus now is his new family and the responsibility with which he has been entrusted.

Before he died, Hitler executed a last will and testament. After the war that document enjoyed worldwide publication, and its pronouncements are well known. Bormann was the named executor of that will. During our conversation he was quick to quote from its text. He told me exactly what Hitler wrote. I die with a happy heart aware that there will spring up the seed of a radiant renaissance of the National Socialist movement. *Bormann scoffed at such a dream. He harbored no desire to renew the Nazi move-*

ment. He was pragmatic in his declaration that Hitler's idea had been ill conceived and poorly executed. Of course, he said, the benefit of hindsight had made clear all of the mistakes. It was strange to hear him speak in such a manner. Hitler had been a witness at his wedding to Gerda. His firstborn was named Adolf, in honor of his godfather. He served Hitler with the obedience of a guard dog, becoming a willing participant to everything he did.

I asked whatever did he mean and he explained that National Socialism was dead. Communism would not fare any better, he noted. It was inevitable that all of the puppet regimes in Eastern Europe would fail. Hitler foretold that outcome and Bormann agreed. The West would dominate the world, of that he was sure. He did not necessarily concur with such a result, only that politics and history had already determined the victor. He liked to say that any government that must force its citizens to stay within its borders is doomed from the start. Again, another strange comment from a man who helped exterminate millions, many his own countrymen.

I wanted to inquire further, to know what caused such a transformation in this man whom I remembered as obsessed with power. But I remained silent and simply listened as he ranted.

His physical appearance had changed. Still a sallow-skinned face, round and fleshy with broad nostrils, his eyes framed by a perpetual squint, glaring with the same nothingness I remembered from the war. But he'd lost weight. No longer rotund. And muscular, carrying himself with a clear air of contentment. He still indulged in the vanity of dress, sporting a cashmere jacket, proper-fitting trousers, and shiny boots. I recall what Hitler once said of him. "What he undertakes he finishes. Sees that orders are carried out. A brutal man." *So I remained mindful that this seemingly pleasant, country gentleman was indeed a devil.*

On this day, though, Bormann's mood was buoyant. His son was three and had received a pony for his birthday. The animal had been raised on a farm nearby. Bormann bragged that its owner insisted on the gift. No one knows his true identity, the war seemingly forgotten. Bormann just one of countless German immigrants that dotted the surrounding mountains and valleys, some with war ties, most with pasts that were not acknowledged.

The boy seems to love his pony. There is genuine affection from Bormann toward the child. I never thought him capable of emotion. Yet with the child he is different. Perhaps it is the fact that there really is nothing left for him? Yet he would not hear of defeatism. National Socialism was dead, he proclaimed again. But there is room for something different. A movement beyond a bold grasp of power. I asked what he meant. But he refused to explain.

Cotton finished reading out loud from the pages Danny had supplied. These did not bear the Soviet seal. Instead they were typewritten in a font different from the other pages.

He and Cassiopeia had been dropped off in Bavaria near a waiting car. Danny had left with the chopper. Cassiopeia was driving as they threaded a path through the Alpine foothills southeast of Munich. Clearly, if the information in the pages was authentic, its author was someone deep on the inside. Incredibly, that person may have talked with Martin Bormann in 1955. Other meetings were noted in 1957, 1959, 1962, and 1964. Each one was described in detail, with personal observations of the encounters.

He glanced up. "If this stuff is true, Bormann survived long after the war. Amazing."

Outside, beyond the car windows, saw-toothed mountains sprinkled with snow framed the tarred road. He thought of a book he'd found in Milan a few months back, a first edition, leather bound, from the 19th century. And what Rousseau said of the Alps. *Never a plain, however beautiful it may be. I want rushing streams, rocks, firs, dark forests, mountains, paths which lead steeply up and down and fearful ravine beside my way.*

He agreed. The majesty was beyond dispute.

They motored through villages quiet in the late afternoon.

A few miles north of one hamlet, to the east, through trees blooming with late-spring leaves, a lake nestled in the embrace of mighty hills. Gray rock loomed skyward, rising perpendicular above the placid water. Snow continued to whiten the folds of the loftier peaks. Yet it was the water that drew his attention. A rich indigo stain on an otherwise stark landscape, so blue it appeared to bottom out as deep as the heights that surrounded it. He was immediately reminded of a Norwegian fjord, where similar water lay imprisoned at the foot of precipitous heights.

The lake stretched for about a mile, and Cassiopeia, following the directions Danny had provided, paralleled its oblong shore, finally veering from the highway onto a dirt path. The lane led to a concrete dock stretching out into surely frigid water. She parked and he caught sight of a house on the farthest shore. Too small for a palace, too grand for a retreat. Walls of granite and pebbledash. It was three stories with an octagonal cupola rising from its center. It sat on the crest of an incline, dense stands of pine and spruce beyond, verdant grass before, mountains blocking off all access except by water. In the afternoon sun the walls shone like a candle in a darkened room, the inky waters of the lake indistinguishable from the tree shadows beyond. The entire scene was a picture postcard Baedeker would have reveled in recommending. Danny had told them that Chancellor Eisenhuth owned the estate.

A family inheritance.

The silence was broken by the call of a distant cuckoo.

They walked to the dock and a small sloop tied at the end. Two armed security men waited for them. A few minutes later they were speeding across the lake.

He was bothered.

The information being peddled was that Theodor Pohl might be the son of Martin Bormann. Why was everyone taking this so seriously?

Easy.

Because they wanted to believe.

He heard again what Danny had said about Marie Eisenhuth. Brilliant. Competent. A determined woman who'd weathered many a political storm. Twenty years ago a series of financial scandals had toppled most of her party's leadership, throwing the hierarchy into chaos. She rose from the pack and eventually assumed control, ruling Germany as chancellor for the past sixteen years. Only Helmut Kohl and Angela Merkel had matched that longevity. A Bavarian, born and bred into the famed Herzog family, with ties back to the Wittelsbachs. An *Oberbayer*: an Upper Bavarian with a deep Catholic tradition. Her father had been an industrialist during the war, tried at Nuremberg but acquitted. Afterward his company, Herzog Concern, helped rebuild Germany, part of a forgiveness the West offered to many Germans in light of the more pressing threat of communism. Albert Herzog's industrial complex had been needed to resurrect West Germany's tattered economy. Forget about former slave labor and human rights violations. The war was over, the West required its champions, and the rewards were clearly bountiful, he thought as he stared again at the magnificent manor across the lake.

But he, too, was wondering.

Why *were* the current chancellor of Germany and the former president of the United States taking all of this so seriously?

CHAPTER TEN

CASSIOPEIA WAS IMPRESSED WITH THE *SCHLÖSS*, ADMIRING HOW another wealthy woman, through inheritance, had managed to express her good fortune. Like her own French château, this German estate had been lovingly restored and decorated in a style that reflected a long heritage.

They were ushered into a salon lined from ceiling to floor with elaborate oak bookcases. A colorful carpet protected a plank floor, and the pale-red velvet upholstery of the chairs and sofa complemented an unusual shade of light blue on the walls. Oil paintings, blackened by time, depicted hardened men of past centuries.

Marie Eisenhuth rose from the sofa.

She was an elderly woman—seventy-five was what Danny had said—short and slender, her silver hair trimmed in a no-nonsense bob. She wore a black woolen suit and studied them with a gaze that signaled strength and confidence. Danny had explained that there was a folksy manner about her people liked.

And he should know.

That had been his trademark, too.

Nothing superficial or manufactured, though. Just an honesty, which seemed undisputed. Enough that she'd managed to survive four hotly fought German elections and acquire the loving nickname of *Oma*.

"I greatly appreciate you both coming," she said in German-accented English. "Danny and I have known each other quite some time and I trust his judgment. He says you are both excellent at what you do and can be depended upon."

They both shook her hand and sat.

Their hostess pointed. "He also said that President Fox was not, as he described, on your Christmas card list."

Cotton smiled. "That would be a diplomatic way to put it."

"He's no friend of mine, either," the older woman said. "For some inexplicable reason, he ordered my phone calls monitored."

Which had been big news.

A few months back a whistleblower had revealed that the NSA had spied on Eisenhuth's and other world leaders' cell phone calls. Why? It had not been explained. But the White House had not denied the claim, either. It seemed a clear breach of trust. Allies should have no cause to spy on one another.

"I simply do not trust him," the chancellor said.

"I am curious, though, why not use your own intelligence service for all this?" Cotton asked. "Why would you need us?"

"Let us say that my relationship with the Bundesnachrichtendienst is . . . strained, at best. Nonexistent, at worst. The BND disagrees with a great many of my policies, and sometimes they do their best to undermine them. We also have reason to believe that they may have been complicit with Washington in spying on me. So I choose not to involve them. This situation requires the utmost secrecy."

Cassiopeia got that part, but, "They do all work for you."

"That seems to mean less and less anymore. People have their own agendas now. I prefer to keep this matter close, which is why I was grateful for Danny's assistance. Have you read what he provided?"

"On the way over," Cotton said.

"And is it ingrained now in that eidetic memory of yours?"

Cotton smiled. "It's there. A gift from my mother's side of the family."

"A precious one, too. I must confess that, at first, I thought this whole thing was a joke, a fraud, that there was an opportunist, nothing more, trying to be important. But now I am not so sure, given the murder of the woman in Partenkirchen."

"Do you honestly believe Martin Bormann and Eva Braun survived the war?" Cassiopeia asked.

"Why not? Mengele did. Eichmann did. Barbie and a thousand other war criminals did."

"The Israelis searched decades for Nazis. Private hunters like Simon Wiesenthal looked, too. Would Bormann not have surfaced?"

"How much about Martin Bormann do you know?"

"I've read a lot about him," Cotton said. "We both have, in fact."

Cassiopeia nodded.

"He was an extremely secretive man," the chancellor said. "Hitler's private secretary, a shadow, the faceless party chief, always lurking in the background. He was certainly someone good at disappearing. He was also the gatekeeper to the Third Reich. Nobody talked to Hitler unless they first passed through him. He possessed a network of informants scattered all across Germany who kept him apprised of everything. He received written reports from them every Saturday night. Of late, I have read some of those. They are fascinating in their detail. He also controlled all of the local governors, the *Gauleiters,* who ruled the occupied territories. That gave him enormous power.

"By February 1943 Bormann knew the war was lost. That is when he began to make plans. One was Aktion Aderflung. Project Eagle Flight. A complex scheme to smuggle gold, gems, stocks, and other assets out of Germany. The other was Aktion Feuerland. Project Land of Fire. Designed to secure a safe refuge for select Nazis in South America."

Cassiopeia was familiar with both, having read about them.

"We know for a fact that enormous amounts of money and valuables were transferred from this country. During the war the Nazis plundered the national bank of every country they conquered. Records show that Argentina's gold reserves grew from 346 tons in 1940 to 1,173 tons by 1945. That is a massive increase during a world war, and it all came from Germany. Bormann was in charge of the party's finances. He knew where every asset was located, every hiding place."

"But the accepted conclusion is that Bormann was killed in

May 1945 trying to escape Berlin. After Hitler died," Cotton said. "I've read the accounts. The testimony came out at Nuremberg. There were eyewitnesses who said an explosion killed him. And as I recall, DNA tests on bones found in Berlin in the 1970s confirmed that it was his skeleton."

"All of those accounts of his death have been contradicted," the chancellor said. "There is no way to know what happened when Bormann tried to flee Berlin. The Russian army was everywhere. He was surrounded."

"So how did he get out?"

"I have no idea."

"And the DNA?" Cotton asked, pushing the point.

"In 1998, when those tests were run, we did some lying of our own. We wanted Bormann dead. There was nothing to be gained by keeping alive the myth that he survived. So the remains were 'identified' through DNA as belonging to him. Part of that deception was to entice some sort of denial from Moscow and a release of information from its restricted archives contradicting those supposed results. But nothing happened. Only silence. So we cremated the remains and scattered the ashes in the Baltic Sea, ending the matter."

Cassiopeia heard what she'd not said.

So they could never be tested again.

"Now new information has been delivered to me," Eisenhuth said. "Unsolicited, I might add, which seems to come directly from those restricted Soviet archives. Our experts say the documents are authentic."

"You think Gerhard Schüb was *das Leck*?" Cotton asked. "He was working for the Soviets during the war?"

"It is possible. And he may be living in Belarus. But I am told you were not able to find much there."

"That's a bit of an understatement," Cassiopeia said. "We learned how to jump out of a plane with one parachute."

Eisenhuth seemed impressed. "Sounds exciting."

"It is."

"Does the information you received explain how Eva Braun escaped the bunker?" Cotton asked.

"Only in general terms. And please remember, there has never been, to this day, a positive identification of any remains belonging to Eva Braun. Nothing at all. And the so-called Hitler skull fragment, supposedly found in 1945 at the grave site in Berlin, was DNA-tested a few years ago. The results revealed it was the skull of a woman under forty, not Hitler's. And it was not Braun's, either. There is no forensic evidence to support a finding that Hitler or Braun died in the bunker."

"But you think that some anonymous information, sent to you by who-knows-who, is authentic?" Cassiopeia asked, not hiding her skepticism.

"If it is fake, why was Hanna Cress killed? Who went to all that trouble to silence her? And with cyanide-laced cigarettes? That shows a certain level of sophistication, would you not say?"

No question on that count.

"Let's be frank," Cotton said. "You think revealing Theodor Pohl as the son of Martin Bormann will end his political career."

"The thought has crossed my mind. Is that so bad?"

"You tell me."

Eisenhuth grinned. "You are quite direct."

"Occupational hazard. Especially when people are asking me, and others, to put our asses on the line for them."

"A fair point. And yes, I want to end Pohl's career. By whatever means. With all of the immigration issues, high unemployment, and inflation sapping the economy, the German populace is vulnerable."

"So you're taking the easy way to victory? Just smear the opponent out."

A flush of anger finally rose in Eisenhuth's face, then quickly faded as she regained control. "*Nein,* Herr Malone. I am trying to learn the truth, which the people of this nation deserve. Would you not agree?"

"I do. Which is another reason I'm still sitting here. What do you want us to do?"

"I need independent corroboration of all this information, and it seems that might exist in Chile. After the first contact, I hired an individual, with my own funds, to investigate." She paused. "He is in Chile, but not making the best progress. I want you to go there and take over that investigation. I need to determine if the information we have is true or false. An unsubstantiated allegation would be disastrous . . . for all concerned."

"And if we find out that it's true?" Cassiopeia asked.

"Then we will let the German people decide if they want the son of Martin Bormann as their chancellor."

CHAPTER ELEVEN

COTTON STARED AT MARIE EISENHUTH AS THE ROOM WENT SILENT for a moment. Beyond the windows, the cuckoo from earlier called again in the distance.

"I realize how this must seem," Eisenhuth said. "It all sounds quite fantastical. But we know that, thanks to Project Land of Fire, thousands of Nazis made their way to Argentina after the war. Why could Bormann and Braun, or even Hitler himself, have not done the same thing? And please know that I was ready to dismiss this all as fiction, until that murder. Hanna Cress was killed for a reason and, at a minimum, I want to know what that was."

"That's the first thing I've heard," he said, "that makes good sense."

His gaze drifted to the windows and the lake beyond.

Eisenhuth rose from her chair and approached a table on the far side of the room. Framed photographs angled from the lacquered top.

"Please," she said, motioning for them.

They stood and approached her.

She pointed to an aged black-and-white image of a young girl and an older man. "That is my father. Though acquitted at Nuremberg, he never forgot that humiliation. The cowards who ruled this country and caused all of his misery either killed themselves, were hanged, or fled.

Other men, the ones who were simply compelled to participate, like my father, had to stay and endure their punishment."

He stared down at the photo.

Albert Herzog was smiling at his young daughter. He was a tall, thin man, the face weather beaten, the hair sparse and black. With a diffident and unassuming gaze, his right arm wrapped around the little girl's shoulder, he stared at the camera with the look of a loving father. The tiniest smile creased his thin lips. How many German industrialists had succumbed to the lure of free labor and ready markets? Hitler offered both slaves to run their factories and a war machine to consume their goods. The profits had been too lucrative and too easy to resist. Car companies, steel mills, armament shops, banks, building contractors, clothiers, research laboratories, and countless other concerns simply could not refuse what the Third Reich offered. And none, to his knowledge, willingly returned a mark in compensation after the war. Whether Albert Herzog was different, he'd never know. The only important point, at the moment, was that his daughter believed him a victim.

Marie Eisenhuth's face seemed set for combat, and he saw the will of a woman who fought to the end for what she believed.

That he admired.

"I want to know if Martin Bormann survived the war," Eisenhuth said. "It galls me to think that he may have lived to an old age. It further galls me that his and others' lifestyles may have been financed with assets stolen from plundered countries and countless victims. I hope none of that is the case. But I want to know, even if there is just a shred of truth here."

"Do you seriously think that Eva Braun was pregnant, married Hitler in the bunker, then left with Martin Bormann to have a child?" Cotton asked.

"I do not know, Herr Malone. The information we have is quite sketchy on that point. But I do believe she and Bormann may have escaped, as the documents indicate. We simply have no idea what happened in the bunker. All we know is what we have been told happened."

"Even if Bormann survived, he'd be over a hundred years old," Cotton said. "Long dead."

"But his son may still live." Eisenhuth drew a breath. "In the information you have read, Bormann's son was born in 1952. So was Theodor Pohl. Did you know that Martin Bormann's father was named Theodor? And the woman who died yesterday. Her last word to Danny was *Kaiser*. Did you know that many in Pohl's inner circle call him the same thing? Kaiser. Emperor. Some sort of term of respect, I am told. Also, as I am sure Danny has told you, is it not odd that much of this same information surfaced a few years ago in Chile, with another American agent? Even the same source. Gerhard Schüb."

That was curious. And puzzling.

"I assume Pohl's past has been fully checked out?" he asked.

"It was the first thing we did. Records show that he was born in Hesse to long-standing citizens but, as you have been told, those records may not be accurate. There are questions. Our wartime and post-war documents are replete with discrepancies. Missing data, incomplete files, forgeries, little in the way of verification. As an adult, Pohl has led a fairly public life. Went to university in Heidelberg, and into business thereafter. All self-made ventures that became quite profitable."

"I assume he has money?"

She nodded. "Quite a bit. He bought several German publishing houses at a time when the industry slumped. He held on to them, consolidated, and created one of the largest publishers in the country. He's also heavily invested in banking and serves on several corporate directorships. I can supply you with a full dossier."

"Does he pay his taxes?" Cassiopeia asked.

He knew that was the Achilles' heel of most successful people.

"He does, with no issues our auditors could determine," the chancellor said. "Everything is in order. His only excess seems to be his politics. But he is a populist, and they tend to lean toward the extreme. I am sure you can see how, at a minimum, all of this has piqued my curiosity."

He had to admit, he was intrigued, too.

Not your ordinary run-of-the-mill mystery.

"The past three-quarters of a century, since the war, has been tough on Germany," the chancellor said. "First the Nazis, then the communists separated and brutalized us. Currently, both legacies seem to have merged in the anger of new-right extremists. When we were divided,

West Germany openly discouraged fanaticism. East Germany, though, took a different tack. The communists merely suppressed everything, thinking hate would no longer exist simply because they would not allow it to be there. After reunification, when that suppression ceased, hate groups from the old East Germany blossomed. Opportunists like Theodor Pohl now exploit that collective frustration."

He sensed her sincerity. This woman of obvious privilege, owner of a secluded estate beside an Alpine lake, seemed in tune with what ailed Germany.

"In 1920 the National Socialist Party was thought to be a joke," Eisenhuth said. "By 1933 it ruled Germany. If history has taught us nothing else, we have learned that we must defend ourselves against extremism . . . from the beginning."

The logic was sound, and he could think of no good rebuttal.

"Time has an annoying way of removing tarnish," Eisenhuth said. "If any of the information I have been provided proves true, exposing Pohl could have a chilling effect on the new-right movement rising not only here in Germany, but throughout the European Union. Or at least we can hope."

He felt compelled to say, "Or the opposite could happen and he becomes a rallying point."

"It is a danger. But I do not want my legacy to be that I led this country into ruin and disgrace. That I paved the way for a man like Theodor Pohl."

"We've already told President Daniels that we will do what we can," he said. "He's a tough person to tell no. As are you."

Eisenhuth smiled. "You are a charmer." She pointed. "I was warned. But I am delighted to have your assistance. When can you leave for South America?"

"Immediately," Cassiopeia said.

MARIE WATCHED FROM THE LIBRARY WINDOW AS THE BOAT carrying Cassiopeia Vitt and Cotton Malone eased from the dock and disappeared across the lake. Part of her security detail watched them leave, too.

She could not decide if she was apprehensive or relieved that soon she might have an answer to the question of her opponent's lineage. Was she doing the right thing? Perhaps it would be better to simply let the matter go. What had Hanna Cress told Danny Daniels? *"There are people and things, from the past, that still have meaning today. Tell Oma to be diligent to victory."*

What a strange warning.

She glanced again at the table and the photographs of her father and mother. What would they think of her? Both had been dead a long time. Neither lived to see her rise in politics, and never would they have conceived that one day she would be chancellor of Germany. A poem came to mind. One her father had quoted often. The words were glued to her conscience.

> *The towers stand in flames*
> *The church is overturned*
> *The town hall lies in ruins*
> *The stalwarts are hacked to bits*
> *The maidens are deflowered*
> *And everywhere we look*
> *Fire, plague and death*
> *Press the heart and soul.*

The writer could easily have been talking about Germany after World War I or II. Or East Germany after the communists. But instead Andreas Gryphius penned his words in 1648, at the end of the Thirty Years' War.

She knew her history.

Over a third of the population had been slaughtered, the nation devastated, towns razed, the collective conscience marred with violence and hatred. Such madness seemed the course of Germany. To some, the quest for empire, the desire to expand, remained perpetually overpowering. And just when victory appeared at hand, greed and arrogance had always caused a downfall. Holy Roman emperors, Prussian kings,

Bismarck, and Hitler all made the same mistakes. None learned from the others, though each preached an appreciation for those who'd come before them. Germany was once again a united nation with another chance to exist as a body politic.

And that scared the world.

What had someone said?

"I love Germany so much I'm glad there are two of them."

But Malone's words rang again, too.

"So you're taking the easy way to victory?"

God knows she wanted to win. That she could not deny. She was not ready to be sidelined. And if proving Theodor Pohl the son of a monster would derail his reputation, then yes, she'd take the easy way to victory. On the other hand Malone's observation could also ring true. Exposing Pohl's heritage might galvanize the other side, making him even more palatable.

Germans were funny on that count.

The opinion polls were close, the people evenly divided. And her fate, Germany's fate, perhaps even the European Union's fate, might rest entirely on something that may or may not have happened in 1945.

She turned from the scene outside the window and considered the weeks ahead. So many possibilities. No guarantees.

A multitude of risk.

"God help us all," she whispered.

CHAPTER TWELVE

POHL SAT BY THE WINDOW AND ENJOYED HIS WINE. IT WAS A LOCAL variety, the grapes cultivated on terraced slopes above the Rhine in soil that had nourished sprouts since Roman times. He liked the blend, tart but not bitter, a reminder of years ago, at university, when he drank a similar grape and first realized that he wanted to rule Germany.

He was enjoying a rare quiet evening after the speech earlier in Cologne. A multi-state swing was scheduled over the next six days. First north to Bremen, then east to Mecklenburg, south to Stuttgart, ending with two days in Saxony and Dresden. He was growing accustomed to the American style of campaigning, yet it was complicated by the intricate German electoral process. There were no primary elections. Political parties named the candidates. Voting was strictly along party lines. Financing was solely through the parties, with no individual contributions allowed. Even how the money could be spent was subject to rigid control. Posters, billboards, leaflets, mailings, and rallies were permitted. Television ads were practically free. Rules all supposedly designed to stop a demagogue.

Yet the system was perfect for manipulation.

Spend enough money wisely, particularly on direct voter contact—mailings, door-to-door canvassing, political events—and unless the other side did the same with equal vigor, practically any election could be commandeered.

Which was precisely what he intended to do.

He sipped more wine.

The bay in which he sat was part of a towering Renaissance window that overlooked the castle's inner courtyard. He'd bought the property a quarter century ago after a succession of owners had neglected its maintenance. Little by little squatters had invaded and partitioned the interior like a beehive, tearing away fixtures, removing doors, even burning the wainscoting for warmth. That, combined with centuries of wind and weather, had taken a toll. He'd spent a decade refurbishing the ancient buildings and modernizing with plumbing, climate control, and electricity.

He loved the end result and named the finished structure Löwenberg.

Lion's mount.

Which seemed appropriate.

From his lofty perch, on a precipice that pitched off into space on three sides, forest stretched forever. He loved Hesse. A place of such exquisite variety. Between the low ranges of the Taunus hills in the south, with their beechwood groves and broad vales, and the magnificent northern woods of Westerwald loomed the loveliest spots of all—the Lahn Valley and *bergland* (hills) where blueberries ripened in summer and mushrooms sprang in autumn. Ancient citadels and medieval villages lay in abundance, as did health resorts and spas dating back to the time of the Prussian kings.

Home for his entire life.

He was enormously pleased with himself. How could he not be? The campaign was proceeding precisely according to plan. The polls were positive and momentum was clearly on his side. He was glad he'd hired political consultants. They'd so far earned every euro paid to them, and in the weeks ahead their abilities would surely be challenged, but they seemed up for the task.

He even liked his new physical image.

They'd recommended losing ten kilos and gradually adding a dash of auburn to his silver mane. The result had made him look a decade short of his nearly seventy years. His blue eyes, which once seemed misty, were now more alive thanks to a plastic surgeon who'd tightened the folds without anyone being the wiser. Another surgeon eliminated the need for glasses, while a nutritionist counseled him on how to maintain stamina through a vegetarian diet, though he secretly varied from that regimen on occasion. His face, adorning posters all across Germany, now projected the look of a determined statesman. His right-angled nose, taut cheeks, and tight brow were, he thought, imposing. Definitely German, in every way that mattered.

He savored another sip of wine and allowed the alcohol to soothe his sore throat. He'd lost count of the number of speeches he'd delivered over the past few weeks. It seemed like he was forever trying to convince someone that his vision for Germany was best.

Soon, perhaps, he would be chancellor.

Below, a car eased into the courtyard and parked. Headlights extinguished and the driver's door opened. Josef Engle stepped out, illuminated by the courtyard lights.

His associate had driven with him from Cologne, but had left Löwenberg a couple of hours back. He never questioned the details of how things were done, nor were they offered. Engle simply handled his duties with expert precision.

And he appreciated that dedication.

He needed zealots.

They operated from principles ingrained into their psyche like gravel melded with cement. Which provided the one trait he simply could not do without, whether from his employees or the German people.

Absolute loyalty.

He finished the last of the wine and continued to enjoy the solitude.

His life so rarely included quiet. Since his divorce twenty years ago women had become a nuisance. A marriage was necessary during the early years when image outweighed experience. Voters simply felt more comfortable with a married man, but a succession of politicians with domestic problems, a few ending in bitter divorces, had desensitized the populace and eliminated the unofficial requirement of a family to qualify for election. He was grateful that hypocrisy was over. Second and third marriages were a norm now and Germans, like citizens of every other Western nation, seemed willing to allow their leaders the same latitude with their personal life as they took with their own.

And he was glad.

Ridding himself of Gabriele had been necessary. She was a bother, wanting children, which was the last thing he needed. His focus was the party and winning elections. Not by the smallest of margins, either. He wanted mandates. Victories that signaled change. But not a new Reich. That word still carried the stench of a previous failure.

Which, to him, was Hitler's worst legacy.

Every law in Germany had been written to avoid a usurpation of individual rights to the benefit of the state, the idea being that nationalism never again be used as a rallying point. But that didn't mean the individual triumphed. It now simply fell to bureaucrats and judges and local officials, the people charged with actual law enforcement, to either ignore or modify the rules to suit their perception of what was best for Germany. Which explained the steady rise in ethnic violence, especially in the old East Germany, and Marie Eisenhuth's inability to stay its growth.

A weak point.

One he intended to exploit. Along with several others.

The heavy oak door across the room eased open. In the blackened window before him he caught Engle's reflection as his associate entered. He turned and asked what he wanted to know: "What happened?"

"An American, Cotton Malone, and a woman, Cassiopeia Vitt, met with Eisenhuth at her *schlöss*. They talked for an hour. Malone and Vitt are now headed to Chile."

They had spies within Eisenhuth's household.

Good ones.

"Strange, how she so quickly involved the Americans."

"Ex-president Daniels is a friend. She's quite distrustful of our intelligence people and even her own security team. It appears the seeds of paranoia we planted are sprouting."

He smiled. All part of the web they'd so carefully spun.

"I checked on Malone," Engle said. "He's an ex-operative. Highly regarded. Not an amateur. Vitt, too, is experienced. She's the sole owner of Terra."

He knew of the French conglomerate.

"They are headed to find the operative Eisenhuth sent to Santiago," Engle said.

"Let's make sure they find his body."

"I'll handle it myself."

Good to hear. "Is the American government involved?"

"No indication. This seems a private matter with Daniels, at least for now. Which makes sense. Eisenhuth would not want any of this to be public. She'll keep it close, as we predicted."

Until circumstances forced it public.

"Pour yourself some wine," he said to his associate.

Engle accepted the offer and moved toward a table.

"Tell me more of the conversations."

"The chancellor is anxious to learn the truth about you and Martin Bormann. She told Malone about her father and showed him pictures. As we already knew, she clearly resents what happened to him."

"So they know of Albert Herzog?"

Engle nodded. "They saw the pictures. No need for us to make sure that information gets to them."

He could not be more pleased.

Exactly what they wanted was happening.

"Her media event with the trees and the swastika played well on the evening news reports," he said. "She has to believe that exposing my supposed lineage will force me to withdraw. She can feel reelection within her grasp. A fifth term. Not since Helmut Kohl has anyone managed that. That sensation must be tantalizing. More than enough for her to take the bait we are offering."

Engle enjoyed a swallow of alcohol. "The presence of the Americans could raise problems. We did not anticipate this level of assistance. Bad enough we had to deal with Hanna Cress."

"Any indication as to what that woman told Daniels before she died?"

Engle shook his head. "It doesn't seem much other than one word."

He waited.

"Kaiser."

He knew Cress had been hired in Belarus as the envoy to deliver the information to Eisenhuth. At some point, original documents would have to be produced, and that moment came last Friday. She'd then been arrested, which had been a bit surprising, but not wholly unexpected. So they'd arranged for her death in a dramatic fashion. That act alone should be enough to spur Eisenhuth's curiosity and send her on a fool's quest.

But he was curious. "Why would Cress utter *'Kaiser'*?"

"She apparently did her research and learned that you enjoy the label."

"But how did she know I was involved?"

All of their contacts had been through third parties. Neither he nor Engle had ever spoken to Cress.

Engle shrugged. "That, I do not know."

Which bothered him.

The nickname was only used here at his residence, or by a few of his closest associates. Men and women who wanted to benefit from his rise to power. How had Hanna Cress known?

And was she even referring to him?

"It is good she is dead," he said.

"There is still the matter of the Americans."

"I don't see how they will matter," he said. "We'll lead them, too, and in the end Herr Malone and Fräulein Vitt will be two more casualties of Eisenhuth's ambition. I'm sure you can adapt the web to include their deaths."

Engle nodded. "But the Americans could have access to information we and Eisenhuth don't. They have vast resources available and the ability to reach many more. They also have diplomatic connections that can gain access to restricted data banks."

"As in South America?"

"Precisely. This whole endeavor hinges on our controlling the information flow."

"Which only means we need to spur them along quickly. Let's not give them time to learn more than we desire."

"I'm leaving for Santiago in two hours by private jet."

He moved toward the wine carafe and poured himself another glass. "Keep a tight hold on this, Josef. It's imperative this plays out as we envisioned. Timing is critical."

"These two Americans might not be as easily led."

He did not want to hear any pessimism. "It all depends on what they find. Make it tantalizing. Irresistible. Remember, they are anxious and time is running short for them, too. The election is fast approaching."

He sipped his wine and thought a moment, considering his adversaries.

"They'll follow. Of that I'm sure. But after their usefulness has waned, kill them both."

CHAPTER THIRTEEN

CHILEAN LAKE DISTRICT
WEDNESDAY, JUNE 12
3:40 P.M.

COTTON WAS GLAD HE'D SLEPT ON THE PLANE. DANNY DANIELS arranged a ride for them on a military transport out of Ramstein Air Base that had flown directly to Santiago. Not the smoothest flight and Cassiopeia had taken a little longer to adapt, but by the time they reached cruising altitude over the Atlantic she'd comforted herself with lots of bottled water, headphones with music, and a nap.

A LATAM Chile commuter flight south to Puerto Montt finished off the nearly 650 miles between Santiago and Chile's popular lake district. The view from the air was one of verdant forests, deep-violet lakes, and towering volcanoes, their snowcapped cones tinged in ruby red. A four-wheel-drive jeep was waiting for them when they landed, and he drove as they headed north, out of town.

"How far to the coordinates?" he asked her.

"About an hour. It's near Lake Puyehue, almost to the Argentine border."

In the information Hanna Cress had provided were GPS coordinates for a location in the Chilean lake district. Google Maps had verified that a dwelling stood there. Or a hacienda, as it would be called here. The plan was to head there first, then connect tomorrow in Santiago with the man Eisenhuth had hired. They'd made contact by phone and provided him with everything they knew, including what had happened in Chile a few years before with Jonathan Wyatt. The investigator concurred in their plan, saying he was working on some things and should be ready to share everything with them by tomorrow.

The highway forked and Cassiopeia motioned right.

He veered and realized they were now headed northeast and climbing in altitude. Huge ulmo trees lined the dark asphalt, and a thick understory of quila and fuchsia carpeted the ground beneath.

Ahead, a skunk fled the roadway.

"All this talk about Bormann has made me think of Henrik," he said.

Their friend Henrik Thorvaldsen had been gone awhile now. Killed in Paris. He missed the old Dane. They hadn't parted on the best of terms, a regret Cotton would harbor for the rest of his life.

Henrik had hated Germans.

And for good reason.

At 4:00 A.M. on April 9, 1940, eighty thousand Wehrmacht soldiers swarmed north across the Danish border into southern Jutland. At the same time, thousands more emerged from German colliers berthed in Copenhagen's harbor. Parachutists dropped down. Bombers dotted the sky. Danish Life Guards at the palace fought to protect King Christian, but the monarch called off the fight at 6:30 A.M. and allowed Denmark to be occupied. By 1943 the occupation had turned brutal and Danes were slaughtered by the thousands in an effort to restrain the population.

"Martin Bormann was the man who issued the order to terrorize the Danish people," he said. "Machine guns were turned against civilians. All of the local police were sent to concentration camps. Terrorist gangs ran free throughout the country. Henrik's father, mother, uncle, aunt, and three cousins were killed in the madness."

"I never knew that," she said.

"He rarely spoke about it. But he told me the story once."

A logging truck roared by in the opposite lane. Ahead an ox-drawn cart filled the dirt shoulder, and he veered into the other lane as they passed to avoid a man wearing a large sombrero. A lake appeared ahead, its verdant banks dense with trees.

"I'm glad you're here," he said to her.

She smiled. "Words of affirmation?"

He nodded. "Is that so bad?"

He knew she'd recently read a book. *The Five Love Languages.* Supposedly, everybody absorbed love in five basic ways. Quality time. Receiving gifts. Acts of service. Physical touch. Words of affirmation. There was a test in the book, which they'd both taken, to determine which one applied to them. He discovered that his love language was physical touch. Holding hands. A gentle caress. Sitting close to each other. Gestures like that spoke volumes to him. Hers was words of affirmation. Simple, straightforward comments that made someone feel appreciated.

Like *I'm glad you're here.*

"I meant it," he said.

"I didn't realize you'd paid such close attention."

"I don't miss much when it comes to you."

She smiled. "You're getting good at it."

"I'm a fast learner."

"There," she said, motioning ahead. "Turn on that side road."

They were using his phone for navigation.

He slowed and eased onto a rocky path that wound up a short incline. After a hundred yards trees blocked the way.

He stopped the car and reached for the door handle. "Looks like we walk from here."

He knew they were no more than a dozen miles from the Argentine border, and the chilly, thin air reminded him of the Alps. The late-afternoon sky hung clear. Thankfully, they'd dressed right with long sleeves, boots, and jackets. They walked through the woods on a defined trail. After a ten-minute hike, mostly uphill, the forest ended. Just as advertised, a hacienda stood on the precipice of a grassy cliff. Beyond, miles away, rose the blue-tinged pyramid of a volcano, its steep slopes clad with a mantle of forest.

"Quite a sight," she said. "And so conveniently isolated."

He agreed.

It reeked of a trap.

They headed toward the house.

Both of them reached beneath their jackets and withdrew an automatic pistol, courtesy of entering the country on a military flight blessed with diplomatic clearance.

The fields surrounding the house were overgrown with brown spindly grass and dense weeds. Barbed-wire fence had long rusted away and the remains of a rotten wooden fence, encircling what was once a corral, lay scattered. A few of the windowpanes were shattered. A wide crack snaked a path down one of the exterior walls, evidencing, he assumed, the earthquakes that sometimes rocked the region. They walked around to the rear of the building where the mountain view was even more spectacular. A brick veranda choked with grass led to a cracked open door.

"This place has been deserted a long time," he said.

Inside was dim and cold.

They stepped through a large kitchen littered with debris and headed toward the front of the house. The rooms were sparsely furnished, everything sheathed in mildewed cloth coated with layers of dust emitting a sour musty aroma. The farthest wall contained sheets of thick plate glass that framed a stunning view of glacier-capped peaks and a broad grassy meadow. The locale on a high, windswept plateau made him think of the Berghof in the Alps.

Hitler's mountain retreat.

Another whitewashed villa with big rooms, thick carpets, and a terrace commanding magnificent mountain views. To the eye there wasn't much difference in the volcanoes of the Andes and the saw-toothed peaks of the Alps. Nor were the forests all that varied. Coigue, ulmo, tepa, and tineo trees were every bit as evergreen as fir and pine. Both locales telegraphed an image of distant majesty. One, he knew, Hitler used to convey to visitors that the ruler of Germany was lord of all he surveyed.

The ulmo trees outside rustled as the wind continued to molest them. He glanced down at the floor, trying to see if the dust had been disturbed, but only their footprints were outlined.

They left the parlor and stepped through a foyer, following one of the hallways toward the rear, passing more rooms dotted with sheathed furniture. Most of the wall coverings bubbled from the elements. An ornate red marble fireplace captured his attention. The paintings on the walls cast a nothingness from their cloth coverings.

At the dining room they hesitated and studied the faded wood paneling, crumbling in places from an assault by insects. Then they turned and gazed down a long corridor. A room at the end of the passageway seemed to draw them forward. He was careful to again check the floor. Dust covered the surface like frost. No footprints.

They stopped in the doorway to the room at the end of the hall. It, too, possessed a stunning view of the serrated Andes through a dingy plate-glass window.

A condor soared in the distant sky.

The furniture, as in the other rooms, was sheathed. What appeared to be a desk faced away from the view, toward the doorway. Deer antlers dotted the taupe-colored walls. Brown sheets had been draped across what appeared to be bookcases, but had partially fallen away. He saw that the black wood shelves, thick with cobwebs, were lined with old volumes. Editions on art and architecture. Philosophical works of Nietzsche and Schopenhauer. Greek, Roman, and German histories. Goethe. Ibsen. Librettos of Wagner's operas. Nordic mythology. Military history.

Something nagged at his eidetic memory.

A familiarity.

On the opposite wall Cassiopeia freed one of the dust-infected sheets and revealed a wooden pole, surmounted by a metal eagle, atop a wreathed swastika. From a black-and-silver nameplate hung a tattered red silk banner framed by a black, white, and red border, the fringe worn, its tassels caked in dust. On it was a black static swastika atop a white circle, the word DEUTSCHLAND above, ERWACHE, below.

Germany. Awaken.

He read the words on the nameplate.

ADOLF HITLER.

"You don't see that every day," she said.

He agreed. Then his mind resolved the tug at his memory. "Those books on the shelf were some of Hitler's favorites. I'm surprised there aren't copies of Karl May, Hitler's favorite writer. He wrote cowboy adventure novels, but May's vision of our West was anything but accurate. The man never set foot in America. I have three in the shop. Collectors pay a lot for them." He again perused the shelves. "Hitler was passionate about books. He possessed a large personal library that was crated and sent to where he stayed for extended periods. Most of those volumes ended up being captured by us when we took Bavaria."

He reached up and withdrew one of the volumes and parted the binding.

"These aren't Hitler's, though. There's no nameplate. Hitler had all his books inscribed." He replaced the book onto the shelf. "These are something else altogether."

He stared around the room, then out the dingy windows, watching trees rustle in a freshening breeze. Something caught his gaze in one of the corners. A glimmer in the sunlight. He walked over and bent down. Dust wrapped an object in a tight embrace. A toy soldier. Metal. An SS man in full uniform, each article of clothing painted the appropriate black, maroon, and silver. He lifted the soldier from the floor and blew away the mites.

Cassiopeia came close.

"The toy of choice for any budding Nazi in the 1930s," he said.

"And here it is, eighty-five years later, in the middle of Chile."

Something shattered from far off in the house.

They whirled toward the doorway, guns in hand.

He quickly pocketed the toy.

"Company," he whispered.

CHAPTER FOURTEEN

Josef Engle strolled down a tree-lined boulevard, follow-ing his target, surprised at the destination.

Where the antique-book store once stood.

The spot was located near the Plaza de Armas, in the heart of the city, about midway down an arcade of picturesque boutiques. Next door sat a café that displayed an assortment of lovely Camembert and ched-dar cheeses in its plate-glass window. He'd dined there several times on past visits and greatly enjoyed the spicy sausage and salami, which the owner bragged were made on-site. He doubted the claim, yet admired the pander, since brashness was a quality he'd learned to accept.

He knew Cotton Malone and Cassiopeia Vitt were in Chile. Yester-day he'd been assured that everything was ready in the lake district, and a preliminary report should be making its way to him anytime.

Which was good.

Good preparation led to good results.

From a cathedral at the far end of the boulevard a bang of bells sig-naled half past the hour. Storm clouds were rolling in off the volcanoes to the west, the late-afternoon sun gradually fading behind a bank of thick cumulus. Rain would surely arrive by nightfall.

His target stopped and studied the street.

The bookshop was gone.

Exploded a few years back when some nosy American eyes and ears had crept too close. Its owner, a Chilean named Gamero Dichato, had been the son of a German immigrant. His father, along with countless others, had filtered into Chile in the difficult years after World War II. Some possessed relatives living in the area, descendants of the original German émigrés who, with the encouragement of the government, had flooded into central Chile during the late 19th century. Gamero's father had been a high-level diplomat in the Nazi foreign service, blessed with living abroad during the war, mostly in South America, capable afterward of denying, with impunity, any involvement with war crimes. The bookshop had been a magnet for the faithful, one of many repositories scattered across South America. Unfortunately, thanks to an American agent named Jonathan Wyatt, it had become necessary to sacrifice Gamero.

Nothing new there.

The web had always required protection.

So Gamero had been killed and his shop burned to the ground, all in an effort to dissuade any further investigation. Back then the idea had been to maintain secrecy. Now the goal was something altogether different.

His target apparently was familiar with that prior situation. An investigator, hired by Marie Eisenhuth, here in Chile now for over a week, his every move had been monitored. Perhaps the American influence explained his newfound knowledge? They would certainly know of this site. Access to that level of intelligence was precisely what he'd warned Pohl about.

He noticed that the land upon which the bookstore had stood remained vacant. Odd that no one had purchased the property and rebuilt something. Once there'd been a vault inside the old shop that protected eight filing cabinets filled with information from long ago, every page organized and indexed. Documents far too dangerous to be removed from Chile. Much had gone into their secretion, and the last thing anyone needed was for some customs agent to request a crate inspection or, even worse, for the materials to be lost or destroyed. So repositories were created throughout Chile, Argentina, Paraguay, and Brazil. Only a few then knew their exact locations, and even fewer knew them now.

Those file cabinets were gone.

Burned in the fire.

Most of their contents, though, had been preserved.

And thank goodness, since they were needed once again.

He'd personally supervised the destruction of Gamero's shop, hating that the man had to die, but understanding its necessity.

Now he was back.

In need of more bait to attract more predators.

He'd taken an early supper in one of the local *picadas,* the atmosphere friendly and relaxed, the tables full of families. He wondered what drew him to such tranquility. Perhaps it was the instability of his own life, a mother he hardly knew and an unknown father. His stepfather had been an ardent communist who assimilated his new family into eastern society. Eventually they all became like the state, emotionless and sedate. From childhood he'd been taught that results were all that counted. And at primary school, then secondary, the military, and finally in the Stasi, he'd performed and become noticed. His current benefactor, Theodor Pohl, was a lot like his former communist bosses. Amoral, relentless, with absolutely no conscience.

Which made things so much easier.

Principles had a nasty way of interfering with results.

His stomach burped from the empanadas he'd enjoyed earlier. The waiter had recommended a filling of minced beef, onions, olives, and a hard-boiled egg, and the suggestion turned out to be excellent. He'd enjoyed three of the pastries and, to remind him of home, his dessert had been a crumb cake topped with fresh whipped cream. The Chileans called the sweet küchen, one of many reminders of the German influence that persisted throughout the country. He'd always called it *mit schlag* and, as a child, he recalled that even the communists could not ruin its enjoyment.

The evening loomed chilly. Nearly winter in the Southern Hemisphere. He'd spent an enormous amount of time traveling Chile, Argentina, and Brazil. A lot like Germany, just with different expectations. Public officials were, overall, quite negotiable. Thank goodness. Pohl's demand for perfection meant he needed friends in certain places.

Particularly now.

They were on a tight schedule.

His target moved on, walking down the street.

Keeping pace with both him and the two Americans in the south was imperative. But as Pohl had noted about Malone and Vitt and this investigator, *"Let's make sure they find his body."*

Indeed.

That should not be a problem.

CHAPTER FIFTEEN

CASSIOPEIA ASSUMED A POSITION RIGHT OF THE DOORWAY. COT-
ton crept left. The crashing sounds had not been repeated. Her gun led
the way as she slipped from the room. The corridor ahead was cast in
deep shadows. A chill swept over her from both the unknown and the
stale air. They inched forward to the end of the passageway, stopping in
the foyer.

A sound came again. Scraping.

From the right.

She eased past Cotton, crouched low, then glided across the darkened foyer to an archway that opened into what was once surely a stately
parlor. A steely determination filled her gaze, her weapon aimed ahead.
She was alert and tense, but not afraid, especially with Cotton covering
her.

Another sound. Metal on metal.

From the rear of the house.

There were two inside?

Her gaze focused right, to the corridor that led back to where they'd
entered through the kitchen. She motioned that Cotton should concentrate on the parlor, and she'd take the other visitor. She did not want
their flank unprotected. Cotton nodded in understanding.

She crept down the hall and decided a rushing advance might give her an advantage, particularly after whoever it was continued to announce their presence with a steady *rat-tat-tat*. She sucked a breath, readied the gun, then bolted into the kitchen.

On one of the counters, three meters away, a puma stared back at her. The graceful cat was about a meter long with a tail half its length. Its small head was topped with rounded ears, the coat a tawny color, lighter underneath, with a white chin and throat.

A snarl seeped from the animal's half-opened mouth.

Sharp canines came into view. Hind legs tensed.

She considered shooting the mountain lion, but really didn't want to do that unless necessary. After all, she was the intruder here.

A shriek came from the front of the house. Not human. Animal. Then a series of low-pitched hisses and growls.

A gunshot echoed.

The puma leaped from the counter and bolted outside through the open kitchen door. She followed the animal with the muzzle of her gun, then rushed back to the front of the house.

Now she understood.

There were two local cats inside. Not unexpected considering the vacant house would provide excellent shelter.

Cotton was nowhere to be seen. She dashed to the archway leading into the parlor. Empty.

"Where are you?" she called out.

"Here," came the reply.

She crept down the corridor, toward the study. In one of the bedrooms Cotton stood just inside the doorway.

"I chased the cat out the open window with a shot," he said.

She nodded. "Mine left on his own."

The room was sparsely furnished with a poster bed, no mattress, a small dresser, and a nightstand, all sheathed. Framed photographs dotted the walls. Grimy black-and-white images of varying sizes, all ravaged by time, the images grainy and overblown, the glass dust infected.

They studied them.

People and places from the area, as the foliage and mountains looked familiar. In one a man stood holding a small boy. Cotton found his phone and retrieved the images of Martin Bormann that Eisenhuth had supplied.

"That's him," he said. "No question."

The boy couldn't be more than two or three.

"It's postwar, too," Cotton added. "His appearance has changed."

She compared the two images. On the phone Bormann was broad shouldered, stocky, knock-kneed, with thin strands of dark hair. A bit bloated, with a scar on the left cheek.

"The fleshy jowls are gone," she said, pointing to the picture on the wall. "His physique is much thinner, the hair is still sparse but longer. But look. No scar on the left cheek."

"Things like that could be fixed, even back then."

Another of the framed photos showed a woman, her wavy hair long and dark. She wore a gathered skirt with a flowery print. Her thin chest was covered in a tight-fitting, short-sleeved blouse. A light-colored apron wrapped her waist. She had high cheekbones, a stiff brow, pencil eyebrows, and modest nose.

"That's Eva Braun," he said. "Her hair is longer and darker. The face is a bit worn, but it's her. Postwar."

He showed her an image of Braun at Hitler's side on his phone.

"Not all that different," she said.

The wall image was tight, revealing virtually nothing of the background, other than an outdoor scene with what appeared to be a wooden structure behind her.

A few of the other photos were similar. Bormann with the boy. Braun and Bormann together. None revealed much about their exact location, and there was nothing written on them, front or back, that offered any explanation as to time or place.

"This is what we were sent here to see," he said.

She agreed.

A new sound disturbed the silence.

A car engine.

Grinding out its gears, coming closer.

They both headed for an open window. A pickup truck was plowing its way toward the house, through the tall grass, the chassis taking its share of bumps and grinds. It was too far away to make out much detail, but two men stood in the bed. It came no closer than thirty meters, where it turned hard right and stopped. Rifles appeared in the hands of the two men and shots were fired at the house, one shattering the window in the room next door.

They ducked for cover.

Before they could return fire, the truck roared back into the trees.

They rushed outside.

"Who the hell was that?" she asked.

"Good question."

CHAPTER SIXTEEN

Munich, Germany
9:00 P.M.

Marie was tired but knew she could not let the audience sense her exhaustion. The day had been grueling. She'd given four speeches in different sectors of the city, then attended a huge rally at the municipal fairgrounds. She'd spent several hours there shaking hands. Dinner had been in the Schwabing, the district just north of the university, and now, in her final appearance of the day, she faced a young, intellectual crowd, eager to embrace an active debate.

"What dangers do you perceive from the new right?" The question came from a young woman with scraggly blond hair and a silver nose ring.

She faced the questioner. "Tell me, since the war has Germany ever seriously been threatened with a radical-right party?" She paused an instant as her rhetorical inquiry played across the audience's minds. "No. We have not. Sure, there is an abundance of vitriolic dialogue, but the radical right is smeared with the same tar that consumed Hitler, and thankfully there is no way to escape that stench. It is a smell that tarnishes their message, but unfortunately it does not dissuade people from listening. So we must be vigilant in making sure that their message of hate does not take hold."

"What of the violence?" another asked. "That's more than rhetoric."

She was ready with her response. "Before we reunified, radicals screamed that no one possessed the will, or the ability, to unify Germany but them. They were the answer to all our troubles. Then the people themselves brought about the downfall of the communists and an emergence of one Germany. The radical right had little to nothing to do with reunification. Now the *new* right has to react to something else. Something different. This is imperative, as they need hate to survive. So they channel anger toward immigrants and foreigners, blaming them for everything they claim is wrong with Germany. Those are the actions of cowards. Not patriots. Violence is the manifestation of their anger. It's on the rise. Yes. But together we can stop it."

She had to be careful with her words.

Bavaria was a Theodor Pohl bastion. The region had always leaned conservative. The embryonic Nazi Party was born not five kilometers away from where she stood. Local beer halls still proudly proclaimed Hitler's former presence without any hint of guilt. Nuremberg, to the north, became a center of Nazi celebrations and the place where the odious race laws were eventually enacted. Her own opinion polls showed Pohl leading the state by a dozen percentage points, but she was determined to at least nibble away at that edge.

"Do you want this nation—our unified Germany—to again fall from grace?" she asked the crowd. "Don't fool yourselves. Xenophobic feelings are clearly on the rise. Jewish cemeteries are disgraced weekly. Memorials at concentration camps have been defaced. Attacks on ethnic groups are increasing. Are we to allow terrorists to dominate our society? Is the world to know Germany by its hatred—or by its decency? Our country, this nation, is only as strong as the people's commitment to peace and freedom."

Heads began to bob in agreement.

The audience was far more receptive than she'd anticipated.

She glanced at the clock hanging in the rear of the hall. She'd been taking questions for nearly two hours, and her years in politics had certainly taught her when to shut up. So she thanked them, shook a few hands, then retreated to the street and a waiting car that took her across Munich.

"What about tomorrow?" an aide sitting across from her asked. "Still leery?"

"To say the least. What are the latest poll numbers?"

"Nationwide you have a 3-point lead. But the margin of error is 4 percent, so it's still dead even."

"Tomorrow is quite a risk. To my memory, no one has ever been so bold in a chancellor's race. There could be a backlash."

And she meant it.

The car turned onto busy Maximilianstrasse and melded into brisk night traffic.

"Pohl's message is taking hold. Its resonance is frightening. Silence at this point could be fatal," her aide said.

"As could what I'm planning to say tomorrow."

She wanted to hear from Malone and Vitt and know what was happening in Chile. That could be her answer. Yet nothing had come, so far, from across the Atlantic.

There really was no choice.

Not to act now might be the worst mistake of all.

Fifteen minutes later she was climbing a set of oak stairs to the second floor of the Karlshof, an elegant two-hundred-room hotel with spectacular views of the nearby Karlsplatz. Her suite was a three-room affair, for which she was grateful since her husband, Kurt, had accompanied her from their nearby lakeside *schlöss*.

"*Guten abend,*" he said to her.

She turned from closing the hotel room door. Kurt was ensconced in one of the suite's Regency chairs, reading the Munich newspaper.

"I left after dinner," he said. "I assumed you were aware. That crowd was not my type."

She'd noticed his exit and was glad for it.

He tended to talk far too much when he drank.

He folded the newspaper and gazed over at her. "Did you notice the waiter who served us dinner? The man repeatedly tried to speak with me. For what, I do not know." He shook his head. "Disgusting. This country is overrun with brownies. They are destroying the fabric of our society."

She, too, had noticed the waiter and spoke to him briefly. He was a citizen, born here to immigrant parents who'd arrived from Turkey four decades ago in one of the first waves of guest workers—those invited to Germany to help alleviate a then-serious employment problem. His family remained after the visa time had expired and now considered Germany their home. "I certainly hope you continue to confine those remarks, and your slurs, to you and me."

"Oh, not to worry. I would do nothing to jeopardize your position or campaign. I am the husband of the chancellor and I keep my opinions to myself."

She wondered how eight million Turks could possibly dilute seventy million Germans, but unfortunately her husband's xenophobia was shared by an alarming number of people. And a declining birth rate among Germans only contributed to that fear. While Turks, Kurds, and a multitude of other émigrés encouraged large families, Germans seemed the opposite. One of the new right's more recent rallying cries proclaimed that within a few decades Germans would become a minority within their own country.

"Why is it necessary for you to hate?" It was a question she wanted to pose to the nation as a whole.

He tossed his newspaper on a side table. "I don't. Not at all. I simply question why *our* country has to be the dumping ground for all of Europe."

"Perhaps because we attempted twice in fifty years to dominate Europe. Not to mention the six million Jews and millions of others we slaughtered in two wars. I would think there is a need for reparation."

Which was why she'd welcomed over a million asylum seekers into the country during her time in office. People from Syria, Afghanistan, and Africa fleeing violence and oppression. But that open-door policy had coalesced her enemies into a cohesive opposition, one Pohl had exploited.

Kurt threw her one of his condescending smiles. "Marie, all of those atrocities are the sins of our fathers and grandfathers, not ours. You, I, and 99 percent of every German alive today have never harmed a soul. Yet we continue to pay the price for their mistakes."

She sat in one of the chairs, tired, but still wound up from the forum.

"You truly frighten me, Kurt. You and all of the others who tear people down to make yourselves feel strong. Why is that necessary? It seems a tragic fault. You cannot be proud of yourselves unless it is at another's expense."

"I am seventy-six years old and proud to be German. I would not want to hurt or harm a soul. Not ever. I simply question the need for continued, indiscriminate immigration into this country."

She reached for the newspaper. One of her advisers had briefed her earlier on the day's events.

"Did you read the story today about what happened in Thuringia," she said. "Forty skinheads, kids, sixteen to twenty-four years old, went on a rampage. They assaulted a Turkish merchant, stole his money, then physically attacked three Spanish tourists. They ended up at Buchenwald and desecrated the concentration camp with vandalism for two hours before police *finally* decided to arrest them. All were subsequently released and the charges dropped. And you see no problem there?"

He shook his head. "As I said, the people are tired of atoning for the sins of another generation. They see foreigners as a constant reminder of that. Can't *you* see? Continuous apologies only fuel the fires of discontent. What is reported there in the newspaper is a prime example of what I am saying. Acts of violence like that are merely reflections of a collective frustration."

She stared at her husband and wondered about him. Only in the last couple of decades had his true feelings manifested themselves. But his radicalism disgusted her. He was akin to a group of twenty-year-olds who, in the 1920s, conceived National Socialism and eventually convinced a nation to follow their lead.

That was her greatest fear.

Germans followed far too easily. Only a few dared to lead while all of the others, like ants in a mound, blindly fell into line. One example of that collective fault had been hammered home earlier when her pollster told her that, even though the communists had utterly destroyed eastern Germany, a surprising bloc of easterners favored its return. *Fewer choices* was the main reason they offered.

Which exposed a fundamental flaw in her society.

Where Americans or the British never fully trusted their government and used skepticism to keep officials at bay, Germans seemed to embrace their leaders with an unfettered devotion.

The man sitting across from her was a prime example.

His father had been an ardent Nazi, an industrialist who not only financed Hitler, but became a willing partner. The only thing that saved him from prison after the war was that Eisenhuth-Industrie had been deemed vital to the rebuilding of the new West Germany. So the family was spared a forfeiture of their assets in return for cooperation, but her father-in-law died twenty-five years ago still fervently believing Hitler had been right.

"Are you still going tomorrow?" he asked her.

She heard the resignation in his voice.

He would never understand so she said nothing.

"I take it from your silence that you are. God help you, Marie. You are making a huge mistake."

"That's your opinion. Keep it, and all of the others, to yourself."

And she meant it.

She stood and headed to her bedroom. His room was on the other side of the suite. They'd not shared a bed in a long time.

"I do keep my opinions to myself," he declared. "But that is the benefit of this great democracy you champion. I may possess whatever belief I desire. You are entitled to yours and I to mine."

It was useless, as always. They'd engaged in similar discussions before, each time with the same results. Him being condescending and her walking off. The man whom she'd married four decades ago had evolved into a total stranger. She'd always thought him different from his family, a progressive German, the son of a Nazi but not an inheritor of those warped ideals. Yet he was exactly like his father. Luckily, Kurt was harmless. He seemed content to oversee the family businesses, read his newspapers, and debate with her. As long as that was the extent of his political efforts, she was fine. She recalled what her aide said in the car.

Silence at this point could be fatal.

So tomorrow had to happen.

But her conflict with Kurt brought into focus the dilemma many

German homes faced. Differing philosophies, differing objectives. Men and women, children and parents, perched on opposite ends of the political spectrum. Such a shame German politics perennially divided families.

And that realization chilled her.

Yet there was something else—sad but true.

Her husband frightened her even more.

CHAPTER SEVENTEEN

Cotton drove the jeep into town. A road sign a hundred
yards back identified the hamlet as Los Arana. The asphalt highway
split the place nearly in half, houses to the south, shops north. Lime
trees dotted a central plaza. The cone of the volcano loomed in the distance, perfectly centered between the domes of a church. The streets
were quiet but it was early evening, the workday over.

He parked near a busy café.

Inside, they ordered food and studied the photographs they'd freed
from their frames at the hacienda.

"This is at least partial confirmation of what Eisenhuth was told,"
Cassiopeia said.

"Provided they're real."

"It won't be hard to determine."

No, it wouldn't.

He turned his attention back to his sandwich. The spicy meat was
hearty, the bread fresh. He hadn't realized how hungry he was. His gaze
caught a man and a small boy at another table, the man using a napkin
to clean the kid's face of sauce. Thirty-seven years had passed since the
two navy officers had come to the house the day after his tenth birthday.
He'd sat in the living room beside his mother while they explained that
the submarine his father had commanded had sunk with all hands lost.

His stomach always churned at the memory of his mother's tears. His father's body was not recovered, the sub's wreckage never found, until decades later. He still missed his father, but had come to terms with the loss. Life had taught him that everyone made choices in their life. Good and bad. He'd made his share.

His father, too.

Cassiopeia lifted the photos from the table and studied each image again. "This is proof Martin Bormann and Eva Braun survived the war."

He sipped his bottled water. "But what happened to that little boy? Did he grow up to become Theodor Pohl?"

"That's a good question."

He'd meant what he said in the car. He was glad that Cassiopeia was with him. If not for Danny Daniels appearing on Sunday, she'd already be back in France after a long weekend in Denmark. That seemed the extent of their relationship. A few days here and there. Then, occasionally, a job together. It certainly made for great reunions. But he had to admit, he'd begun to miss her when she wasn't around. He had few friends in the world—a result of both the nature of his former occupation and the isolation he'd intentionally sought by moving to Denmark in the first place. His son, Gary, remained close and visited at least three times a year.

Which he really enjoyed.

The boy had a good head on his shoulders. They'd talked some about his future, and he'd been surprised when the seventeen-year-old mentioned the navy as a possible career. Sure, he'd chosen that path, too. But that was a boy reacting to the death of a father, trying to honor him in any way possible. What was Gary's motive? Hard to say. His son was tight-lipped. But there was still a year or so to go before any decision would have to be made. He had to admit, though, having his boy join up would be wonderful.

The front door creaked open and two uniformed carabineros swaggered into the café. Both were young and armed with holstered pistols. They strolled to the counter and spoke with the man who'd taken their food orders a few minutes back. Cotton kept both policemen in his peripheral vision as he finished off the last bites of his sandwich.

The two turned and motioned at Cotton and Cassiopeia.

The man behind the counter nodded, and they walked over.

"Excuse me," the one carabinero said in English. "We need a word."

Cotton wiped his mouth with a napkin. "And what word would that be?"

A smile formed on the man's lips. "Weapons. Are you armed?"

He did not like where this was going. "We are."

"Please place your guns on the table."

"We are sanctioned to carry our firearms," Cassiopeia said.

"That may be so," the other carabinero said, "but we want the weapons on the table."

"And if we refuse?" he asked.

The man drew his pistol and pointed it directly at him.

"Then we shall do this another way."

CHAPTER EIGHTEEN

LÖWENBERG
STATE OF HESSE, GERMANY
10:15 P.M.

THEODOR POHL STUDIED THE FIGURE SITTING ACROSS FROM HIM. He was a portly stump of a man with sparse brown hair and the face of a walrus. But he'd been assured that Waltraud Klein, a senior judge in the local state court, was quite reasonable, and at the moment he was in need of a negotiable jurist.

"I must say, Herr Pohl, it is an honor that you have taken the time to speak with me," his guest said.

A tinge of tobacco accompanied Klein's words. He hated the scent. It was the smell of habit, of weakness. But he held his emotions in check. This man did not need to know what he truly felt.

"I asked you here, to my home, as I am aware of the trial that is forthcoming next week in your court."

A city official had been accused of incendiarism after writing an inflammatory letter to the chairman of the Central Council of Jews. In the letter he urged the man to leave Germany and take the entire council membership with him. Such statements had long been banned by German law, so the official was promptly arrested. The case had generated national attention, quickly involving many of the political parties in the debate.

"It will be quite a trial," Klein said, seemingly proud of the fact he would be involved.

He decided to get to the point. "I am told that you broke away from mainstream politics long ago."

Klein nodded. "Past governments were far too friendly with the communists for me."

"On that point we agree. I, too, believe Helmut Kohl and his successors were Marxist sympathizers." He paused a moment, hoping he'd gauged this man correctly. "I am also told that you are a believer."

Klein's pudgy face revealed nothing. The jurist simply stared back through oily eyes. "My father was a member of the Nazi Party. So was my grandfather. They are two men I greatly respect."

"As you should. But are you a believer in what they stood for?"

He needed to know.

"I am." There was pride in the declaration.

"I am also told that many in the judiciary feel the same way."

"There are others who do not think the past so bad."

Numbers flashed through his mind. Statistics he'd memorized. Recent national polls indicated that 42 percent of Germans believed the National Socialists once offered both good and bad qualities. Sixty percent were convinced that prejudice against the Jewish people would continue. Forty percent acknowledged themselves as right-wing sympathizers. Twenty-seven percent thought Germany superior to other nations, and another 17 percent were undecided. A solid one-half of the populace liked the sound of *Fatherland,* while a quarter felt there were still Nazis living among them.

He rattled off the percentages to Klein, then said, "Most telling is that 7 percent of Germans would actually vote for Hitler again. Nearly 30 percent believe that, without the war and the Jewish problem, he would have been labeled a great statesman. It irks me that a succession of governments have masked their own incompetence by perpetuating the belief that somehow we still owe the world for what happened eighty years ago."

"Assuming it even happened."

"Precisely."

He did not for a moment believe the Holocaust never occurred. He realized, though, that many, like the fat judge sitting across from him, fervently thought Jewish extermination was, if anything, small scale or nonexistent, a myth created by the Allies to deflate postwar German nationalism. He'd actually read some of Klein's legal opinions, rendered over the past twenty-four years he'd served on the local court, where he once called the Holocaust a "historical thesis," and lamented that Germany must still be forced to atone while other countries slaughtered people with no consequences.

"Your defendant in the coming trial is a respectable man," he said. "His political convictions are matters of the heart. He is no terrorist. No Nazi."

"So I am told," Klein said, with an appraising stare. "May I inquire as to your particular interest?"

"Votes, Judge. There is a large segment of the population that labels this trial an injustice. Nations all around the world have free speech. We proclaim the same, yet routinely censor the thoughts and feelings of many Germans, this defendant being a prime example. He was simply expressing his opinion."

Klein did not respond, and the room lapsed to quiet. He knew that the judge had taken a late supper, alone, in a hotel nearby, then had been secretly brought to the castle. Privacy was essential. The last thing either of them needed was a suspicious reporter lurking around.

"I have followed your campaign with great interest," Klein said. "Your words make sense."

Exactly what he wanted to hear. "I need your assistance. Your defendant must be freed. Make a statement with your decision. Draw a line. I am told that your reversal rate is less than one-half of one percent. That's admirable. Make this decision appellate-proof. Be clever with your words, but don't mince the message."

"That could start riots."

"And the problem?"

Klein registered his understanding with a smile. "Unrest that you would oppose in action, but not in principle. An appeal to both ends of the spectrum."

"And to the all-important middle, Judge. At present, the race for control of the Bundestag is far too close. It will be the middle-ground voter who decides who prevails. The German that, in his heart, believes as we do, but would never voice the same. That German, though, can speak volumes in the voting booth. There, only God knows how they vote. My prediction is they will do as we say, 'Germany for Germans. Foreigners out.'" He reached to the table beside his chair and grabbed a folder. His staff had done an excellent job in preparation. Their assumptions about Waltraud Klein had proven correct. "Are you aware of other criminal cases presently pending?"

"Similar to my defendant?"

He nodded, then opened the folder and explained.

Six youths in Stuttgart had beaten a man to death in his home with a baseball bat. He was a twenty-year resident of Germany, but a Croat by birth. They considered him an "inferior element." All six were about to be tried for murder.

Three men torched an apartment building in a village near the Czech border, members of an ultra-right group that targeted asylum seekers. A ten-year-old girl was horribly mutilated in the fire. All three were about to be tried for arson. The judge in that trial had already dismissed attempted murder charges.

In a tiny village southwest of Berlin the most grievous incident of all had occurred. Seventy-three Africans were moved by the government into an abandoned building. The local villagers were openly opposed to the action. Written protests were filed. Meetings held. Letters posted. All to no avail. Fearing violence, guards were stationed at the building but inexplicably one night, the previous April, while guards were not present, Molotov cocktails came through the windows. The local fire brigade took twenty minutes to respond and, when they finally arrived, did nothing more than prevent the blaze from spreading, allowing the building to burn completely to the ground. None of the Africans were hurt, and they were subsequently moved to another town, but two locals were eventually charged with arson. Their trial started in four weeks.

"I am familiar with the last situation," Klein said. "I am told the defendants have alibis. Good ones."

"True. So acquittals should be easy."

"But the unrest would continue?"

"That is the idea. Then, after the election, we can turn our attention to all these 'asylum seekers' and resolve all conflict with finality."

Klein folded his fleshy hands across his lap. He knew the man's background. A nothing lawyer who'd managed to make it to the bench through a variety of political cronies who saw in him a personality they could manipulate.

"The Beer Hall Putsch of 1923 all over again," Klein said.

Klein was making all the correct connections.

Pohl needed him to identify with the past. Fanatics required linkage. It somehow gave legitimacy to what may otherwise be, at least for them, a bold assertion. He knew that, for some, the putsch of November 9, 1923, continued to be remembered with an almost religious fervor—when a young Hitler, Göring, Himmler, and Hess led three thousand storm troopers to the War Ministry in Munich trying to overthrow the Bavarian government. Police ultimately confronted them and shots were fired. Göring was hit and Hitler dislocated his shoulder. He was subsequently arrested and sentenced to five years in prison, serving only one, after another judge molded the law to suit his own political sympathies.

"You, too, have an opportunity to participate in the infancy of something great," he said. "Something special for our nation."

"I am not a Nazi," Klein declared.

He almost smiled. Many believed what the Nazis had preached, though few wanted the label. "Neither am I. The Nazis are gone. Their movement failed. There shall be no resurrection. But that does not mean some of their thoughts are not useful."

"What specifically would you have me do?"

A smile curled on his lips.

"Many things, Judge. Many important things."

CHAPTER NINETEEN

Los Arana, Chile
6:00 P.M.

Cotton and Cassiopeia were led from the café at gunpoint and driven a few miles out of town to a Tyrolean chalet, engulfed by dense woods, that seemed straight out of Bavaria. He recalled his previous experiences with the local law enforcement. The Carabineros de Chile were of long standing, with a national jurisdiction and a mandate to maintain order. Twice in the past he'd worked with their Ministry of Public Security and found everyone to be highly proficient and totally professional. But that was in Santiago. He was now six hundred miles to the south, in a rural region with a history of German influence dating back to the 19th century.

"Commander Malone. Senorita Vitt. Please, take a seat."

Their host stood in the center of a great room, its ceiling open to the roof of the A-framed structure. He was dressed in a dark business suit cut close in the European style. His black hair was long and wavy and gleamed from heavy brushing. He was lean and hard looking with a patrician nose, mustache, and small hands. The two carabineros quickly withdrew, which telegraphed that this man was in charge.

"I am Juan Vergara, deputy minister of investigations for Chile. I apologize for the intrusion on your dinner. But I am wondering why an American Justice Department lawyer and a billionaire from France are in my country, without my knowledge, with weapons."

His English was clear and nearly devoid of an accent. There was a charm to his manner that made Cotton question the strong-arm tactics.

"I'm wondering why the deputy Chilean minister of investigations is so concerned with us," Cotton said. "Surely you have more important things to do."

"Your vehicle was seen in the vicinity of a local hacienda earlier. One we have been aware of for some time. Gunshots were reported. A diligent farmer in the vicinity noted the license plate on your vehicle. We determined that it was a rental, paid for by a local importing company that I just happen to know is used as a front for American intelligence."

Okay, now he saw the reason for the interest.

"My government cooperates with yours, Commander Malone, on a great many things. We are allies. Some I do not understand, nor particularly agree with, but I am a willing servant. But this? We are totally unaware. So please, what is your business here in Chile?"

Cotton sat. "You seem to know a great deal about me. I haven't been in the navy for a while."

"You are a known commodity."

"It's always nice to be appreciated. And by the way, I'm retired from the Justice Department, too."

"Interesting the way you spend your retirement years."

He caught the message but offered nothing more.

"Where are our weapons?" Cassiopeia asked as she sat.

"They are being held, pending answers to my questions." His tone indicated that he wasn't backing down, either.

Cotton decided a little cooperation might go a long way. So he told Vergara about what happened. He then displayed the photos from his pocket and asked, "Recognize anybody?"

The Chilean studied the images carefully. "They appear quite old. I am only forty-one, and these seem to have been taken long before I was born."

That inquiry was going nowhere so he shifted gears. "Why the dog-and-pony show with the policemen and guns?"

"Your intentions were unclear. Is this an official visit? Now that you say you are retired, are you rogues? Inciting trouble in my country? Until I learn more, caution seemed warranted."

"Does your agency maintain immigration records going back to the 1940s?" he asked, deliberately changing pace again.

"That is a curious inquiry. Why would you be in need of such obscure information?"

"It concerns our business here."

"Until I learn what that may be, I will not be answering any more questions. On the contrary, you will do the answering."

"Our business here is sanctioned by the German government," Cotton declared. "Make whatever official inquiries you desire with Berlin. The chancellor herself is involved. By all means, talk to her office. Then I need an answer to my question."

He decided to leave Danny Daniels out of the equation.

For now.

"I shall do just that."

And Vergara retreated from the room without saying another word.

"He apparently knows more about us than he's saying," Cassiopeia whispered.

No question. "This house is impressive."

He glanced around at the interesting mixture of Bavarian pinewood and Scandinavian furnishings, none of which was bargain-basement stuff.

He wondered if the place was Vergara's or the government's. And had someone really spotted them leaving the hacienda and recalled the license plate? A bit much, he thought.

Twenty minutes passed before the minister returned.

"They connected me directly to the chancellor. A charming woman. She explained your presence and officially requested our assistance." He sat. "As I said, you have a fascinating retirement, Commander Malone. And you, Senorita Vitt, the sole owner of a multinational European corporation. Interesting how you spend your time, too. Be that as it may, what might my agency now do to help you both?"

All that was a little too easy for Cotton's taste, but he decided to play along. "We're looking for two Germans who immigrated to Chile after the war. The two in the photographs. A man and woman. It's doubtful, though, that they entered officially, and most certainly aliases were used."

"And who might these Germans be?"

He hesitated, then decided what the hell. "Martin Bormann and Eva Braun."

A crease of amusement flashed across the policeman's face. "You can't be serious?"

"Would I kid you?" His attempt at humor seemed lost on Vergara, so he motioned to the photos. "Like you said, those shots were taken a long time ago, we think in the early 1950s."

"Both of these individuals were hunted worldwide."

"Not true, Minister," he said. "Both were presumed dead. Braun committed suicide in the bunker with Hitler. Bormann was supposedly killed the next day by Russian artillery when he attempted to flee the bunker. No one seriously hunted either one of them."

He did not voice what he was thinking, what he recalled from his reading on the flight over. In 1947 Bormann was actually tried in absentia at Nuremberg, found guilty, and sentenced to death. Corpses were not generally afforded such special attention. And—

"Bormann was not declared legally dead until 1973. The official listing even contained a curious qualification that death *had not been completely established.*"

Vergara sat silent for a moment. His expression was stoic, a studied manner, as if running through a memorized routine.

"I may have some information on this," their host said. "There was a Bavarian who lived here in the late 1930s. A man named Peter Graf. He'd been a minor German official who lost all his posts when the Nazis assumed power. So he moved to Chile and amused himself by publishing a newsletter on politics and economics. I know this because, as a junior carabinero, I once was involved in an investigation that caused his file to come across my desk. History is a hobby of mine. In 1948 Graf was visiting a Count von Reichenbach. He was another German refugee who owned a large estate in the south, near the Argentine border. One day Graf was walking in the rain forest near the estate when three horsemen appeared wearing ponchos and sombreros. He recognized one of them as Martin Bormann. He knew him from before the war. Supposedly, Bormann also recognized Graf, cried out that fact, then fled toward the border. Graf reported the incident, but nothing ever came of the sighting, as far as I know."

"I imagine that is not the only sighting Chilean records indicate," Cassiopeia said.

Vergara nodded. "I have read others and been told of many more. And not just Senor Bormann. There were many criminals from the war who supposedly chose Chile as a safe haven. All of us in the police were aware of that reality. Our government then was most sympathetic to their needs. Why? I have no idea. Today attitudes are different. We have gladly assisted foreign governments with apprehension and extradition of anyone suspected as a war criminal. The hacienda you just visited has long been associated with Germans. It is why we still, periodically, check on it."

"Nazis are still hunted here?"

The policeman shook his head. "Not much anymore. They are all dead by now. But as I said, from time to time we cooperate with foreign governments who do still hunt. As I am doing right now."

"Was there ever any serious effort made to verify Bormann's presence in Chile?" Cassiopeia asked.

"I have no idea. That I would have to make inquiries about."

"Which would be welcomed," Cotton said.

Vergara shrugged. "I would be glad to do it. There exists no sound reason to harbor secrets any longer."

Maybe not. But that did not explain the murder of a woman inside a Bavarian police station. Information delivered to the German chancellor that revealed a pregnant Eva Braun and a son for Martin Bormann. And the photographs, books, and other memorabilia that they'd been directly led to find.

"Any idea why all that Nazi stuff was in the hacienda?" he asked.

"It is not uncommon. Memorabilia like that turns up all the time. There are dealers who routinely peddle it. Our laws have long made it illegal, and we do enforce those. But the practice still occurs."

Cotton recalled an Argentine news article from a few years ago where a secret room had been discovered in a Buenos Aires house, filled with hundreds of Nazi artifacts. The largest cache ever found anywhere.

"Who owns that hacienda?" he asked.

"A German émigré who has been dead twenty years. His family continues to possess the property, but they do not reside in Chile. One of many absentee owners."

"Someone is using that location," Cassiopeia said.

"I have already ordered surveillance of the grounds."

Cotton was tired. The day had been long. Jet lag was taking a toll. And tomorrow wasn't looking like it was going to be any better. "If we're done, could you take us back to town? We need some sleep."

"There is no need for that. You may stay here. I am returning to Santiago tonight by plane. I will leave the two carabineros who brought you here at your disposal. They will retrieve your vehicle from town."

He appreciated the gesture.

"What of our weapons?" Cassiopeia asked.

An enjoyment dawned in Vergara's cold brown eyes, then a charming smile formed on his lips. "Of course, they will be returned."

Yet the voice carried a tinge of irritation.

Not much.

But enough.

CHAPTER TWENTY

Cotton stepped from the shower and reached for a towel. He'd slept well, and the hot water had felt good. As usual, he shaved in the shower, a habit he developed in the navy that not only helped with nicks but saved time, as shaving ranked on his favorite to-do list just below a root canal.

The chalet was two stories, the upper floor containing two spacious bedrooms, though they'd only needed one. Vergara, true to his word, left last night and the two carabineros had slept downstairs. He'd sensed nothing unusual during the night and Vergara had returned their weapons, as promised. He wasn't overly impressed with the deputy minister of investigations. Too many questions and not enough responses. He needed to contact Danny Daniels, so he wrapped the towel around his waist and headed toward the bedroom.

"Hey sailor, new in town?" Cassiopeia asked, tossing him a wink.

She was sitting on the edge of the bed waiting her turn for the bathroom.

"The shower is all yours," he said, giving her a quick kiss.

She smiled and stood but, as he walked by, she managed to free the towel at his waist, which fell to the floor.

He shook his head and retrieved it.

She gave his bare chest an appraising glance and motioned at a jagged scar below his left pec, where the hair had refused to return. "Every time I see that, I wince a little. That had to hurt."

He glanced at the old wound. "Took forty stitches."

From his last assignment with the Magellan Billet, a supposedly cushy mission in Mexico City. Supposedly no danger. Court time. Witness interviews. Being a lawyer, instead of a field officer. But it had turned into chaos. Four people gunned down. He managed to kill three of the gunmen, but one shot him.

"How about I make it feel better later," she said.

He grinned. "I'll hold you to that."

And she headed for the bathroom.

He found his laptop in the travel bag. Standard Magellan Billet issue and specially programmed for coded transmissions. Along with the phone and his watch, Stephanie had supplied him with the most current model. One of her rules required regular reports from agents, since she liked to know what her people were doing. And she particularly liked to know about problems before they became catastrophes. He didn't work for her any longer, but he figured Danny Daniels wanted the same. So he opened a scrambled text to the number Daniels had provided and typed, Anybody home?

About time I heard from you. Eisenhuth told me that the Chilean police called last night for a reference.

Juan Vergara. Pushy fellow. Lots of questions, little information. Two of his carabineros escorted us at gunpoint to him. Not my idea of the Welcome Wagon. He turned on the charm and gave us a chalet to stay in for the night with a couple of babysitters. He then flew back to Santiago. You know anything about him?

I do now. People I called say he has a bit of an attitude, but is competent.

We found some confirmation of the information. Photos. They seem authentic. I'll forward images to you.

Good to hear. Work with Vergara. We need local assistance. Use your charm, that warm and fuzzy everyone finds so irresistible. I'll report all this to the chancellor. Keep in touch.

Yes, sir.

He deleted the scrambled text. He knew the information would not languish in a trash bin or on any server. It was gone forever, another feature programmed into the computer, per government specifications.

The shower was still running in the bathroom.

While he had a moment, he decided to study up a little. No such thing as too much information. Using a search engine, he located hits on Eva Braun. He'd read about her through the years, nothing more than a bit player to Hitler and the rest of his cronies. Then he found a page devoted to the woman who, in April 1945, became Mrs. Adolf Hitler:

Born in Munich in 1912 to a middle-class Catholic family, the daughter of a schoolteacher. She first met Hitler in the studio of his photographer friend, Heinrich Hoffmann, in 1929, describing him to her sister as "a gentleman of a certain age with a funny moustache and carrying a big felt hat." She worked as Hoffmann's office assistant, later becoming a photo laboratory worker, helping to process pictures of Hitler. Blond, fresh-faced, and athletic she was fond of skiing, mountain climbing, gymnastics, and dancing.

After the death of Geli Raubal, Hitler's niece with whom he maintained a long love affair, Braun became his mistress, living in his Munich flat in spite of her father's opposition. In 1935, after her abortive suicide attempt, Hitler brought her to a villa in a Munich suburb, near his home. In 1936 she moved to Berchtesgaden where she acted as Hitler's hostess. She led an isolated life in the Alpine retreat and later in Berlin. Every effort was made to conceal her relationship with Hitler, since the Führer was supposedly devoted solely to the nation. Few Germans knew of her existence. Even Hitler's closest associates were not certain of the nature of their relationship, since Hitler preferred to avoid suggestions of intimacy and was never wholly relaxed in her company. In fact, he would often degrade and belittle her intelligence. She spent most of her time exercising, brooding, reading cheap novelettes, watching romantic films, or concerning herself with her own appearance. But her loyalty to Hitler never wavered. After he survived the July 1944 assassination plot, she wrote an emotional letter, saying, "From our first meeting I swore to follow you anywhere, even unto death, I live only for your love."

In April 1945 she joined Hitler in the Führerbunker, and eventually died with him as part of a suicide pact. She was heard to say, "Better that ten thousand others die than he be lost to Germany." The rest of her family survived the war. Her mother, Franziska, who lived in an old farmhouse in Ruhpolding, Bavaria, died at the age of ninety-six, in January 1976.

He typed another request into the search engine and scanned three sites on Martin Bormann before he found a concise summary:

Bormann was born in Halberstadt on June 17, 1900, the son of a former Prussian regimental sergeant major who later became a post office employee. He dropped out of school to work on a farming estate in Mecklenburg. After serving briefly as a cannoneer in a field artillery regiment at the end of World War I, he subsequently joined the rightist Rossbach Freikorps in Mecklenburg. In March 1924 he was sentenced to one year's imprisonment as an accomplice in the brutal vengeance murder of Walther Kadow (his former teacher at elementary school), who had supposedly betrayed a Nazi martyr to the French occupation authorities in the Ruhr.

After his release he joined the National Socialist Party, becoming its regional press officer in Thuringia and then business manager. From 1928 to 1930 he was attached to the SA Supreme Command and in October 1933 he became a *Reichsleiter* of the party. A month later he was elected as a Nazi delegate to the Reichstag. From July 1933 until 1941, he was the chief of cabinet in the office of the deputy Führer, Rudolf Hess, acting as his personal secretary.

During this period Bormann, diligent, adaptable, and efficient, began his imperceptible rise to the center of power, slowly acquiring mastery over the Nazi bureaucratic mechanism and gaining Hitler's personal trust. In addition to administering Hitler's personal finances, he acquired the power to control the living standards of *Gauleiters* and *Reichsleiters,* the men who administered the various lands in the Reich. His brutality, coarseness, lack of culture, and apparent insignificance led top Nazis to underestimate his abilities. His mentor Rudolf Hess's flight to Britain opened the way for him to step into Hess's shoes in May 1941 as head of the party. Until the end of the war Bormann, working in the anonymity of his seemingly unimportant office, became the fierce guardian of Nazi orthodoxy. He was an arch-fanatic when it came to racial policy, anti-Semitism, and the *Kirchenkampf,* the war between the churches.

Increasingly, he controlled all questions concerning the security of the regime, acts of legislation, appointments, and promotions, especially if they concerned party personnel. Everything required his approval. By the end of 1942 Bormann was Hitler's private secretary. Always in attendance, taking care of tiresome administrative details, and steering Hitler into approval of his own schemes. He eventually displaced all rivals, including Goebbels, Speer, and even Eva Braun. Ordered by Hitler "to put the interests of the nation before his own feelings and to save himself," Bormann fled the Führerbunker on April 30, 1945.

Accounts of what happened afterward vary widely. According to Erich Kempka (Hitler's chauffeur), Bormann was killed trying to cross Russian lines by an anti-tank shell. Doubts, however, have persisted and numerous sightings of Bormann were reported, beginning in 1946. In that same year his wife, Gerda, died of cancer, though his ten children survived the war. One account says Bormann escaped to South America and settled in Argentina. Other accounts placed him in Brazil and Chile. Nothing was ever confirmed.

Two fascinating people.

Each had played a role in a conspiracy that terrorized the world for twelve long years.

Was there more to their story?

His phone buzzed, interrupting his thoughts. The display indicated the caller to be Juan Vergara. They'd exchanged numbers.

He answered.

"A man was murdered here in Santiago last night. Brutally stabbed to death. He is the same man the chancellor told me about last night. An investigator in her hire. She told me he would be working with you and Senorita Vitt and I should extend him the same courtesies."

"Where did it happen?"

"In his hotel room. I'm sending you a photo."

Which loaded onto his phone. The edge of a body filled the right side of the screen. Blood on the floor. To the left of the corpse lay a knife. No. A dagger. He enlarged the image with his fingers. The weapon was black and silver, the SS motto engraved on the blade, runes and eagles etched in the grip. He knew its history. Created by Himmler himself, the knives were bestowed onto each new SS inductee during a ceremony in a Thuringian castle. He'd seen photographs, but never an actual blade.

"Do you know the significance of that blade?" he asked Vergara.

"I have been told. Which is one of two reasons why I'm calling you."

"And the other?"

"There are things here you need to see."

"Can't you tell me?"

"Not on the phone. I will send a plane."

"All right. At least one of us will come your way."

"And the other?"

"They'll stay here and see what else turns up."

CHAPTER
TWENTY-ONE

DACHAU, GERMANY
2:40 P.M.

MARIE WALKED THROUGH THE GATE AND ENTERED THE concentration camp. Her emotions swirled from fear, to anxiety, to outright anger. The motto that once greeted all new arrivals flashed through her mind.

Arbeit Macht Frei. Work brings freedom.

Another Nazi lie.

She was taking an enormous gamble with this pilgrimage to one of the few remaining remnants of National Socialism. Dachau, particularly, garnered a special place in the national history, since it was the first of Hitler's murder factories, the model upon which all the rest were based.

Her conversation with Kurt last evening still plagued her. She'd woken several times during the night, bothered by his attitude and her apparent indifference to him. She wondered if she even loved him any longer. More, she pitied him for holding on to such inexplicable anger that so clouded his judgment.

Yet his sentiments were not uncommon.

Theodor Pohl was opening a wound that had never healed. His politics of hate, couched in terms of patriotism, would only send Germany backward. Someone needed to speak out. And at the moment, she was the only spokesperson who could command a national audience.

But the risks were real.

Modern Germans were confirmed pacifists. They wanted no mention of the former wars, either directly or indirectly. By and large they were consumed with historical guilt, bleeding their anguish in rivulets of pride.

But could that wound be mended?

The next couple of days might provide an answer, but the thirty-minute drive north from Munich that she'd just endured seemed to have served as a sobering prelude. Few road signs had pointed the way, as if the concentration camp was better left unknown. Her staff reported that, over the past few years, there'd been a sharp decline in German visitation. The vast majority of visitors to Dachau were either tourists or students. Schoolchildren came simply because German law proclaimed they must, yet Pohl was openly advocating a switch to voluntary school visits, something recent opinion polls indicated nearly 40 percent of the people favored.

Which was another disturbing trend.

She recalled when, at age eleven, she'd made her obligatory visit. Her mother had tried to explain the madness, and she'd reacted with the innocence of a child. Her adolescence was spent in postwar Germany amid a nation in ruins. She'd watched cities rise from rubble and the countryside re-emerge from wholesale destruction.

And the worst of all.

The creation of two Germanys.

One free. The other enslaved. One looking west. The other east. Barbed wire, land mines, and armed guards kept one population contained and the other from doing anything about it.

What a waste. And all for nothing.

She turned her attention back to the scene before her. The day was warm with a low bank of pewter cumulus rolling in from the Alps to the south. The wire perimeter, concrete administration buildings, and watchtowers of the former camp still stood. But the barracks were gone, torched by Allied liberators. All that remained were rectangular gravel plots marking their foundations, arranged in rows side by side, like semi-buried coffins, and one replica barrack rebuilt to illustrate the horror that was Dachau.

One of her aides motioned and she stepped toward a memorial sculpture, a grotesque metallic representation of bodies gnarled like knots in a barbed-wire fence. A podium stood facing south. The camp would provide a backdrop for the cameras now focused on her. Usually she spoke extemporaneously, but today handwritten notes were waiting at the podium.

She approached and stood straight.

"*Guten tag.* I came here today, to this place of evil, to speak my mind. My remarks will not be popular, but sometimes a person must take a path others shun." She paused a moment. "I want to continue to lead this nation, not only forward to a glorious future, but away from a shameful past. Confronting that past, dealing with truth, is the only way, I believe, to relieve ourselves of a burden that another generation so recklessly forced upon us." She motioned behind her. "How did this place come about? How was it possible that something this horrible could exist where farmers, for centuries, innocently tilled the soil and artists plied their trade?"

She answered her question, telling the reporters about the end of World War I and the dictates in the Treaty of Versailles that forced the closing of a local munitions factory. Afterward Dachau possessed the highest unemployment rate in Germany.

"And Hitler exploited that misfortune. He used collective despair for his own political gain. When local authorities were told in 1933 that a concentration camp would be built nearby, employing a staff of three thousand, they were elated."

She held up a copy of the *Dachauer Zeitung,* the local newspaper of that time.

"The press proclaimed the event *a great economic advantage.* Townspeople called the camp a *legitimate institution.* A place where those alienated from society—communists, socialists, union leaders, clergy, and, later, Jews—could supposedly be reeducated."

She hesitated and let her words take hold, knowing that everyone clearly knew what *reeducated* meant.

"Let me read something from *Dachauer Zeitung,* published in the June 15, 1933, edition. *At 11:00 A.M. a stand-up concert took place before the concentration camp. The prisoners, closely packed behind the gate, were engrossed in listening to music from a dashing storm trooper band. Around 3:00 P.M., a strong SS detachment trailed the ringing instruments of the storm trooper band, in procession, from the concentration camp through the city to the Ziegelkeller restaurant where a big concert took place. The camp commandant was in the lead, high on horseback. It was a heart-quickening picture.*"

She stared at the crowd and cameras.

"Now, you might say those are the words of a press afraid to publish anything contrary to the Nazi Party position. And to some extent, that observation would be correct. Unfortunately, though, there is more.

"At the time there was a great contest between Dachau and the nearby villages of Prittlbach and Etzenhausen over which township would take administrative possession of the camp. Press reports speak of the taxes to be made from beer and goods sold at the camp, along with a solidifying of a relationship with the personnel."

She hesitated again.

"And there is more. Every day from 1942 to 1945 a thousand or more prisoners marched to factories and businesses in this area as slave labor. Russian and Polish internees were routinely beaten as they made their way from the railroad station. I have read the testimony of one Polish inmate who said, *All the way down Friedenstrasse we were spat upon. Some threatened us with fists and had to be pulled back by the SS. We were spat upon by women and youth, especially young males. It was terrible.*"

A few of the reporters, those who had covered her extensively over the past few months, were gazing in wonderment. She imagined what they were thinking. Never had a candidate for national office taken such an aggressive stand with the nation's past. But she was banking on her pollster's conclusion that the vast majority of Germans would never go back, no matter how appealing Theodor Pohl's rhetoric may be. Standing here, at a place where thirty thousand people were meticulously slaughtered, not counting innumerable Russians and Poles who were butchered immediately upon entering, she was hoping to set herself completely apart from her opponent.

"Let me make one thing clear. I don't want it to be said that there were not acts of kindness and defiance by decent people who recognized the horror of Dachau. There are many reports of food being smuggled to slave laborers. Even accounts of SS guards who took pity on their charges. Sadly, though, those incidents were few and far between."

She was coming to the heart of her message. Bait for the supposed son of Martin Bormann. Danny Daniels' earlier call had confirmed that there was indeed photographic evidence to support the accusations. Eva Braun and Martin Bormann may have parented a son.

But was it Pohl?

That remained to be seen.

She held up a copy of *National-Zeitung,* a 1950s extremist publication of the ultra-right DVU Party.

"In here is described the absurd account of how Allied soldiers compelled SS prisoners, after the war, to build the gas chamber and ovens here at Dachau. What exists here today, the windowless gas chamber labeled Shower Bath and four brick crematory ovens, are deemed by this account *a dummy without documentary value.*"

She motioned to one of her aides who'd been standing on the far side of the memorial. The man pushed a stainless-steel cart draped in a crimson cloth toward the podium. Wheels clunked along on the rough cobbles. He stopped, slipped the cloth from the cart, then withdrew.

Stacks of books lay atop.

"These publications, in one way or the other, also deny what history has so clearly recorded."

She reached below the podium to where a book rested. One of her staff had placed the volume there in preparation for this moment.

She held the book high.

"They are all similar to this publication. *Germany Through the Ages.* On these pages, concentration camps are described as *necessary* and the murder of Jews is characterized as merely *an act of disrespect.* The author likewise finds no flaw in the claim that the ovens and gas chambers here at Dachau were built by SS prisoners *after* the war. He also expresses doubt over whether the postwar trials of forty camp guards were fair. He claims the accusers were all *professional witnesses,* and the guards stood no chance since not a single defense witness could be found. That, of course, ignores the fact that ninety-four defense witnesses actually testified at the guards' war crimes trial. The book goes on to condemn the eventual execution of twenty-eight guards as *wholesale murder.*"

She lowered the book.

"This so-called account, *Germany Through the Ages,* and all the books stacked here before me, were published by my opponent. This is the type of fantasy from which Theodor Pohl derives profit. The type of fiction he endorses as history. This is the man who wants to lead Germany."

She paused to grab a few quick breaths and gather her thoughts.

The gauntlet had been thrown.

A line drawn. No turning back.

"The people of this nation must ask themselves one simple question. Are you prepared to rise above the indignities our forefathers thrust upon us? To do that we have to be honest with ourselves. Denial is akin to condonation. We are a great and mighty people. Our history is one of achievement and glory. The twelve years of the Third Reich cannot, and should not, be allowed to utterly obliterate our ancient culture. That can only happen if we, as a nation, succumb to the temptation of denial and the lure of fabrication. What happened, happened. We cannot undo that fact. Nor could we ever atone, for the horror was simply too much. But what we can do is not allow our emotions to be exploited, our fears to be heightened, or our sense of well-being to be denied. Those among us who use fear and hate to lift themselves above the fray must, and should, be rejected. It is the only way to assure our future."

She stepped from the podium and, following the advice of her press secretary, did not take questions.

Her words would be her message.

Inquiries could only dilute the impact of her extraordinary statements. Instead a tour was now planned of the camp. She'd be seen at the gas chamber, examining the ovens, and walking among the international memorial. After that, she would leave Bavaria and start a two-day swing through western Germany.

By tomorrow she'd either be the clear front-runner—

Or so far behind it would not matter.

CHAPTER
TWENTY-TWO

Santiago, Chile
11:30 a.m.

Cassiopeia exited the car onto a busy sidewalk. A dazzling
pattern of grand buildings rose around her, but thick smog burned her
throat with every breath. The Plaza de Armas was crowded with midday shoppers, the city alive with business and activity. The hotel stood
three doors down, where a uniformed carabinero guarded the front entrance. Juan Vergara waited patiently in the shade of an elm tree near
the curb, smoking a cigarette. True to his word, a plane had come south
to ferry her back to the capital. She would handle things on this end,
while Cotton dealt with the other.

"Welcome, Senorita," Vergara said, adding a smile she instantly
found more irritating than polite. He stubbed out his smoke on the
trunk of the tree. "I see Senor Malone stayed behind. Hopefully, he will
have a productive day. Here the body was removed hours ago, but everything else has remained untouched. Awaiting your arrival."

She followed him inside.

Dust mites hung in the blue shafts of sunlight that spilled in through
the dingy front windows. A small sidewalk façade concealed a spacious
lobby with tall ceilings and paneled walls, all of it a bit run-down, but in
a nostalgic kind of way. A stairway led up to the second floor where another carabinero stood guard at an open door. Just inside a dark splotch

stained the hardwood. She noticed its irregular shape and size. Apparently the victim had lost a lot of blood.

Vergara pointed to the floor. "The body was found there, stabbed in the chest, the blade pulled up into his heart. As you might imagine the wound bled profusely." He stepped over to a rattan chair and grabbed a plastic bag. "This was found beside the body."

She studied the bloodstained SS dagger.

"Those are certainly not seen every day," Vergara said. "A unique murder weapon."

"Any witnesses?" she asked.

"Not that we can determine. Unfortunately, this is an old hotel with no cameras. Time of death was early this morning or late last evening. So far no one has come forward, but the investigation is young."

She could see that he wanted to ask more. So she volunteered, "We never met the guy. As you know, he was in the personal employ of the chancellor. The plan was for us to connect with him today."

"Perhaps his dying last night may have been designed to prevent that from happening."

She agreed. It was possible. "Was anything found here? Notes? Papers? Laptop? Cell phone?"

Vergara shook his head. "Not a thing. Whoever killed him most likely claimed all that, too. Do you plan to explain any more as to what is happening? The situation has definitely . . . escalated."

"We will. When we can. You told Cotton that there was something we needed to see?"

"The deceased made some phone calls from this room. We traced them to an apartment across town. That is what you need to visit, but I wanted you to see this first."

She rode with Vergara to a corner of downtown in the Providencia district. There were lots of quiet neighborhoods, all not far from the city center, most devoid of traffic. Shopping and restaurants dominated, along with a slew of both new and older apartment buildings.

She stepped out of the car.

Autumn leaves rattled like tin along the sidewalk.

Vergara joined her. "Primarily older residents live here. A few blocks away are some of the most expensive former homes in the city, now converted to offices. Many of the foreign embassies are there."

The five-story brick edifice before her looked like one of the older buildings, but in pristine condition.

A uniformed officer waited at its front door.

"Is your point that this is an expensive place to live?" she asked.

He nodded. "Exactly."

They entered and climbed stairs to the third floor and an open apartment door, guarded by another officer.

"We are looking for the apartment's owner," Vergara said.

"You think the owner is the killer?"

"It is possible."

"If so, he seems to have left an easy trail to follow."

The Chilean smiled. "At the moment, we only want to speak with him."

She surveyed the immaculate surroundings. There was a living room, dining room, kitchen, utility space, two bedrooms, and two baths. Light, cream-colored walls, laminated-wood floors, and a modern décor dominated, with all of the expected appliances and conveniences, including an elaborate built-in stereo system. She caught the impressive view out the windows. "He or she does live well. This is lovely."

"I checked with the landlord. The owner pays the rent, with cash, on time, every month. He's lived here for six years."

"What do I need to see?" she asked.

"This way."

He led her down a short hall to a bedroom that had been converted into an office with a small desk, sofa, and three glass cases that displayed an eclectic collection of knickknacks.

Several caught her attention.

One, a heart-shaped silver gorget upon which was affixed a gilded eight-point sunburst. Within the sun were an eagle and a *Sonnenrad*. She knew the sun-wheeled swastika had been a popular Nazi adornment. Beside it lay a bandolier and some gauntlets. On another shelf sat a typewriter, its black metal casing rusted and battered. She noticed the keys.

The number row served its usual dual function, the switch activated by the shift key, accommodating common punctuation as a second alternative. But above the 5 was a double sig rune. SS. Quite a specialization.

A porcelain statue sat on the top shelf. Athena in a flowery robe, a column rising from her open palm. She lifted and studied its underside. Two interlocking sig runes were etched into the porcelain, which meant it had been produced by camp labor as part of one of the SS's collateral industries.

"They're all obscene," she said.

"I agree. We've been interviewing the neighbors. None suspected the owner of being a Nazi enthusiast. But none had ever been inside here, either."

She was irritated at his trickling of information. "There has to be more than this for you to bring me here."

"There is." And he motioned to a metal filing cabinet. "Everything in those four drawers is war related."

"You studied them?"

He waved off her question. "A cursory inspection only, enough for me to know you should see them. Please."

And he motioned for her to take a closer look.

She stepped to the cabinet and opened one of the drawers. Rows of files were packed tight. She slipped out a cluster from the center, took them over to the desk, and scanned through the brittle pages. All typed. Mostly carbon copies. Many contained the seal of the Third Reich. Most were records of financial transactions. Gold transfers. Deutsche Bank, Deutsche Orientbank, Banco Alemán Transatlántico, and Banco Germánico most prominent. Dated from 1942 to 1951.

She studied more of the pages.

Corporations were mentioned.

Siemens. Krupp. Mannesmann. Thyssen. IG Farben. All German entities that supported the Nazi war effort, along with Schweizerische Kreditanstalt, apparently a bank in Zurich that accommodated transfers from those corporations to banks in Chile.

Vergara studied them over her shoulder. "What do they say?"

"You don't speak German?"

He shook his head. "Only Spanish and English. Are you fluent?"

She nodded. "How did you know what these were?"

"I called in an official translator who gave me an overview of what they contained."

She kept looking.

Four words caught her attention on one page.

Spende der Deutsche Wirtschaft.

Fund of German Business.

Or, as history had dubbed it, Hitler's Bounty.

Moneys derived from German industrialists—some of whom contributed willingly, while others required encouragement. It was the price paid for the privilege of profiting from the Reich, and it became Hitler's personal treasure chest, making him the richest man in Europe.

A token of gratitude to the leader.

That's how she recalled it being explained.

The moneys mainly were paid in the form of a one-half percent tax on a company's payroll, along with a tariff levied on every ton of steel or barrel of oil produced, all payable directly to the Führer. Historians all agreed that Martin Bormann exclusively controlled those funds—hundreds of millions of marks—which disappeared after the war. And here was incontrovertible evidence of foreign transfers, including account numbers and authorization codes, most approved by the scribbled signature of M. Bormann, that related directly to that fund.

"Is there anything of importance mentioned?" Vergara asked, noticing her interest.

She decided a lie was better than the truth. "Nothing yet, but I want to see it all before I conclude this was a waste of time."

She spent the next two hours going through the files. There were hundreds of asset transfers, along with deeds to real estate in Paraguay, Uruguay, Brazil, Argentina, and Chile. Patent records, too. Along with pages that dealt with what was called the Cultural Fund, moneys paid by people and entities who used Hitler's image on things like posters and stamps, which generated many more millions of marks. All transferred from Germany to Chile and Argentina from 1944 onward.

Vergara came in and out of the office, noticing some of what she was doing, but otherwise leaving her alone. She should speak with Cotton.

But not now.

"I'm going to need to box up all these files," she called out to Vergara.

He stepped into the office, and she decided to share a little.

"They show an enormous amount of wealth coming from Germany to South America. When you find the owner of this apartment, we're going to need to ask him a lot of questions."

"I understand. We are actively searching and should have some results shortly. I will say that I have dealt with this type of financial matter before. One of our local institutions, the Banco del Estado, has repeatedly been implicated with war-related transfers. I know of several investigations that were conducted into its past activities."

That name was familiar.

Some of the records she'd just examined evidenced transfers to that bank in the 1940s. Maybe a visit could be productive.

"I'd like to go there," she said.

Vergara's face remained deadpan, and she wondered how much practice it took to control one's emotions so effortlessly.

"All right, Senorita. I can arrange that."

CHAPTER TWENTY-THREE

POHL WAS AMAZED. HE'D NOT THOUGHT MARIE EISENHUTH capable of such a bold political move in calling out his publications and implying he was a Holocaust denier. He'd clearly underestimated her, and he resolved never to make that mistake again.

"Are we ready?" he asked one of his aides.

"We will be by five, as promised."

"Has the press assembled?"

"They are waiting."

He adjusted his tie and combed back his wavy hair. Though his blood pressure had always been elevated and his weight fluctuated, baldness was not something he'd ever needed to worry about. He stepped over to a table where an early dinner had been provided by the hotel. Though he'd yet to experience problems with cholesterol, his doctors had recommended a strict vegetarian diet. Unfortunately, he loved the local Westphalian ham, the meat coarse and rich, so he carved off a slice and reached for a chunk of pumpernickel bread.

He sat in a chair by the window and enjoyed the sandwich.

Outside, across the street, the Bürgerpark was green from elms, oaks, and beech trees that clearly recognized warm weather had arrived. The surface of the lake beyond was disturbed only by ducks.

Bremen was truly a lovely part of Germany. A free city. A sovereign state all to itself. The smallest in Germany. A place that traced its roots straight back to Charlemagne.

He so admired political independence.

Small doses were excellent fuel for vast social movements. Large doses, though, could be disastrous. People definitely needed latitude, but they also required discipline. He so wanted German glory restored to that before World War I, when there was no Versailles humiliation, no Weimar Republic, and none of the absurdities from World War II. Back to a point where hopes and dreams were not tainted by stupidity and greed. Hitler had been a political maniac who mangled a good idea and destroyed any chance of it ever succeeding.

Clearly that evil needed to be ignored.

But not forgotten.

Hitler's name alone, in many, still evoked a deep sense of duty, and obedience should never be underestimated. In fact, it was the one trait of the German people he was absolutely counting on.

He finished the sandwich and stepped back to the food cart. He poured a half glass of schnapps and downed the strong, clear liquid in one swallow.

A knock at the door and another aide indicated that it was time to go.

Good.

He was ready.

They drove in silence to the *marktplatz*.

His campaign staff was bright and efficient. They'd carefully analyzed the situation and quickly devised an effective response to Eisenhuth's earlier show at Dachau. Their efforts adhered to a rule learned from American politics.

Never let your opponent speak unilaterally.

That was the fastest way to lose an election.

Public opinion stayed fluid. The days of Joseph Goebbels and the Soviet Politburo, when a few could easily control the thoughts of millions, had faded. The press today was diverse and hungry, fueled by independent corporations and unimaginable sums of money. And the internet added a whole new dimension to the art of propaganda, both good and bad. Manipulation today required a varied approach, combining the skill of a film director with the abilities of an actor, while simultaneously exhibiting the wisdom of a philosophy professor.

A tough assignment. But he was good at it.

And getting better.

The car stopped and he stepped out onto the square.

Bremen's impressive *rathaus,* replete with bas-reliefs, rose on one side, the town's Gothic cathedral on the other. Both would serve as back-drop, like Dachau had for Eisenhuth. Instead of a victims' memorial for a focal point, his staff had chosen the statue of Roland that graced the *marktplatz* with a podium standing within its shadow. At its base, facing a throng of reporters, were stacks of books, about two hundred in all.

He paraded from the car straight to the podium, buttoning the coat to his Evan-Picone suit as he walked. He glanced up at the ten-meter-high stone statue. Roland, the nephew of Charlemagne, stood brandish-ing a sword of justice and a shield upon which he knew was inscribed, FREEDOM DO I GIVE YOU OPENLY.

The symbolism seemed perfect.

"Guten abend," he said into the microphones, once at the podium. "Earlier in the day my opponent saw fit to openly accuse me of being a Nazi sympathizer, a man who derives profit from the denial of recorded history. She produced copies of books that have, through the years, been published by houses I either own or control." His gaze focused tightly on the crowd. "I do not deny her charges. How could I? Those books exist. They were placed on the market and sold for profit. That is the way of business. I make no apologies."

He raked the crowd of reporters and the camera lens with his gaze.

"My opponent's personal attack, though, is puzzling. On the one hand she advocates free debate. She demands vibrant discussion as a way for us to confront our past and deal with our legacy." He paused a mo-ment. "So why do books that advocate a premise so patently contrary to documented history cause her concern? Are not these authors entitled to the same opportunity to air their positions? Free speech does not mean censorship of what we, individually, might find ridiculous, absurd, or offensive. The right is available to all, without qualification, and my publishing houses have never taken on the role of censor."

He motioned to the books stacked on the cobbles before the podium.

"All of these volumes have likewise been published by my companies. They were written by noted historians and Jewish advocates, and detail all that occurred from 1933 to 1945 in the minutest of detail. They are not in any way flattering to this nation, but represent what each individual author has determined to be the truth. Many of these have won awards and are recognized as definitive historical works in their field."

He hesitated again, catching his stride.

"Behind me rises the statue of Roland, the symbol of this city, which represents Bremen's long-standing tradition of independence and tolerance. It is said that so long as this statue stands Bremen will remain free. I believe in freedom. It is paramount to my political philosophy. But unlike my opponent, I do not see the need to filter that freedom through a sieve that traps ideas that I, personally, find offensive. Instead I trust the German people to read, study, and evaluate what they want, when they want, and how they want. Reject the absurd, accept the logical. That is your right."

Several of the reporters he'd long ago concluded were friends bobbed their heads in unison. This was turning out to be a great day, especially after Josef Engle had reported that everything in Chile was proceeding precisely according to plan. Just a few more days and the world press would have a story of epic proportion, all verified by a former American Justice Department lawyer and an ex-president. Marie Eisenhuth's puny attempt at political grandstanding would be totally forgotten.

He swept his arm in an arc and motioned at the statue rising behind him. "On this monument is proclaimed, FREEDOM DO I GIVE YOU OPENLY. It is the motto of this city-state and has served the citizens of Bremen for centuries. Roland was a brave, dynamic individual. He was not afraid to lead, but he was equally courageous in trusting the people. I believe the same. For every Nazi, neo-Nazi, right-wing sympathizer, or Hitler fanatic there are tens of thousands who think otherwise. My opponent's brazen insult to the people of Dachau, her lament that no one cared about that suffering, was uncalled for and wholly unnecessary."

He stared straight at the cameras and provided the sound bite his public relations people assured him would make the news.

"Winning an election should not entail the disparagement of a great nation."

Satisfied, he stepped from the podium and, unlike Eisenhuth, indicated that he would take questions. The reporters swarmed close, aiming their cameras, thrusting forward their recorders. Now the evening news broadcasts would contain two reports. One from Dachau in the south, the other from Bremen in the north. Viewers could decide for themselves which message they embraced, and the overnight polls would confirm their decision.

Tomorrow could truly be a new day.

CHAPTER TWENTY-FOUR

CHILEAN LAKE DISTRICT
12:15 P.M.

COTTON EMERGED FROM A WOODED PATH ONTO THE GRASSY HILL-ock where the hacienda stood. Everything was sodden from rain that had passed over during the night. Spears of sunlight broke through remnants of low gray clouds and stabbed the far-off mountains in shafts of gold, eventually becoming lost in vast evergreen forests below. A swarm of pastel-colored birds fluttered in the warm, moist air. A strong autumnal nip suggested winter might be early this year.

He'd driven himself from Los Arana.

One of the carabineros had transported Cassiopeia south to the airport at Puerto Montt. The other policeman had offered to accompany him but he'd refused, preferring instead to work alone. Surprisingly, the officer had not made an issue of the matter and said he'd wait at the chalet for him to return, available by phone if needed, supplying a contact number.

The house appeared quiet, just as yesterday.

He studied the surrounding terrain and noticed a pasture off to the west, the field overgrown with wild grass. Was this once a Nazi hiding place? A refuge where men fleeing postwar justice hid along their own personal path to obscurity. Interesting how so many, who so willingly pledged themselves, so quickly fled the cause. Few after the war stood by their supposed beliefs. Once power and status faded, so went their enthusiasm. Truly rats on a sinking ship. Was one of their safe harbors now standing before him?

Maybe.

He was on the hunt.

Which he loved.

Like bookselling, which was actually his current occupation. Plenty of hunting to do there. Three months after he opened his shop he was lucky enough to find an 1806 copy of Lord Byron's *Fugitive Pieces.* Then he found an excellent first printing of Arthur Conan Doyle's *A Study in Scarlet* and Robert Frost's *Twilight.* He sold all three to collectors for nearly three hundred thousand euros, netting enough to carry him through the first year of business. Those deals also cemented his reputation as a man who could find what somebody wanted.

Which was exactly his mission here.

Near the house, movement caught his attention.

A man. Middle-aged.

Thoughts of the two men with rifles yesterday advised caution. His weapon was tucked tight at his spine and he folded his right arm back, ready to palm the gun.

A stiff breeze blew up a snuff-colored poncho, but an oversized black hat stayed put thanks to a chin strap. The guy wore a leather apron the color of his sunburned skin, a sheathed knife dangling from his left hip. The face was lined and furrowed, a splotch of a mustache evident beneath a hooked nose. The newcomer was busy inspecting the walls.

"Buenas tardes," Cotton called out. The man turned, spied his visitor, then strolled over through wet grass. "Do you speak English?"

"Of course. Does not everyone?" A smile accompanied the observation, revealing upper teeth so badly mangled it looked like two rows.

"You a gaucho?" From the dress he thought the man might be one of the famous cattle handlers from a nearby ranch.

"Hardly. They exist only for tourists. But there was a time when I would have wanted to be one."

Cotton introduced himself and explained why he was there.

"I watch over this place. Carabineros found me yesterday and wanted to know about some Nazi things inside."

"What did you tell them?"

"The last time I was here those things were not."

"When was that?"

"A couple weeks back. I come only when I have to."

He sensed something in the declaration. "Why is that?"

Off to the east, at the edge of dense woods, a uniformed carabinero emerged from the thickets, a rifle slung over one shoulder. He recalled what Vergara had said about having the house watched.

"I noticed him when I first arrived," the man said. "This place breeds trouble. It's a *racupillán*."

He gave him a quizzical look.

"A local Mapuche word. House of the devil."

"Sounds like you've been around awhile."

"My whole life." He swept an arm out into the air. "All this was for Germans. They bought this land long ago."

"Where are the owners?"

"They don't live in Chile. Not good enough for them."

"If you feel that way, why look after the place?"

The guy shoved the hat from his head. The chin strap held it in place against his shoulders. He ran his fingers through oily sandy-blond hair. Along with a dusting of dandruff, he seemed to have an adequate supply of chips on his shoulders, too. "This was a place for them to come, have picnics, ride horses. Not to take seriously." The man shrugged. "But I need work."

"Doesn't seem like there's much to watch over. The house is a wreck. The pumas have taken over."

The man chuckled. "I let them squat here a long time ago. They make excellent guards. You're right. The house has fallen down, mainly over the past few years. No funds for repairs, not like in the old days."

"When was it last occupied?"

"Decades back. Germans came and went. Many of them. Stay awhile, move on. I worked here. Tended the cows and horses. Quite a hacienda back then."

He fished the photographs from his pocket and handed over the one with Bormann and Braun. "Ever see those two here?"

The man studied the images, then shook his head. "Who are they?"

"Just some people I'm looking for." He estimated the cowboy's age at no more than fifty. Too young to know anything firsthand about post-war Chile. "Is there anybody nearby who lived here in the 1940s. Someone who might recognize the people in the photos?"

"You police?"

He shook his head. "All I want is information."

"We get people like you every once in a while. I don't like them any better than Germans."

The message was clear. "I'm not a bounty hunter or anything like that. Just looking for information."

The man remained silent for a moment and he wondered if he really knew anything at all. "Ada was here then."

Interesting. "Where does she live?"

He pointed south. "Tilcara. It's down the highway forty kilometers south. She might know the people in the picture."

"Why do you say that?"

"Ada is old. She knew all the Germans, and they knew her."

CHAPTER TWENTY-FIVE

COTTON SLOWED AS HE ENTERED TILCARA. LOTS OF SHOPS, CAFÉS, hotels, and tourist agencies. The simple gray buildings lacked the rustic roughness of a village or the tarnished elegance of a city, but they were charming nonetheless. Another volcano loomed in the distance, and the snout of a blue lake intruded to the south. Palms and mimosa cast a feel more of Spain than Chile.

The gaucho had told him where to find Ada, so he drove straight to the Church of Our Lady. It stood solitary just beyond the town limits, a frescoed façade between two bell towers, a long, low wing to one side made of whitewashed bricks. A convent was attached that housed the Good Shepherd Sisters, who ran a home for the elderly next door. He'd been told that Ada was not a nun, but she had for a long time helped them operate the convalescence center.

The facility wasn't much. One story. Cement-block walls painted a pale blue with a gabled tiled roof. It sat among the trees with flower boxes protruding below every window. Simple, but well maintained. Luckily, his mother would never need to live in such a place. His father had been gone a long time and she'd learned to manage on her own, still running her family's onion farm in middle Georgia, as she had ever since his grandfather passed. Financially, she was set. Truth be known she was most likely a wealthy woman. They spoke about once a month, and he knew he should call more. But communication was a two-way street, one she seemed equally satisfied traversing only occasionally.

He entered the building and was told Ada could be found in the church. He crossed the street and opened the stout oak doors, the arch above adorned with a half-obliterated Christ and angels with piteous faces. Inside was a single aisle, the nave high and broad, the walls displaying a masquerade of differing styles. A woman knelt in a pew clutching a rosary, a hooded cloak of white enfolding her head, her lips mumbling as if muttering a spell.

He sat in another of the wooden pews and waited.

"*Buenas tardes,* Senor Malone."

The greeting momentarily startled him.

"I received a call from a friend," the old woman said in deep, gritty Spanish-accented English. "I was told to expect your visit."

No surprise. "That gaucho was there on purpose, wasn't he?"

She stood from the pew with some effort and turned to face him. "I wanted to speak with you. Alone. Thankfully, you reappeared today without your escorts and made this invitation easy to extend."

He had to admit, the guy's spiel had been delivered with the aplomb of a first-rate actor who knew his lines. "You're not a fan of the police?"

"On the contrary, I am a firm supporter of law enforcement."

She stepped closer and pushed back the veil. She was thin faced, cheeks sunken, the skin around the blue eyes crinkly with advanced age. She had a low forehead and crooked shoulders poorly concealed beneath a loose-fitting black dress. Her gray hair was tied back with a silver scarf into a ponytail.

He stayed seated as she approached closer down the aisle. "What do you do here?"

"I spend time with the residents. Go on walks. Participate in activities. Work in the kitchen. Support the staff. Visit residents who end up in the hospital. It is a rewarding life for a widow."

"How long have you lived here?"

"Over seventy years. My parents arrived just after the war."

As long as his presence had been anticipated, he produced the photographs found at the hacienda and showed them to her.

"I see you found what I left," she said.

Her admission did not surprise him.

She motioned with the images. "Those two lived near Lago Todos los Santos, at the Argentine border."

"What were their names?"

"He was the Brown Eminence."

He made the connection. The term was one attached to Martin Bormann during the war because of his influence over Hitler. A derivation from the Red Eminence, Cardinal Richelieu, King Louis XIII's chief minister, who dominated the monarchy and effectively ruled France. Richelieu's assistant, Father Joseph, dubbed the Gray Eminence, was, like his superior, a shadowy figure adept in quiet diplomacy and covert power. Red and gray referred to those prelates' robes. Brown was the color of Nazi uniforms.

"They lived on a remote farm and kept to themselves. He called himself Luis Soreno. But my father knew his real identity. He handled all of the Brown Eminence's business matters."

"And the woman?"

"Rikka was the name she used. But we all knew she was Hitler's widow. Eva Braun."

He pointed to the photos. "Was the child born here?"

She shook her head. "That's where the truth deviates from the story in the pictures. No child existed here. There was a child, but not born here."

"Where then?"

She hesitated, sat silent for a moment, then said, "Africa."

"You weren't supposed to tell me that?"

"I'm supposed to tell you that the child, a boy, died here."

"So that there would be no son of Martin Bormann still alive to search for?"

Ada nodded. "That was part of the purpose of the Kaiser's web. To throw you off that trail."

"You know Theodor Pohl?"

"Unfortunately, I do."

"Not a fan?"

"Hardly. He is an evil man."

He'd circle back to that topic. Right now, he wanted to know the rest of her story. "What happened to Bormann and Braun?"

"They stayed here awhile, then moved on. The Brown Eminence was constantly paranoid, afraid someone would recognize him. No one cared about the widow. Few even knew her face or name. But him. That one people would have wanted. A *quetrupillán*."

He did not recognize the word.

"Mute devil," she said.

He realized that the world was a different place in the 1940s. No massive amounts of television. No internet. Hiding was simpler, and many war criminals were quite successful at simply fading away. Especially two people most of the world already thought were dead. "Where did they go?"

"As I said, Africa."

"How do you know this?"

She stared at him with eyes that seemed misty under hooded lids. "My brother went with them and took care of their needs."

He waited.

"When he left Chile, he quit using his Spanish name, the one we all were given when we arrived. Instead, he reverted back to his German birthright and once again became Gerhard Schüb."

That name again.

But now he knew who the man was.

Provided this old woman was not more misdirection.

He studied her nothing face that made little impression, perhaps because it was kept so empty of expression. But every instinct within him said she was telling the truth.

So he asked, "Why tell me this?"

"The Kaiser cannot succeed. He fancies himself an emperor. A reminder of Caesar, I suppose." She spat on the floor. "That's what I think of him. You are being used. The Kaiser is spinning a web into which you are being drawn. Look around you. This church was built by Jesuits in 1672. It has been raided, destroyed by bandits, burned, and ravaged by earthquakes. Yet it still stands. There are things at work here that have withstood an equal amount of assault, and they still stand, too."

He could see she had more to say.

"I am an old woman who has found that life's amusements fail to amuse me any longer. Food hurts my stomach. Play makes me nervous. And memories disgust me. All my life I have lived by duty and I am tired of serving. Little by little my mind has been freeing itself from the prejudices in which it was reared. It's been a difficult endeavor, but I am coming to the end. I understand that you have no reason to believe a word I am saying. So tell me, Herr Malone, would original writings help convince you of my sincerity?"

He nodded. Why not? He'd come this far.

"I have many."

"Are they part of the Kaiser's web, too?"

She smiled. "Some were supposed to be."

He caught the message. "But not all?"

"Hardly."

"Then I'd like to see these writings."

CHAPTER
TWENTY-SIX

SANTIAGO
1:00 P.M.

CASSIOPEIA ACCOMPANIED VERGARA INTO THE ELEGANT BANCO del Estado, its neoclassical façade an unflattering shade of pale yellow. Across the street, in a tree-shaded plaza, a band was entertaining a group of listeners. The music faded as heavy glass doors eased shut behind her.

Vergara had explained on the drive over that the bank was a venerable Chilean institution dating from the 19th century, surviving countless revolutions and even the communists. The documents they'd found repeatedly mentioned the bank as the recipient of money transfers, and Vergara had thrown his weight around and arranged an immediate meeting. The managing director was expecting them, so they were quickly ushered into a second-floor office where a tall, lean man with wispy brown hair greeted them with handshakes and introduced himself as Vicente Donoso. He was dressed in what she recognized as an expensive Fabio Inghirami suit with a striking Gucci tie.

"I have conveyed your request for documents to our legal counsel and, while it is being considered, I have been directed to speak with you," Donoso said in English. "We pride ourselves on cooperating with the police. This bank has a long-standing relationship with the government. So please, explain precisely what it is you desire."

She sat in the proffered chair and told the banker about the documents she'd just spent the past few hours reviewing. "I have in my possession German war records that indicate various accounts were opened in this bank from 1942 to 1951. They are in a variety of individual and corporate names."

"Might I see these documents?" Donoso asked.

She opened the briefcase Vergara had provided and extracted a sheaf of twenty pages. She'd culled through the files and narrowed her interest to certain memoranda, all from Martin Bormann, authorizing the transfer of various amounts in gold and cash out of Germany to the Banco del Estado. She handed the papers to Donoso, who scanned each page with obvious interest.

"You read German?" she asked.

He looked up. "My mother insisted I learn her native language."

He flashed her a toothy smile before returning to his reading.

"Fascinating," he said when he finished. "I have read many versions in books of Nazi moneys being sent overseas, but none from firsthand information. And Martin Bormann himself approving so many. Extraordinary."

"He was directly in charge of Hitler's Bounty," she said. "Hundreds of millions of marks were collected, and only Bormann would have known where those funds were ultimately deposited." She gathered the pages back from Donoso. "Do your records go back to the 1940s? I have some account numbers for this bank."

"Let us find out."

"I thought we needed to wait on the lawyer," she said.

"I don't believe it will hurt for me to have a look. Do you? May I have the account numbers?"

She handed him a sheet of paper. He turned his attention to a desktop computer, began typing, then studied the screen. "Most of the accounts noted are long closed. A few are still active."

Had she heard right? "Still active?"

"*Sí.* Three of the accounts you have identified are currently open."

"Meaning moneys are moving in and out?"

"You understand I cannot answer that question. We would have to wait for the lawyer. On the dormant or closed accounts, from fifty years ago, I have no problem discussing those. But something active, that is a different matter altogether."

"Senor Donoso," Vergara said. "We require information on those active accounts. It is important to a murder investigation. Do I make myself clear."

"Without question, Minister, but the law mandates I cannot reveal anything on an active account. Surely you are not saying I ignore the law."

Vergara straightened in his chair. "I would never advise anyone to do such a thing. But I can secure a judicial order to allow the inspection of records."

The banker nodded. "As my legal counsel informed me earlier. I suggest that be done."

Vergara motioned to the computer terminal that sat adjacent to Donoso's desk. "If you will access your electronic mail I think you will find a transmittal of an order that I requested three hours ago. I was assured it would be forwarded directly here by the court."

The banker threw them a curious look before rolling his leather chair closer to the computer and again tapping on the keyboard. The screen faced away from Cassiopeia. A moment later Donoso glanced over and said, "You are correct. It is signed by the magistrate and allows for a full inspection. The original is being delivered as we speak."

"Must we wait?" Vergara asked.

"No, Minister. All of the legal requirements seem to be in order."

The banker stabbed a button on a telephone console and spoke Spanish into the receiver. Cassiopeia understood every word of the instructions for an assistant to gather up the documents.

"It will only be a few moments," Donoso said to them when he finished. "We have had some experience with this type of matter before. About ten years ago there was an international lawsuit that involved a subpoena for our records. I handled that matter for the bank. It was fascinating to learn what happened during the war. Reading the documents you just provided brought all that back to me. Are you familiar with Aktion Aderflung?"

She recalled the words from speaking with Marie Eisenhuth. "Project Eagle Flight. Bormann's scheme to get wealth out of Germany."

Donoso nodded. "An enormous undertaking. And ingenious. I learned about it in that lawsuit."

She listened as he explained how, from 1943 to 1945, over two hundred German corporations set up South American subsidiaries, mainly in Chile and Argentina. Cash and assets were moved through shell companies in Switzerland, Spain, and Portugal to South American branches of German banks. Manufacturing facilities were constructed and businesses were either purchased or opened new.

"I was privy to the Mercedes-Benz situation," Donoso said. "They built the company's first plant outside of Germany in Argentina. And devised a clever scheme to launder money. The Argentine office of Mercedes-Benz would charge the German office higher production costs for each vehicle made. If the true cost of making a car was three thousand marks, Mercedes-Benz of Germany paid five thousand marks for the components needed to make the car. The difference was then secreted into a South American bank for use later, after the war. Hundreds of millions of marks were stashed away like that, all of it untraceable. Of course when you have the full cooperation of the banks and the government in the conspiracy, you can do whatever you want."

She agreed.

"And all of those German corporations operating on this continent also provided employment for fleeing war criminals. Eichmann, for example, was working at the Mercedes-Benz plant in Argentina when he was captured."

"You know a lot on this subject," she said.

"World War Two has long been an interest of mine."

She listened as the banker continued to explain more.

On August 10, 1944, Bormann called a mass meeting of German industrialists, business leaders, and party officials in the French city of Strasbourg, at the Hôtel Maison Rouge. Representatives of Krupp, Messerschmitt, Rheinmetall, Büssing, IG Farben, Volkswagen, and many other companies were there.

"Bormann was not," Donoso said. "But he sent an emissary who told the gathering that the war was lost. It was only a matter of time before it ended. What mattered was that Germany survive afterward. No one wanted the nation's assets laid bare for the victor, as happened in 1919 after the First World War."

So alliances with foreign firms were encouraged. Cash and assets moved. To facilitate that, Bormann waived the Treason Against the Nation Act, passed in 1933, which imposed the death penalty on any German violating foreign exchange regulations.

"And the flood began," Donoso said. "The flow of capital out of Germany was enormous. Gold, silver, platinum, gems, stocks, patents, bearer bonds. All of it moved to banks and safety deposit boxes around the world, many of which were here on this continent."

"I never realized it was so systematic," she said.

"Key corporate manpower was also diverted overseas, especially to neutral countries. Little would be left for the victorious Allies to feast upon—and in the end little *was* left. In fact, the Allies themselves eventually rebuilt Germany with their own money."

A soft knock came to the office door and an older woman with auburn hair deposited three thick folders on the desk.

"I requested a printout of the open accounts' activities over the course of the past fifty years." Donoso opened the top folder and reviewed the pages. "The three active accounts were all opened in the latter part of 1946. At that time a respectable amount of gold bullion was deposited. By the 1970s that amount had been converted to cash, U.S. dollars to be exact, and had multiplied in value."

"How much?" Cassiopeia asked.

"All total, nearly seven hundred million dollars."

The information grabbed her attention. "How was that possible?"

"Simple valuation increases account for a large portion of the increase. Gold, after all, was not worth then what it now brings. Also, there were investments that paid handsome returns. Some of which the bank supervised. We pride ourselves on portfolio management. This is an example of our success."

She wasn't interested in his pandering. "Is someone still utilizing the accounts?"

"It would appear."

Vergara reached over the desk. "May I see the records?"

The banker slid the folders across. The minister perused each page carefully. Cassiopeia noticed everything was in Spanish—her first language, as she was raised near Barcelona.

"What of the closed accounts?" Vergara asked. "What happened to those?"

"According to our records, those were all dormant by 1980, their balances taken to zero. Only these remain. Unfortunately, our records from that far back do not reflect if the accounts were simply closed or the assets transferred to another account or bank."

"All three of these accounts were opened by a Luis Soreno," Vergara said as he read from the folder.

"Is that name familiar?" she asked the policeman.

"The hacienda you were at yesterday. From 1946 to 1953, it was owned by an L. Soreno."

She faced the banker. "How active are these three accounts?"

"There have not been all that many transfers over the past fifty years. More so in the last twenty than the first thirty. Several corporations were involved."

"Any of them individually?"

He shook his head. "None noted. All were to corporate accounts."

She tried to recall the information Marie Eisenhuth had provided about Theodor Pohl's business affairs. He owned four German conglomerates, all related to the publishing business, along with two Dutch concerns and one Belgian. He likewise possessed interests in three German banks. The dossier was on her phone as an email attachment.

"Mind if I look at the pages?" she asked.

Vergara handed her the folders. Her gaze scanned the sheets, noting that indeed there were financial transactions out.

She noted the locations.

The expected Switzerland, but Rome, London, New York, the Cayman Islands, Andorra, and Luxembourg were also mentioned. The payee on each transaction was listed in a separate column. She opened the attachment on her phone and compared the information. No names matched. Then two transactions on the printed page caught her attention.

Names she knew.

Eisenhuth-Industrie, Hannover.

Herzog Concern, Frankfurt.

Then she saw the designations again. And again. She started counting. Over two dozen entries. Transfers made from Banco del Estado to financial institutions located in Germany with accounts in those corporate names.

She was in shock.

A quick search on her phone and she learned that Eisenhuth-Industrie was owned and controlled by Kurt Eisenhuth. Husband to the chancellor of Germany. Herzog Concern was once the property of Albert Herzog. Father to the chancellor of Germany, the same woman who'd sent them to Chile to find the truth.

"This can't be," she whispered.

CHAPTER TWENTY-SEVEN

COTTON FOLLOWED ADA THROUGH THE CHURCH, OUT A BACK door, into an egg-shaped courtyard lined by a rough stone wall. Turf carpeted the space, withered and full of bare spots. A concrete walk led out to the convent, but they did not go that way. Instead they followed another zigzag path to a small, squat house set among the trees.

"My home," she said as they walked.

It was a quaint cottage with walls of pebbles and bricks crossed in a tapestry-like design. Dormers dotted the tile roof, each with stone mullions. Inside was typical Bavarian bourgeois. Heavy tables, chests, and upholstered chairs, the colors dominated by green and gold. Much of the wood was gaily painted with folk art and geometric designs. They took a seat in a parlor accumulated with the clutter of a lifetime. Two windows shaded by flowery curtains admitted the midday sun. A luminous dust danced in the cool shadows.

"You are being played for a fool," she said.

No shocker there. "By who?"

"The Brown Eminence."

"He's long dead."

"Not his successors."

"Does that mean Theodor Pohl?"

She smiled, her cheeks colored by only a slight warmth. "They don't want you to know of Africa. They want you to think Bormann and Braun lived and died here. But that is not true."

If not for events of the past few days he would have dismissed her as insane.

She glared at him. "How old do you think me?"

He'd been wondering the same thing. "Eighty to eighty-five."

She smiled. A first. "You flatter me, Herr Malone. I am ninety-three."

"You age well."

"Aryan genes, perhaps. But I was never one to believe in all that racial superiority." She paused. "My father worked in the Reich's Security Office in Stuttgart at the local Gestapo headquarters. He was an envoy who traveled all over Europe, performing various duties. What those might have been, I have no idea. I was sixteen when the war ended. Everything around us was in shambles. One day in 1945 my father went away and never came home. My mother, brother, and I had no idea what happened to him. Dead? Alive? We did not know. He was just gone. Then, in 1947, my mother told us we were leaving Germany and moving to Argentina. I was astounded. I had never ventured more than a hundred kilometers from Stuttgart. But I must admit, I was pleased to go. Germany was in ruins.

"We first went to Italy, then sailed from there to Buenos Aires. We were given new names and identities, which we all thought strange. I became Margarita. But I abandoned that fiction long ago and took back my birth name. Ada. A few days after we arrived, my father appeared. Safe and healthy. It was astonishing. He took us by car west until we saw the Andes Mountains. We traveled up into the foothills and eventually came to an iron gate that was opened by armed men, who allowed us inside. A few days after that we came to Chile."

"You've been here ever since?"

She nodded. "I was young and somewhat naïve, just glad to be away from war. Eventually I came to learn that powerful men require others to implement what they need done. Those others are not important people, just ones the powerful can rely upon. My father was that for Martin Bormann."

Now he was intrigued.

"He handled many tasks. Personal and business. One of his duties was to provide protection. So he created many Bormanns. In Europe, Asia, across South America. Those who searched for the Brown Eminence found most of them, but never did they come close to the actual man."

He recalled more of what he'd read on the internet earlier. For decades after the war Bormann sightings had been regularly reported throughout Brazil, Argentina, Bolivia, and Paraguay. Even Vergara described a possible encounter. A few of the Bormanns even turned themselves in to authorities, claiming a need for justice in their old age, but all were eventually confirmed as either deranged or delirious. Never had a serious lead developed that Martin Bormann was alive.

"Your father did a good job."

"That he did. It was his idea to move Bormann and Braun to Africa. He'd been told of the Orange Free State, and Bormann finally agreed to go."

He was trying to gauge her, deciding if she could be believed. But she'd gone to a lot of trouble to get him here.

"I hate Nazis," she said.

"Your father was a Nazi."

"That's true. And for a daughter who wants to remember him fondly, that fact has been difficult."

It seemed she wanted to speak her mind, so he let her.

"I went once and heard Hitler speak." A sadness laced her declaration as memory seemed to take hold. "He paraded into the hall to some lively military tune, wearing his brownshirt uniform and the shiniest boots I'd ever seen. Everyone stood while he spoke. It was required. He had a voice like thunder and he reveled in mocking his enemies, telling us the latest outrage the Fatherland had suffered. He loved to use mythology and antiquity to emphasize a glorious destiny. The crowd laughed, applauded, and shouted approval for two hours. It was hideous."

He heard the disgust in her voice.

"He was an evil man who thought little of women. He came to our house once. I heard him tell my mother that a woman must be a cute, cuddly, naïve little thing, tender, sweet, and dumb. Their duty was to birth children and please their husbands. He was a pig."

"And Bormann?"

She spat on the floor. "Even worse. A sloven bastard. He treated Evi miserably."

He made the connection. *Evi*. Eva Braun's nickname, which only her closest friends used.

"Back then, living here, in southern Chile, was like being in Germany," she said. "We all spoke German in school. The walls of our classrooms were decorated with swastikas and portraits of Hitler. We joined the youth organization and learned to respect hard work and authority. We read *Mein Kampf* and old copies of *Das Reich*. We studied Goebbels' speeches and were trained as avengers, told one day we would be part of the next great struggle for a new Germany. What nonsense. But we did all live together, growing our own food and taking care of one another in what many called Hitler's Valley. It stretched across Patagonia with three main communities: Deutschland, Heimat, and Vaterland."

Germany. Homeland. Fatherland.

"It was quite lovely," she said. "Bormann was in charge of it all. Until he left. Then my father took over. When he died, all of the responsibilities passed to me." She surveyed him with an insolent air of triumph. "Many have come before you, searching. And we have always dealt with them. The last encounter happened a few years ago. Two Americans. One died. One was deceived."

Jonathan Wyatt. Chris Combs.

"You were part of that?" he asked.

"I arranged the entire deception."

"Why?"

"It was part of my duty. But the Kaiser ordered one of my friends murdered in the process. A wonderful woman named Isabel. For that there is no forgiveness. I no longer owe that disgusting man anything."

"So why did you agree to be a part of what's happening here?"

She smiled. "My last opportunity to repay the Kaiser."

"Pohl has led us the whole time? To right here?"

She nodded, her face a blend of confidence and calm. "But I have now assumed control of your leash."

"To what end?"

She gestured with a disdainful sweep of her hand, then pointed. "That you will discover in the plastic bin, there, on the table."

He glanced through an archway into a small dining room and saw the container.

"I prepared it just for you," she said.

How convenient.

"Please take it, and go."

Apparently the meeting was over. So he stood, walked over, and grabbed the container. But before he left he removed the toy soldier from his pocket, the one he'd found at the hacienda, and set it on the table.

"I believe this is yours."

CHAPTER TWENTY-EIGHT

ENGLE EASED HIS CAR CLOSE TO ANOTHER VEHICLE PARKED ON THE shoulder of the road in a thick stand of araucaria trees. He stopped directly adjacent to the driver's-side window and rolled down his own window.

"What happened?" he asked the man in the other car, whose window was already down.

"Malone came three hours ago. He and Ada spoke in the church. I snuck in through a rear door and got close enough that I could hear."

He listened as his spy reported all that was said.

None of it good.

"Malone did not get here by way of the path we set up," his man reported. "Ada led him on her own."

Even worse.

"Then she took him to her house. I could not get near them without being seen."

So they had no idea what else was said.

Ada was, at best, difficult. That's why he'd ordered the extra surveillance as an added measure of assurance. He'd had no choice but to involve her. It was imperative that the messenger be of the right age and right nationality. Nearly all of the Originals were dead. Only a handful remained, and none in the lake district save for Ada.

"They stayed inside the house for about thirty minutes, then Malone left, carrying a plastic bin."

Containing what? Another disturbing piece of information.

"Anything else?"

His minion shook his head. "It's been quiet ever since."

Which left only one course.

He motored back to the highway and drove the remaining mile to the Church of Our Lady. He found the cottage out back and stormed in through the front door without knocking. The old woman was perched on a large couch with blue satin cushions.

Waiting.

"You think yourself so clever," he said in German.

"I have known you far too long, Josef."

"Why was it necessary to mention Africa? Or Herr Pohl? What are you doing, Ada?"

"Why was it necessary to spy on me?"

"So I can be aware of your treachery."

"Your Kaiser will not succeed."

His fears were rapidly becoming reality.

She continued to sit still, at moments seemingly far away in another place. He kept his voice calm and asked, "What did you tell him?"

"I told him that Bormann and Braun went to Africa."

"He was supposed to learn that the son died here, nothing more." Everything he'd so carefully planned seemed now in dire jeopardy. He needed to know something else. "What of the container he left with? What did you give him?"

"Information he needed to know."

Never had she been this emboldened in the past. "What's changed, Ada?"

Her gaze knifed through him. "Everything. And you changed it, Josef. When you shot Isabel. For no reason, other than to protect your precious web. I appreciate you granting me the opportunity to right that wrong."

"You never said a word about Isabel when it happened."

"No. I simply buried her, then vowed that when presented with the right opportunity, I would avenge her death. Unlike yourself, I knew the Brown Eminence. He was a dreadful man. But I learned from him about keeping things to myself."

And she'd done an excellent job.

"It was necessary for that old woman to die," he said to her. "The Americans had to be convinced."

"Her name was Isabel. She was a dear person. My close friend. She only participated in that endeavor as a favor to me."

His patience was wearing thin. He'd obviously made a huge mistake involving this old woman, and he was going to have to answer to Theodor Pohl for the miscalculation. At a minimum their timetable was disrupted. At worst, the whole endeavor could collapse. And the election was fast approaching. Pohl was not accustomed to catastrophic mistakes.

Nor was he.

And the bitter soul calmly staring at him had just dealt them both a deep blow.

She fixed him with a glare that signaled nothing but hate and resentment. "I hope you, your Kaiser, and the Brown Eminence all rot in hell."

Ada's job had been to stage the hacienda, planting the photographs and other memorabilia, then spur Malone and Vitt along, reconnecting today and informing them that the son of Martin Bormann and Eva Braun, supposedly shown in one of the pictures, was dead. After that, the next stage of his carefully crafted *konundrum* was already in place, ready, but it would now have to be postponed indefinitely. He could not allow this woman any more opportunities with Malone.

Time to end the problem.

He reached beneath his jacket and palmed the grip of the Browning automatic he'd obtained yesterday in Santiago. No sense belaboring the point. He aimed the pistol.

And heard a click.

Behind him.

He turned.

Standing in the archway to the dining room were two men, both with rifles aimed at him. The same two fair-haired youths who'd shot at the hacienda yesterday from the pickup truck, hired to keep Malone and Vitt moving along.

"I think not, Josef," Ada said.

He lowered his gun.

"I am not Isabel," she declared. "And killing you here and now is not enough to satisfy my anger. Instead, I want you to taste failure. Then the Kaiser will deal with you. Tell him that this will not turn out as he planned."

He felt the power of the threat, and realized she meant every word.

"His web will be broken."

CHAPTER TWENTY-NINE

COTTON RETURNED TO THE CHALET OUTSIDE LOS ARANA. HIS carabinero babysitter gave him a curious look when he plopped the plastic bin down on the tile floor beside the dining room table. He'd stopped in town along the way and grabbed a quick lunch. He still had not heard from Cassiopeia and was curious about what was happening in Santiago, but he assumed she'd check in when there was something to report.

He dragged a chair close to the table, bent down, and opened the container, which was filled with faded-white envelopes, all addressed to Ada and bearing postage stamped SAU.

He recognized that designation.

South African Union, the name of the country prior to its late-20th-century political reform into the Republic of South Africa. He lifted the top envelope from the stack and withdrew three sheets of pale-blue paper, each in remarkably good condition.

He gently opened the folds.

The writing was all German, in a feminine scroll. He read the first paragraph, but the text was tough to translate. Not the fluid German he was accustomed to seeing. This was rougher, the words more difficult to associate. Like what slang could do to English.

The carabinero ambled over.

"Won't do me much good," Cotton said to the policeman. "I can only understand so much of this."

The man glanced down over his shoulder. *"I hope this note finds you in good health. It is a shame I cannot say the—"*

"Apparently you don't suffer from my infirmity."

"That's Old German. I studied language at university." He seemed proud of the accomplishment. "It can be difficult, if not accustomed to the verbiage."

"Then maybe you could assist?"

The man smiled. "That's why I am here."

"Pull up a chair and start reading out loud."

Cotton glanced at his watch.

Nearly 7:00 P.M.

He'd been listening to the carabinero for nearly three hours. The letters were all apparently written by Eva Braun, signed in the alias of Rikka Soreno, the name Ada had mentioned earlier. They had been sent to Ada from the latter part of 1949 to 1952. Apparently Braun and Bormann fled Chile in 1947 to live in the Orange Free State, part of the then South African Union. He was amazed at their choice of refuge, his memory recalling details about what was now simply called the Free State.

Dutch white settlers, Boers as they were eventually labeled, fled to a region in northwest South Africa during the 18th century. They obtained independence from Britain in the mid-19th century when they created a Boer Republic dedicated to white rule and racial segregation. Even for a nation married to apartheid, Orange Free State politics was right of right. Women could not vote. Africans possessed no privileges. Asians could remain within the country no longer than twenty-four hours. A bloody war with England at the turn of the 20th century finally imposed subordination. But it was only in the 1990s, when the African National Congress assumed power, that the state was purged by a black-majority government and renamed, dropping the *Orange,* which carried connotations of a Dutch racist past.

Prior to that time, though, the region would have offered a nearly perfect sanctuary for one of the world's most wanted war criminals. World War II in Africa was little more than a press account, the conflict not spreading much beyond the Sahara region, thousands of miles to the north. Martin Bormann would have been a nobody, and Luis Soreno would have been an even greater shadow. From the letters it appeared Bormann had continued his wartime policy of staying out of the limelight. The letters talked of giraffe, eland, zebra, and springbok. The Sorenos lived in a ranch house with sandstone walls and a corrugated iron roof. A sweeping veranda overlooked flat mountains and aromatic cherry orchards. But there was a sadness to the prose, one that signaled a troubled life.

"Who was this woman?" the carabinero asked, after finishing reading another letter.

He knew he could not answer truthfully. "A disappointed wife. Not happy."

"The husband seems a brutal man."

He could not argue that fact, especially concerning someone who claimed the Holocaust on his résumé.

He reached into the container and lifted out the final two bundles of letters. At the bottom lay a single sheet of white paper, the blue ink crisp, the script feminine.

Clearly recent.

He lifted out the note and read the English.

You now understand the pain the Widow endured for the love of her true husband. She should have died with him in the bunker, but he demanded she flee. As a wife did at that time she obeyed her husband, but her sorrow was a life without him. However we might feel about Hitler, she loved him. Go to Africa and the place mentioned in the letters. There, all will become clear. I am sure you think me either obsessed or insane. Who could blame you? There is no reason for you to believe me, after all my entire purpose for being here was to deceive you. But I do hate the Kaiser and you are being manipulated. If possible, please allow me to offer one last bit of verification. In the mountains near here, beside the

north shore of Lago Girasol, stands a schlöss. A place where the fol-
lowers once gathered. It is an old place, known only to a few. Going
there will show you that I speak the truth.

Another prod to move him forward along some carefully chosen
path. Part of the Kaiser's web? A trap? Or a genuine offer of proof?

Who knew.

His thoughts were suddenly interrupted by the opening of the front
door. He looked up to see Cassiopeia enter, followed by Vergara. An
anxious look filled her eyes. One he did not like.

"Trouble?" he asked.

She nodded and they retreated upstairs where they could talk in
private. She explained about financial records and a link to Eisenhuth-
Industrie and Herzog Concern.

He asked, "How much was transferred?"

"Nearly a hundred million euros over a long period of time."

He now understood. "We were sent here to find those records. This
whole thing is not about Pohl being Bormann's son. It's about Marie
Eisenhuth. We're here to find the evidence that will take *her* down."

He told her about Ada's duplicity.

"Pohl fed the original information to Eisenhuth, using Gerhard
Schüb's name, so the chancellor would come looking," he said. "Then
they killed Hanna Cress and that investigator to keep us interested, and
made sure *we* found those financial records. Only Ada's improvisations
seem unexpected."

Cassiopeia sat on the edge of the bed. "So there probably is no son
of Bormann and Braun. Why would Pohl risk that exposure with this
plan?"

"He wouldn't. This is about the Eisenhuth and Herzog families being implicated with Nazi wealth. And what better way to prove authenticity than by it being found by us."

He told her about Ada's handwritten note. "She has to be telling the
truth. Nothing in the stuff sent to Marie Eisenhuth mentions Africa.
But thinking back on it now, they don't really mention any locations at
all. Just details of encounters that could have occurred anywhere. Ac-

cording to Ada, Bormann and Braun left Chile in 1947 and never returned. And the letters from Braun bear that out."

"Provided they're authentic."

"They are." He had no doubt about it.

"That means the financial information on Marie Eisenhuth's husband and father is true. Why else point us straight at it?" Cassiopeia said.

He nodded. She was right.

"We need more information," he said.

And he knew where to get it.

"Let's go see Ada again."

CHAPTER THIRTY

8:15 P.M.

THE SUN WAS GONE BY THE TIME COTTON AND CASSIOPEIA LEFT the chalet and drove toward Tilcara. It was a forty-minute ride through dark, forest-clad mountain roads. Vergara offered to accompany them, but they declined.

This trip needed to be made alone.

He slowed and entered the small town, easing past darkened buildings. Streetlights illuminated only the intersections. Then he sped out, the headlights cutting tight cones into the blackness ahead.

He spied the church from earlier.

Every window was a colorless rectangle. If not for a half-moon high in the eastern sky the building would have been nothing more than a splotch in the night. He parked again out front and they walked around to Ada's cottage. No lights burned there, either, but the front door was cocked open. Cassiopeia apparently sensed trouble, too, and they both reached under their jackets for guns.

I'll take the front, he mouthed. *You double around back and see if there is another way inside.*

He headed toward the door.

Cassiopeia rounded a corner toward the rear of the house. He stopped short and listened, searching for movement. No wind disturbed the trees. Frogs croaked out a concert in the distance, joined by the rattle of crickets. He hugged the jamb and peered inside, but the blackness was absolute. He remembered details of the parlor from earlier. No overhead light, only lamps scattered on tables. To switch one on would require him to be inside and vulnerable.

So he opted for the direct approach.

"Ada," he called out. "It's Cotton Malone."

He waited, but there was no reply.

"Ada."

Still no reply.

Suddenly the inside was ablaze with light.

"Come on in," Cassiopeia said.

He entered.

She stood across the room, gun at her side.

On the floor lay a man. Young. Dressed in jeans, shirt, and jacket. A red dot marred his forehead, hands crossed on his chest holding a sheet of paper upon which was written FOR ISABEL.

"My guess is he works for whoever Pohl hired to lead this endeavor," he said. "Ada said they killed her friend. Now she returned the favor."

"That's a bit much for an old woman working at a convalescence home."

He agreed.

Undeniably, they were dealing with something much more.

But first.

"Let's search this place."

JOSEF ENGLE PARKED THE CAR AT THE CHALET.

He'd watched from the road as a vehicle with Cassiopeia Vitt and Cotton Malone sped away. He was still unnerved from the encounter with Ada. All of it would have to be reported to Pohl, and he was not looking forward to that call. But first he had to deal with another matter.

He exited the car and followed a graveled path to the front door. A moment later Deputy Minister of Investigations Juan Vergara answered his knock.

"Where did they go?" he asked.

"They went back to see the old woman. After Malone read the letters."

Good. His man, on the scene, watching Ada's cottage, would keep an eye on what happened. "Where are these letters?"

He followed the Chilean into another room where a plastic bin lay open on the floor. A table was littered with envelopes. A uniformed policeman sat in one of the chairs casually reading.

This just kept getting worse.

"Anything interesting?" he asked the carabinero in Spanish, adding a smile.

"*Sí*, Senor. Much. The writer of these was a German woman. Proud. But so unhappy."

He could not care less, except for the fact this stranger knew more than he should. He faced Vergara. "Tell me about Malone and Vitt."

"They went upstairs when we arrived from Santiago and talked privately. I assume Vitt was reporting what she learned in Santiago. Then they left, saying they were going to see Ada again."

"Tell me about Santiago."

"Vitt found the financial records, as you wanted, and the bank confirmed the information. Senor Donoso at Banco del Estado performed perfectly, as I knew he would."

"And what was your reaction?"

"I told her that Chilean law requires that I make official inquiries to anything that relates to Nazis. I then contacted the Bundesnachrichtendienst and informed them of what had been discovered. I provided them documents by email and requested an official BND inquiry."

Precisely what he wanted to happen. Federal Intelligence Service experts in Berlin would quickly confirm that all of the information was accurate. Since, after all, it was. Which would add more fuel to the wildfire he was quickly spreading.

Finally, something had gone right.

He'd first met Vergara five years ago and had disliked the Chilean from the start. Men of vague principle and excessive greed disgusted him, and Vergara possessed an overabundance of both.

Not to mention an uncontrollable curiosity.

Vergara would not even have his post but for Theodor Pohl's inter-vention with certain Chilean officials. Nowhere, though, in their ar-rangement was Vergara, or any Chilean, to be privy to so many intimate details, especially those not part of the original plan, like letters kept by an old woman fueled by revenge.

"There is something else," Vergara said. The minister handed him a handwritten sheet. "This was in the bottom of the container."

He read Ada's handwritten words.

Dammit.

What a disaster.

The house adjacent to Lago Girasol was strictly off limits, not some-thing Cotton Malone and Cassiopeia Vitt should ever go near.

Africa the same.

Ada had truly sabotaged everything.

He made a decision.

The kind the East Germans had taught him to make when risk far outweighed reward. A lesson he'd learned long ago.

Nothing is ever gained from recklessness.

So the course was clear.

CHAPTER THIRTY-ONE

COTTON HEADED INTO ONE ROOM, CASSIOPEIA ANOTHER.

The house was less than a thousand square feet.

He noticed more of the German décor. A faded porcelain pitcher, painted with a gristmill in a white-and-brown motif. Lamps with Hummel shades in needlepoint. Painted candlesticks. A wooden crucifix on the wall, beneath a little peaked roof, made of cypress or cedar. He'd seen similar memorials across Bavaria.

In the bedroom they found an antique dressing table with a mounted oval mirror. Toiletries and creams lined the top. A dresser was covered in knickknacks that obviously had meaning. Cotton started there, rummaging through the drawers. Lots of clothes but, in the bottom one, he found an old scrapbook with a tattered leather cover. The pages were a stiff linen, the pictures held in place with little black glued corners. He hadn't seen those in a while. His grandmother had similarly glued old pictures in scrapbooks back in Georgia.

He scanned through the pages.

One immediately caught his attention.

A black-and-white of Adolf Hitler, striking a defiant pose. Not a manufactured image or something created for PR.

A personal photograph.

Ada had said that Hitler once came to her father's house.

A popular lampoon from the early 1940s came to mind, one that accurately described the exalted German leader. *He who rules in the Russian manner, dresses his hair in the French style, trims his moustache English-fashion, and wasn't born in Germany himself, who teaches us the Roman salute, asks our wives for lots of children but can't produce any himself—he is the leader of Germany.*

Cassiopeia came into the room and saw the photo. "You don't see that every day."

He agreed, and kept paging through.

There were lots of old black-and-white pictures of people and places, many fading away with time. One recurring image was of a tall, virile man wearing an SS uniform. No emotion showed on his face, only a blank stare, as if a smile would almost be painful. The shore of a lake loomed in the background, tall trees surrounding him.

Another image caught his eye.

Of children, each around seven to eight years old. Two boys and three girls, dressed as if going to church in suits and skirts, posing together in a happy gathering. He studied their young faces, but none were recognizable as Bormann's supposed son from the other photos in the hacienda.

He kept perusing.

Another picture dominated a single page.

Two men. The first was the same face from the other photo, this time minus his SS uniform. He wore lederhosen, the leather shorts supported by suspenders joined by an ornamented breast band that displayed a shiny swastika. A light-colored shirt covered his chest, knee-high stockings embraced his legs, a woolen cape draped his shoulders.

This time he flashed a smile.

The other man was short and heavy-chested with sparse black hair. He wore a double-breasted suit with a Nazi armband wrapping his left biceps. Cotton studied the older face closely, noting a contrived smile that showed no teeth, a tight jaw, and a cagey gaze.

He'd seen it before. "Am I right?"

"That's Marie Eisenhuth's father, Albert Herzog."

Which they'd seen at Eisenhuth's *schlöss*.

"First the money transfers. Now this." He stared around at the bedroom. "Chancellor Eisenhuth is not going to like any of this."

"We need to talk with her."

"I think we ought to check one more thing first. Ada went to a lot of trouble to steer us to Lago Girasol. We owe her a visit to that house by the lake. Let's do that tomorrow."

"You realize it could be a trap."

The thought had already occurred to him. "We do live a dangerous life."

She smiled. "That we do."

They finished their search and left the house, taking the scrapbook with them. Back at the vehicle he noticed something lying on the driver's seat. Something not there a few minutes ago when they arrived.

A stack of envelopes.

His senses went alert. "Seems our return here was anticipated, too. We were meant to find that body, the scrapbook, and these."

He removed the rubber band and counted fifty-three. All with South African postmarks, this time in a masculine hand, addressed to Ada in Tilcara. He opened one and, in the cabin lights of the jeep, scanned the handwritten page.

"It's signed Gerhard."

"The dates on the envelopes?"

He shuffled through the stack. "All over the place, from the late 1940s to the '60s."

"Clearly, she wants us to read these, too," Cassiopeia said.

He agreed.

But the question for the night was, why?

Cotton woke from a fitful sleep, surfacing through layers of wobbling dreams, and glanced at the luminous dial of his watch: 3:45 A.M. He'd been asleep about two hours, ever since he and Cassiopeia had returned from Tilcara. They'd reported the corpse but decided to keep the scrapbook and the new envelopes to themselves, secreting them within a canvas knapsack found in the jeep and hiding them beneath the bed.

Cassiopeia slept peacefully beside him.

A lot was happening here, and he could not seem to unscramble his thoughts. Why did he persist in spending the prime years of his life traipsing across the globe solving other people's problems? He'd once been a lawyer in the strangest sense. His clients were not people with problems sitting across from a desk. Instead, he'd represented causes, policies, nations.

A player in a global game.

The Magellan Billet had been his firm. Stephanie Nelle the senior partner. His assignments had been some of the most important the Billet were delegated.

And for good reason.

Stephanie had trusted his abilities.

And now so did the chancellor of Germany.

He pushed back the soft vicuña-skin comforter and rose from the bed. The only light that illuminated the room leaked in from beneath the door leading to the hall.

Something had stirred him.

A sound.

He reached for his gun on the bedside table and crept to the door, slowly turning the handle. The corridor beyond was lit with wall sconces splashing amber light toward the ceiling. He stuck his head past the doorframe and peered both ways.

There was no one in sight.

A railing overlooked the ground-floor great room.

The chalet was designed in the Alpine style of pitched ceilings, with lots of windows and plenty of space. In his boxers and undershirt, he tiptoed across the carpet to the wooden railing, keeping back from the edge, glancing downward, the gun at his side.

The two carabineros were sprawled on the sofas, fast asleep. Light splashed into the great room from the dining room where Vergara sat at the table, engrossed in reading Eva Braun's letters.

A cell phone on the tabletop suddenly began to vibrate.

The unit jiggled across the wood with a *rat-tat-tat* he recognized as the sound that had disturbed his sleep.

"*Ja.* What is happening?" Vergara asked in German, answering the call.

Interesting. Cassiopeia had said that the man was not familiar with the language.

There was a pause as the caller spoke.

Vergara kept talking in German, the words coming in a hushed whisper, fast and furious. Cotton caught only bits and pieces of the conversation.

"A . . . made sure . . . take me . . . necessary . . . if not for happening in my country . . ."

Another pause.

"My responsibility . . . gratitude . . . Plane . . . all will be . . ."

Vergara ended the call and went back to his reading.

They'd told Vergara about Lago Girasol, showing him Ada's note. The deputy minister had said he was familiar with the lake, but had no idea if any house sat on the north shore. He noted the area was sparsely populated and abutted one of the many national parks that dotted the lake district, near the Argentine border. He'd offered to dispatch a team to investigate, but they'd declined, preferring to go themselves. They did accept his offer of transportation and any additional information about the site.

New alarm bells rang in his brain.

He watched a few more minutes, then retreated to the bedroom and gently closed the door.

"What is it?" Cassiopeia whispered, awake and waiting for him.

"More trouble."

CHAPTER THIRTY-TWO

Cotton finished another muffin lathered with palm honey and washed his breakfast down with some tart orange juice. He'd woken half an hour ago to songbirds perched in a nearby mimosa tree. The tranquility of the setting belied the fact that he was surrounded by enemies. Vergara was certainly suspect. If Ada was to be believed, nearly every move he and Cassiopeia were making had been anticipated. And the local deputy minister of investigations could certainly be part of that. Unfortunately, to shift the situation into reverse gear he had to play out today's trip to Lago Girasol, if for nothing else than simply to confirm what he believed about Juan Vergara.

"Ready to go?" he asked Cassiopeia, who was also having a second muffin.

The plastic container Ada had provided still lay on the floor, the letters stacked on the table.

"What do we do about those?" Cassiopeia asked.

"Leave 'em."

"You think they will be okay?"

"I imagine that if anything was going to happen to them, it would have already." He wished he could say the same for them. "Have you seen our host this morning?"

They were in the downstairs dining room, the two ever-present carabineros relaxing nearby in the main salon. Food and drink had been waiting on the table.

"I heard him leave about an hour ago," she said. "We need to stay sharp. Traps are never a good place."

He smiled. "Especially for the prey."

A soft chime came from the front room. A phone. A few moments later a beep, then footsteps. The taller of the two carabineros strolled into the dining room. "Senor Vergara is ready for you at the lake. The plane is there."

"Good," he said. "Lead the way."

The drive from the chalet took less than fifteen minutes. The lake lay just north of Los Arana's main plaza. A light fog steamed from the still water and filtered a rising sun, casting the normally cobalt-blue water in a tinge of pewter gray. Far off to the west, above the fog, sunshine splashed the cone of a flat-topped volcano, its crimson flanks seemingly smeared with blood. Oyster-colored clouds dotted the sky above.

The plane was an up-wing, twin-engine amphibian, one of the old Twin Bees, built like a tank with long lines of rivets, hefty struts, and thick walls of sheet metal. The hull rested in the water like a boat, the lake gently lapping its sides, sunlight gleaming off its shiny façade.

"Now, that brings back memories," Cassiopeia said.

He agreed. They'd flown one in China a few years ago.

"I've already been blown out of the sky once this week," she noted.

He smiled. "I'll try to be more careful."

Vergara waited at the foot of a short gangplank that led to a rubber-covered dock. "I am told the fog is low level and will be gone by 9:00 A.M. There should be no problem landing once you reach Lago Girasol. It is high in the mountains. The air there is thinner. Are you positive you will not require a pilot?"

"I can handle the controls," he said. The last thing he needed was more babysitters. "What about the body from last night at Ada's house?"

"He's been identified as a local man. We are still working on his connection to the old woman. She's now missing, too."

He wasn't worried about Ada. Clearly she could handle herself. His problem was standing right here.

"Lago Girasol is 120 kilometers to the northeast," Vergara said. "There is a chart in the plane, which I have marked. I assume you can navigate as well?"

"They had a course or two on that at the Naval Academy."

And he added a grin.

"Of course, how silly of me not to realize. There is, indeed, a house in an inlet on the north shore of the lake. No roads lead to it, the only approach is from the water. It is isolated. I left some information on it, along with images from Google Maps, in the plane."

"Is she fully gassed?"

"I personally ensured the tanks were topped."

He was not comforted by that assurance.

"Have a good flight," Vergara said. "I will be interested to hear your report."

Cotton followed Cassiopeia onto the pier. She toted the canvas knapsack that held the scrapbook, the letters left for them, and the photos from the hacienda.

They climbed into the cabin.

Two leather seats sat side by side with a bench behind. The instrument panel did not extend to the passenger side, which gave them a wide view ahead through the forward windows. He strapped himself in and studied the controls then reached overhead and adjusted the throttle controls, props, and fuel mixture. He glanced down at the keel plugs and noticed the compartment seemed watertight. He fired up the twin engines, adjusting the fuel mixture until the props spun firm. He twisted the elevator and rudder trims and adjusted their angles.

The plane glided from the pier.

He grasped the yoke with both hands and maneuvered out onto open water. There was plenty of space, the lake several miles long, the fog light. The Twin Bee glided across the surface and the controls tightened. As the wings caught air the plane lifted, smooth and steady.

The lake ended and forest raced past below.

They cleared the fog and found sunny sky at six hundred feet. Distant volcanoes, rising like boils on the landscape, vanished as the windshield filled with a salmon sky rapidly deepening to blue. He banked right and adjusted course toward the northeast.

Cassiopeia studied the map, seemingly comfortable with his piloting. "There are several lakes and two towns along the way."

Below, fetid forest stretched forever. Any mist seemed confined to only where there was water. "We should be able to ground-track there and back."

"Assuming this chart is correct."

He saw her point.

"Vergara's assurances were not that reassuring," she said.

He motioned to the gauge on the control panel. "Unless he tampered with that, we have eighty gallons in the main and sixteen in the auxiliary. A full load. Besides, there's water everywhere down there. Plenty of places to land."

He liked being back in the air.

"Let's forget about all this gloom and doom for a while," he said. "Read me a few of Gerhard Schüb's letters."

CHAPTER THIRTY-THREE

ENGLE WATCHED VERGARA AS THE MINISTER SPOKE ON A CELL phone. A radio receiver rested on the dining room table amid stacks of Ada's letters. The two other policemen had brought the unit inside the chalet a few minutes ago and were now busy connecting an antenna and finding an extension cord. He'd passed the time by reading some of the letters Ada had first supplied to Malone and Vitt.

He recognized the name Rikka Soreno and the South African location. But in all of the briefings that Pohl had provided, no mention had ever been made that Eva Braun maintained such extensive contact with South America. No long-lasting friendship with Ada was ever noted, either. But he should not be surprised. Too many players. Too much time had elapsed. Too little information. Anything was possible.

And usually was.

The body found in Ada's house had been the man he'd stationed to watch her. The old woman had killed him and let her feelings be known.

FOR ISABEL.

Another old woman whom he'd eliminated a few years ago to chill another trail that two American agents had tried to follow. He'd never realized that death had been such a problem. No mention of dissent had been made from anyone here in Chile about what happened then. But Ada definitely held a grudge. He had to find her.

Fast.

Also, he could not allow Vitt or Malone to leave Chile alive. Pohl had told him to deal with them once their usefulness had waned.

And that time had come.

He turned his attention back to the telephone conversation.

"This is Minister Vergara. I have information of a drug flight presently ongoing toward the Argentine border. An attempt was made to stop the plane on the ground, but failed. I have the course coordinates and description of the plane. I need an intercept scrambled immediately." A pause while Vergara listened. *"Bueno. Gracías."* A pause. "Excellent. I will monitor communications. You have my phone number. I will keep the line clear. You do the same." The Chilean hung up the phone and turned to him. "A fighter is on the way."

"What is the procedure?" He needed to know the details.

"We have radar agreements with the Argentines. There are many unauthorized flights along the border. The Americans even assist in our endeavors with a mobile radar platform."

"Have you involved them?"

He shook his head. "No need. This is being done on my order, with local resources."

"What about radio contact with the amphibian?"

"Commander Malone and Senorita Vitt will discover their unit receives quite well, but is deficient in transmitting."

"I assume it is not unusual for drug traffickers not to respond by radio?"

"Quite common. They try to avoid interception. Some are good at navigating the mountains. Others are not as skillful."

"Does the interceptor understand what to do?"

A sly smile came to the man's thin lips. "His superior does."

COTTON LISTENED AS CASSIOPEIA READ A FEW OF THE LETTERS aloud. Each was a fascinating account of a man thrust half a world away, serving a cause he only vaguely understood, far from his sister.

February 7, 1949

. . . our arrival in Bloemfontein was uneventful. This is a
strange place. Nearly five thousand feet above sea level, the air
clear and light. Patches of Europe are everywhere. Waterwheels,
homesteads, rose gardens, stout buildings. There is a nearly
perpetual battle with drought, pests, and bankers. Luis com-
plains incessantly. He does not particularly like the choice of
location. This Union of South Africa is a strange nation. It
possesses two capitals. Johannesburg, to the north, is the political center. Bloemfontein here in the Free State is the judicial
center. Why this is so no one can adequately explain, though
there is talk of merging both here in Bloemfontein. The Free
State is replete with Dutch influence. They, in the form of
Boers, settled here. Many still talk of the Anglo-Boer War,
which only ended less than fifty years ago. They still remember the concentration camps. Luis likes to tell me that the
British invented the concept right here when they slaughtered
thousands of women and children during the war. All things
British are still hated with a deep passion, which pleases Luis
greatly.

I wish you could see this country. It is truly beautiful.
Grayish-brown plains dotted with what the locals call peppercorn
bushes, the flatness broken by iron-colored kopjes. Mountains
line the edge of the sky, their tops shaved level. Storms settle
over the land for hours, the rain falling in thick sheets. But by
morning the sky is wiped clear by a warm sun. We have taken a
house on the outskirts of town. It stands in the shade of fir and
gum trees. You would love the bougainvillea that climb its walls.
Behind is a barn and stable. Water mills revolve over springs
and fill tanks and make life possible. Without water there would
be nothing but barren veld for hundreds of miles. Nighttime is
the best of all. The veld goes silent and silver in the moonlight.
Darkness is absolute, the trees like cardboard cutouts. Our dogs
congregate beneath the open windows. It is good they are there.
They keep the lions away. The dogs are fearless and I envy their
courage.

May 23, 1949

Time is nearly irrelevant here. This forgotten land is truly a paradise in many ways. The whites control everything while the Africans toil the land. I witnessed a curious sight a few days back. Luis and I drove to a town a few miles west of our farm. Not much there besides a red-roofed store, a Dutch Reformed church, and a petrol station. A small farm was for sale and Luis wanted to be present when the mortgage was called. What a strange sight. Furniture piled in the sunlight, the money lender leading the auction, the mortgagor in shabby clothes, his wife and children in tears, their house and possessions all gone. I noticed that only a fence of prickly pear would soon separate them from the Africans beyond. I asked Luis about the matter. His bid was deemed too low and he failed to secure the property, so he was not in a good humor. He lectured me that there is no place in this world for the weak. They clutter the strong with the vice of sympathy and for that they must be eliminated. He felt nothing for the family that would sleep on the earth that night without the protection of shelter. I felt for them, though. How could one not? But Luis seemed filled only with contempt. He is a hard man, fueled by hate and even more by regret. Rikka is having a difficult time. He will not take her swimming at the Mazelspoort or for a boat trip down the river, or simply sit beneath the trees and enjoy the day. She tries to make life bearable, if not for him certainly for herself. He tries to please her with luxury. Their house is full of silver, mahogany, and books. No one comes to visit, though. He will not allow visitors. His suspicions have increased since we arrived, a phobia of doubt that consumes his every day. He is so dependent on me. Odd, actually. This man of power and wealth so needing me. I am his eyes, ears, and legs. Doing, saying, seeing all things he cannot. He is paralyzed by fear and part of me is glad.

January 14, 1951

We have moved again. This time closer to the border with Basutoland in the eastern highlands. The years are passing slowly.

I was promised my release from service by Christmas, but I am now told that Luis will not let me go. He still depends on me. I seem to be the only one he trusts, if that attribute can be applied to a man such as him. He will not let me leave, though I plan to broach the subject again with him soon.

Our new farm is lovely. It is an estate bought with profits from the gold mines. Luis was smart to invest. He has earned a fortune, but continues to live a solitary life. I am still the messenger who travels into Bloemfontein to report on any news. Books are my main duty. He consumes more than a dozen each month. I order what he demands and drive to town every three weeks when a shipment arrives. Mainly American book clubs provide the bulk of his taste. It is his one pleasure and Rikka encourages the endeavor since it spares her the wrath of his boredom. He is truly an evil man, of that I am sure. He does not deserve any luxury in life. If not for my duty I would end this charade. But I can't. It is not my nature, as I am sure you understand.

Cassiopeia read on and Cotton listened with fascination as Gerhard Schüb recounted life in South Africa. The letters were scattered over a wide breadth of time, all written in German, the insights profound as Schüb analyzed his employer. Clearly he did not care for Martin Bormann, but he continued to perform his duty with diligence. Each letter was duly signed with the salutation, *your loving brother, Gerhard.*

"Schüb seems to have hated Bormann," Cassiopeia said.

"That's the great paradox of Nazism. While hating everything about it, so many willingly gave themselves so completely."

Cassiopeia thumbed through the remaining envelopes. "The last letter is dated in 1961."

Ahead he spied a large splotch of cobalt-blue water framed by shores of verdant scrub and copper-colored beech trees. A mist flashed back and hung in the air, fighting against the burning sun. Craggy peaks of gray and purple rose on three sides, houses tucked away in the folds. Beyond, thick dark alpine forest oozed in all directions, the landscape green as an emerald, dripping with moisture. He estimated the lake was several miles long and equally wide.

Lago Girasol.

Dense forest lined the shore.

He spied an inlet. Narrow. Jutting into the treed landscape. A small, forested island protected its mouth, atop which stood a masonry tower.

What a strange sight.

They flew over it.

"That's a guard tower," she said.

He agreed. Like something overlooking the Rhine in Germany.

Tucked among the trees, he spotted the *schlöss*. Similar in look and style to Marie Eisenhuth's. Huge. Remote. Inaccessible. Built of stone. Far more European than South American. More forest protected the house on three sides. Only from the lake, facing south, was the house visible. He saw no signs of anyone. No vehicles. No smoke from the chimneys. Nothing.

A pier extended out into the blue water.

"We can tie up to that dock," he said.

And he headed in for a landing.

CHAPTER THIRTY-FOUR

ENGLE COULD TELL THAT VERGARA WAS PLEASED WITH THE RADIO reports.

"Target is down on the lake," the fighter pilot reported over the radio, in Spanish. "Landed and tied to a dock. Two people headed ashore toward a large house."

Vergara acknowledged the information with a nod, then said to him, "These transmissions are being monitored by a great many governmental agencies. It is important that we establish that a drug trafficking flight was en route. They have stopped near the border for who-knows-what. Radio contact is impossible since the target would not respond to hails. Chilean protocol requires that the plane be brought to the ground. Standard procedure does not call for planes to be destroyed in the air. Too much risk of ground casualties. Instead, the idea is to force flights down."

"But it is already on the ground."

"Which is good for us. Now we deal with your problem."

CASSIOPEIA FOLLOWED COTTON ASHORE, BRINGING WITH HER THE backpack with the letters, scrapbook, and photos. Neither one of them wanted that evidence far from their sight.

They both studied the magnificent house.

A three-story, polished-stone structure with ornate rococo iron trim. Rows of windows overlooked the grounds and the lake, each protected by sturdy, wrought-iron bars. A sign at the end of the dock proclaimed in Spanish PRIVATE PROPERTY.

"You don't see mansard roofs like that in South America," she said.

He agreed. Much more common in Europe.

They trudged up through a slope of damp, manicured grass toward a stone terrace. Tall, clean-trunked trees lined the outer perimeter. Baroque statues, each encircled with autumn flowers, stood periodically on display. The absence of activity was noticeable, the stillness in the chilly air a bit unnerving.

"This is beautiful and well maintained," she noted.

"Which makes you wonder."

She heard the haunting cry of a nightingale, like a warning alarm. The skies had turned gray and fatigued, the sort of overcast day that promised rain but never delivered. An unrelenting breeze swooped out of the mountains and chafed their faces, the air hanging fresh and thin with a taste of pine. The terrace was immaculate, the furniture covered in canvas protectors. Not a speck of mold or mildew anywhere.

Cotton approached the glass doors.

Locked.

"I see no reason to be subtle," he said.

Neither did she.

He found his gun and used it to break one of the glass panels, then he reached in and unlocked the door.

Inside was spectacular.

A great hall occupied a large portion of the ground floor. Dark hunting trophies contrasted with the cream-colored walls. Tapestries draped two walls, mostly hunting scenes. Stucco decorated the ceiling with images of birds and animals. Colorful rugs protected the parquet floor. A tall white ceramic stove filled one corner, outfitted with a gleaming brass door. Everything had a medieval feel, the heavy styles proclaiming power and wealth.

"This screams Europe," Cotton said.

She agreed.

A vase of freshly cut flowers sat at the center of a large clothed table in the dining room.

"Are those here for our benefit?" he asked.

Good question.

They kept exploring the ground floor, which seemed to ramble on. Aside from a spacious kitchen and a light and airy dining room, there was a gaming room with a billiard table, and a study, one similar to the hacienda's, only much larger, its mood set by mellow-oak bookcases, the red velvet upholstery of the chairs complementing pale-tan walls. Above the cases hung oil paintings in heavy wood frames.

Cotton studied the canvases.

"What is it?" she asked.

"That's Richard Wagner," he said, pointing to one of the images. "Hitler's favorite composer. Those paintings over there are from Franz Stuck and Carl Spitzweg. Two more of Hitler's favorites. The three paintings of drunken monks over there are by Eduard von Grützner, whom Hitler loved, too."

"You know your Nazi art."

"Just stuff that sticks in my brain from reading. Sometimes it has to come out. None of those artists ever achieved much fame, which always baffled Hitler. Did you notice the books on the shelf?"

She stepped closer.

The subjects varied from literature to history, science, architecture. Then she saw a row that looked familiar. Editions on art. Philosophical works of Nietzsche and Schopenhauer. Greek, Roman, and German histories. Goethe. Ibsen. Librettos of Wagner's operas. Nordic mythology. Military history.

"They're the same as the hacienda's," she said.

He nodded. "Exactly the same is my guess. Taken there for our benefit by Ada."

She walked over to the windows. Slatted sunshine spilled in past the blinds. An enormous mahogany chair with thick cushions sat before one of them, facing outward.

"You have to wonder who sat here," she said. "It seems like the king's chair."

It also brought to mind another mansion she'd read about, not all that far from here, across the border in Argentina. Near San Carlos de Bariloche, in the Andean foothills, on the southern shore of Lake Nahuel Huapi.

Residencia Inalco.

Popular lore liked to say that Hitler and Eva Braun escaped the Führerbunker in 1945 and managed to make it to Argentina, where they supposedly lived for a time at Inalco. Most agreed the tale was fiction, created to bring more tourists to Patagonia, but the story survived thanks to a variety of books and television shows that offered much in the way of speculation and little in proof. Yet Bariloche *had* harbored war criminals. Lots of them. And they would have felt right at home. Plenty of Alpine-style architecture thanks to Germans who settled there in the late 19th century. Combined with a cool climate, deep-blue lakes, and snowcapped mountains, the area was a veritable slice of Bavaria. History noted that Juan Perón, who headed Argentina after the war, had allowed the secret immigration of some thirteen hundred Nazis fleeing Europe. Now here she was beside another South American lake that reeked with suspicion, inside a place that had the feel of a museum, unlived in, untouched by human warmth. What was this? A residence? A gathering spot? A memorial? All financed with gold stashed in South American banks by former Nazis intent on living until old age?

And why did it still exist?

World War II had been over for a long time. Nearly all of the German participants were dead. Any who still lived would have been lesser lieutenants, the lowest of the lowest echelon, conscripted in the dying days of the Third Reich. Young men then, many just boys, who tried to impress their Führer by slaughtering civilians. Nuremberg labeled their efforts "crimes against humanity," and they'd been hunted ever since— not with the same dogged determination a Mengele, or an Eichmann, or a Klaus Barbie commanded, but hunted nonetheless.

"It's spooky," she said.

"I agree. Reminders of the Third Reich are all here, only subtle. Nothing overt. You have to know what you're looking at. Let's check upstairs."

A door opened somewhere in the house.

Loud.

Obvious.

They both reached for their weapons.

Footsteps thumped down the outer corridor, approaching the study.

There was no place to hide, so they assumed a position behind the open door that led out to the hallway, guns ready.

Two men with rifles entered.

Then Ada appeared and turned their way.

"*Guten morgen.* We must go. Now."

CHAPTER THIRTY-FIVE

Stuttgart, Germany
1:00 P.M.

Pohl completed the last interview, pleased with the past hour. News coverage was clearly the most effective tool in German politics. Silly restrictions on paid television advertisements limited the number of political spots and the time when they could run, as well as requiring a somber announcement that they were all partisan statements. Needless to say, few watched and even fewer listened to those messages.

Talk shows, interviews, and news programs, though, were different. As was the internet. There were no rules or limitations, which made them perfect for disseminating propaganda. His policy, instituted from the first day of the campaign, was to make himself available for at least an hour each day to answer questions. Of course, he was selective about the correspondents afforded the time, and his staff quietly doled out the privilege as a reward for favorable coverage. It was one of the ways he made reporters' jobs easier. A way for them to ingratiate themselves with their editors. And so far the chosen group had responded to his generosity with a barrage of coverage that had translated into positive percentage points in the polls.

But he wasn't all that surprised.

Unlike in the United States and Britain, where most of the press leaned left, the fourth estate in Germany was tilted right.

And for that he was eternally grateful.

He glanced at his watch and noted the time. The last interview, with a news crew from Hamburg, had run a bit long. He needed a few minutes of privacy, so he asked his staff to excuse themselves on the pretense of having a short nap. The rest of the day was going to be arduous with stops scheduled in Killesbergpark, the university, and the Institute of International Relations, where he was scheduled to speak after dinner. Tomorrow would take him to the Daimler factory in the eastern suburbs and some handshaking at the front gate. Six hundred thousand people lived in and around Stuttgart. Two of his publishing houses were headquartered south of town, along with a respectable chunk of the remaining German publishing industry. Though he was a local employer with connections that ran deep into city politics, and his latest polling numbers showed him strong in both the city and surrounding countryside, he'd still scheduled two full days in the area—no sense taking chances—and he intended for the newspapers and television to be saturated with him over the course of today and tomorrow.

He was headquartered at the Hotel am Steigenberger. The proprietor, a longtime supporter, had provided a suite that overlooked the Palace Garden. As the last of his staff filtered from his second-floor room, he reached for the phone and dialed the number he'd long ago memorized. Per a message sent last night through an aide, his call would be expected.

One ring.

Two.

"So good of you to be punctual," the voice said on the other end after the third ring.

"It is a virtue, I am told."

Kurt Eisenhuth laughed. "With you, everything is a virtue."

"I am but a humble publisher. Not the grand industrialist you are."

"You flatter me, Theodor. But we have a problem."

"I suspected as much from your request that we speak immediately."

"It is Marie."

"How is *Oma* today? She can't be pleased."

His pollster had already reported that the overnight numbers showed a clear 2-point gain for him. In the "battle of the books," as the media had dubbed yesterday's affair, it appeared he'd emerged the clear winner.

"She plans more of what happened yesterday," Kurt said. "She is not backing off."

"Excellent." And he meant it. "Do encourage her."

"You take her too lightly."

"Spoken like a devoted husband. I assure you, Kurt, I do not underestimate your wife. She's both capable and intelligent, which is reflected in her ability to hold on to power for so long. That makes for a dangerous combination in a political adversary. I assume, though, you have more to tell me than that. Your message said this was important."

"I came across some notes she made from a telephone conversation. Two Americans are presently in Chile looking into something concerning you. What, I do not know. But I thought you should be made aware."

He couldn't say that he was already well aware. That, in fact, he was orchestrating everything happening across the Atlantic. So he simply said, "Interesting."

"The notes mentioned finding some photographs, nothing more. Do you know what that is about?"

"Not to worry. It has nothing to do with me."

And he meant it.

As Marie Eisenhuth and the hapless fool on the other end of the phone would soon discover.

"She is quite restless. Troubled even," Kurt said.

"As she should be. That stunt yesterday was foolish. Please, as I said, encourage more of the same."

"I am afraid she listens to nothing I have to say."

"Oh, there you are wrong, old friend. She listens and promptly does the opposite. Remember that. An angry dog is best led by its tail."

Kurt laughed. "I will keep that in mind. But you seem unconcerned that people may be investigating you."

"It would not be the first time, nor I am sure the last. It comes with running for public office. I have nothing to hide, so let them investigate."

"Are you going to win this election?"

"That is the goal."

"Marie believes you to be a demon. The embodiment of everything she abhors."

He could not care less. "She cannot grasp much beyond her own centrist philosophy. To her, anything contrary to that is a return to the past. She will soon learn that Germany is stronger than she believes."

"But is it strong enough to survive what you have in mind?"

He chuckled. "I assure you, Kurt, this nation has the backbone for anything, as history has proven."

Men like Kurt Eisenhuth could never comprehend what he envisioned. They were followers. He was the leader. The emperor.

The Kaiser.

"Spoken like a chancellor-to-be," Kurt said. "I will not take any more of your time. I simply thought you would want to know the information." A touch of resignation laced the declaration.

"I appreciate your efforts."

And he hung up.

CHAPTER
THIRTY-SIX

COTTON AND CASSIOPEIA FOLLOWED ADA AND THE TWO ARMED men back through the house. He'd seen the urgency in the old woman's face and realized that she was there to help.

So they had not argued.

"I have learned that this place has become a target," Ada said. "We must hurry and leave."

They crossed the ground floor and found the kitchen. Through a storage room a door opened to a staircase down into a cellar. Incandescent bulbs lit the way. The air turned progressively cooler as they descended.

"What's happening?" he asked as they hustled down the stairs.

"Minister Vergara is doing the Kaiser's bidding," the old woman said. "Theodor Pohl wants the two of you dead. Now."

Always a bit disconcerting to hear.

They came to the bottom, and he saw an expansive basement that seemed to traverse the entire ground floor. Tools and other equipment were neatly piled everywhere. Doors opened into a laundry and a refrigerated wine cellar. Furnaces, too, for winter heat. Other doors stood closed with hasp locks. Ada seemed to know exactly what she was doing as they threaded a path toward a far wall of cement block.

"This house was built in the late 1940s," she said. "But it has been modernized several times since."

She stopped before the wall and pointed to one of the men with rifles, who seemed to know what to do. The young man handed off his weapon, then jumped up and grabbed hold of one of the metal pipes that ran along the ceiling beneath the floor joists. He pulled himself up and slammed a fist into the side of the joist.

A panel in the cement block wall swung open.

"The men who frequented this house for decades always required an emergency exit," Ada said. "In case of trouble."

"Like Nazi hunters closing in?" he said.

"That certainly would have qualified."

Everyone hustled through the open portal into a tunnel about three feet wide and six feet tall, straight as an arrow for a long way, bulbs every twenty feet or so lighting the way.

"Move quickly," Ada said. "Don't worry about me, I'll keep up."

She wore a coffee-colored dress that fell just past her knees with a thick jacket covering her midsection. She carried a walking stick, which seemed to help with her balance. And she moved surprisingly fast for a woman in her nineties.

The panel shut behind them.

They were now encased within a tight space, nothing but earth and rock around them. A familiar panic swept over him and he felt Cassiopeia's hand on his shoulder, reassuring him. She knew how much he hated this kind of enclosed space. But there was no time for phobias. Thankfully, they were moving fast, headed away from the mansion, the tunnel angling downward.

To take his mind off the uncomfortableness he studied the construction. Horseshoe shaped. Rough brick walls. Dirt floor. Most likely not a tunnel, but built into a trench dug from the house, then filled over to conceal it.

Which brought no comfort.

They rushed ahead for about fifty yards, where the route veered slightly left and dropped sharply downward. More bulbs illuminated the way for another thirty yards.

He steeled himself and kept pace.

At the end rose a metal ladder. One of the young men scaled the rungs and pushed open a wooden door in the ceiling.

Everyone followed him upward.

They were standing in what appeared to be a barn. Two tractors, hand tools, and a riding lawn mower filled the shadows. The only light leaked in from a dingy window high up on one wall.

"This shed is away from the main house," Ada said. "And below it, past a berm."

Cotton nodded at Cassiopeia and they both withdrew their guns, aiming them at the other three.

"Lay those rifles down. Nice and slow," he ordered.

The young men complied.

"Herr Malone," Ada said. "There is no need for that."

"Forgive me if I'm a little distrustful."

"Might we go outside?" the old woman asked. "There's something you should see and hear."

He glanced at Cassiopeia, who shrugged. *Okay. Why not.*

"Lead the way."

A side door was opened and they stepped out into the cool morning. Branches of old-growth trees interlocked overhead, creating a barrier against the cloudy sky. He saw that they were indeed away from and below the main house, a treed berm rising up on one side. A narrow dirt road led away from the barn. Patches of sunlight striped through the trees. Overhead, the sky rattled with a distant roar.

A familiar sound.

"A fighter jet?" he asked.

Ada nodded. "It followed you here on Vergara's order."

Nothing about that sounded good.

A thunderous boom broke the silence, followed by a scorching wave of hot air that engulfed the sky above them.

An explosion.

Instinctively, they all ducked and shielded their faces.

The treetops were cuffed by the ripple of disturbed air, flung back on the wave of a detonation. Luckily, they were far enough away, and below, that the blast did not affect them. He heard the crash of rubble, the crackle of fire, and the *flit-flit* of debris falling through the trees.

He waited for it all to subside, then hustled up the forested incline.

Cassiopeia followed.

The house was engulfed in a ball of flame, reduced to a crumpled, glowing form, the cindered shape of what had been an elegant *schlöss* gone. Fire probed up through the dirty smoke, roiling and billowing. Debris littered the ground in all directions.

"Air-to-ground missile," he said.

A roar approached.

Growing louder.

They stayed hidden among the trees.

High-caliber rounds strafed the burning rubble and thumped into the wet ground beyond the house. The fighter shot passed overhead, disappearing up into the cloud cover.

"Making sure we're dead," he muttered, staring at the smoldering ruins. The air hung thick with the stench of charred wood.

The fighter returned.

But farther off.

Then a second explosion in the distance.

"Your plane," Ada called out from below.

He turned and asked, "You knew this was going to happen?"

"Lucky for you I have friends who alerted me."

Yeah. Lucky for us.

They descended off the berm.

"What now?" he asked.

"We walk," Ada said.

They followed the dirt road to a hardpan trail that snaked beneath the trees, Ada and her two acolytes leading the way. After a few hundred yards they came to another path that diverged. Clear and defined. Which they took, passing through a moonscape of bracken and heather. A thick carpet of leaves provided a springy softness to the earth and soundproofed their footsteps, allowing songbirds to be heard. The trail narrowed, then dead-ended at a patch of low ground. A rose-colored ibis sprang forward, its ostentatious wings flapping as they grabbed air.

Wild violets colored the clearing's perimeter. Cotton noticed a scattering of slate and granite rubble across the rough grass.

"Those are graves," Cassiopeia said.

He stepped into the cemetery and immediately saw that all of the markers had been hammered to gravel. He bent down and examined the remnants. "I imagine a few war crimes files could be closed by identifying the dead here."

"You would be correct," Ada said.

He tossed one of the shards of rock aside, then glanced around at the tall beech and thick araucaria trees. Bars of sunlight cut across the treetops in golden shafts.

"Who the hell are you?" he asked Ada.

"Someone who just saved your life."

ENGLE WATCHED AS VERGARA SPOKE ON HIS CELL PHONE. THE LAST report from the fighter pilot indicated that house had been obliterated.

Vergara ended his call. "The seaplane was likewise destroyed, as you requested. The pilot says there is nothing left of it or the house. He also strafed the ruins with high-caliber rounds."

There'd been no choice. The *schlöss* had to be eliminated with zero traces of anything remaining. A shame, too. He'd visited several times and it was quite magnificent. Pohl would not be pleased, but there was no other option. Malone and Vitt also had to die and the trail from here turned ice cold, just as he'd done before when others ventured too close.

"Local carabineros were alerted to the explosion by boaters. They are headed there now across the lake, but it will take them an hour or more to get there. We can explain the house's destruction as an errant shot." The minister smiled. "These things happen. Senor Engle, your problem appears to be solved."

"And I am most appreciative. This was above and beyond what we expected from your services."

"*Gracías.* It is a pleasure to serve Herr Pohl. He is a generous benefactor."

The two carabineros sat on the other side of the table. They'd listened to everything with interest. He knew these were not mere policemen, but instead were part of Vergara's personal staff, both also on Pohl's private payroll. Their task over the past few days had been to monitor Malone and Vitt and report everything. But they'd gone too far reading Ada's letters. Now they were loose ends. As was Vergara. Thankfully, everything that had happened here traced back to these three.

Nothing led to either him or Pohl.

He reached beneath his jacket and gripped the pistol, its safety already released. He removed the weapon and fired two shots, one each into the carabineros' foreheads. Vergara seemed at first stunned, then reached for his own sidearm. But Engle placed two bullets into the minister's chest. He finished the job with a third above the nose that sent the deputy minister of investigations to the floor.

He checked all three for a pulse.

None.

Vergara and his nosy minions were no longer available for questioning. Cotton Malone and Cassiopeia Vitt were dead, the house by the lake gone. All of the financial records from the file cabinet Vitt had seized yesterday were back in Santiago in Vergara's office.

Which was perfect.

They wanted those found and exposed.

Perhaps Vergara's death would be linked to them. The few records that Vergara had emailed to Germany would serve their intended purpose and spur the German authorities along. Ada was definitely a problem, and the letters she'd provided were still a concern, but she'd most likely gone to ground. Finding her now would be both risky and difficult.

He'd deal with her after the election.

At the moment there was another pressing matter.

One he was going to investigate on his way back to Germany.

So he calmly tossed the letters into the plastic container, snapped it shut, and left the chalet, deciding to burn them along the way, then enjoy a quick meal in town before flying on to Africa.

CHAPTER
THIRTY-SEVEN

COTTON WALKED ALONG THE PATH.

Ada led the way, still gripping her rustic walking stick, the ground becoming riddled with holes from its sharp point as it helped her make her way. Cassiopeia kept pace behind him, still shouldering the backpack. He heard the sound of rushing water, and the trail began to run along the edge of a swollen stream, through dense entangled thickets. They were headed away from the *schlöss,* black smoke still pouring up into gray sky. Finally they emerged from the woods onto a wide dirt road that led back toward the lake.

"We had not the time for a proper introduction," Ada said. "You must be Fräulein Vitt. It is a pleasure to meet you."

"I have to say, it's an even greater pleasure that I meet you. Thank you for what you just did."

"I wrote that note and encouraged you both to come here, unsure as to exactly what Minister Vergara might do. But then I received a call about what Vergara wanted done, so we came immediately."

"You are incredibly well informed," Cotton said. "Especially for a person who merely works at a convalescence center."

"Lucky for you that I have such varied interests."

He smiled.

"Thankfully, we had sufficient time to act. I was told they would wait a few minutes after you entered before sending the missile. They wanted both you and the house gone."

"Since you were never supposed to mention that place, right?" he asked.

"That's correct. Once I did, I knew Vergara would act. How? I was unsure. But they also would not want you going to Africa."

"Who is *they*?" he asked.

"Theodor Pohl and his associates."

"He wants us to tell Marie Eisenhuth that her father and husband are connected to lost Nazi wealth," Cassiopeia said. "He also wants the German people to see those documents and hear that truth. Vergara couldn't wait to get out of that bank and make an official report."

"The question seems to be, are you going to allow that to happen?"

"What are our choices?" he asked.

"Go to Africa."

"Why?"

"The truth awaits you there."

"We read the letters you left," he said. "Your brother, Gerhard Schüb, lived a long time there. But the last letter we have is over fifty years old. What happened since? How do you know anything about Africa?"

"Is it not enough that I do?"

His patience was wearing thin. "We're standing here in the woods, near what was once some sort of Nazi shrine. One you knew all about. Then there are these young men with rifles, who clearly take orders from you. By your own admission, your father worked for Bormann. Then you took over—"

"Herr Malone, this area of Chile, and over the border into Argentina, was once filled with Germans from the war. Many fled here legally to escape the destruction there. They were not Nazis. Many more came illegally to hide, trying to be inconspicuous. They required assistance."

"Some of those were war criminals," he said.

"And most of them were eventually caught. Bormann implemented Aktion Aderflung and Aktion Feuerland as his plans to get key people and assets out of Germany. And yes, my father headed up those efforts here in Chile. My brother, though, had a much tougher assignment. Yes. We were Nazi caretakers. But my brother and I performed our duties in honor of our father, whom we both loved dearly."

"And what was the house we just saw?"

"A place for the old ones to enjoy. There are only a few left, but they still came here from time to time. Especially on April 20."

"Hitler's birthday," he said.

She nodded. "You know your history."

"I know when I'm being played. And we've been played from the start. But we allowed it so we could move this along."

"I ended that."

He chuckled. "No. You just started a new tune for us to dance to."

"Herr Malone, I was asked to stage what happened at the hacienda you visited. And I did. I admit that."

"Using some of the books from the *schlöss*?" he asked.

The old woman nodded. "That and the banner. Much of the old memorabilia was stored in the basement. But that is now gone, too."

"You don't sound sad," Cassiopeia said.

"It is like losing a cancer."

He agreed.

"I was told to spur you along from the hacienda. Which I did, when these young men fired on the dwelling. I was told to provide some photographs in an inconspicuous manner. Those were left for you to find on the wall inside. They are of Bormann and Braun. But they were not taken here. The child you saw with Bormann is a stranger. Some letters were to be supplied to reinforce my statements that no son of Martin Bormann exists." The old woman smiled. "But I changed that part."

"You left those letters in the car last night?"

She nodded. "They were important for you to read. The Kaiser has no idea they exist, nor does he know that Eva Braun and I corresponded secretly for many years. My brother facilitated that on his end in Africa. She needed a friend. Someone to confide in, and I served that need."

Cassiopeia slipped off the backpack and showed the scrapbook. "You wanted us to find this, too?"

Ada nodded. "I had the Kaiser's spy killed and left there as a message to Pohl's man. I assumed you would come back, looking for me, then search the premises, so I left that for you to find."

"You want it back?" he asked.

"No. Take it. You will need it."

"And the financial records?" Cassiopeia asked.

"Those they definitely wanted you to find, so you were led right to them. The chancellor's investigator was murdered to add emphasis to your search. The dagger was obtained from another repository and used as the murder weapon. You would be shocked at how many of the Nazis' things remain on this continent.

"Unfortunately, there's more than enough in those financial records to implicate the current chancellor of Germany with the stink of the Third Reich. They are not fake. It is all true, and the chancellor will have to deal with that sad reality." She paused. "Can we just say that, for me, things have altered. Where once I aided the man who likes to be called Kaiser, that is no longer the case. I am taking a great personal risk in helping you, one that may eventually cost me my life. And as you've just seen, your lives are also in danger. But I have been told that you both are more than capable of handling yourselves."

"And who told you that?" Cassiopeia asked.

"Someone who knows."

"This one is the queen of cryptic," he said to Cassiopeia.

"Subtlety is a lost art," Ada said. "There is another matter, though."

She motioned and one of the younger men handed her a cell phone, which she passed to Cotton. He saw the image of a man. Mid-fifties, tanned skin, a Vandyke beard dusted with streaks of silver-gray.

"His name is Josef Engle," the old woman said. "Remember the face. He is the Kaiser's right hand." She paused. "He's the one who killed my friend Isabel. He killed the investigator the chancellor sent to Santiago, too. The man I had killed last night worked for Engle. It was Engle who paid Vergara to kill you both. Once he knows that effort failed, I assure you, he will move to eliminate you again."

He locked the man's features into his brain.

"My father served the Brown Eminence until Bormann left in 1947. I never saw Bormann or Evi again. They became my brother's responsibility. My father continued to deal with the needs of those who had fled here as a refuge. Bormann created many accounts at many banks, and my father was the trustee of them all after he left, responsible for maintaining the balances and disbursing what was needed. Regular reports were made to Africa until my father died, and Bormann stayed involved with all major decisions. But once my father died, I was placed in charge, and I chose to make no more reports. That was never challenged. I assumed Bormann was dead by then, too. I have been *der regler* of those moneys for a long time. Senor Donoso, whom you met yesterday at the bank, is a man of questionable morals who works for whoever might pay him. Vergara has been his benefactor for many years."

"So you allowed those financial records to be found?" Cassiopeia asked.

The old woman nodded. "To stop that would have stopped all this from moving forward. I am sorry that Chancellor Eisenhuth will pay a price, but it is a price long in coming. It is time she knew the truth."

"How do you know Theodor Pohl?" Cotton asked.

"He and I have been associated for many years. From time to time he would ask for favors. Those occurred mainly when people came here investigating the past. We've had all sorts. Governments, bounty hunters, writers, journalists, moviemakers, even an American television series that dealt with a wild theory that Hitler somehow lived a long peaceful life here. We dissuaded them all and sent them off chasing shadows."

"To protect the money?" he said.

The old woman shook her head. "To protect the past. The last problem came a few years ago. Two American agents. Which led to Isabel's murder. I knew then that I would one day make the Kaiser pay for that callous act. And, make no mistake, Juan Vergara participated in Isabel's murder. He is likewise responsible. They will all pay."

"There's a lot of bitterness in you," Cotton said.

"It comes from a life of poor choices."

"What do you want us to do?" Cassiopeia asked.

"Follow the letters I have given you," Ada said. "They will guide you in Africa."

"Why should we believe anything you're saying?" he asked.

"I just saved your lives. If I wanted you dead, you would be."

He did not doubt that observation.

"Why did you and your brother never reconnect?" Cassiopeia asked.

"I never said we didn't."

"So is your brother alive?" he asked.

"The answer to that question awaits you in Africa. Let me say that there is far more at stake here than you realize. When Pohl decided to entice Marie Eisenhuth to come here and uncover those financial records, he never imagined the doors he was opening. He never comprehended the extent of the hate and resentment that awaited him. As arrogant pedantic fools often do, he thought himself the smartest and the cleverest. He wove a web that has now been tangled. It only remains for the two of you to untangle it. To do that or not is your choice, and yours alone."

The old woman paused.

"Choose wisely."

They were taken by boat across Lago Girasol, then by car the 120 miles back to the dock they'd left from earlier. Their jeep was still there, and they used it to drive to the chalet. Two police vehicles were parked out front. That meant the carabineros and Vergara were there. They approached the building with caution, peering through the rear deck's plate-glass windows to take stock of the inside. Surely their appearance was going to be a surprise. Particularly if Ada was to be believed and Vergara had been involved with the attempt on their lives.

The great room was empty, but the dining room told a different story. The two carabineros lay sprawled in chairs, Vergara on the floor.

All of the bodies bore bullet holes.

"You think it was Ada?" Cassiopeia asked. "Or Pohl's guy Engle?"

"My money is on the latter. Tidying up loose ends."

They entered through unlocked French doors.

A radio receiver sat on the table.

"That wasn't there earlier," she said.

No, it wasn't. Then he noticed. Ada's letters were gone.

Cassiopeia saw it, too.

"That definitely means Pohl's man, Engle, handled this hit," she said. "Ada wanted us to have those. He didn't."

Right on.

Thankfully, in his eidetic mind he could hear the words of the carabinero as each one was translated for him. Dates flashed in rapid succession: 1949, 1951, 1962. Places. Names. And they still had the other letters, scrapbook, and photographs.

He glanced at his watch: 2:35 P.M.

"The good part is we're dead," she said. "Just not as permanently as these three."

"But the $64,000 question is, do we go to Africa?"

She nodded. "We've come this far."

He agreed.

CHAPTER THIRTY-EIGHT

GERMANY
3:30 P.M.

MARIE DREADED SUMMER. WHEN SHE WAS YOUNGER JUNE ALWAYS meant a welcome relief from the dreary cold, a time of warm days, inviting evenings, and a sun that lingered long into the night.

But all that changed nearly fifty years ago.

On June 14.

The day her parents died.

A Boeing 707, from Athens to Rome, crashed into the Ionian Sea. All eighty-eight people aboard were killed, thanks to a bomb hidden in the cargo hold that sent the plane into the ocean.

All because of the Middle East.

The Palestinian Liberation Organization had been ousted from Jordan, so it relocated its headquarters to southern Lebanon, where it easily enlisted militants from the nearby refugee camps. At the time south Lebanon was known as Fatahland, thanks to the dominance of militant organizations that used the region to stage attacks against Israel. Fatah was the most ruthless of the Palestinian liberation groups and, eventually, was linked to the bomb that killed her parents, though nothing was ever proven.

But eighty-eight people were gone.

Two of them the most important in her life.

Especially her father.

She'd worshiped him.

Before the campaign started she'd informed her staff to keep the afternoon and evening of June 14 free. She offered no explanation, nor was one requested. Each year she made a pilgrimage to the cemetery. It sat beside the ancient Kloster Egern, a great abbey founded by Holy Roman Emperors and still home to a contingent of Benedictine monks. For the past forty-six years she'd come and lit a candle in the small church. After, she would walk to the graves and leave yellow roses as her way of honoring two people, stolen from her far too soon. For years, Kurt had accompanied her. But not so much for the past decade.

She struck a match and maneuvered the flickering flame toward the candle. The wick took a moment to catch. The candle's fragile light barely pierced the semi-darkness that surrounded her. The church itself was a statement in simplicity. Red stone with dignified decoration, a quiet place to come once a year and question heaven on what purpose was served by two such early deaths.

She knelt in one of the pews.

The monks were kind enough to close the building for the afternoon and afford her privacy. Only two security men had accompanied her, both outside guarding the doors. It was not often that she prayed. Though both her parents had been devout Catholics, religion had never been an overpowering force in her life.

But neither was it a stranger.

The rear doors creaked open, and she wondered about the interruption. She lifted her head and turned to see her husband standing at the gate to the main vestibule.

He stepped into the chapel. "With the campaign, I thought maybe this year you might not come."

"The better question is, why are you here?"

"I wonder if these yearly reminders of grief are healthy?" he asked.

"I appreciate your concern, but they were my parents."

"I meant no negativity. It's just been a long time since they left us."

She understood what he meant. At some point the living must let go of the dead. "I may never be able to let them go. They were murdered for nothing."

And she made no attempt to mask the bitter resignation in her voice.

"I agree. I mourn them, too."

At these moments Kurt was most like the man she remembered from so long ago. Dashing. Handsome. Adventurous. They'd married young. Two offspring from wealthy families. A merger of old money and power. Their life had been one of constant privilege, which she'd managed to convert into a successful career of public service. But Kurt had matured into someone she simply no longer knew. Where she developed compassion and a global view, he cultivated prejudice and nationalism. Instead of trying to understand his odd metamorphosis, she withdrew, which allowed them to drift farther in opposite directions. They became like poles on a magnet, bound together but forever separated by forces neither of them could affect. At this moment, though, staring at him through the pale light of the church, the good memories urged her to take his hand and comfort him. But the bad ones screamed that was no longer possible.

So she simply said, "They died because of hate. Thankfully, the Middle East is a different place today than it was fifty years ago. Progress has been made."

"Marie, Jews and Arabs have been killing each other for five thousand years. It's never going to stop. That hate has spilled out to the entire world, and that's not going to stop, either. I wonder, what would your father think of your tenure in office?"

Being this close to her parents' bones always seemed to give her an added measure of strength. It was, perhaps, another reason why she came each year. A rejuvenation. One she needed. Even at her advanced age.

"They would have been proud," she declared.

"You can't really believe that. I doubt your father would have endorsed an open-border policy that allows anyone to come into this country. I seriously doubt he would have bent to the will of the United States or placated Russia. He hated NATO and thought it horrible that Germany was entirely dependent on foreign powers for its external protection. He and I discussed all those subjects on more than one occasion."

"My father lived in a different time, with different views. Above all else, though, he was a German patriot, as am I."

202 | STEVE BERRY

"One who is fighting for her political life. That stunt at Dachau backfired. You insulted half of Bavaria. What were you thinking, labeling people uncaring racists. Is insulting a nation your way of leading? You made it easy for Pohl to pivot away."

"Then perhaps he's finally earned your vote?"

He shook his head. "There it is. If I don't agree with you, I'm immediately your enemy."

Anger flushed through her. "This is not the time, or the place, for a political discussion. We should stop."

"Perhaps your father wants to hear what you have to say."

She resented his pressing, so she said again, "My parents would have approved of whatever I did."

"Can you say that with clear impunity?"

She wasn't going to debate him here, in this sacred place, on this solemn day. So she stepped toward the gate, but he blocked the way.

"Will you flee the Bundestag when your policies are questioned? Is dissent that repugnant to you?"

A wave of uneasiness swept through her. "Move out of my way."

"Do you have any idea what you are doing?"

She was not accustomed to being spoken to in such a manner. Especially from her husband. "Go to hell, Kurt."

"I feel like I'm already there."

His aggressiveness was something new. Which puzzled her. "What is it, Kurt? What troubles you?"

He said nothing.

She wanted to know. "If I repel you so, do you desire separate lives?"

"We already have those."

"Do you want a divorce?"

"I do not."

"Then why berate me? Why belittle me? I've governed this country for sixteen years. Germany is strong and vital. My leadership is respected around the world. I know precisely what I'm doing. So why not simply leave me alone? Live your life, with your ideas, and allow me to live mine."

"I wish things were that simple."

There was a sadness about him that troubled her. Which was also new. Pursuing that, though, seemed a waste of time. She simply did not care anymore. "I want to go to my parents' grave. Will you please move from the gateway and let me pass. Or do I need to call my security detail?"

"On your own husband?"

"If that's necessary."

He remained frozen in place. It would be better for them both if they went their separate ways. But circumstances bound them together.

He retreated out the doorway.

She brushed past him.

He grabbed her right arm and stopped her advance.

Their eyes locked.

"Keep on and you will destroy us all," he spit out.

She wrenched herself free.

And walked out.

CHAPTER
THIRTY-NINE

Cotton focused his attention out the plane's side window at the panorama below. He'd rented the two-seater Cessna in Durban, after a long flight from Santiago on the same military transport that had ferried them from Germany to Chile. A call to Danny Daniels had made the overseas flight instantly available. They'd also explained all that happened, including the damaging financial records that had been sent to Germany by Juan Vergara, which could be fatal for Eisenhuth. Danny had indicated he would deal with those records from his end.

The Free State lay three hundred miles west of Durban, in the interior, across some of South Africa's roughest terrain, the fastest and safest mode of transportation to there by air. According to the navigation chart, they'd passed over the Free State's eastern boundary a few minutes back. Below spread a rugged terrain of sandstone outcroppings, soaring peaks, and deep river valleys. The sun, white, not golden, lit the rocky earth with the brilliance of magnesium. Eland, grey rhebok, and reedbuck grazed on the mountainsides between lightly forested kloofs. Ahead, he saw hills and trees give way to table-like mesas, grasslands, and more sandstone.

A town appeared.

Compact, with no trees, and shadowless thanks to the searing, vertical sun. Heat pulsated from a tarred road and off the red clay rooftops. On the side of one of the sandstone mounds, beyond the town, a pack of black-and-tan goats leaped over rocks, perhaps spooked by the plane overhead. The scene cast the look of a drained aquarium, and if not for the unique wildlife he would have thought he was flying over the American Southwest.

He followed a curve in the Modder River toward Bloemfontein, the Free State's sprawling capital. The sky was clear with only patchy, high clouds. The plane's wings were level, the nose up, the flight smooth. Cassiopeia was reading him more of the letters that Ada had supplied, translating the German text and revealing Gerhard Schüb's innermost thoughts and feelings. She'd culled through the fifty-three envelopes on the transatlantic flight and had been rereading parts of the ones she considered most interesting.

November 19, 1951

. . . this land is not a place for vegetarians. It is instead a feast for carnivores. I have learned that steaks, chops, and cutlets roasted outside on the fire and eaten beneath the stars with your fingers taste far better than anything inside on a plate. I have grown accustomed to being outside, though here it can be so unpredictable. Storms break over the mountains with force. Lightning is more vivid than I have ever seen. The thunder cracks like artillery and shakes the earth with shudders. The rain falls in thick sheets, then can end in an instant. After, thousands of frogs rejoice in croaks that are deafening. Oh, Ada, it is a glorious place.

Two days back we traveled to a farm in the south still within the Orange Free State jurisdiction. Luis never ventures far beyond the borders. We were told by another guest to not speak of the Anglo-Boer War. The Afrikaners who lived on the farm suffered humiliating family losses at the hands of the British and still harbored deep resentment. The war has been over for fifty years so I wondered about the warning. Despite our efforts to avoid the topic, our host willingly spoke of the war. How the British rounded up all the white women and children and forced them into camps. Thirty thousand died of disease and starvation. It was their way of breaking the Boers, forcing the Kommandos into surrendering. Yet it had the opposite effect. The Boers fought harder. It was only when captured Kommandos were enticed to fight against their former compatriots with the promise that their loved ones would be released from the camps that the Boer back was broken. Many accepted the invitation, and it was their treason that eventually cost the Boers victory. Our host had a name for those men. Hensoppers. I asked what it meant and he told me, "Ahands uppers." Then he spit upon the ground to show me what he thought of them.

March 15, 1952

I have driven north to Johannesburg on my trip to retrieve Luis's books from the mail slot and obtain what specialties Rikka desires. She has lately taken an interest in crochet. Her finished products are quite lovely, though there is little need for scarves and sweaters here. She seems to craft them simply to irritate Luis, as he berates her constantly for the waste of time. She seems to delight in his discomfort.

Johannesburg is so different from the Orange State. It is a young city, less than sixty years old, full of tall buildings, buses, trams, neon lights, shops, and limousines. Perhaps the strangest sight is the pyramids at the end of the long streets. They are the gold-mine dumps, ore taken from the ground waiting to be processed. They are to here what the Acropolis is to Athens. They draw the eye at every opportunity and symbolize the untold wealth of this region. Luis has invested heavily in the mines and is reaping enormous profits. His benefactors are most generous and he has even shared a tiny morsel of that wealth with me, enough to allow me to purchase an adjoining tract of land and build a home. It is a sandstone building with a clay roof surrounded by a cherry orchard. It also has a stoep where I sit in the evenings and watch the zebra, topi, and gazelle. Indian craftsmen worked the interior decoration. It is my home and for once I am grateful to Luis.

June 23, 1956

Luis has been in an awful mood for several weeks. He has been reading books about the war. In one Goebbels was quoted as having said, "Bormann is not a man of the people. He has not the qualifications for the real tasks of leadership. He is but a mere administrator, a clerk, nothing more." He fumed that those were bold words from a coward who killed himself and his wife and children, all for the rantings of a crazed man. He speaks horribly of the Führer. He has nothing but contempt for him. He tells me that every political movement needs a revolutionary. Someone to acquire power by whatever means. Yet once it is acquired, that power gradually passes to those more capable of organization and control, those with the ability to administer, and it is they who ultimately rule. "Take pride in being a bureaucrat," he tells me. "For clerks rule the world."

Hitler, he says, lived in a fantasy world. One that was easy to manipulate. Especially once he knew all of Hitler's weaknesses and understood how to nourish the man's self-satisfaction.

"Never let anyone know your weaknesses," he cautions. "It is fatal."

In another volume, a book about him, he took great delight in all the inaccuracies. "Everyone should be allowed to read their own biography," he says. The writer described him as "a personality without needs," calling him "overly diligent, eager to serve, and could easily assume another's idea without distorting it with his own." With that conclusion he was quite amused. National Socialism, he tells me, was merely an instrument for his ambition, not a cause to die for. Which was why he was still alive and Hitler, Goebbels, Göring, Himmler, and all the rest were dead. He tells me nothing of what he desires. I know that he meets regularly with a group of local men, but I am not included in their discussions. Which is fine. I do not care to know anything.

A rusty condor flapped its wings in the sky ahead.

Cotton banked the Cessna and overflew metropolitan Bloemfontein. It was a city of nearly six hundred thousand, the buildings a delightful hodgepodge of British, Mediterranean, Renaissance, and classical architecture. A tree-filled central square served as the nexus for what appeared to be the oldest part of town. Cars, trucks, and buses clogged the highways like ants on a log. The airport sat about five miles east of town and he contacted the tower for landing instructions. The tower responded to his radio contact and told him to circle the field once, then await instructions.

Two commercial flights were ahead of him.

He vectored north and began a long swing around the runway.

An SAA Airbus lumbered in the sky a few miles to the east, landing gear down, making its final approach to a pitted tarmac.

The tower told him to follow it down.

And land next.

CHAPTER FORTY

ENGLE UNFASTENED HIS SEAT BELT AND ROSE. THE SAA FLIGHT from Cape Town to Bloemfontein in the aging Airbus had been rough, nothing like the smooth crossing of the Atlantic by private jet. He'd caught the flight in Buenos Aires after a short hop across Argentina on a LATAM commuter from Puerto Montt. He was grateful to get a seat. The experience with Ada, if nothing else, had hammered home the value of vigilance and the price of expediency.

He stood in the cramped cabin and allowed other passengers to make their way out. He wasn't in a hurry, so there was no need for appearing to be. Theodor Pohl's rebuke from yesterday still rang in his ears. He'd called his employer and reported all of the deaths, along with the bad news of what had happened.

"*You realize there is little chance of restarting this matter in time,*" Pohl had said. "*That insane old woman may cost me the chancellorship.*"

"*We've used her before with no problems. But the last time there had to be a killing, which you approved. She took that personally.*"

The loss of the *schlöss* had not been received well, either.

"*That house has stood for sixty years,*" Pohl had said. "*It was a special place.*"

"*But it presented a risk, once exposed by Ada. I decided to eliminate it.*"

"*How generous you are in destroying expensive assets. It was worth millions. And what of Ada?*"

"I will deal with her when this is over. Right now, I've already booked a flight to Cape Town. I'll be in Africa tomorrow."

"Find out if there is anything on that end that requires attention. There should not be, but that old woman knew far more than she should. And I'm worried. There should be nothing in Africa that poses any problems. Gerhard Schüb is dead. But God knows, I don't want any more firsthand evidence surfacing. No more letters. Or any writings. Understood?"

"Perfectly."

"Make sure Africa is sterile. The good thing is that the financial angle is now in play. At least that went right, and it may be enough to accomplish our goal. Deal with Africa, then get back here. And Josef." Pohl paused for a moment, and he knew what was coming. "Don't disappoint me again."

The last of the passengers filed out toward the front of the plane.

He followed.

He would not disappoint Pohl again. But more important, he would not disappoint himself. He'd planned everything so carefully. It should have worked. It was working. Just one miscalculation with Ada. At least he'd eliminated Cotton Malone and Cassiopeia Vitt. Juan Vergara, too, and his nosy minions. Only Africa remained.

Which should not be a problem.

He mentally clicked off what needed to be done in the hours ahead.

Clear customs. Retrieve his luggage. Rent a car.

Then drive south to Nohana.

And make sure there was nothing to find.

COTTON WAS DRIVING A RANGE ROVER RENTED AT THE AIRPORT. Cassiopeia sat in the passenger seat and navigated them down President Brand Street in central Bloemfontein. The boulevard was clogged with slow-moving traffic. They'd made one stop at a department store and purchased changes of clothing, since they'd traveled from the relative cool of the Chilean mountains to the heat of southern Africa. Light cotton pants and shirts and a supply of thin socks and hiking boots made for a decided difference. Cotton also detoured to an ATM and obtained enough rands to get them through the days ahead.

The information they knew with certainty was sketchy.

Martin Bormann and Eva Braun, alias Luis and Rikka Soreno, along with Gerhard Schüb had apparently lived in and around Bloemfontein from their arrival in 1949 until sometime in 1952, when they moved deeper into what was then called the Orange Free State. Schüb's letters repeatedly mentioned the town of Paarl, yet that location was no longer denoted on any map for the current Free State. So the first thing they needed to determine was Paarl's present designation.

After parking the Range Rover on a side street, he and Cassiopeia searched the array of drab concrete government buildings, but everything was closed for the weekend. They did locate a tourist office that was doing a brisk business with visitors milling in and out. Inside, a smiling African woman unrolled various old 20th-century maps of the local district and found Paarl, lying about fifty miles southeast of Bloemfontein, but by the late 1980s its name had been changed.

"That's Nohana today," the woman said. "A lovely town. Near the mountains, where it is cool. Oh, how I wish I were there."

"Are there farms in the area?" he asked.

"Many. It is a fertile place. Lots of trees and hills. I have many times visited."

She told them more about the area and suggested a route south on highway N6, then up into the mountains on R26. They thanked her for the information and left. Outside, in the stifling heat of midday, Cotton, too, wished he was in the mountains.

"We should have asked her about death records," Cassiopeia said, "and where to find them on Monday. You never know. We could get lucky."

He agreed.

So they stepped back inside and learned from the woman that birth and death records were maintained statewide in a building three blocks over.

"But entries are not the best from that time," she said. "Only recently has the state started keeping quality records. Many once died on the veld, their deaths never recorded anywhere."

And he'd be shocked if there was a death entry for Luis or Rikka Soreno. It would have been unlike Martin Bormann to take such precautions in life, then leave a remnant of himself so easy to find in death. He, along with Braun, probably died on the veld, buried in an unmarked grave.

Outside on the sun-blanched street, he swiped his brow with his hand.

"Only one thing left to do," Cassiopeia said. "Like the woman said, south on highway N6 to Nohana."

He stared up at the stark sky. Heat seemed to settle all around him like a lid to a boiling pot. Not unlike middle Georgia, in summer, from his teenage years.

"I hope the mountains really are cooler."

CHAPTER FORTY-ONE

SchlÖss Herzog, Bavaria
12:30 P.M.

Marie slipped her arms into the jacket and finished dressing. Last night she'd done something she'd never done before.

She locked the door to her room.

For over a decade she and Kurt had lived together, but separately, each content with their distance. But sometime after midnight, amid a clatter of thunder and the patter of a summer rain, she'd slipped out of bed and locked the door. At first she thought it all a dream, her senses drifting from what was perceived to what was real.

Why do such a thing?

In her state of semi-awareness she'd slipped back a quarter century, to a time when she and Kurt once enjoyed each other. When love and passion were an element of their relationship that both of them seemed to cherish. Yet so much had happened since. And particularly yesterday. She could still feel his tight grip on her arm.

They tried for years to have a baby.

Finally, testing revealed that it was a mutual issue. He was low on sperm, she was incapable of producing viable eggs. Science had not progressed to the point of today, and by the time it had, they were too old to be having children.

She'd many times thought that loss began their decline.

Perhaps.

Or maybe they should have never been together from the start.

Kurt was the first man she'd ever given herself to, and he would be the last. She was seventy-four years old, way past what anyone would consider the prime of life. Not old. Not finished. But definitely tired. Yet now, staring at herself in the mirror, she concluded that time had certainly been kind, somehow sparing her the indignity of a bulging midline and skin marred like creases in a crumbled sheet of paper. Physically she'd weathered life well. Emotionally depended on the time of year.

June was perennially her month of renewal.

She should have probed Kurt yesterday and found out why he treated her with such contempt, query him on his anger and bitterness, perhaps even try to understand his resentment of all things foreign.

But as always, she'd kept silent.

When she woke this morning she'd quickly unlocked the door, ashamed of herself for being so mistrustful.

Thankfully, no one had noticed her transgression.

A light rap brought her mind back to the present.

She heard the bedchamber door open, then close.

She stepped from the closet and saw Kurt crossing the parquet floor toward her. He was dressed in a striking three-button Zanetti suit with a white Charvet shirt and a Façonnable silk tie.

"I wanted to apologize for yesterday," he said. "It was inappropriate what I did, speaking that way and grabbing hold of you."

She appreciated the concession but had to say, "Yes, it was. On both counts."

"It won't happen again."

She could see that he was being sincere.

"You look lovely," he said.

She'd dressed conservatively, choosing a navy tailored jacket, pleated skirt, and ivory silk blouse. Back to the campaign trail today.

"Is the rain gone?" she asked, trying to make some sort of small talk.

"I was just outside. Sunny and warm. The skies are clear." He, too, seemed to be searching carefully for the right words.

She found the situation puzzling. They were behaving like two adolescents after their first date. In one sense it was comical, in another tragic.

She approached her jewelry cabinet and found a string of Mikimoto pearls, a present from Kurt one Christmas decades ago.

"Let me help you," he said.

He stepped close and she caught the familiar miasma of his after-shave, pipe tobacco, and cloves from the gum he loved to chew. He moved behind her and reached across her shoulders, gently clipping the pearls around her neck. He then softly kissed the skin below her right ear. Her eyes closed at the gesture. She was glad he could not see her reaction.

Enough.

She stepped away and faced him.

"What is all this?" she asked both him and herself.

"A husband showing his wife affection." There was a caressing quality to his tone that she did not like.

"After yesterday?"

"For which I just apologized."

"Which I thanked you for. But that doesn't change what happened."

He clasped his arms behind him and stood straight like a warrior. A wave of apprehension shuddered through her.

Here we go again.

"Marie, we are both old. Time is slipping away from us. Perhaps, before we die, we should try to forget politics, to forget our differences, and enjoy what little life we have left."

"I've never known you to possess a death wish. You are quite healthy and could live another twenty years."

"No, Marie. I can breathe for another twenty years. Living is an entirely different matter."

"What is it you want, Kurt? Can't you understand why I'm perplexed?"

He lowered his head and stepped close to the window. There was a boyish attitude about him that seemed at odds with his grown-up intentions. He seemed a man in a quandary, and she desperately wanted to understand his dilemma.

"Marie, you are perhaps about to become the longest-serving leader of this nation. Have you truly comprehended what that would entail?"

"I don't want to have a philosophical debate with you."

"Neither do I. But I do want us to face reality. We are at a cross-roads. You and I. The culmination of your entire life may occur in the next few weeks."

"*May? Perhaps? About?* So nice to hear the confidence my husband has in my chances of winning."

The corners of his lips turned down. "I meant no disrespect. Of course I want you to win."

"That's the first time I've heard you say that."

"I am not your enemy."

She wanted to believe him, but years of rebuke and the numbing agony of his prejudices had erected unassailable barriers. Strangely, while her marriage faltered, her political career had prospered. She'd found ambition a powerful barbiturate, dulling everything, including caring. The man standing before her, casting a façade of aristocracy, was in many ways unknown to her. But unlike him, she'd not abandoned her conscience.

And she remained highly suspicious.

Why? She could not say.

"You say you're not my enemy. Who is, Kurt?"

His face registered nothing at the inquiry, and he seemed to be searching for the right words. For an instant she sympathized with Germans who'd once faced her identical dilemma. Families wary of one another. Not knowing who, or when to trust. A collective paranoia, encouraged by authority, that, in the end, paralyzed the nation. What was it Martin Bormann once said?

Fear is necessary.

Kurt's eyes narrowed and hardened like iron. "The answer to your inquiry is quite simple. You have no need for enemies. You play that role for yourself with perfection."

He turned for the door.

And left.

CHAPTER
FORTY-TWO

COTTON WAS SURPRISED BY NOHANA. HE'D HALF EXPECTED A desolate frontier hamlet, full of poverty and dilapidated buildings, but instead the town was a bustling center of nearly ten thousand people, dotted with trendy art shops featuring local Basotho crafts. A number of the stores catered to the nearby cherry and asparagus farmers. There was also a tinsmith, tobacco shop, and two churches, one Dutch, the other Anglican. The Red Mountains offered a spectacular backdrop to the sandstone architecture, gleaming in the sun as if made of metal. The peculiar tone of native music, coming from a band playing in the main square, added a festive atmosphere.

The cool air was filled with an aromatic scent from thousands of cherry trees, a waft Cotton found inviting after the stifling heat and sulfuric stench of Bloemfontein. In one of the craft shops they learned that many of the workers from the nearby Highland Water Scheme lived in and around Nohana. The multi-dam project was just over the border, in neighboring Lesotho. He wanted to ask the clerk about the Sorenos and Gerhard Schüb but thought better. No use spooking the locals. They decided to take a few minutes and rest in a café across the street. The lady at the craft shop told them about some delicious Boer breads, pastries, and tea.

Inside the café, perched at a table beside the front window, they enjoyed a quick lunch. The car sat in sight, just outside the front window, the backpack with all their evidence locked inside.

"We have to handle this carefully," he said.

Cassiopeia agreed. "We don't want a repeat of Minsk."

He grinned. "You don't cut me a drop of slack, do you?"

"About as much as you cut me."

He grinned. "Two strangers looking for people dead for decades will certainly raise warning flags." He was keeping his voice low, though the café's proprietor was busy in the kitchen and only a couple of other tables were occupied, both by couples who seemed interested only in themselves.

What was it about loving someone unconditionally? He and his ex-wife had once cared for each other that way. But something changed. Slow and steady. Which led to cheating and estrangement. On both their parts. What happened when two people shared everything? Was togetherness a precursor to division? That exact doubt was what kept him on edge with Cassiopeia. Lives were tough to intertwine. Personalities never seemed to mesh completely. Instead the ordinary act of living forced people apart. Many times it came from everyday pressures, most times through simple excess. He'd succumbed. His ex-wife, too, though she'd be loath to admit it.

He downed the rest of his tea. "Let's split up and meet back here in an hour. Less suspicious if we hit the shops separately. Hopefully, if we're clever, somebody will remember Luis Soreno or Gerhard Schüb."

CASSIOPEIA HEADED FOR ONE OF THE ART GALLERIES ACROSS THE street, deciding to start there. Inside was an eclectic mixture of sculptures, tribal shields, and framed dye bolts of Zulu wool. The female proprietor was a tall, svelte woman with short-cropped silver hair who was especially proud of the rock paintings on display that depicted animal, human, and supernatural motifs. Replicas, the woman explained, produced by local artisans from the originals nearby.

"Quite extraordinary," Cassiopeia said.

"The originals are thousands of years old. If you have time, do go out and see them."

"I may do that. I'm here to study the local art. Do you have anything by Gerhard Schüb?"

She watched carefully for any reaction. None.

"I am unfamiliar with him. Is he from here?"

"I was told he lived in this area some time ago and was quite talented."

"I have lived here all my life and have never heard that name."

"How about Luis Soreno? I was told his work is quite excellent, too."

The woman shook her head. "Wherever that information came from, it was not related to Nohana. That name is unknown to me, too, and I like to think I am familiar with all our local artists."

She'd thought the ruse might work, but nothing in the woman's words or manner suggested that she was being untruthful. Cassiopeia continued to browse a few more minutes, then thanked her and left. Two more galleries produced the same results. The fourth was an attractive white-sided building with a covered stoep supported by decorative ironwork and roofed, like the rest of the building, with corrugated tin. Inside was an elaborate photographic display of the Bantu, Zulu, and Swazi tribes. The black-and-white pictures were extraordinary, and Cassiopeia found herself captivated by the images.

"Most were taken with a box camera," the male attendant said. "It is how the Boers and the original 1820 settlers saw the natives in the 19th century, before any European influence."

She'd already noticed a raw edge to the images, more African than worldly.

"It is impossible today to take a photograph of a native without there being some European reminder, either in clothes, appearance, or heritage," the man noted.

She continued to study the photos. The man stayed at her heels, perhaps sensing a sale as signs indicated that copies of the pictures were available.

"Once a native dons a piece of European cloth, it seems to stay. Customs fall by the way quickly," he said.

She was about to ask about Schüb and Soreno, using the same ruse as before, when she glanced out the front window to the busy street. A light-colored coupe slipped into a parking spot, and the driver's door opened. The man who emerged was tall, mid-forties, and tanned. His hair and Vandyke beard were a gleaming black, flecked with bits of silver-gray. He wore a lightweight khaki shirt with blue cotton trousers.

She knew the face instantly.

From the image Ada had shown them.

Josef Engle.

CHAPTER FORTY-THREE

Engle took a moment and studied the town he knew was formerly labeled Paarl, now called Nohana. Along with the obligatory churches, there was a lawyer's office, a schoolhouse, a post office, cafés, several feed and supply stores, and too many art galleries to count. It seemed a place of age, charm, and character with an air of success reflected in clean streets, manicured shrubs, and trimmed trees. Apparently prosperity had taken root in this corner of South Africa.

He'd rented a car at the Bloemfontein airport and driven directly south. From Pohl he'd heard the stories of all that occurred here after the war, but this was his first visit to the African continent. He needed to determine if there were any lingering concerns, resolve them, and return to Germany. Earlier on the phone, Pohl was adamant that he was needed back as some alternative plan would have to be activated. Encouraging was the fact that Pohl seemed to be rising in the polls thanks to Eisenhuth's blunders, but his employer was not prepared to bet the entire outcome of the election on the other side's mistakes.

"That's the quickest way to lose," Pohl had said. *"We need to make this happen."*

And he agreed.

A glance at his watch showed it was nearly 3:00 P.M. He'd not eaten since the transatlantic flight hours ago. So he decided to take a few moments and visit the café across the street.

No hurry.

This trip was his alone.

CASSIOPEIA APPROACHED THE FRONT WINDOW, KEEPING HERSELF where she could see Engle but he could not see her. The gallery's proprietor was still staring at one of the pictures, prattling about its authenticity, but she heard nothing he was saying. She watched Engle as he surveyed the town and studied a clear azure sky. He carried himself in a casual manner, unconcerned about being seen. Which was understandable. He believed both she and Cotton to be dead in the *schlöss,* six thousand kilometers to the west.

So why was he here?

She suddenly became aware of the gallery owner.

"Is there something out there?" the man was asking.

She turned and faced him with a smile. "I was simply admiring the town. A lovely locale."

He seemed to like the compliment. "We are quite proud of our community. It has developed into a thriving place."

As she turned back to the window and the street beyond she saw Engle stroll toward the café she and Cotton visited earlier.

What had Cotton said?

"We'll split up and meet back here in an hour."

She couldn't allow Engle to see either of them. The element of surprise was finally on their side. She faced the gallery owner again. "I'll come back in a little while. After I look around a bit more. You've been most helpful."

She stepped to the door and exited just as Engle entered the café across the street. She hustled two doors down onto the covered stoep of what appeared to be a closed government office. She retreated into the front door alcove and made sure she could see both the café and the street in both directions.

She could not risk openly searching for Cotton, so she found her cell phone to call him.

No service.

So she decided to stay put and hope she saw him before Engle did.

COTTON WALKED THE STREETS AND SENSED AN UNDERLYING German texture to Nohana. In one of the cafés, two blocks from the place he and Cassiopeia had visited, he heard a patron hail the waiter with *Herr Ober.* He noticed on the posted menus at several eateries German beers and Teutonic cuisine. In the shop windows were Hohner harmonicas, cuckoo clocks, and Zeiss optical supplies. There was what appeared to be a German club, which seemed expensive, along with a theater and, surprisingly, a small orchestra house. He passed two jewelry stores that were stocked with a variety of semi-precious stones, garnet being the most notable, a stone quite prominent in southern Germany.

Just beyond a small laundry he came to a curious establishment with the catchy name of The Boer's House. He turned a brass knob and entered what appeared to be a museum. There were lots of bandoliers, stuffed wildlife, stones, and fossils, along with pictures, books, cuttings, and relics that told the local story. Thinking there might be someone inside who could be helpful, he casually began studying the various exhibits, his mind absorbing the details.

From the placards he learned that the label *Afrikaner* was tricky. It in no way implied African, but instead was any white person of non-British descent who spoke a twisted form of Dutch known as Afrikaans. Most Afrikaners were Dutch, Flemish, French Huguenot, or, most interesting, German. Boers were those of Dutch extraction, mainly farmers, who initially forged the Free State. Boers hated the British, the British hated the Boers, and they both hated natives, which was how Africans seemed to have been labeled.

The displays showed some of the bawdy, bursting tent towns, then villages leaping to life, then the coming of the white magnates. The slant was distinctly Boer, and the concentration camps from the Anglo-Boer War were vividly depicted. Just as Gerhard Schüb had said in his letters to Ada, thousands of women and children died in the British camps between 1899 and 1902. Interestingly, although photos showed that Africans likewise were interned, little to no mention was made of their suffering.

But African culture was not ignored in the exhibits.

Perhaps, he thought, it was a concession to the black majority government that now ruled both South Africa and the Free State. The various grainy images depicted the Africans as a handsome people with aquiline noses, low brows, and stern expressions. Many of the women wore Victorian dresses that swept the ground, and the men enjoyed an obvious regality. He started to notice more of the captions beneath the photographs and how they captured, though certainly not intentionally, a similar attitude for both natives and Boers.

Both had sought freedom and peace.

And been denied.

One prayer that a local chief was quoted as saying seemed to fit each group perfectly.

O Lord, help us who roam about. Help us who have been placed in Africa and have no dwelling place of our own. Give us back a dwelling place. O God, all power is yours in heaven and earth.

"May I help you?"

He turned. A white man, about fifty, with a knotted face like solidified glue stood before him. His English sounded like Cockney and German combined.

"Just trying to absorb some of the local flavor." He tried to make light, but his host seemed intent on solemnity.

"You will not find a good taste here."

"Your exhibits are informative."

"They are propaganda. Forced upon us."

A strange observation from a white man in Africa.

"Our new government wants everything non-biased. We must present a fair view of our heritage." Sarcasm laced his declaration.

"I take it you are not pleased with majority rule."

"I am no liberal."

And he believed that observation. He decided a direct question might be the best approach. "Do you know of a man named Gerhard Schüb?"

The curator shook his bulbous head. "Never heard of him."

"How about Luis Soreno?"

The man shook his head. "Sorry. No."

He could sense the conversation was going nowhere, so he said, "Think I'll look around a bit more. If you don't mind."

His host swept his arms out into the air. "Enjoy it all." Then the portly man retreated across the room.

He turned his attention back to the displays and came to a series that dealt with gold. It wasn't until after the war, in 1947, that vast amounts of ore were mined, then exported, earning millions annually. Owned exclusively by whites, but worked totally by blacks, the gold mines built the Orange Free State into a fifty-thousand-square-mile bastion of ultra-apartheid. Just as in the gold rush days of the American West, whole towns owed their existence to the proximity of a nearby mine, and he noticed that Nohana/Paarl was not among the benefited communities. Most lay to the west and north, on the other side of the Free State.

He was gazing at a series of photographs concerning the diamond mines when a face in one of the images caught his attention. Three men stood in a parlor upon a wood floor dotted with lion and zebra skins. They wore safari shirts, light-colored trousers, and wide hats. Each was tall, lean, and proud. There was a gaiety in their expressions, as if the issues that worried most people—famine, poverty, oppression—meant nothing to them. It was the face of the middle man that brought instant recognition.

Albert Herzog.

Marie Eisenhuth's father.

He stared close to be sure.

The eyes, nose, and mouth were the same from the photos he'd seen at the chancellor's *schlöss* and at Ada's house.

Apparently all had been taken in relatively the same time frame.

Postwar.

Another connection.

The case against Marie Eisenhuth was not looking good.

He wanted to ask the proprietor about the picture but decided that even if the man knew something he was unlikely to obtain any useful information, so he opted to find Cassiopeia.

And decide then what next to do.

CHAPTER
FORTY-FOUR

CASSIOPEIA HUGGED THE ALCOVE'S WOODEN WALL AND TRIED TO
appear like she was seeking a respite from the midday sun, but her attention continued to focus on the café across the street. Josef Engle had
been inside nearly fifteen minutes. A couple of patrons had come and
gone, but Engle had yet to be seen.

Her mind raced with the possibilities.

Engle was here for a reason, and surely it concerned Gerhard Schüb.
What else would have brought him to Nohana? It was the only explanation that made sense. Engle certainly possessed more information
than she and Cotton had uncovered. What was it he knew that they
didn't? In his letters Schüb had sounded like a reluctant participant in
Bormann's grand scheme, but with Nazis, whether willing or drafted, it
seemed safe never to assume anything.

No matter.

Josef Engle was a current reality. Here. In Nohana.

Across the street.

She reached behind her jacket and felt for the gun. The pistol was
nestled against her hip in a reassuring embrace. Both she and Cotton
had decided to stay armed.

Good choice.

Particularly now with a man who may have killed Eisenhuth's investigator, a Chilean deputy minister, and two carabineros nearby.

She glanced at her watch: 3:35 P.M.

Their car remained parked in front of the café. Her gaze raked the street searching for Cotton. There were a number of people milling about. He'd said an hour, and the time for them to meet was rapidly approaching. She could not allow Engle to see either of them.

She had to intercept Cotton.

But he was nowhere to be seen.

She noticed a banner pulled across one of the storefronts that advertised, in English, a race that was to occur in a few days' time to the top of a nearby mountain. A cherry festival was likewise announced from another placard. Beyond the low-slung buildings spread a plain where green kopjes broke in the distance. She spied farms among the trees with shiny, revolving waterwheels. Change the fauna and the topography and the locale wasn't a lot different from southern Germany or the Chilean lake district. Both were cool, green spots among mountains where Aryans seemed to congregate.

She risked another look.

The café was still quiet.

She could not cross the street—Engle's view out the restaurant's main window would be unobstructed. Though they'd never met he surely knew their faces, as they did his.

He might be their best lead to finding whatever there was to find. They needed to be the pursuer, not the pursued.

Another glance at her watch.

Cotton appeared from around one of the street corners.

Heading straight for the café.

ENGLE ENJOYED HIS LUNCH OF A HOLLOWED-OUT HALF LOAF OF white bread filled with curried chicken, beans, and rice. A bit spicy, but tasty and definitely filling. He washed everything down with a thin lager that was quite bland, but ice cold and refreshing. Food was a pleasure he truly enjoyed. Luckily, his employer was generous and allowed him to spend what was necessary to accomplish his tasks in comfort. He thought he could easily have a weight problem if he did not adhere religiously to an exercise regimen. His hectic lifestyle also aided his metabolism. The past few months had been particularly intense. Pohl had warned him that there would be much to do. Two years of planning had gone into the decision to run for chancellor. Now the election was less than sixty days away. Unfortunately, little had developed as he and Pohl envisioned, and to restart the endeavor would require every one of those sixty days. Luckily, the financial revelations could, in and of themselves, work. But in their two conversations since yesterday, Pohl had seemed concerned.

"Just make sure there is nothing in Africa to cause us problems," was his simple instruction. *"That old woman tried to send Malone and Vitt there for a reason."*

He assumed they would also now resort to the same sort of tactics used in the past. Political blackmail, bribery, intimidation, and the hint of violence—enough to keep the opposition off guard, but not enough to lose control. Pohl's steady political rise had been aided by a careful mixture of all those elements, and the result was a cadre of clerks, ministers, reporters, and politicians who owed him, in one way or another. Maybe those debts would be enough, by themselves, to catapult Pohl into the chancellorship?

He could only hope, since his efforts had borne no fruit.

He stood from the table and tossed down a few rands, then headed for the door.

No need to worry about any of that at the moment.

Time to go to work.

CHAPTER
FORTY-FIVE

POHL ROSE FROM THE ROCOCO CHAIR, HIS GAZE LOCKED ON THE Belgian tapestry that draped the far wall. He liked the scene. It depicted the start of an autumn hunting expedition complete with eager dogs, dense forest, and noblemen full of anticipation. It was a gift from one of his Rhineland associates, a housewarming present from someone who could afford the price 17th-century tapestries commanded. He liked men of money. They exuded a confidence peculiar to those accustomed to having their way.

In a few hours his campaign was going high tech with an elaborate internet event. An online town hall where he would interact with the participants, chatting and responding to their questions.

He liked the idea.

No need to travel from town to town.

Far better to talk to the whole nation at one time.

He'd asked earlier not to be disturbed, at least for another hour, and knew that his chief steward, the man who ran Löwenberg, would make sure he was afforded privacy. He stepped from the chair toward a leather-topped table that dominated one corner of the oblong room and grabbed an apple from a pewter bowl. His groves produced them by the bushel every year.

A colossal tile stove bearing the date of 1651 reached nearly to a ceiling held aloft by crossbeams fashioned by hand. His bed was enormous, supported by stout mahogany legs. Angels, homely with bulging cheeks and wings sprouting from their ears, adorned the four posts. He'd liked their attentiveness from the first time he spotted them in a Frankfurt antiques store.

He crossed the bedchamber and entered an alcove that once, six hundred years ago, had served as a bathroom. There'd been a stone toilet carved into the outer wall with an opening that allowed whatever was deposited to free fall to a collection container three stories below. Primitive surely, but he assumed the methodology was infinitely better than squatting over a hole dug in the earth. The toilet was gone, as was the hole in the curtain wall. A decorative bench now jutted below a mullioned window that offered a stunning view of the forested valley beyond.

One other anachronism, though, remained from ancient times.

The noblemen who originally built the castle in the 15th century were nearly fanatical in their fear of being trapped by an invader. So every nook and cranny possessed at least two ways in and out. The bedchamber behind him was no exception. In fact, it was afforded the utmost in security for the time.

A secret escape.

He approached one of the inner stone walls and applied the right amount of pressure to one of the mortar joints. A section revolved, revealing a spiral staircase that wound down in a steep counterclockwise direction.

He flicked a switch affixed inside, and a series of low-voltage lamps illuminated the path below.

He entered and shoved the panel closed.

The stairs were narrow, the descent nearly vertical. He'd discovered the stairway prior to his purchase of the estate and its presence, along with spacious rooms carved out of the ground below, had sealed the deal. Back then there had been one other way into the subterranean chamber at ground level, but he'd recently closed that path. Now only the staircase provided an entrance.

At the bottom he flicked another switch, and a series of decorative pewter fixtures dissolved the darkness. The air was climate controlled, and an industrial humidifier made sure no moisture left a lasting impression. The floor was polished slate framed by thin lines of black grout.

He fished a knife from his pocket and started to carve the apple. The blade itself was special. A gift from his father. He'd carried it since childhood, delighting in periodically sharpening the edge, oiling its surface, tending to it like a jeweler with his tools. He walked in the silence and slipped a moist chunk of apple into his mouth.

This was where he came when he needed to think.

A lot was about to happen.

He'd planned for so long.

It was imperative he remembered all of his lessons, especially concerning the Third Reich.

There'd been precision in planning there, too, which might have borne fruit save for reckless greed and inexplicable stupidity. Why was it, he'd often wondered, that no fanatic governed long? The answer was easy. Either unacknowledged excesses or inherent weaknesses hampered good judgment. Both flaws were consistently fatal, and no despot ever recognized their deficiencies. The democratic process, for all its chaos, forced leaders to face their own mistakes. There was public debate. Attention. Spectacle.

The battle itself kept a person sharp.

No dictator had ever survived such scrutiny.

The nature of absolute power demanded absolute loyalty, and unfortunately an ability for self-examination was simply not inherent in either autocracy or the personality of someone able to achieve absolute power. The thin air at the top of the mountain seemed to always cloud the brain.

He sliced another apple wedge and smiled.

The trick was not to fall victim.

He imagined what it must have been like to stand on the balcony of the Berghof, the Alps in the distance, Hitler musing about his latest idea, uniformed officers milling about enjoying Rhineland wine and French champagne, hanging on his every word. What a romantic notion. But after all, that was the whole idea. The Nazis had been good at coating the rotten with a supposedly sweet veneer. And Hitler was the master. Failed putsch leader in 1923. Jailed 1924. Reich chancellor 1933. Total power acquired 1934.

An unparalleled political rise. Textbook.

One to be envied.

From 1933 to 1941 practically everything Hitler undertook he achieved. In 1935 he thumbed his nose at the Treaty of Versailles by conscripting a military. In 1936 the remilitarization of the Rhineland breached the Treaty of Locarno. In 1938 Austria was incorporated without a single bullet fired and the Sudeten territories acquired with France and England's permission. In 1939 Bohemia, Moravia, and Memel were occupied, and Poland defeated. In 1940 Denmark, Norway, Holland, Belgium, Luxembourg, and France were conquered with little effort. In 1941 Greece and Yugoslavia were overrun.

By 1942 a total domination of Europe.

Remarkable for a man with strange ideas, mainly borrowed from others, who did nothing more than proclaim the end of despair.

He tossed the apple core into a nearby metal trash bin.

If only Hitler had stopped.

He folded the blade and pocketed the knife.

Twelve years of victories. Followed by four years of utter failure. What changed? Certainly not Hitler. He remained single-minded until the moment he pulled the trigger in the bunker. No. What changed was the strength of his opponents. Sadly, the man was only able to defeat that which was already wavering, nearly dead. His gift, though, the true sense of Adolf Hitler, was his uncanny ability to spot those weaknesses.

And that was what needed to be learned from the Nazis.

The weakness of others would be his ally.

He thought about the new unified Germany. Three hundred and fifty-seven thousand square kilometers, half farmland, a third forest. Eighty-three million people. Eighty-one percent German, the rest a mixture. Ninety-nine percent literate. A gross national product in the trillions of euros. Less than 2 percent inflation, and just over 5 percent unemployment.

So what was the weakness to be exploited?

That 19 percent of foreigners.

A mixture of other Europeans, Asians, Africans, Turks, and Arabs.

A basic underlying hatred for foreigners was already there, and only fuel was needed to spark the fire. Hitler was smart to stimulate a hatred of Jews. He stoked a hatred that stretched back to Martin Luther and the Reformation. But in the 21st century, in order to reap the benefits from a collective hate, he would have to take a new approach.

The enemy carefully chosen.

Turks were part of that 19 percent and, by and large, were Muslims. Not only did a few of those inherently hate Jews, their presence further diluted the political strength of the scant few Jews who remained within Germany.

No German today need hate a Jew.

Some of the Turks seemed more than willing to take up the cause.

So let them.

Germany no longer possessed the military might to enforce an ideology. But what he knew to be true—what he must never forget—was that the German psyche had evolved little since the last war. For appearances' sake his new German state must suppress anti-Semitism, for the world would tolerate nothing less. Yet the same world community never seemed to mind when the Arab was oppressed.

So the course was clear.

Let the Turks hate the Jews and let the Germans hate the Turks. If those two extremes were played off each other skillfully, power could be both obtained and maintained. But to achieve success he needed to learn from one more of Hitler's mistakes. While dominating Germany, playing off the populace's fears, pitting one group against the other, Hitler managed to drain the nation of one of its most precious resources.

Knowledge.

One-third of all the world's Nobel laureates prior to World War I came from Germany. But most fled after 1933 to America and Britain. Physicists, chemists, biologists, mathematicians, biochemists, engineers. Twenty-seven eventual Nobel Prize winners. The names became a roll call of the world's best. Fermi, Born, Bloch, Haber, Einstein, Stern, Pauli, Teller. America developed the bomb, went to the moon, and became a superpower thanks, in part, to German minds.

That mistake could not be repeated.

The world would not flourish while Germany languished.

He smiled to himself.

No.

The world, in fact, had made its own share of mistakes.

German mass murderers implemented the Holocaust with machine precision. Yet what happened? Within ten years of the war ending German sovereignty was restored and the country was rebuilt with Allied money. Many of those who aided and abetted the atrocities were enlisted to fight Stalin. The German nation should have been extinguished, erased from the map, its territory absorbed by its neighbors with no chance of any resurrection. But instead the threat of communism took precedence over common sense, and Germany was allowed to survive.

How utterly foolish.

He knew what had to be done.

Start the fire. Fan the flame. Watch the blaze. But never allow it to burn out of control.

And keep in mind what Goebbels said.

Make the lie big, make it simple, keep saying it, and eventually they will believe.

He stared ahead.

The subterranean labyrinth ended at a solitary wooden door. He always completed his visit here.

Beyond was true inspiration.

He stepped forward, grasped the iron handle—

And prepared himself.

CHAPTER FORTY-SIX

FREE STATE, SOUTH AFRICA
3:50 P.M.

COTTON HOPED CASSIOPEIA WAS WAITING FOR HIM AT THE CAFÉ. He was encouraged by the image of Albert Herzog he'd seen in the museum. At least they were in the right place and on the right track.

He kept walking and stared up into a flawless cerulean sky. The sun was starting its westward retreat, illuminating the nearby mountains in brilliant hues of crimson and taupe. He turned a corner and confronted a cloud of dust, oil, and fumes from three trucks that lumbered past, chasing the sun, heading out of town for the main highway.

He caught sight of the Range Rover still parked beyond the café. The sidewalks were filled with a variety of Africans, Indians, and whites, most of the men in lightweight tropical clothes, some with sun helmets, the women in colorful dresses below the knees. The chatter was open and friendly, some English, some Afrikaans. He understood no Afrikaans. It was a difficult dialect, resembling Dutch in the way that slang resembled English, a synthetic substitute borrowing from Flemish, French, and German.

He focused again on the street and suddenly spotted Cassiopeia. She appeared from an alcove under a covered stoep, across the street, and waved him off.

"Go back. Around the corner and wait," she called out.

It took an instant for him to digest her command, and before he could say or do anything she disappeared into the shadows. He turned and retreated around the corner, following her instruction, trying not to attract attention. He allowed a couple of women with shopping bags to pass, then eased back to the corner and peered around the edge of a low-slung stone building.

Still no Cassiopeia.

Strange.

Then he saw a man leave the café and step toward a Ford compact. Affixed to the front windshield was the same orange sticker that appeared on the Range Rover, designating the vehicle a rental. The beige exterior was powdered with road dust. The man climbed inside, then U-turned the car so he was headed west, back toward the main highway.

He knew the face.

Josef Engle.

Cassiopeia raced across the street to the Range Rover.

He followed her.

She slipped behind the wheel and was cranking the engine as he flung open the other door and jumped in. She gunned the accelerator and U-turned the utility vehicle.

"This just keeps getting better and better," he said.

ENGLE FOLLOWED THE DIRECTIONS THEODOR POHL PROVIDED yesterday on the telephone. He motored west for six kilometers, then turned north, the highway in surprisingly excellent condition, each side lined with gum trees, wattle, and clusters of dense jacaranda.

The elevation steadily rose as he headed deeper into the mountains, nearer the border with independent Lesotho. He imagined what life must have been like here after the war, when South Africa was a fragile union held together by little more than hate. He'd read about some of the history. Where the Nazis and communists failed, the South African Nationalists succeeded, creating for nearly a century a split of the country into one for blacks, the other for whites.

Such a shame that endeavor had not worked.

He wondered, gazing out the car windows at the rich farms, what the current black majority government would do with all of this. He'd listened to Pohl talk of such matters and knew how his employer felt about white supremacy. How did he feel?

Hard to say.

But being here, feeling what was surely a salient pull white men had felt for centuries about this land, he could see that it was something worth fighting for.

COTTON KEPT HIS EYES AHEAD, OUT THE WINDSHIELD.

"I spotted him going into the café. He was casual and open," she said.

He told her about the The Boer's House and the photo of Albert Herzog. "Add one more in the negative column for Marie Eisenhuth."

"So why is Engle here? To find Gerhard Schüb? For what? We don't even know if he's still alive."

"Ada was quite obtuse on that." He pointed. "Ease a little toward the shoulder so I can look around ahead."

They were following a large truck on the main highway. She allowed the Range Rover to drift right, and he spied Engle's car still moving at a leisurely pace two cars forward.

She angled back into the middle of the lane.

"We're headed north," he said. "Into the mountains."

In the distance he studied the terrain, which seemed a mixture of Wales and Switzerland. Patches of Europe sprouted everywhere. Waterwheels, homesteads, attractive farm buildings, even a rose garden adjacent to one house.

"I think he's here to mop up," she said. "If Schüb is alive, he may want him eliminated. If dead, then he's after any lingering reminders of his life. Ada wasn't supposed to tell us about Africa. So he's here to make sure all is quiet on this front."

Which made sense.

They crossed a long girder bridge that cast a reticulated shadow across muddy water hundreds of feet below. The trees on either side of the highway thickened to a dense forest that hugged the slopes of rapidly rising ridges. Cotton found a South African road map in the glove compartment and determined that the highway led northeast, over the border, into Lesotho, toward the Highland Water Scheme, which explained what a heavy transport was doing on the road ahead of them.

Cassiopeia again eased the Rover toward the center. "Engle seems to know where he's going."

"I'm glad one of us does. We're nearing Lesotho."

He'd been there before. A mountain kingdom. Fiercely independent and brutal. Even the old South African Nationalists left them alone. On assignment a few years back he'd gotten into a nasty scrap with their national police, whom he found both cruel and corruptible. Two of their officers were killed, and it had taken State Department intervention to calm the matter.

"It's not a place I want to visit," he muttered.

"We may not have a choice."

She was right.

They would have to go wherever Engle led.

CHAPTER
FORTY-SEVEN

ENGLE SLOWED THE CAR AND SWEPT AROUND A SHARP TURN AT A controlled pace. The road was a twisting path up a steep incline, one side lined with stones, the other with trees and loose rock. The transmission whined and rattled like metal to a grinder stone. He was looking for the dirt lane that, by Pohl's directions, should appear at any time.

His instructions were clear.

Ascertain the situation, assess the risk, and report.

He'd entered the country unarmed, but there should be no need for guns. All of the African participants were dead. That included Gerhard Schüb, who supposedly died two years ago. Which was why they'd used Schüb's name in the contacts with Eisenhuth. Yet Ada had directed Malone and Vitt here. Why? Pohl knew that Ada and Schüb were siblings. So what did she know that they didn't? If anything? It could all be a ploy. Simply a way for Pohl to waste time chasing ghosts. Perhaps even to make a mistake. The situation required investigation, but the history into which he was delving involved people possessed of a volatile combination of fanaticism and cleverness. As with positive and negative charges, the resulting merger created nothing but sparks.

So he told himself to stay alert.

Be ready for anything.

He'd already decided that once he made an initial assessment, he'd find a comfortable inn. The proprietor at the café mentioned a lovely lodge in a nearby valley with thatched rondavels set amid a peach orchard, the food supposedly excellent. A night of relaxation would be welcome. Usually his trips were laced with apprehension and fraught with anxiety.

Perfectionism was indeed a stern master.

Once he returned to Germany the weeks ahead were going to be especially hectic. Pohl would have him scurrying from one person to another determining their loyalties. He was actually quite good at persuasion, even better at ensuring that he meant what he said.

Ahead he spotted a graveled road framed on either side by a stone wall that flared at each end, forming a distinctive entrance, one that matched the description Pohl provided.

He slowed.

COTTON MOTIONED. "HE'S TURNING."

Cassiopeia's foot came off the accelerator.

"No. Go past. Keep going."

She gained speed and continued to follow the truck ahead of them. He watched as Engle's vehicle veered left. He peered carefully past Cassiopeia, out the driver's-side window, as they passed the turnoff. The rear of Engle's car was obscured by a cloud of dust that whipped up in his wake.

Cassiopeia drove another half mile down the road, then U-turned on the highway. They reapproached the lane and stopped. Affixed to the elegant stonework that outlined the entrance was a carved wooden sign that read ALLESVERLOREN.

"What does it mean?" she asked.

"I assume it's the estate's name." He found his phone and typed in the word, asking Google for help. "Everything lost." He stared at her. "What an odd name for a house."

"Perhaps someone is trying to send a message?"

"We need to know who lives here."

She was right. He glanced at his watch. Nearly 5:00 P.M. He motioned ahead. "Pull up into those trees."

She drove the car a quarter mile farther up the road then eased to the opposite shoulder.

"You stay here and keep an eye on that entrance."

"Where are you going?"

"Back to town to play a hunch and get some information. I'll return within the hour."

She opened the door and stepped out. "Okay. Give it a try, Sherlock."

He slid over. "Let's hope that's the only entrance to wherever Engle's going."

"And if he leaves before you get back?"

"Then we're screwed."

He gripped the wheel and gunned the accelerator, heading back toward Nohana.

He thought again about the name.

Allesverloren.

Everything lost.

Fascinating.

ENGLE DROVE TO THE END OF A WILLOW-LINED LANE. BEFORE HIM a one-story house sprawled out under a bower of bushy trees. The ground beyond fell sharply toward a rock-strewn stream, and he watched a squadron of swallows dip under a wooden bridge that crossed the swift-moving water. To the west spread a plain that never varied, a low kopje, kilometers of grass, the Free State stretching toward a horizon dotted with blue shadowed ridges that, in the clear air, appeared to be within walking distance but were surely many kilometers away. Cherry trees filled an orchard toward the south. In a fenced meadow, ostriches meandered in an awkward gait.

He parked and stepped out into cool air.

He'd definitely risen in elevation, his breath thin, a challenge to savor. He was impressed with both the house and the view.

Quite an estate.

The obligatory covered stoep, which seemed a part of every Free State house, was especially spacious and dotted with rocking chairs, some facing west toward the spectacular view, others overlooking the fields and mountains.

Through the front door a soggily built man with a pale face and heavy hands stormed across the stoep's wooden planks. He was nearly bald and bespectacled, his features projecting a note of taut command. Engle instantly assessed a hot mind and a cold heart, a smile coming perhaps as often as an oyster cracks its shell.

"*Goeinaand,*" the man said.

"I'm sorry. I do not speak Afrikaans," he replied in German, testing the waters a bit.

"*Guten abend,* then."

"You are fluent in my native tongue?" He stayed with German.

The man shrugged and gestured with his hands. "It's a language I took time to learn."

He stopped at the base of wooden steps, coated, like the rockers, with a thick layer of gray paint. A rottweiler slept against the stoep's far railing and commanded part of his attention. His host seemed to notice his interest.

"Not to worry. She's quite docile." The man paused. "Most of the time."

He decided to get to the point. "Are you related to Gerhard Schüb?"

The man gave him a curious look of appraisal. "Now, that is an odd way to introduce oneself."

"My name is Josef Engle. I have come on behalf of Theodor Pohl."

Crickets trilled in the distance as a moment of silence gestated into something that suggested suspicion. Concern laced the other man's rotund face. "That is a name I have not heard in a while."

"I need to speak with you. In private."

The big man chuckled and gestured with his thick hands. "Then come inside, Herr Engle. We will talk and maybe you might learn what I know. Then again, maybe not."

CHAPTER FORTY-EIGHT

COTTON DROVE STRAIGHT TO THE BOER'S HOUSE. HE WAS GOING to see if the tight-lipped proprietor could offer any information about the owner of Allesverloren. He hoped the museum stayed open past 5:00 and was pleased to see that it did not close until 6:00.

"Remember me?" he asked when he entered.

No one else was inside.

"My inquisitive visitor from earlier. Did you find Gerhard Schüb?"

Interesting he recalled that specific inquiry.

Maybe his hunch was right.

"Let's cut through the crap, okay?" He explained who he was, why he was there, then produced seven hundred rand, part of what he'd received from the ATM. "This is surely more than you earned here today. Certainly more than enough for you to help me out."

"Do all Americans think everyone is for sale?"

"Not all, just me. Usually I'd be more subtle, but I'm in a hurry and I sense you're a man who knows things."

He dropped the crisp bills on the counter. The man raked them toward him with pudgy fingers laced with grime. "What is it you desire?"

"Who lives at Allesverloren?"

"My, my, you have been busy. That's fifteen kilometers out of town."

"I know the geography. Answer the question."

"That estate is titled to Jan Bruin. A Boer patriot. His family has owned the land for a long while."

"Since the last world war?"

"After that time."

"Strange name for a place. Everything lost."

"I did not realize you were fluent in Afrikaans. So few bother with our language. Especially Americans."

"Call it a hobby. And it's more German than Afrikaans. Now answer my question. What's in the name?"

"That I cannot answer. I assume the meaning is something special to the family. Most of the large farms are named, and all are quite personal."

"Tell me about Jan Bruin."

"His mother was of old voortrekker stock. Dutch. A kind, gentle woman who played a lovely violin. His father was German."

That information grabbed his attention. "What was his name?"

"Thomas."

"Thomas Bruin does not sound like a German name."

"Now, that is rather stereotypical, don't you think? All Germans don't have to be called Hans and Dieter."

He brushed away the criticism with a question. "What do you know of the father?"

"Why is this so important?"

He was becoming impatient. "Was he an immigrant?"

"Now I see. Perhaps from the former Reich? That's a tired premise, wouldn't you say?"

"Humor me."

"I truly know little of the father. He died two years ago. The mother passed a few years before that. The son is another matter. He is a patron of this museum, and makes a generous contribution each year in his mother's name. A gentleman for whom I have only praise."

"Then tell me more about the son."

The man gave a noise that ranked somewhere between a cough and a laugh. He appeared annoyed. But the message was clear.

Hand over more rands.

He did.

"Jan was born here, in the Free State, educated in England. He started in the diamond business as an office boy at Dunkelsbuhler and Company. It is a large London merchant house. He returned here to run the fields for the company and eventually bought a couple of mines himself. He was our mayor for a time, and now represents the Free State in the national assembly."

"How old is he?"

"My age. Mid-forties." The man motioned across the room. "Come, let me show you something."

He followed him to one of the photographic displays, where his informant pointed to a photograph of a brilliant blue-white stone. "Forty-six carats. There are only three blue diamonds that size in the world. It was found in one of Bruin's mines. Incredible, isn't it?"

He studied the picture, a full shot of the sparkling stone under what was surely brilliant light. The steel-like blueness seemed faintly sinister, even menacing. Perhaps like its owner. He turned to the proprietor. "I asked you before. Ever heard the names Gerhard Schüb or Luis Soreno?"

"I was not being coy. Neither is familiar."

"They supposedly lived in this area in the 1950s and '60s."

"Before my time. But even so, I have lived here all my life and neither name is one I recognize."

He sensed that he'd gained all the information he could. He needed to get back to Cassiopeia. "I appreciate your time."

He meant it, though he'd paid for the privilege.

"Come back, when you will. I enjoy doing business with you."

Outside, he stepped toward the Range Rover, but a little voice in the back of his head told him to not be so hasty. So he rounded the vehicle and approached one of the street-side windows for the The Boer's House. Carefully, staying to one side, he peered inside.

Just as he suspected.

The proprietor was busy dialing a telephone.

CHAPTER
FORTY-NINE

MARIE UNFOLDED THE NOTE HER AIDE HANDED HER. THE FEMI-
nine handwriting informed her that a gentleman wanted to see her.
He'd driven seventy-five kilometers from Frankfurt and had patiently
waited at her hotel all day. She immediately recognized the name and
decided time would have to be allocated, since this man never appeared
unless there was something important to discuss. She turned back to
the aide and gave her a whispered instruction, then focused again on the
people around her.

She'd just spent two hours at the country's oldest synagogue with
about twelve hundred people who'd attended an open forum. The
synagogue was originally founded in the 11th century as the home to
a sizable Jewish population, but the Nazis razed the building in 1938.
Nearly a quarter century later the walls rose again, and the resulting
structure, completed in the 1970s, was certainly impressive. Directly
adjacent to the synagogue was the Jewish Museum, which detailed the
history of the local Jewish community, a mixture of pain, sorrow, hope,
and joy. She'd been asked to appear weeks ago and, after the display at
Dachau, her advisers felt the event would be consistent with her message of truth and hope. Though Jews made up only a minuscule portion
of the German populace, in a close election no one could be ignored.

And her pollsters were still warning that the whole contest was simply far too close to call.

She needed to focus.

But all day she'd been bothered by Kurt's earlier display. He'd stormed from her bedroom and promptly left the *schlöss*.

Had she pushed too hard?

Maybe he was right.

They were both aging. Their time in this world about over. She'd loved him once. Maybe even still. Perhaps she could continue to do so in the future. Then, perhaps not. Their differences were great, and politics seemed to constantly dictate their relationship. But no matter. He was gone for now. And if history was any indication he would stay away a few days, then reappear, never mentioning the tiff that had caused his absence. She'd often wondered what he did during those times.

Were there other women?

Probably.

Once she'd almost hired someone to find out, then decided it was better not to know. She wasn't much of a wife and he wasn't much of a husband, no sense trying to place the blame on someone else. If Kurt possessed a mistress, perhaps that was best, provided he was discreet. One thing for him to indulge his needs, quite another for her to know, and intolerable if the public became aware.

She lingered another twenty minutes, then excused herself and left the museum, pausing for a moment at the street. The limousine that she'd instructed her aide to arrange rounded the corner and motored to a stop.

The rear door opened and she climbed inside.

Her security detail followed in a separate car.

Erwin Brümmer sat comfortably in the rear seat.

"You are a patient man," she said as she settled into the black leather beside him.

"It was I who desired your time. You are a busy woman."

The once basso profundo tone, Brümmer's legendary trademark, was now tempered by the effects that eighty years of life left on vocal cords. Like the voice, Brümmer's body seemed to be succumbing to age, too, though the derisive gaze, disheveled hair, and dark, unblinking eyes remained. Perhaps it was the cigarettes he refused to surrender, or the diabetes she knew was ravaging his kidneys. Still, the ancient *Herr Doktor* clung to life, his mind sharp as ever. Her father chose him as the family's lawyer long ago, and he'd always been a fixture in her life, offering the kind of sound advice and guidance she'd come to rely upon.

She wanted to know why he'd come, but knew he would tell her when ready. He could not be rushed. Not ever.

The car pulled from the curb and the driver raised the Plexiglas partition that separated the rear compartment from the front seat.

"I've received some disturbing information. I thought it best to speak with you before approaching Kurt."

The declaration grabbed her attention.

Brümmer had long ago expressed his apprehension regarding Kurt. Both Eisenhuth-Industrie and Herzog Concern were exclusively managed by her husband. With regard to Herzog, that had been mandated by her father's will, though Brümmer had been appointed the executor of the estate. The consolidation of the two corporations' management was done at her insistence, yet Brümmer had always kept a steady eye on every major decision, particularly as it related to the Herzog side. For all his political faults, Kurt had run the companies reasonably well. What troubled her at the moment was that rarely had Erwin Brümmer come directly to her. He was from the old school, the one that demanded a chain of command be rigidly respected.

And Kurt was in that chain.

She waited for him to explain.

"The BND has made inquiries at our banks. The requests for information came as the result of an official inquiry from the Chilean police and a man named Juan Vergara. Certain aspects of our financial records have been subpoenaed. Those official inquiries are supposed to be private, but the banks thought it best I know. We do a lot of business with them."

"What kind of financial records?"

"Overseas transfers of cash into our corporate accounts. Specifically, from a Chilean bank account that was opened by Martin Bormann in the 1950s."

"Erwin, you must explain yourself."

She could not hide the astonishment in her voice.

"Millions of euros have passed from the Banco del Estado in Santiago, through Luxembourg, Liechtenstein, the Netherlands, and Switzerland, to banks here in Germany, into accounts our companies control. There is absolutely nothing suspect about the transfers themselves. Similar transactions occur on a daily basis from banks around the world. What makes these unique is that they are now directly linked to Martin Bormann and Hitler's Bounty. I don't have to tell you the implications of that."

No, he did not.

What was happening?

Cassiopeia Vitt and Cotton Malone were supposed to be finding a connection between Theodor Pohl and Martin Bormann. She'd heard nothing from them, or Danny Daniels, all day. Now there was a trail that led to her? One that could sink her candidacy on the mere allegation.

"Where did the money go?" She wanted to know.

"Impossible to ascertain. The funds were commingled with other corporate assets. No one in the accounting departments thought much of the transfers. As I said, many are made between our affiliates worldwide every day."

"How are you sure that the money is tainted?"

"My sources in the BND confirm that there is a current investigation of both Eisenhuth-Industrie and Herzog Concern. The Chileans provided them information that establishes the link beyond any doubt and requested action be taken. There are former Nazi documents that authenticate the money's source. It is a priority investigation, one that few are privy to. That could help keep this out of the media for the immediate future." The old man hesitated, and she caught the look in his eye. "I'm told that there is an ex-American intelligence operative and another woman, in the field, working together on an assignment that you requested. Do you want to tell me what's going on?"

She realized not much would have to be said. He knew almost everything. As always. The weight on her shoulders seemed to have doubled over the past few minutes. This was turning into madness.

The car eased across Worms to her next appearance.

She faced the old man and told him everything she knew.

"It would seem," he said, "that the hunter has now become the hunted. That tainted money clearly went into our accounts."

"I need to speak with Kurt."

"I should say so."

"I know nothing about any of those transfers. Absolutely nothing."

"Obviously. Why send people to utterly destroy yourself? Time is a problem, though. This can be contained for only so long. You have enemies within the security forces who will relish this opportunity."

On that point he was right. "I'll find Kurt."

Brümmer heaved a sigh and settled back into the seat. "Do that. But I do not envy your task, Marie. Not in the least."

CHAPTER FIFTY

FREE STATE, SOUTH AFRICA
6:15 P.M.

ENGLE STARED INTO THE AQUARIUM. A HUGE PINK ANEMONE writhed gently in the agitated water as a squadron of orange-and-black clown fish wiggled between its opaque tentacles. The elongated game room dominated the house's east side and was lined with built-in aquariums, each one displaying a variety of colorful saltwater and rather dull-looking freshwater species. Books and globes added more of the taste of an adventurer.

"The freshwater species in the other tanks are far more expensive," his host said after he commented on the difference. "They come from a variety of habitats here on the continent. Some are quite rare."

And his host was apparently an avid collector. On the walk from the front door he'd spied a Cézanne, a van Gogh, two Diego Riveras, Kangxi porcelain, and a variety of African art, which he knew little about. Wall cupboards and a camphor cabinet were filled with elaborate silver. He'd also learned that the big man's name was Jan Bruin, the estate's owner, the precise individual Pohl had instructed him to find.

They sat and a thin African retainer dressed in a stiff-looking shirt and tie appeared, then retreated with drink orders. He settled onto a sofa that faced an ensemble of leather club chairs. An elaborately carved table supported by four gleaming tusks filled the space in between and displayed what appeared to be a mother-of-pearl chess set. The surrounding walls were clad in Elizabethan panels and dotted with trophies and photographs from past hunts. The room seemed a place to sit and remember.

"A bit politically incorrect," he said in German, motioning to the table, then to the lion, elephant, and rhino heads on the walls.

"Not here," Bruin declared in English. "Hunting was a way of life for us. You are correct, though, in one respect. Those days are over. Today we stalk with cameras. But I remember, as a child, how exciting a hunt could be." Bruin tossed him a penetrating gaze. "You said outside that you have come on behalf of Theodor Pohl. How is the Kaiser?"

The steward returned with the drinks, and Engle took a moment to enjoy a few sips. The wine was tart and tasty.

"Excellent wine," he said.

"Made here in South Africa. Now, could you answer the question."

He decided he'd had enough of the pretext, especially since this man knew Pohl's nickname. "He is engaged in a bitter election fight for the chancellorship of Germany."

"I read about that. You do know that he and I have never met."

"I know that. But, Herr Bruin, I am aware of your lineage. Your father was a man named Gerhard Schüb. He immigrated to South Africa after the war, arriving from Chile with another individual named Luis Soreno, along with Soreno's wife, Rikka. I understand your father passed on two years ago."

"He did. He lived a full life. My mother died before him. She was fortunate."

"In what way?"

"To have a long life, too. What else?"

He let the remark pass and asked, "Have you had any contact with your aunt Ada, who lives in Chile?"

"I'm at a loss. I never knew I had an aunt."

"Your father never spoke of her?"

"My father was a most secretive man. He kept many things to himself. I was unaware we had any living relatives on his side of the family."

"Did your father leave any papers behind? Letters, perhaps? From his sister, Ada."

Bruin's brow creased in amusement. "That would have been most unlike him. The Kaiser knew my father well, so he knows the answers to these questions. My father was not one to keep things. And as I said, I had no idea I had an aunt, so there were no letters to find."

"Did he leave any papers concerning a Luis Soreno?"

"Did you not hear me? My father left no papers when he died. Nothing. Why is this of concern now? I have heard nothing from Germany in a long time. Now this interrogation."

He chuckled. "Did I say anything was a concern?"

"You did not have to. Your presence here says it all. I must tell you, Herr Engle, I do not like anything even remotely associated with new-right politics."

"Such a strange position from one who lives in the Free State. Was this not the original bastion of apartheid? Its birthplace."

Bruin dismissed the observation with the swipe of a big paw. "Before my time. I have never adhered to those policies. Not every South African is a racist or a white supremacist. My father was neither. He was a good man who did his duty until he died. He never supported any of those policies. Quite the contrary, in fact. He and I both have little patience with fanatical causes."

"I represent no such cause."

"Really? Here you are in South Africa, in my home, asking about Nazis from over half a century ago. What possible relevance could any of that have today?"

"Why did you mention Nazis?"

Bruin shook his head in apparent disgust. "As you say, let us not play games. You and I both know of Luis Soreno. And Rikka. That much I was made aware of."

He let the moment pass by, retrieving his drink and sipping more wine. "I think it best neither of us speak of them."

"I agree. The last thing I want is for the world to descend on this house. Let him, and his bride, rest in their graves. There is no danger of me ever speaking of that. It would be the last thing I would want."

"How do you know about them?"

"My father told me, right before he died. It mattered not by then. Everyone was dead. But he made it clear that it was his affair, not mine, and it was over, and had been for a long time."

So why had Ada directed Malone and Vitt here?

Bruin pointed. "Go back and tell the Kaiser that there is nothing for him to fear here. He can become chancellor of Germany and I will not give it a second thought. I, too, am in politics. I represent this area in the national assembly, but only with a minimal zeal. I prefer to stay to myself, grow my cherries, and raise ostriches. Both bring me much more joy."

"No wife?"

"I have never married. I live here alone, save for my dogs, my birds, my fish, and a few employees." He seemed proud of the fact.

"Let me ask again. Your father left no papers? No correspondence? Nothing?"

"Herr Engle, my father was a private man who only in the last few months of his life opened up to me. That was hard for him, but he wanted me to know who he was and what he believed before he died. He despised Luis Soreno and all that the Brown Eminence represented. My father came to Africa for one reason, but he stayed for quite another."

He swallowed more wine as he allowed the man to talk. "And what was that?"

"He loved this country. It became his home. He managed to accumulate some wealth and bought this land. Today I have a fortune invested here. He wanted my life to be different from his, and it has been. Let the Nazis remain dead and gone. No one need ever be concerned with them again. I for one waste not a thought on their folly." There was a hesitation, as if a memory interjected itself, then faded. "Now, could you tell me precisely why you are here?"

"I have been sent to make sure what you and I know does not have the ability to manifest itself."

"I have known this for many years and have kept the information to myself. There is no reason to doubt I would not continue."

On that conclusion he was still debating.

Ada had to have learned whatever she knew from somewhere.

Was it from this man?

He realized, though, that killing Jan Bruin could prove risky. Pohl had provided some of the personal history. Bruin was being modest. He was actually a politician of some note. Not a celebrity in the sense that his actions were subject to great scrutiny, but well known nonetheless. A violent death could attract a lot of attention. Perhaps Bruin was right. Let it lie. But that was not his decision to make. He needed to consult with Pohl and let his benefactor decide the next course. So he finished the wine and tabled the glass. "You are correct. Let us leave things as they are. I will report what you've said." He stood from the sofa. "I appreciate your time. And I thank you for your discretion."

Bruin rose and led him back to the front door and onto the covered stoep. The rottweiler still slept against the railing.

"Are you staying the night in Nohana?" Bruin asked.

"I thought I might. Then leave tomorrow."

He noticed words etched into the pediment above the main door.

RUST-EN-VREUGD.

Bruin caught his interest. "Rest and gladness. It was the wish my father had for all who entered."

"Appropriate, I'm sure."

"I have always thought so. They seem particularly applicable at this moment."

He caught the message.

Evening was descending, the air steadily releasing its heat with the sun's westward retreat. He took a moment and admired the distant mountains and emerald veld.

Impressive.

He said his goodbyes and headed for his car. As he reached the stoep's steps, the rottweiler wrested itself from sleep and stood.

Bruin came close and stroked the animal. "Herr Engle, tell the Kaiser that I am no threat, but I can be quite formidable if roused."

Maybe he was right.

Like the rottweiler Jan Bruin continued to pet, sleeping dogs, especially those aggressive and unpredictable, were best left alone.

CHAPTER
FIFTY-ONE

COTTON LEFT NOHANA AND DROVE BACK NORTH TO ALLESVER-
loren. He watched the road carefully for Engle's vehicle, but it did not
appear. He found Cassiopeia where he left her, in the heavy brush just
off the highway.

He checked his watch: 7:20 P.M.

The sun was vanishing, the shadows lengthening.

"Engle left about ten minutes ago. He went north, toward the border," Cassiopeia said as she climbed into the Range Rover. "Learn anything?"

He told her what the man at the museum had related.

"I assume it's our turn to visit Jan Bruin?" she said when he finished.

He angled the car toward the estate's entrance. "Yep."

He drove about half a mile down the dirt lane before parking in front
of what could only be described as a mellow old home adorned with
splendid stone and woodwork. Red-brick walls were at places thick with
vines, the paned windows numerous, a lack of symmetry clear proof of
decades of determined remodeling. A copper turret at one corner, green
from age, was topped with an ornate weather vane. Three stone chimneys reached for the evening sky. The intense whirring and snapping of
insect wings from all around brought to mind the crackle of wood in a
fire.

A heavyset man dressed in jeans and a long-sleeved shirt stepped from the covered stoep. His sparse hair, which seemed bleached by the sun, was the color of hay. The width of his shoulders and breadth of his chest suggested he was accustomed to hard work. He introduced himself as Jan Bruin. Cotton quickly explained why he and Cassiopeia had come, deciding the direct approach would be best.

"I assume you received a call from the man at The Boer's House," he said to Bruin in English. "He was dialing the phone as soon as I left."

"I did. He wanted me to know of your inquiries."

"We need some answers. Do you mind talking?"

"Why don't we sit on the stoep. It's lovely out here this time of day."

They followed him up a short flight of stairs, and each of them took a seat in a high-backed rocker made of what Cotton believed was stinkwood. An odd description he'd always thought considering the wood possessed no odor. Off to the west the blood-red globe of the sun purpled the distant ridges.

"There's a woman," he said, "her name is Ada. She lives in the Chilean lake district. Is that a name you are familiar with?"

Bruin seemed to consider the inquiry a moment before saying, "I have never been to Chile."

"That doesn't answer my question."

"The answer is no. That name is totally unfamiliar to me."

"She sent us here," Cassiopeia said. "Or should I say, she sent us to Africa and the trail led here."

"Trail to what?"

Cotton wasn't going to offer too much. Instead he decided to see how truthful their host was going to be. "We believe that a man named Josef Engle will come to see you. Has that happened?"

Bruin shook his head. "No one by that name has visited."

"He could have used an alias," Cassiopeia said, and she described Engle as he appeared not an hour ago, then asked, "Has a man fitting that description been here?"

Bruin slapped away the inquiry with the back of his hand. "Same answer. No one like that has come. In fact, I have had no visitors in several days."

He watched Bruin's urbane mask of self-control as he lied. Cassiopeia kept her face rigid as well, and neither of them revealed anything.

"He may stop by," Cotton finally said. "We have reason to believe that he's here in Nohana."

"What am I to do if he appears?"

"We'd like you to find out what he wants," Cassiopeia said. "Then we'd like you to tell us."

"What is all this about?"

"The man at The Boer's House said your father's name was Thomas Bruin and that he was a German immigrant. Was Thomas his birth name?"

"Now, Mr. Malone, that question could be construed as intrusive."

The voice sounded mildly irritated.

"I can be that way sometimes. Occupational hazard. But could you answer the question?" He wasn't going to back off.

Bruin considered the rebuke with clear amusement. "My father was born Thomas Bruin in Stuttgart. He immigrated to South Africa after the war. So did a number of others, none of whom were Nazis or war criminals, just men and women who wanted a better life somewhere else. Germany was, after all, in shambles."

"Does the name Gerhard Schüb mean anything to you?" he asked.

The question hung in the air a moment as Bruin hesitated with his response. "The name has no meaning. Is he another immigrant?"

"We're not sure," he said. "We were hoping you would help us out and we could learn more."

"It appears that you both know precious little."

"Exactly why we traveled all this way," he said. "To learn."

A soft whir passed overhead, followed by the slow flap of wings. An owl returning to its perch in a nearby tree. More insect wings quivered in air that was chilling by the minute. A flock of rosebushes hugged the house's foundation, just beyond the railing, and the creamy-yellow blooms trembled in a burst of wind. On the horizon, far off on the veld, a cloud of dust rose.

"Wildebeest," Bruin said. "Heading for water. Huge as a Buddha and powerful. I so enjoyed shooting them."

"Why don't you anymore?" Cassiopeia asked.

"There's no sport to it."

He wondered about the comment. Strange coming from a man born and raised in a place where wild game abounded. Bruin continued to rock in his chair, staring off into the distance. A few moments passed before Bruin said, "Is there anything more?"

"The name of this estate. *Allesverloren.* Everything lost. How was that chosen?" he asked.

"What relevance could that have?"

"None. Just curious."

"My father chose the name. He never explained why."

"You didn't ask?"

"I was not in the habit of questioning my father."

He saved the best for last. "One more name. Luis Soreno. That familiar?"

Their host's jaw tightened a moment with what Cotton briefly perceived as antagonism. But Bruin kept his manner detached, his face cold and deadpan. More deception? Hard to say for sure considering how effortlessly the man had lied a moment before.

"That name, too, is foreign to me. Sounds Spanish, and we have precious few Spaniards in this region."

He could tell that they were going to learn little. The frontal approach was not working. Time to slip in through the back door.

But not now. Later.

He stood from the rocker.

"We won't trouble you anymore. We appreciate your time." Bruin rose, too, along with Cassiopeia. "If Josef Engle appears, I advise caution. He may have killed several people, including a deputy minister of the Chilean police. He's not a man to toy with."

"I appreciate your concern. But I'm afraid his trip, like yours, would be a waste of time. I know nothing, and will tell him that if he appears."

CHAPTER
FIFTY-TWO

Marie found Kurt quicker than she thought possible. She first called the *schlöss* and was told that no one there had heard from him. A call to Eisenhuth-Industrie's headquarters revealed that Kurt had not been on-site since early afternoon, but he'd indicated that he intended to stay in town for the next few days. The company maintained an apartment in the Sachsenhausen district amid the pubs, restaurants, and shops of the old town. So she abruptly canceled her evening engagement in Worms, claiming a sore throat, then borrowed an aide's car and, after dark, had one of her security men drive her north into the city.

She knew the apartment well.

It belonged to her parents. They'd lived there after the war once the building had been resurrected from the bombing. It was not her childhood home—that had been the Alpine *schlöss*—but a place where her mother and father had lived later in life.

When her father changed.

She recalled how morose and introverted he became, saying precious little, smiling almost never, consumed by something not acknowledged yet always there. Many were just like him. Later, psychologists coined a name for their affliction. Post-traumatic stress disorder. The natural, psychological result of a sudden debilitating trauma. In the chaos of the post–World War II world there were no fancy names for the malady, only a realization that its effects were real and widespread. The eight months her father had spent incarcerated at Nuremberg, awaiting trial as a supposed collaborator, seemed to have exacted an enormous toll on his psyche. He was never the same. Was he ashamed? Humiliated? Was his reaction guilt at the horror that was the Third Reich? If so, he never spoke a word that indicated either recognition or remorse.

Over the past three years she had only rarely visited the apartment. It was used mainly by Kurt when he stayed in Frankfurt. If it was also a love nest for his mistresses she did not want to know. It was another of their unwritten rules, more of their separate privacy that neither voiced but each demanded, a once liquid commandment that had solidified in the past decade.

But the matter now weighing on her mind was far different from a cheating spouse. Hitler's Bounty. Martin Bormann. South American accounts. Eisenhuth-Industrie. Herzog Concern. Connect the dots and a line joined those seemingly unrelated things into an unspeakable image. She'd called Danny Daniels and learned that she'd been set up, the whole thing a trap to get her to dig deep in Chile, where the financial records were offered up to law enforcement on a silver platter, garnished with the blood of her dead investigator, along with the Chilean inspector who'd requested the inquiry. What a colossal mistake she'd made. But what did Kurt know?

She had to find out.

Her driver let her out on a side street two blocks from the familiar row of adjoining burgher's houses. The gabled façades reflected a medieval flair that this section of the city exuded. She told her security man not to accompany her upstairs. He did not like it, but obeyed. On the first floor she found the paneled door and rapped lightly.

Not a sound stirred from inside.

She knocked again, this time harder.

Still no answer. Was Kurt inside with someone?

Downstairs she heard the main door open, then close, and footsteps started up the stone-and-brass staircase.

She waited.

An older couple crested the landing, then turned on their way to the second floor. She gave them a glance, then knocked on the door for a third time. Once she had possessed a key, but it had been years since she'd last seen it. The couple stopped their climb and she could feel them staring at her.

She turned and faced them.

"He's not there, Frau Bundeskanzlerin," the man said, acknowledging the feminine form of her official title. "He is at the Knoblauch, having dinner. We just came from there."

A wave of uneasiness passed between them. She wanted to ask if Kurt was alone, but knew better. The man seemed to sense her quandary, almost divining her thoughts with a look reminiscent of her father's derisive gaze.

"He eats there regularly, when he is here. Always alone, before 8:00 P.M. A creature of habit, your husband."

The man said nothing more and the old woman never uttered a sound. They simply turned, arm in arm, and began their ascent to the upper floors. She wanted to stop them, ask their names, thank them, play the role of candidate, but instead she simply listened as the footsteps faded away.

The Knoblauch was located three blocks from the apartment. The restaurant filled the cellar of what was once a Carmelite monastery, decorated with hewn-wood tables, wrought-iron lamps, and aromatic candles. The establishment's name, which meant "garlic," was immediately apparent upon entering, sharp scents permeating the thick air with an enticing aroma.

Kurt was sitting alone at a far, corner table, reading a newspaper. Only a few of the other tables were occupied. She'd come alone, her minders outside in the car. She ignored the maître d' and walked straight over. He glanced up, and the lack of surprise on his face worried her.

Had he expected a visit?

She sat. "We need to discuss a matter."

"I don't think here is the place to debate our personal life."

"It's not about this morning." She kept her voice low. The melody of a harp from a far corner added background to the muted conversations of the other guests. They should go outside, but she thought remaining in public would prevent him from getting angry and walking away.

"The federal police are investigating our companies' finances."

His eyebrow rose in disbelief. The information apparently grabbed his attention. He seemed surprised.

She explained in a low voice what Erwin Brümmer had told her. "The Chilean authorities have made a formal request for information, and subpoenas have been issued. I want to know, Kurt. Is there any truth to this?"

A waiter brought his dinner, but he instructed that it be taken back to the kitchen. He sipped from his water goblet and asked if she wanted anything to drink. She dismissed his offer with another inquiry as to what was happening.

"Marie, we have customers in Chile, Argentina, Paraguay, and Brazil. We also have investors, customers, and banks on that continent. Money coming from there is not unusual. But I have no knowledge of any connection to Hitler's Bounty or Martin Bormann."

She was trying to gauge his response for truthfulness, but their personal distance had dulled her ability to know for certain when he was deceiving her. She'd ignored him for so long—simply allowed him to have his way provided he never interfered with her feelings or emotions. Now she cursed her indifference. "You do see the ramifications here?"

"If true, it will destroy everything. You and me both. How was Brümmer informed before me? I was at headquarters all day and no one said a word."

"The inquiries have only come to our banks. They are bound by secrecy and cannot reveal the investigation. But Erwin learned through contacts there."

"If he knows, others do, too. Maybe even the press by now."

That prospect was causing her gut to churn. "No inquiries have, as yet, been made to my press office."

But it was only a matter of time.

"Marie, our companies escaped the war reparation suits. There were numerous investigations, you know that, and many corporations were implicated, but not us. How is it that now, mysteriously, we are implicated with Hitler's money? Something must be in error here, or is this dirty politics from your opponent?"

She wanted to tell him about the information that had originally spurred her interest, and Cassiopeia Vitt and Cotton Malone who were somewhere in Chile, and how it all now seemed a trap, but thought better. He would simply say that she had no one to blame but herself and, in one respect, he was right.

After all, she'd taken the bait.

Obviously, the original premise that Theodor Pohl was the son of Martin Bormann and Eva Braun had been fiction.

Now all of it had turned around to her.

"Kurt, this is serious. Not only for the political implications, but for the moral ones. If our companies accepted money, whether knowingly or not, that is traceable to Bormann and the Third Reich, we are no better than they. Our fortune, our lives, have at least in part been built with blood. It is a stigma that we will never be able to shake."

"I am no Nazi," he softly declared.

"But you, and I, may have benefited from their evil."

"That is preposterous."

His naïveté was beyond irritating. Bad enough that she had to endure his racist overtones and German superiority, but combine those absurd propositions with political blinders and the result was the type of fool Theodor Pohl cherished as a supporter.

"I assure you, Kurt, if the allegation is true the result will be anything but preposterous. I don't have to remind you what happened to other companies caught up in the reparation suits."

She knew he was aware of the horrible publicity and the millions of euros spent by a dozen or so German corporations found to have profited from slave labor during the war. It made no matter that those suits were litigated fifty years after the peace. The plaintiffs' venom had been just as potent, the results just as devastating, the effects just as awful.

"Come now, Marie, this is not about me. This is about your political future. You could not care less about the companies."

She resented his accusation of selfishness. "No, Kurt, it is about what is right and wrong. I could not live with myself knowing that any funds came to us from the Third Reich."

He seemed unimpressed with her convictions. "Tell me what you know of the money transfers."

His sudden shift of subject caught her off guard.

Was the move calculated?

"Erwin says they have occurred over a sixty-year period."

He sat back in his chair and faced her with a look she found both irritating and disconcerting. "You understand what that means?"

Of course she did. "My father might be implicated."

Albert Herzog ran the company personally until the day he died. Though there was a management board and various advisory committees, he'd been in complete charge. Any transfers prior to his death would have most certainly been approved by him.

Disturbing thoughts swirled through her mind.

Her father's far-right-wing philosophy. His refusal to ever speak ill of the Third Reich. His insistence that Germany was no better off postwar than prewar, and in fact—as he'd many times voiced—a divided Germany was worse than anything Hitler ever did. She'd dismissed his beliefs as those of a man who'd known a Germany unfamiliar to her. Many of his generation felt the same. Few of them were left. But as a child and into her teenage years, those men and women had dominated Germany.

"You must tread lightly here," Kurt whispered.

"I will cover nothing up."

"Even if it means the end of your political career and the besmirching of both your own and your father's memory?"

There was something unsettling about Kurt's tone. "You never told me whether you were aware of the source of those Chilean funds."

"I believe I said that I possessed no idea of any connection to Hitler's Bounty or Martin Bormann."

"Which answers nothing."

He shook his head. "Perhaps it eases your conscience to think me your enemy. Does it help you justify your rejection of our marriage, and me?"

She cautioned herself that they were in public. Her tone and demeanor must be controlled. He was good at baiting her. She needed to be better at not taking the offer. "I have rejected nothing," she whispered. "You are the one who cannot support me."

"I am entitled to my beliefs, as you are to yours."

"We have progressed way beyond beliefs, Kurt. This has international implications."

He shrugged. "Which do not concern me."

"You're rather enjoying the possibility of my failure, aren't you?"

"I don't relish any pain coming to you. But I am no Nazi, nor have Nazis financed our business. I will personally investigate this tomorrow and find out what is happening."

But she wasn't so sure.

There was something in his desultory tone that triggered alarm.

Being linked to Hitler, in any way, repulsed her. The thought that her father may have participated, and profited from evil, sickened her. But something else nagged at her conscience. For once she was glad that she'd come to face Kurt. To judge for herself his reaction. To watch his eyes and see his face.

And that was the problem.

He knew more than he was saying.

CHAPTER FIFTY-THREE

COTTON WAS IMPRESSED BY THE ACCOMMODATIONS.

The lodge sat in an oak woodland overlooking a darkened plateau. The rooms were separate sandstone cottages that dotted a grassy space beneath a canopy of trees, like mushrooms in the shade. The clerk explained that inside the largest thatch-roofed rondavel, set off to one side, an excellent dinner was served until 10:00 P.M.

In the room they'd each showered away dust and fatigue. Cassiopeia lingered in the hot water longer, apparently enjoying a few minutes of peace. He used the time to connect his laptop to the wireless internet and let Danny know the situation and that he would report more tomorrow. He then changed into more of the clothes they'd bought earlier. For him that meant a pair of stone chinos and a solid button-down shirt. He noticed that Cassiopeia decided to dress for dinner, too, emerging from the shower wearing houndstooth trousers and a lightweight silk blouse, both in shades of gray and olive, the fit slim and sporty.

She stood across the room and towel-dried her long dark hair. Her gun lay on the bed, and she tossed the towel aside and checked the magazine. He'd already done the same with his weapon, which was now tucked inside his belt beneath a lightweight jacket. He passed by her, and the fragrance of the soap from her shower lingered in his nostrils longer than it should.

"I could get used to this," he said.

"What? Sharing a room?"

"Sharing everything."

"Careful. You're approaching that dreaded M-word."

That he was.

Her face softened. "I could get used to it, too."

And they both seemed fine to let it go at that.

For now.

"You haven't said a word about Jan Bruin lying to us," she said.

He hadn't broached it, because he was still mulling over what to do. "Clearly he's involved with whatever is happening here, or he wouldn't have lied."

"But we don't know which side he's on. He could tell Engle all about us, and there goes our advantage."

"We knew that risk when we approached him. We're in Bruin's sandbox. This could get rough."

She reached for the towel and finished drying her hair, then stepped to the mirror and lightly combed the damp strands into place. "How about we get some food, then some rest. With Engle and Bruin around we're going to have to be cautious. I'll take the first watch, you can have the second."

"And I thought we were going to have a lovely walk on the veld in the moonlight then . . . later—"

She tossed him a mischievous grin. "Who knows, be a good boy and you might just get that walk."

Dinner was excellent, a mixture of African and European delights. And reasonably priced, too. Cassiopeia shunned wine, recognizing the need for a clear head. He didn't drink at all, having never acquired a taste for alcohol.

He still did not know what to do next.

They were at a crossroads.

Perhaps it was time to involve official channels. Danny could brief the State Department and request intervention. The Justice Department still maintained a prosecutorial unit devoted to war criminals, and there were treaties among nations, South Africa included, that would allow extradition. Engle and Bruin both could be questioned, the press alerted, a lot of attention thrown on the situation, perhaps enough to flesh out what was really happening and implicate Pohl.

Thankfully, they had some proof.

The photos. Scrapbook. Schüb's letters. All were safely locked in the lodge's house safe. The other letters Ada had provided from Eva Braun were gone, but he recalled every word read to him by the carabinero. Unfortunately an eidetic memory would not be enough evidence to convince the court of public opinion, and it would be that jury's decision alone, in the end, that would matter.

They left the restaurant and headed back toward their cottage. Stars blinked and fluttered in a brilliant night sky, while a wind disturbed the branches with the soothing softness of a lullaby. The path was lit by a string of lanterns suspended from trees, which cast the way in swaying shadows. Lights from the adjacent cottages dissolved more of the darkness. A dog bayed in the distance, and the harsh discordant wail of a hyena announced the animal was hungry.

"Tomorrow we'll see what more we can learn on Jan Bruin," he said. "He's our best lead at this point."

"What about Engle?"

He wanted him, too. But he did not want the trail to stop there. The prize remained Theodor Pohl, who'd been jerking everyone's chain from the start.

His cell phone vibrated.

Danny was calling.

Directly. No encrypted text. Not good.

He answered.

"All hell has broken out," Danny said. "The BND is actively investigating the chancellor on those money transfers. She's in a vise. A bad one. Can anything be salvaged on your end?"

"That remains to be seen. We were sent here to Africa for a reason. I'm just not sure what it is."

"Keep digging until you hit bedrock. It's all we have left."

"That's the plan."

The call ended.

"He's not happy," he told Cassiopeia.

"There's not much to be happy about. We handed Pohl exactly what he wanted."

They kept walking, the path lit by more lanterns. Ahead he saw their cottage, the entrance lit by an amber wall fixture. A man stood beside the bench just before the front door on the brick path. He was short, thin, and old, dressed casually.

They approached.

"Good evening, I am Gerhard Schüb. I understand that you want to speak with me."

CHAPTER FIFTY-FOUR

ENGLE SETTLED INTO THE CHAIR BESIDE THE BED AND TAPPED IN the number for an overseas call to Germany. He'd taken the café proprietor's advice and reserved one of the thatched rondavels, set amid a peach orchard, about twenty kilometers from Nohana, near the Lesotho border. The food was, as promised, superb. He'd enjoyed the oxtail in red wine sauce, washing it down with a heavy lager that reminded him of home. He'd delayed making contact until after dinner since he was reasonably sure what Theodor Pohl would say.

The private line in the Hessian bedchamber at Löwenberg was answered on the second ring.

"I have been waiting," Pohl said.

"I needed to know the situation before calling. I did not think a partial report was what you wanted."

"I'm listening."

He told his employer precisely what had occurred since his arrival in South Africa.

"Do you think he was lying, that he may have been in contact with Ada?"

"Impossible to say. He strongly denied even knowing she existed. Perhaps he is being truthful. Perhaps Herr Schüb kept that information to himself?"

"It's possible. The old man was tight-lipped. But I can't take that chance. It's too great. I want the situation there handled."

He knew what Pohl meant. Kill Jan Bruin. "That could pose a problem. He is a public figure, a member of the national assembly."

"The Free State is a violent place. The entire country is a hotbed. Bad things happen. Besides, there is little choice. He knows far too much. He and Ada are communicating. I can feel it. His father is gone. The others are gone. This son and his aunt are all that is left out there."

"What if documents survive? As with Ada?"

"I never met Bruin, but I agree with his assessment. Schüb was not a man to keep incriminating things. Besides, without anyone to authenticate them they fall into the realm of pure speculation. That's nothing to worry about. Perhaps an author will write another one of those conspiracy books and one of my houses can publish it. Probably would sell quite a few copies."

Killing Ada? Yes, that he would do. But he disagreed with harming Jan Bruin. The man was the son of Gerhard Schüb, a man who'd loyally served both the Third Reich and Martin Bormann. There was good stock there. They'd done their duties for decades. No reason to think he'd be disloyal now.

"Is that the course you desire?" he finally asked.

"Why the hesitation?"

"Perhaps well enough should be left alone."

"If you had not failed in Chile, Africa would have never been in play. This whole endeavor has become fraught with unacceptable risk. I am tired of evidence and witnesses appearing. So we shall do this my way. The investigation into the chancellor has started. It's only a matter of time before the press learns and her troubles start. Make sure all is good there. Finish your task. Tonight. Then return here tomorrow. We will deal with Ada when this is over and I am chancellor."

The phone call ended.

COTTON STARED AT THE MAN WHO SAID HIS NAME WAS GERHARD Schüb, picturing clearly in his mind the image of the virile soldier, wearing an SS uniform, that he'd seen on Ada's dresser.

Age had taken a toll. The gray-white patina bore a bluish tint, the gnarled tracing of veins clearly visible. The face had drawn into itself pinched and tight, but the pale-blue eyes still seemed alive. Faint strands of silver hair streaked the domed forehead. A steady tremor shook the hands. Sixty years had passed between the photograph and the reality standing across from him, yet he was certain the two men were one and the same.

"I thought it time we talk," Schüb said, the voice nearly inaudible.

Perhaps the whispered tone was intentional, coming from someone who rarely repeated himself.

"You're supposed to be dead," Cassiopeia said.

"As are you."

"Ada kept you informed?" Cotton asked.

"She is a dear and loving sister."

It almost seemed painful for the old man to speak, his vowels reluctant to surrender to consonants, the rasp of cigarettes clear.

"Jan is your son?" Cassiopeia asked.

The old man nodded. "A good boy. He lied to you today about Josef Engle and Ada on my instructions. I still, as of then, had not decided what to do."

"And now?" Cotton asked.

"The others are dead. Only I remain. Perhaps I am meant to end all of this."

"And Ada?" Cassiopeia said.

"She has done a good job in Chile. Now the rest is up to me."

"Why did you never go back there?" Cotton asked.

"By the mid-1960s there was no way I could ever return to Chile. I had lived here for nearly twenty years. This was home. I had acquired property, stature, friends."

"Apparently a wife, too," he said.

Schüb nodded. "Another lovely woman who loved me. Jan was born, and he meant a great deal. So I made the decision to stay. Ada and I both decided to fulfill our duties to our father. Separately."

"Can you tell us how Bormann and Braun came to Africa," he asked, hoping the old man would answer.

Schüb stood silent for a moment, then spoke in the same funereal tone.

"Let us take a walk and I will tell you a story."

Within hours of Hitler's suicide, Bormann donned the uniform of an SS major general, crammed papers into a leather topcoat, and fled the Führerbunker. On the Weidendammer Bridge he encountered bazooka fire, but managed to flee the scene with only minor injuries. He commandeered a stray vehicle and drove to another underground bunker constructed in secret by Adolf Eichmann, equipped with food, water, and a generator. He stayed there a day, then slipped out of Berlin and headed north, dressed in the green uniform of a forest warden.

Across the Danish border he found a rescue group, stationed there weeks before, to aid fleeing Nazis. He had prepared himself for the journey months earlier by burying two caches of gold coins, one in the north, the other in the south. He'd also secreted away banknotes and art treasures in various Swiss vaults that could later be converted into cash. He'd long ago overseen the deposits of huge sums of gold and currency in South American banks. His political position gave him access to planes, cargo ships, and U-boats, and he utilized that privilege in the early months of 1945 to transport out of Germany all of what might be needed in the years ahead.

Aktion Aderflung and Aktion Feuerland were in place.

Projects Eagle Flight and Land of Fire would now serve their function.

By the end of 1945 Bormann was in Spain. He stayed there until March 1946. His face was relatively obscure until October 1945 when, after he was indicted for war crimes, his picture was posted throughout Europe. It was then he decided to leave the Continent, but not before dealing with Eva Braun.

Throughout the war she was intentionally kept in the background, denied the spotlight, and forced to remain most of the time in the Bavarian Alps. Only those in Hitler's innermost circle were familiar with her face, so it was easy for her to meld into the postwar world. She'd returned to Berlin against Hitler's order on April 15 to inform him she was pregnant. Hitler took the news with surprising calm, but delayed fourteen days before finally marrying her. During that time he arranged, through Bormann, for her *escape. By April 22 Hitler knew that he would never leave the bunker alive. He wanted to die a martyr. Braun objected to her surviving. She wanted to die with Hitler. But the Führer would not hear of it, particularly considering she was pregnant.*

Finally, she agreed to do as he asked.

A female SS captain who possessed a similar build and look to Braun volunteered to take her place, proud of the fact that she would be with Hitler in his final moments. That woman entered the bunker on April 30, around 1:00 P.M., an hour before Hitler and Braun were scheduled to lock themselves away for the final time. In the confusion of that day no one noticed the switch. People were routinely coming and going. With Bormann watching, she bit down on a cyanide capsule and ended her life. Her body, clothed in a blue dress identical to one Braun would be wearing, was kept in an adjacent anteroom.

Bormann was the first to enter the bedroom after Hitler died.

He promptly covered Braun's body on the pretense of protecting her dignity. He realized all focus would be on Hitler, and he was correct. Braun's task was to lie still and be dead. It was Bormann who carried her from the bedroom and momentarily deposited her body in an anteroom, after being called by a guard. That act was not prearranged, but it allowed Bormann an easy opportunity to switch the bodies, leaving Braun hidden in the anteroom while her substitute was burned with Hitler in the Chancellery garden above. In the confusion that occurred after, Braun, her physical appearance altered by disguise, and dressed as the SS captain who'd arrived hours earlier, left the bunker.

She was flown out of Berlin to Austria on one of the last flights. From there she traveled by train to Switzerland, no different than thousands of other displaced women. Her face was unimportant. Her name virtually unknown. So her journey, using new identity papers and money provided by Bormann, was quite easy.

Eventually, she arrived in Spain.

They stayed there until the spring of 1946. Transportation out of the country was arranged on an oil transport by a Greek sympathizer, Bormann and Braun arriving in Brazil a month later. Eventually, they traveled to Chile. Nazis had congregated there since the war, most in heavily fortified estancias south of Santiago. All part of Project Eagle Flight. They settled near the Argentine border in the lake district, until the lure of Africa drew them back across the Atlantic.

"I HEARD THAT TALE FROM BORMANN ON MORE THAN ONE occasion," Schüb said. "So much that I know every detail. He ridiculed Braun until the day she died. Belittling and degrading her in a most horrible way. He wanted her never to forget what she owed him. He enjoyed being in the superior position, and liked for people to owe him."

Cotton was amazed at what he was hearing.

"They were eventually legally married here, in the Free State," Schüb said. "Under their assumed names. Luis and Rikka Soreno."

"Why did she stay with him?" Cassiopeia asked. "History says she hated Bormann."

"She became with child again, and no one wanted an illegitimate off-spring. Sadly, Braun loved Hitler. She had a special place for him in her heart. I guess what is said is true. There really is someone for everyone. Even a monster. Hitler made it clear he wanted her to go with Bormann and raise their child. So she obeyed, but Bormann had other ideas. He was most difficult to live with. But she liked to make fun of him behind his back. Her favorite description was as an *oversexed toad.*"

"So she married him for the child?"

Schüb nodded. "As did Bormann marry her. Strange was his person-ality. Capable of murdering millions, yet concerned that his offspring would be chastised as a bastard."

"Did she give birth to their child?" Cotton asked.

"She birthed twin boys. Quite unexpected. And difficult, too."

"When?" he asked.

"Nineteen fifty-two."

The year Theodor Pohl was supposedly born.

"And afterward? What happened?"

"There was no afterward."

He waited for more.

"Braun died during that childbirth. She was far too old to be giving birth. She bled to death in a house not far from here."

He thought back to the correspondence from Eva Braun to Ada and the dates and recalled none past 1952, which was some corroboration of what he was hearing.

"What happened to Hitler's child?" Cassiopeia asked.

He wanted to know that, too.

"She gave birth in January 1946. The baby was robust and healthy. That occurred in Spain. Braun did not arrive in Chile until early 1947. The child never made the journey."

He was puzzled. "What do you mean?"

"Bormann took the baby at birth. Braun never saw the newborn."

"Why?" Cassiopeia asked.

"He wanted no part of Hitler's offspring."

"I assume," Cassiopeia said, "that was not what Hitler wanted."

"Quite correct. Bormann was to take care of Braun and the child. But Hitler's mistake was thinking Bormann could be trusted."

He understood. "Once Hitler was dead, Bormann made his own rules."

"And Braun had to accept," Cassiopeia added.

Schüb nodded. "She was told the child died at birth. No one knew anything to the contrary, save for Bormann and the midwife who handled the delivery."

"And you," Cotton said.

"That is correct. And me."

"What happened to Hitler's child?" Cassiopeia asked.

"Bormann never said. Knowing him, though, he probably killed it."

"You don't even know the sex?"

The old man shook his head.

Doubt began to cross into Cotton's mind. "We have a picture of Braun holding an infant in Chile."

The old man showed his first sign of annoyance. "Just a piece of misdirection. No children of Eva Braun's were ever present in Chile, and she never saw any of the babies she birthed."

A muffled sound filled the air overhead, like a breeze. He glanced up to see birds, not a hurried or confused flight, but a calm pilgrimage, their shadows flitting across the moon.

"Flamingos," Schüb whispered.

"Where do they go?" he asked.

"The night is their refuge. They will return at dawn."

Cotton continued to watch until the last of the shadows faded into the blackness. Then he faced Schüb and said, "We also have a picture of Bormann and a boy. The child was three or four."

"He rarely allowed himself to be photographed. Images were taken only for specific purposes. I took that one myself, here in Africa, long ago, and sent it to Ada a few years back for her use. I'm assuming she made sure you found it in an appropriate way."

"You and she communicate?" Cassiopeia asked.

The old man nodded. "Constantly. Once, only by phone or letter. But now, with modern technology, we can even see each other when we talk."

"An old dog learning new tricks?" Cotton asked.

Schüb smiled. "Something like that. I told her yesterday to send you my way. It was time for me to come back from the dead."

"Does Pohl know of the connection?" Cassiopeia asked.

The old man nodded. "He does. But he firmly believes I am dead."

"So how is Pohl connected to you?" Cotton asked.

"I never said he was."

"You didn't have to. He didn't send his bird dog here out of the blue. That guy Engle came straight to your house."

There was a hesitation while the old man caught his breath. The thin chest barely moved with each breath. "It is a long tale."

"We're listening."

Schüb swiveled his head like an owl and seemed to be looking around for something.

Finally, the old man said, "Be patient, and I will tell you everything."

CHAPTER
FIFTY-FIVE

ENGLE CROSSED THE OPEN PRAIRIE, THE GRASS SHORT AND THICK, and used the cloak of night to reenter Allesverloren. He took in the unusual surroundings. The fitful drone of a beetle's wing, the chatter of a bat, the trill of crickets that masked all sound of his approaching steps. He recalled the rottweiler and assumed there were more dogs, yet so far he'd not encountered any four-legged sentinels.

He kept close to the trees that dotted the plain in patches, always maintaining a course to the shadow of a house that loomed ahead. It was a little past 10:00 P.M. and his assumption about Jan Bruin was proving correct. He was apparently an early sleeper, as not a light shone from any of the windows. He did not agree with his employer's decision to eliminate the South African, but he was not in the habit of questioning his superior, so he resolved himself to handle the task with his usual efficiency, and the dogs be damned.

He made his way through a cherry orchard and found the steps leading up to the front stoep.

An owl unburdened its soul.

He climbed the steps.

Not a sound betrayed his presence.

He'd noticed something earlier during his first visit. While saying goodbye to Bruin, as his host had explained about the motto *rest and glad-*

ness, he'd noted that the front door possessed no dead bolt, no latch, no chain. He'd thought it strange, but purposefully drew no attention to the fact. He simply assumed that a man such as Jan Bruin required no locks for protection. It appeared to be a salient declaration that safeguarding Allesverloren involved much more than a chunk of metal. Come if you want. Trespass if you dare. The risks were all yours.

And that concerned him.

A man such as Jan Bruin knew the ways of his world. Pohl had been right on the phone. South Africa, if nothing else, was a brutal place. Its history was one of senseless violence. Only recently had some measure of sanity asserted itself. Bruin would be thoroughly schooled in the nature of his land, but orders were orders and Engle's were clear, so he crept close to the front door and turned the knob.

It opened.

He entered the darkened foyer and eased the door shut.

The air inside was warm and laced with the scents of boiled tomatoes and a lingering cigar. He stepped across smooth flagstones to the hardwood floor of a nearby corridor and followed a wide hall, past the conservatory and billiard parlor, to the game room where he and Bruin had talked earlier. Everything reeked of ancestry and old money. He noticed more Rouen platters, bits of Delft, and Limoges porcelain.

The trophies on the walls and the aquariums loomed silent in the pitch dark, the only light courtesy of a three-quarter moon. His eyes were fully adjusted and he easily threaded his way through the furniture to the elaborate gun cabinet he recalled from earlier. It was fashioned of the same rich wood, maple he believed, that encased the rest of the salon. He remembered seeing at least a dozen assorted rifles, along with several handguns and a crossbow.

He approached the cabinet and opened the glass door.

Again, no lock and no surprise.

He reached for one pistol in particular. A Webley target revolver— blue finish, six-inch barrel, light, maybe a kilo or so, vulcanite stock. He knew the weapon well. None had been made since 1945.

Perhaps it was an heirloom, he thought.

He brought the gun close and savored a bitter scent of oil, which was confirmation that Jan Bruin cared for his guns. He checked the cylinder. Just as he thought. Six shots. Fully loaded. A man like Bruin would never display an empty weapon.

He gripped the stock and left the room through the nearest doorway. He knew nothing of the house's geography, so he just followed another corridor until he came to an intersection. Doors framed with elaborate molding lined both sides of the hall, each spaced sufficiently apart to indicate that the rooms beyond were spacious. At the far end was a pedimented paneled door, much larger than the other entrances.

He stepped to the door and slowly turned the knob.

The thick slab of ornately carved wood was well hinged and eased open without a sound. He was right. The room beyond was indeed an elaborate bedchamber. He took in the silhouettes that dotted the space. Tall, heavy furniture, a four-poster canopy bed, clothes strewn across a small sofa. A rug filled the center, but from the runner in the hall to the start of the rug was a good five paces. He spied the covers on the bed and noticed a mound in the center, signaling where Jan Bruin was sleeping, the height and width consistent with the big man's girth.

He could approach closer, but the wood floor might betray his presence. So he weighed his options. Before he could decide on what to do, though, movement to the right caught his attention. A squat black form appeared in a doorway, then suddenly lunged forward on all four legs.

A rottweiler.

Finally.

Paws clicked off the floor as the dog raced toward him. A growl grew louder as the dog drew close. White fangs flashed against a light tongue. In the instant before the animal could leap, he pointed and fired the pistol. The retort was loud and a pitiful yelp signaled that he'd found his mark. The dog reeled to one side, crying out in agony.

Another shot and the animal went silent.

Before Jan Bruin could react, he deposited three rounds into the coverlets. Bruin never moved from the bed.

He needed to act fast.

The house was large, and though Bruin had said he lived alone, there were surely servants quartered somewhere. He'd planned his escape through one of the windows, disappearing into the veld beyond, back to his waiting vehicle and out of the region, but he needed to be sure Bruin was dead. There was one bullet left in the target pistol, so he stepped to the bed and reached for the thick covers.

Light flooded the room.

He raised a hand to shield his eyes from the burning rays, trying to give his pupils a moment to adjust.

He turned.

Jan Bruin stood in the hall doorway, a rifle muzzle pointed straight at him. Three other men—broad-shouldered, bronzed, simple-looking fellows—appeared from the remaining doors leading from the bedchamber, they too with guns leveled.

"Did you think me that stupid?" Bruin asked in German.

He said nothing.

Bruin entered the room and moved to the dog, its body bleeding onto the wood floor. He knelt and gently stroked the animal. "Poor Goliath. I had to sacrifice him for you." Bruin stood. "And that makes me angry. Men like you disgust me."

He still held the pistol, though at his side.

"Put the gun on the bed," Bruin commanded.

No choice, so he tossed the pistol down.

"It would give me no greater pleasure than to kill you," Bruin said. "My father warned me many times about men such as yourself. He knew your type. Following orders. Blindly. But unfortunately, killing you would only serve notice for more to come, and that is the last thing I need."

His eyes were now accustomed to the light. He reached down and slid back the covers. Pillows filled the mound that masqueraded as Bruin. "How did you know I would come tonight?"

"Tonight, tomorrow, the next day. One of those would have been correct. You could not, or should I say your employer could not, allow me to remain alive once you were aware that I knew things. That is why I told you what I did."

He slipped a glance at the other three men who each stood impassive, their guns still leveled.

"No need to worry," Bruin said. "They do not understand German. This conversation is between you and me alone."

"What now?" He was interested in the answer.

"You will return to Germany and tell Theodor Pohl whatever you want. I don't care. I simply want to be left alone."

He did not particularly enjoy being caught in a trap, the mouse never did have much fun, but he was in no position to bargain. "I am paid to do as Pohl desires, just as your men are paid to do as you say. I assume you demand loyalty. So does my employer. This is not personal."

Bruin motioned to the dog with the barrel of the rifle. "That was personal, Herr Engle."

"Unfortunate, but necessary. But it was you who conceived this deception. The dog was a player, by your choice."

"Really? Did you not expect to encounter one at some point? What choice did I have?"

"I was becoming suspicious that my progress had been too easy."

"But that didn't stop you. Men like you are difficult to stop. Go back to Germany. Tonight. Tell the Kaiser that I'm dead. Tell him whatever you want. But do not return here. Ever."

"If I do?"

"Then the lions on the veld will enjoy your carcass."

He assessed the threat and concluded that such an outcome was indeed possible. He was alone in an alien land. At a disadvantage. So he did the smart thing. "Am I dismissed?"

"These men will escort you to your hotel to retrieve your things, then to Bloemfontein and the airport. Be grateful that you are more valuable to me alive than dead."

"How can you be so sure that I won't report the truth?"

"You are not a man to report failure, particularly when your every action was anticipated. And coming off the debacle in Chile, that could deem you obsolete."

"You are well informed."

"More than you will ever realize. But I am no threat. So lie, Herr Engle."

"What of your aunt? She is a threat."

"I will deal with her. She will not be a problem for you. Leave her alone."

"That may not be possible."

"Then you, or anyone sent to harm her, will die."

It irked him that this Afrikaner knew him so well. Was he that transparent? Bruin was right, though. First the chaos caused by Ada's insane actions. Now this. Maybe it was better he relied on Bruin's assurances and Pohl knew nothing. "As you say, Herr Bruin. I am in no position to debate. I will report your untimely death."

Bruin turned to one of the other men and spoke in what he assumed was Afrikaans. Then the big man turned back and said, "Be good, Herr Engle. Try nothing. There are many more men, if these three prove inadequate."

He stepped away from the bed. His three escorts followed him.

Before leaving he stopped at the doorway and said, "You may know me, but I know men like you. True, I underestimated the situation. But now that I realize the depth of your connections, especially to your aunt, I see there is much more here. Yet perhaps you are right. All this has remained dormant for decades, and it is better left that way."

"I assure you, Herr Engle. That is truly the best course, especially for your employer and for *your* own continued good health."

CHAPTER FIFTY-SIX

Cotton listened as Schüb talked more about Martin Bormann.

"Chile and South America as a whole, after the war, swarmed with bounty hunters. The Israelis particularly were vigilant. It became increasingly difficult to stay in the shadows, even with local assistance. We learned of the Orange Free State from another German émigré, so in 1947 we managed to convince Bormann to come here."

"This was actually a great hiding place," Cotton said.

Schüb nodded. "That it was. The war was foreign to this place. Little to no impact. Lots of Germans were already around, from when the southwestern territory was colonized decades before. But Bormann never really grew comfortable here. The Widow, though, loved the place."

He was intrigued. "She sounds like a more complicated personality than history portrays."

"It wasn't long after we arrived that Luis and I went on a hunt. The Widow came, too. He never let her stray far from his sight. He shot a rather magnificent lioness who was guarding a single cub. We captured the cub and took it back to camp. Luis wanted to keep and train him, but the animal would not cooperate. Everything seemed to ruffle the cat's temper. He banged his head against the slats of the wooden container. Refused to eat. Bit the handlers. One night the animal butted his head enough to loosen one of the nailed boards at the top of the crate. The board gave way so that he could get his head out and taste just a bit of freedom. Unfortunately, there was not enough room for the rest of the body to squeeze through, so there he hung, his head free, still imprisoned, until he strangled himself to death." Schüb paused and caught a breath. "That's how I found him the next morning. I thought about that cub for many years. The Widow was the same. Part of her free, the rest contained. Eventually that combination killed her."

"Why did Bormann even want Braun?" Cassiopeia asked. "Historians universally agree that he thought her ignorant and shallow. Just let her go. Be rid of her."

"She was Hitler's, and that gave her value. I recall when he learned she was pregnant the second time. He simply smiled and ordered their marriage. He did not love her. He simply wanted to possess her. She never argued with the decision. That was not her way."

He decided to bring the conversation back on a relevant track. "What happened to the infant boys after Braun's death?"

"One was sent away. The other Luis raised, until the boy died in a fall."

"Where was the one who lived sent?" Cassiopeia asked.

"Germany."

"Why did he keep one?"

"He'd fathered ten children by his first wife. He was proud of that. But he hated when all of his children publicly rejected their heritage. His eldest even became a priest after the war, which particularly galled him. So the infant boy was to be his legacy, someone who would worship him unconditionally."

"What happened after the one boy was killed?" Cotton asked.

"It was the only time I ever saw him shed a tear. Quite a frightening sight, actually. The sadness of Martin Bormann."

He caught the sarcasm and registered the resentment. He wanted to understand it further. "I read your letters to your sister. Why did you remain here if you truly hated Bormann?"

"It was my duty. I was young, and that concept meant something to me. Perhaps, on reflection, it was foolish, but it did not seem so at the time. Then, after the Widow died, I stayed for the boy. Luis was immeasurably cruel to the child. He forced him to keep absolutely quiet and punished him severely with a dog whip or, even worse, with kicks. I recall once when he beat him because he was afraid of a large dog. He called it discipline, but it was nothing more than abuse. The boy needed me around. He and I spent a lot of time together. Then after he died, I stayed for myself. By then I'd met my wife, fallen in love with both her and this land. I was somebody here. Thomas Bruin. I would have been nothing anywhere else."

He wanted to know more about Schüb himself. "Why did you fake your death?"

"Two years ago Pohl began to plan his campaign for the chancellorship. He also began to assert himself with me. Prying, wanting more and more information, assistance, money. I thought it best that I leave the scene. So my death by natural causes was announced. There was a funeral, then I left the country and have lived elsewhere ever since. Rarely have I ventured back here."

"Where do you live?" Cotton asked.

"Switzerland. I am another person there, too. An old eccentric who bothers no one. But the possibility that Theodor Pohl could indeed become chancellor of Germany repulses me. He also used my name to entice the current chancellor to investigate things in Chile. Of course, he believes me dead. The entire web he's conceived jeopardizes everything Ada and I have done for the past six decades. I cannot allow him to succeed."

He could sense a man with a mission. "You know everything, don't you? All the secrets."

A distant sound caught his attention, and Cotton jerked his head to one side and focused out into the darkness beyond the trees.

"Hyenas," Schüb said. "Roaming the night. They and the jackals stay close to the gazelles, looking for the weak, but never do they meld. Predators are like that."

He looked back at the old man and waited for an answer to his question.

"*Ja,* Herr Malone. I am the only one left alive who knows it all."

. . .

Schüb strolled down the brick walk. The sun hung high in the African sky and baked the streets and rooftops of Johannesburg with blistering heat. He carried the baby gently in his arms, cradling the infant to his damp shirt, careful to ensure that the sun never found the milky white skin.

He stopped for a moment and studied the child.

The boy was sleeping, wrapped in a blanket and dressed in the christening gown that Eva Braun had labored the past few months to create. No one knew that she was carrying twins, and the midwife's abilities had been severely challenged with the difficult delivery. He'd asked Bormann if a doctor should be called but the demon refused, and the Widow died in a burst of agony as the second infant boy emerged from her womb. Bormann had said nothing afterward, simply staring at Braun's body for a few seconds, then turning his attention to his two sons, studying each carefully, examining their bluish skin, using a damp cloth to swipe away the blood and fluid, perusing their features like a potential buyer might study an antique. "This one seems stronger," Bormann said, pointing to the child on the left.

Still affected by Braun's death, Schüb forced himself to look away from the corpse on the bed, to the crib that one of the Africans had crafted specially for the occasion. "Does it matter?"

Bormann's gaze bore into him. "It matters a great deal."

"Your wife is dead."

"I do not need to be reminded of the obvious."

"You still intend to consummate the transaction?"

"Of course."

"What of your wife?"

"Bury her somewhere that the remains will not be found."

"Should she not be remembered?"

Bormann reached into the crib and lifted the infant on the left. "This one will be mine. He is all the memory I require. Take the other and keep the appointment."

He continued to study that infant, now safe in his arms, the one who'd lain on the right.

The Rejected One.

He was less than four hours old and had already experienced his first car ride on the trip north from the Free State. For the past month the couple had been waiting in

Johannesburg, as Braun's delivery time drew near. All had been arranged months ago, just after Braun had discovered she was pregnant and she and Bormann married. If she'd lived, Braun would have been told that the infant died at birth. He did not agree with Bormann on that issue, but had wisely kept his objections to himself. His employer was not a man given to debate or criticism.

He gently stroked the boy's cheek. The lips suckled as if it was time to feed. He had nothing to offer, so he tightened his grip on the tiny body and stepped to the entrance of the Hotel Maseru. On the second floor, in a corner room, a man opened the door. His round head was shaved clean, as was his genial face. He was heavy limbed with puffy hands and sausage fingers. The woman standing beside him was soft and ample with a pleasant, flattish, slightly masculine face.

"Guten abend," the man said as he closed the door.

The woman rushed to him and gazed at the baby. "Such a precious darling." She held out her arms, and Schüb knew what she wanted.

He handed her the infant.

"Liebling. So wonderful," she said, her eyes watering and tears beginning to race down her cheeks. "What sex?"

"A boy," Schüb said.

"How marvelous," the woman said through her tears. She faced her husband. "A boy. Our son."

The man drew close, his eyes, too, watering. He reached out and caressed the strands of matted black hair on the child's head. "He is a miracle."

Schüb knew he shouldn't. But his orders were clear. "There is one condition. It applies to the name."

The woman glanced up and smiled. "We know. What will he be called?"

"Theodor."

CHAPTER
FIFTY-SEVEN

"Theodor Pohl?" Cotton said.

Schüb nodded. "It was a decade before I saw the Pohl family again. In Germany. The boy was, by then, quite a specimen. Martin Bormann's legacy. Named for Bormann's father. Though he rejected the infant, he still wanted an element of control, so he picked both the parents and name."

"What was the point of sending the child away?" Cassiopeia asked.

"He'd planned that scenario long before he knew there were twins. If Eva Braun had lived, her child would have never stayed in Africa. So he arranged for a German family to adopt it, one who had been loyal to the Reich. But when she died and he saw the two babies, he thought that was a sign. He was superstitious in many ways. So he decided, then and there, to keep one of the infants as a connection to Germany. He was always distrustful of Africa. He despised the natives, and thought little of Afrikaners. To him, one was subhuman, the other an arrogant imitation of Aryan."

Cotton was confused. "So he kept what he perceived to be the strong son."

"That's correct. He was always distrustful of the Widow, which was why he originally planned on giving the baby away. But with her gone, he felt he could keep the child. He possessed a vision for that boy. I thought at the time those plans were ridiculous, but I have come to learn that his dreams may not have been so preposterous."

Cotton asked, "Who were the Pohls?"

"Wilfrid Pohl was a minor party official in Hesse during the war. One of Bormann's many informants, so he rewarded him. But remember, at the time Bormann believed that boy to be the weaker of the two, the one he did not want. So to him, it wasn't much of a reward."

"Until the child he kept died," Cassiopeia said.

"Precisely. Which meant he was given another opportunity with the Rejected One. The weaker, in his mind, of the two."

"He stayed in contact?" Cotton asked.

Schüb nodded. "Throughout the boy's childhood. Then, when Theodor attended university in Germany, after Wilfrid Pohl died, he told the boy the truth."

"Pohl knows who his natural father is?"

"He does, and they became quite close. During the last few years of Bormann's life, he and I spent a lot of time with the lad. Theodor worshiped him. Of course, the boy never knew he was the Rejected One."

"When did Bormann die?"

"He managed to live to old age. It was 1981 before the cigarettes finally killed him."

Cassiopeia shifted on the grass. "You said he had plans. What did Bormann have in mind?"

"He dreamed of his son one day ruling a unified Germany. He hated the Soviets. Despised communists. Loathed Americans. He wanted a Germany different from Hitler's dream, but still similar in many ways."

"Fascism would never be tolerated today," she said.

"Don't be so sure. Jews are tormented throughout Germany routinely, and have been for a long time. Foreigners are abused, even killed. Laws are being changed by the day in slow, imperceptible modifications, but in clear shifts toward the right. It is happening all over Europe. The cycle has begun again. Slow, but steady."

Cotton was not impressed. "The basic law of Germany, its constitution, has checks and balances in place that would prevent the rise of a demagogue."

"You misunderstand," Schüb quickly said. "I'm not speaking of a

Hitler. Or a dictator. Instead, Bormann recognized the need for a duly elected leader. One who comes to power in a fair and open contest. You are correct. The world has changed. Bormann foretold those changes, but he realized that the democratic process could be as effective an instrument of control as totalitarianism. Maybe even more so, since the people would actually choose that leader from a contested slate of candidates. A true popular mandate, if you will."

A mosquito whined near his ear and Cotton swiped the insect away. He kept listening as Schüb exhaled quickly, as if ridding himself of something unpleasant.

"I remember once we went on another hunt. North into Tanganyika territory. We heard breaking vegetation, snapping branches, heavy footfalls at a river's edge. It was dark and Bormann shone his light and found the eyes of a rhinoceros. The big beast immediately broke into a trot across the beam and came within twelve meters of us before stopping and letting out a blast of steam. Bormann started to play the light, which sent the animal into a blinding rage. Back and forth the rhino raced across the rays, charging the shadow at the beam's edge. Strangely, the animal never realized where the beam originated, he just kept marching back and forth, in and out of view. Then all of a sudden he caught the beam in his eye, squared and faced us with his chin out, two horns pointing straight ahead. He took two ponderous steps forward on stump-like feet. He was going to charge. I leveled my gun, but Bormann simply switched off the light and we stood in total darkness. A rhino, the size of a compact automobile, twelve meters away."

Cotton tried to visualize the scene. Not a place he'd want to be. "What happened?"

"The rhino simply walked away. Never did a thing. Just calmly walked away." The old man hesitated. "Bormann's voice came through the dark. He told me to learn from that. Every beast can be led. The talent is in controlling the method and possessing the ability to start and stop, never allowing anyone to know they are being led. He who possesses that, possesses all."

Cotton stared into the flat enamel eyes that apparently had borne witness to much.

"He liked to instruct," Schüb said. "He detested talking to the

Widow and, after she died, he formulated no new female relationships. Once the boy was killed, I was all that remained, until Theodor became older. So he told me a lot. He often prophesied about many things. I was a pupil in his mind."

"But you were never impressed?" Cassiopeia asked.

"Remember, history dubbed him Hitler's shadow. That was quite accurate since the shadow is always darker than the man. This was particularly true of Bormann. I shudder to think what more atrocities Germany would have committed if he had truly been in charge."

The night's peace was defiled by a long shrieking wail. A lot of information was coming their way, but there was one thing they desperately needed to know.

"Where are Bormann and Braun buried?" he asked.

Schüb shrugged with a surprising indifference. "Is that important?"

"It's vitally important. No one is going to believe any of this unless we have evidence. Skeletons are damn good proof. We can trace their descendants and match DNA for confirmation, then tie Pohl to them, too. Being the son of Martin Bormann and Eva Braun will come with political consequences. This is going to have to be demonstrated conclusively to the satisfaction of the world."

"I am not proof enough?"

"Hardly."

The old man went silent in the dark. Finally, he said, "All right. Tomorrow we will go to the graves."

CHAPTER
FIFTY-EIGHT

POHL WAS PREPARING FOR THE FIRST OF FOUR DEBATES WITH MArie Eisenhuth. Each would be televised nationwide starting in twelve days, and his staff had already composed a series of briefing books overflowing with information. It was vitally important that he appear both confident and knowledgeable. The subject matter of their first encounter would be the economy, followed by employment, foreign affairs, and lastly, at his insistence, immigration.

He was surprised Eisenhuth had agreed to the final topic.

Her stance was simple. Germany owed the world for the Holocaust and the price of that repayment had been an open border. No other nation on earth was shackled with such a legal requirement. Only Germany. And all for what happened over three generations ago. Every opinion poll showed that two-thirds of the nation favored a change in policy, and a change was what he intended to offer. Close the borders. Restrict immigration. Limit the rights of those already in Germany and hopefully they'd leave. Careful with oppression, though, just exploit the xenophobic fear that was rampant throughout the Continent. If France, Belgium, Holland, Denmark, Italy, and Spain joined with him, and there was every indication those nations eventually would, then the effort would not be viewed as oppression but popular sentiment. Together they could achieve what individually was barred.

But carefully. Slowly. Methodically.

Remember Hitler's error.

Don't rush it.

He was ensconced on the castle's third floor, the room paneled in native Hessian wood, the ceiling vaulted and tinted in varying shades of green. A Black Forest clock filled one corner and was less than forty-five minutes away from striking a chorus for midnight. Papers were strewn across an oak table ringed by four straight-backed chairs. The chamber was once where electors gathered to cast their ballots, as a previous owner of the castle possessed one of the precious votes for choosing the Holy Roman Emperor. He used the space for staff meetings since it sat in the upper reaches and ensured privacy.

He reached for a pitcher of beer and refilled his stein.

He glanced at the oil paintings on the walls. The scenes varied. Monks in prayer. An armored knight wearing a look as though it pained him, and another with a lord and lady glancing down disapprovingly. Each was an original of some value, not masterpieces, but collectibles. He liked them, and that was all that mattered since he thought it important to be surrounded by things one liked. A light tap on the door and one of the stewards entered and said, "There is a visitor downstairs."

He gripped the stein and started to enjoy the beer. "Who at this late hour?"

"Kurt Eisenhuth."

He showed no annoyance, though the imbecile's presence here, in his home, was a problem. But the meaning behind the man's appearance caused him even more concern.

Something was wrong.

"Bring him up."

As the steward left, he stepped to the window and glanced below. He hoped that, beyond the walls, the media was down for the night. Earlier, his staff had reported that no reporters were camped at the base of the drive leading up to the courtyard entrance, everyone apparently satisfied that the candidate was home until morning. They'd retake their positions early tomorrow, ready for another day on the campaign trail. He was ready, too. Things were finally starting to happen.

And now this.

Kurt Eisenhuth entered the room.

"Close the door," he said, not turning from the window. After the bolt clicked shut he said, "I hope this is important."

"Marie confronted me a couple of hours ago. She wanted to know about large sums of money that have been transferred from a Chilean bank into the company accounts. Money she says came from Hitler's Bounty."

He kept the smile to himself, brushed a strand of hair away, then slowly turned. "And the problem?"

"She was never supposed to learn about that."

He shrugged. "These things happen."

"You said there was nothing to worry about from that inspector in Chile."

"The revelation to her was necessary."

"What does that mean?"

The voice rose with anger. Interesting.

"Just what I said. She needed to know."

"Are you insane? If a connection is established to the past, she and I are both finished."

He stepped to the table and found his beer. "Come now, Kurt. Aren't you being a bit melodramatic? Blame it all on her father."

"I did. But she is also aware of transfers after his death."

"Do you monitor every euro that makes its way into the company coffers? No. Simply say Albert Herzog set all that up and you are only now becoming aware."

Kurt stepped forward, closer, too close. "You and I both know that the majority of that money has come after her father's death. He's been gone a long time."

He savored more of his beer, assessed the threat, and said, "This is no time to become self-righteous. That money compensated for a lot of hard times." He paused. "And bad management. I do not recall any objections from you."

"That was something started by Albert. I simply inherited the benefit and took advantage of it."

"But you accepted the funds. No questions. No refusals. Hitler's Bounty has been quite good to you."

"You are insane. You'll be the ruin of us all."

He tabled the stein. "Your wife must be stopped. Her time as our leader is over. *Oma* must be sent into retirement. She wants to reveal me as some kind of Nazi, but it is she who is the true fascist. She who benefited from that evil. The nation will fully understand her hypocrisy once this information is revealed."

"And you plan to publicize it?"

"I will not have to. That's the wondrous thing about this web I've woven. Once the transfers are confirmed and the source verified, which will not be hard, your wife will do all that for me. Ideologues are like that. Their own sense of personal worth compels them to insane honesty. She will reveal it all for me. I won't have to do a thing, except express my outrage. My party will then be swept into power."

"You perhaps underestimate Marie."

"Spoken like a devoted husband. I applaud your loyalty, though I did not believe you cared."

"Am I to be sacrificed as well?"

Now the real reason for the visit.

He shrugged. "Come now, Kurt. Many German corporations profited from the war and little has come of it, except for some token payments to survivors. They thrive and people forget. I tell you this, I shall reimburse whatever the corporation must pay in reparations."

"With more dirty money?"

"It spends the same as the clean."

"You did not answer my question."

He was witnessing a side to Kurt Eisenhuth never seen before, one that seemed to trigger self-preservation. But, he realized, even the weakest animal was programmed to survive. So he decided to be conciliatory. "No, Kurt, you are not to be sacrificed."

"Marie will not rest until she knows everything. I cannot have her discovering my involvement. I just managed to lie my way through a difficult encounter with her."

"Are you afraid that your weakness will diminish you in her eyes? She will think less of you? I thought your relationship had deteriorated past such pettiness."

"You don't know anything about our relationship."

He leveled his gaze and said, "I know your marriage is virtually nonexistent. I know you have several mistresses. So why not a new beginning for you? No more pretending. Be who you are. Why all this hostility?"

"You want me to turn on Marie? Publicly?"

"Why not? Plead ignorance. Blame her father. After all, he *was* a Nazi."

"She will defend him against all."

"Precisely. To her detriment."

He noticed Kurt's features soften, as if his anger passed as quickly as it matured. He'd read the man correctly.

But that wasn't all that difficult.

He wanted to smile, like a man who'd just solved a devilishly ingenious puzzle, but knew better.

Instead he bore in. "I am the hope for this nation, Kurt. You and I both know that. The time for apologists is over. Our atonement must end. Marie is the product of an era that has passed. I am the one who must fulfill Germany's destiny. We have to deal with reality, Kurt. As much as we may not like that reality, we have no choice." He, too, kept his tone low, like a father counseling a child. "Marie is a disappointment. You know that. Which is why you and I aligned to start with."

"I fully realize that."

The concession came on a breath.

Kurt Eisenhuth was a tool, nothing more, and on that point Hitler was correct. *Like a dutiful farmer, use your tools, care for each, then store them away to be used another day.*

Time to store this one away.

"Kurt, perseverance is what we need. I have the situation under control. So go home. Be patient. And I assure you, your wife will be the only casualty from any of this."

CHAPTER
FIFTY-NINE

Free State, South Africa
Sunday, June 16
7:00 a.m.

Cotton rose from the bed. Cassiopeia was still asleep beside him. He grabbed his laptop and booted up the machine. Danny Daniels needed to know about the new developments, but he wanted to be sure about Gerhard Schüb, or whoever that old man really was last night, before doing so. One constant that had become painfully obvious over the past few days was that nothing was as it appeared. Certainly Schüb had made an impression, a supposedly firsthand witness to the fact that Martin Bormann and Eva Braun survived the war and parented a son, who was now a candidate to be chancellor of Germany.

Exactly what they'd been sent to confirm.

It might be true. Then again, it might not.

So a little homework was in order.

He found the dossier that Marie Eisenhuth had supplied on Pohl and reread the information.

Birth records on file in Hesse indicate a date of birth of March 15, 1952, to Wilfrid and Cornelia Pohl. Wilfrid Pohl studied national economy at the University of Berlin. After World War I he was a founder of the German Democratic Party and advocated national democracy. He was forced to leave that party after an internal scandal. He shifted ideologies and was elected to the Reichstag by

the conservative German People's Party, and became a member of
the Reich Economic Council. Eventually he headed the Reichs-
bank office in Frankfurt until 1941. He then became president
of the senate in Hesse, working for the National Socialists. No
evidence of anything criminal ever surfaced in his past, and he
escaped postwar prosecution. Little is known of Cornelia Pohl.

Theodor was an only child, raised in southern Hesse. He attended university in Cologne but finished his studies in Munich.
Grades average. No honors. Married for a short while, now divorced. He has no known children.

Three interviews with persons in Hesse, who were living
in the 1940s and 1950s, confirm that the Pohls parented a boy
named Theodor. None could recall any specifics of the birth.
Postwar was a chaotic time, they all explained. Each seemed surprised by an assertion that the child may not have been the Pohls',
but all commented that there were many orphans at that time
who needed homes and everyone did their part. All note that the
Pohls were quiet and reserved. None could recall any controversy
surrounding them.

Wilfrid Pohl, though a Nazi Party official, served in the postwar government and aided in restoring the German banking system. Again, nothing unusual since many ex-Nazis were recruited
for postwar government service. The Pohls lived modestly. Wilfrid Pohl died in 1974, his wife in 1977.

Theodor moved into the business world immediately after
university. He was a real estate speculator for a number of years
and made some wise investments in Frankfurt, which turned
huge profits. He financed several massive building projects and
continues to receive generous rent payments. He moved into the
publishing business by age thirty-five and now commands one of
the largest media conglomerates in Germany. Books, periodicals,
radio, television, movies. His net worth was recently estimated by
Stern at 2.5 billion euros. Passport records indicate—

Cassiopeia sat up in the bed and shook the sleep from her eyes. She
was fully dressed, as was he. They'd both slept ready for trouble.

"Pohl has traveled a lot," he said. "But not here. I thought I recalled that detail. Take another look at this."

He passed her the laptop, then stepped into the bathroom and splashed warm water on his face and brushed his teeth. The past few days had been long, and he was still jet-lagged from the flight over the Atlantic.

A lot was happening.

And he was supposed to be retired.

He wondered about his bookshop. He loved that place, its air constantly reeking of old paper and musty leather. The previous proprietor had not kept the stacks in order and he'd worked for three months before opening the doors to rearrange everything, taking his organizational cue from other stores in Copenhagen. Bookselling seemed an art form in Denmark. There was a real appreciation for the written word, one he'd come to admire. He'd even done something unusual for him. He joined the Danish Antiquarian Booksellers Association and made a point to attend their monthly gatherings. Thankfully, he'd hired great people and realized they would keep an eye on things, like always.

He stepped back into the room, patting his face with a towel.

"I think Schüb is for real," she said. "We can put an end to Theodor Pohl. But those financial records will also end Eisenhuth."

"Both these politicians want a firing squad, but they're circling up to fire. Still, something about this doesn't ring right. It's bothered me all night. There's more happening than we can see."

"Any theories?"

Before he could answer, a knock on the rondavel's door drew his attention. Awful early for visitors. He stepped over and peered out the window as Cassiopeia reached for her weapon. Jan Bruin stood outside. Alone.

Cotton signaled all was good and opened the door.

"Good morning," the hefty Afrikaner said in English. "I've come to fetch you for my father."

He stepped back and let the big man enter. Bruin was dressed in jeans and a work shirt. Schüb told them last night someone would come by.

"A cold morning ensures a warm day," Bruin said.

He wasn't interested in a weather report. "Your father seems to be in charge, despite the fact he's supposed to be dead."

Bruin chuckled. "He does look good for a corpse. But I bow to his seniority. He is, after all, my father." Bruin faced Cassiopeia. "And good morning to you, Fräulein Vitt. I must apologize to you both for the deception yesterday. I assumed you were aware I was lying about Herr Engle."

"We were," he said.

"You kept that fact close," Bruin said. "Well done."

"You're a pretty good liar yourself," Cassiopeia said.

Bruin chuckled. "We had to make an assessment. My dear aunt Ada called and told us that you may be coming. She told us all about what happened in Chile and said you were people we could trust. But we've learned to be cautious. Last night I dealt with Josef Engle. I so wanted to kill him, but Father had a much better idea."

Bruin told them what occurred at his home. "Engle boarded a plane six hours ago. He is now on his way to Paris."

"And then to Germany?" Cassiopeia said.

"Most certainly," Bruin said. "I believe Father's assumptions are correct and Engle will not tell Pohl that I am still alive."

"Welcome to the realm of the corpses," Cotton said. "Seems we're all dead. So what now?"

"You wanted to see the graves. I am here to take you. Father will meet us at the cemetery. And bring your things. We will not be returning here."

Cotton had already concluded that the South African connection was played out. "How about we leave in thirty minutes. A shower would be welcome."

Cassiopeia stood from the bed. "I agree."

CHAPTER SIXTY

COTTON MARVELED AT THE RIDE FROM NOHANA ACROSS THE FREE
State, which revealed 150 miles of bleached earth dotted with towering,
chocolate-brown anthills, some six feet high. Occasionally the sparse-
ness was broken by farms, the sun quivering off corrugated iron roofs.

Leaving the Free State, they entered the adjacent province and the
town of Kimberley, just over the border. He was familiar with the locale. The heart of the country's diamond industry and home to the
original De Beers mine, it was brown and ugly with streets laid out
by diggers seemingly in a hurry, their shacks gone, the modern buildings huddled together like a crowd of those miners reveling in a find.
The real wealth of the area was clearly not the land itself, but what was
beneath—gold, diamonds, minerals—enough to have made some men
obscenely rich.

He drove the Range Rover while Cassiopeia sat in the rear and
Bruin filled the front passenger seat. He followed the big man's directions as they wove through Kimberley and turned north, paralleling the
Vaal River, the earth flat, red, and fiery. Then the landscape changed
at the quaint settlement of Christiana. Lines of poplar started to fringe
the riverbank and miles of concrete channels funneled water westward,
transforming the earth into green fields of corn, lucerne, mealie, and
potatoes. They passed through town and found a cemetery to the east,

within sight of the river. A tall white man wearing a dirty sun helmet, a bush shirt, and a pair of shabby trousers approached the car through a partially open iron gate. Bruin climbed out and talked to him, then motioned for them to drive through as the gate swung open.

"Park over there," Bruin said, motioning.

The grassy cemetery was spread out over a large area under the shade of tall gum trees. A low mortar wall edged the perimeter. Crosses, obelisks, and headstones of varying shapes broke the flatness. Shrubs and flowers congregated at spots like mourners around the graves. An assortment of small chapels and mausoleums rose throughout.

"This was officially whites only, until recently," Bruin said.

"Why do I get the impression it still is?" he asked.

"Sadly, there are many in this country who still long for apartheid. Even in death."

A storm was brewing to the west, the clouds thick and black and fed by a blazing sun that refused to be shielded. He stared ahead at one of the marble mausoleums. Gerhard Schüb stood outside an open gate. They walked over to him, past split-slate gravestones and moldering tombs.

"I made the decision to bury them here," Schüb said as they approached. "Bormann owned an interest in several Kimberley mines. He came to this area often. And it was away from Nohana."

"I'm surprised Bormann even allowed his body to be buried," Cassiopeia said.

"He would be, too," Schüb said. "His orders were for his corpse to be burned. Like Hitler's. He did not want anyone finding his remains."

"Why did you disobey?" Cassiopeia asked.

The old man shrugged. "I was no longer required to follow orders. So I did as I pleased. I put him beside the Widow and his son. I thought it fitting that he be in the same innocuous location as they."

"You're a strange man," Cotton declared, not caring if he insulted the German.

"I would agree. My life has been unusual, to say the least. I am ashamed to say that I allowed loyalty, greed, and pride to dictate my decisions. But if I had not, I would not now have Jan, and he is my joy." The old man smiled at his son. "A father should be so lucky."

The younger Bruin said nothing. He didn't have to. The bond between them was clear.

"Wasn't putting Bormann here, by Braun, an insult to her?" Cassiopeia asked.

Schüb shrugged. "It mattered not anymore. Both were dead and it made it easier for me to keep watch."

He was curious. "From whom?"

"I never really knew. I just realized that my task was not over. Something told me this day might come."

They approached the open grille and studied the mausoleum's interior. A simple mixture of marble and granite. Nothing religious or personal. No inscriptions.

"You're not a God-fearing man?" he asked Schüb.

"From all I've seen in my life, if there is a God he's quite terrible at what he does." Schüb came close. "The Widow feared being buried in the veld—that the animals would feast on her body. She many times said she would not want to be anywhere the beasts could find her."

"Bormann never questioned you about what you did with her body?" Cassiopeia asked.

He watched the old man as he considered her inquiry. The eyes were those of someone who'd given up expecting good news.

Which was understandable.

"He told me to dispose of her, and I did. He never asked where. This was my place. My creation. Known only to me." He motioned. "Shall we go inside?"

They stepped from muggy air into a cooler space. A block of dull light from the open doorway lit the far wall. The interior was a rectangle about twenty feet long and nearly that wide. Three raised tombs dominated the interior, two long, one small, clearly a child's.

Schüb seemed to notice their interest. "I read once where Bormann wrote to his first wife during the war and told her that he wanted no cheap exhibitions at his death. They gave a false impression, he said. I believe I honored that request. Besides, many in this land mark their graves sparingly."

He did the math. Braun and the boy would have been dead nearly seventy years, Bormann over forty. Surely, though, some semblance of DNA could be recovered and a scientific verification made on the remains from known descendants that could be matched to Pohl.

He stepped to the smaller of the three sarcophagi and slid back the slab of gray marble that covered the top just enough to peer inside. He expected to see the remains of a small child, maybe five to six years old, the body decayed, only blackened bones signaling that the occupant was once human.

But to his surprise there was nothing.

"It's empty."

"That's not possible."

The old man stepped close and peered inside. For the first time Schüb showed bewilderment. "I put him there. It was so sad. My heart still hurts for him. He was a darling lad."

The pain in the old man's voice was clear.

Cotton stepped to one of the other tombs, this one of light pink marble. He assumed it was Eva Braun's.

"She loved that color," Schüb said.

The lid covering the marble rectangle was thick. He would need help sliding it aside. Jan Bruin came close and together they angled one corner to the left, exposing a dark triangular opening.

"There's nothing here, either," he said.

"I was present when the lid was closed," Schüb said. "I have maintained this mausoleum for decades. It has remained inviolate."

"When was the last time the tomb was checked?" Cassiopeia asked.

"Given my 'death,' it has been over two years."

Cotton moved to Bormann's sarcophagus. He and Bruin slid the white marble lid ajar. Empty, as well.

Gerhard Schüb stood deep in thought, but it was clear that what they'd found was unexpected. "This changes everything."

"I assumed you had something in mind."

"I did, until this. We need to leave."

"Where are we going?"

"To where there are answers."

He and Bruin maneuvered the lids back into place.

"Care to say where?" Cassiopeia asked.

Schüb was standing at the doorway, staring out into the cemetery. Drops of rain were starting to sprinkle down, peppering the mausoleum's iron roof in a steady *rat-tat-tat.*

The old man turned back and said, "Switzerland."

CHAPTER
SIXTY-ONE

Lugano, Switzerland
Monday, June 17
2:00 p.m.

Cotton stood on the terrace and admired both the lake and the surrounding snowcapped Alps. The Italians called the indigo water Ceresio while the Swiss labeled it Lugano, which illustrated the dichotomy of the region since Italy controlled the south shore, the Swiss the north. A great cloud wrapped Mount San Salvatore in the distance with a mantle of cotton haze, its gnarly peak like a great tusk thrusting toward heaven.

Gerhard Schüb's villa dominated fifteen acres of pristine shoreline southwest of Lugano. Its elegant façade was a pale-yellow brick adorned with elaborate painted friezes, and not even the trumpery additions could obscure its grandeur. Rooted periwinkles and creeping ivy sprang from black marble basins. Renaissance doorways, gilded paneling, rich tapestries, and terra-cotta floors completed what was clearly a Mediterranean feel. He and Schüb had arrived in Lugano by military transport, while Cassiopeia and Jan Bruin flew on to Munich. They'd devised a plan. Cassiopeia would speak with Marie Eisenhuth, and Bruin would be the incontrovertible evidence needed to convince her of what was happening and what had to be done.

He stared out at the lake and focused on a zone of reflected light, bright off the distant Alpine peaks, a dazzling radiance that slowly crept across the still water. He remained apprehensive, concerned, a bit confused, and sought reassurance from the tranquil scene, watching two squirrels darting among a scattering of pendent fir cones at the muddy shoreline.

A door opened and Schüb stepped onto the terrace.

The old man walked straight to where he stood beside the balustrade. A few feet below, the lake gently lapped a concrete wall. As the German drew close, two narrow slits revealed eyes that were mild and meek, but, like him, also anxious.

"Here I am known as Simone Tenglemann, an Austrian, retired and living a life of leisure," Schüb said. "That is the wonderful thing about the Swiss. Few questions are asked and privacy is respected."

"A beautiful choice of locale for a dead man."

"The fact that this Swiss town faces south is quite symbolic. In the 1960s Italians flocked here to avoid taxes and the communists. Northern Italy, at the time, was home to the largest Communist Party in the Western world. Workers in Italy possessed the vote, and there was a real danger of a Bolshevik rise. So the rich came here to stash their gold, currency, and assets, most of it smuggled in. Banks sprouted, and they were all quite accommodating. Much more relaxed than Zurich or Geneva. Few rules, which remains true even today."

"You came then?"

Schüb nodded. "Bormann wanted the money in Swiss banks. He left the details to me. Much later, when I decided to 'die' and leave South Africa, this location was a logical choice of where I would live."

"You seem to have profited from your years of service. I would imagine this house was not cheap."

"I had total control of all the funds Bormann once dominated."

"Nazi money?"

"It is. But money, nonetheless."

"And what were you supposed to do with those funds?"

"Theodor was to have it all."

"But you decided that wasn't such a good idea."

"I provided him with nearly 350 million euros in liquid assets."

"What you mean is, you gave him the stuff that was traceable. Interests in the diamond mines, real estate, stocks, and a token sum from the hoarded assets."

A smile crept onto the old man's withered face, the skin yellowed and blistered like ancient vellum. "Precisely. He had no way of challenging me. I was the only one with records."

"How much was left?"

"Hard to say. But it was substantial. Maybe five billion euros."

He didn't doubt that observation, recalling the billions generated from not only the Holocaust, but the war itself. Plunder reaped huge rewards.

He stared across the terrace at the statue of a naked young man, his limbs wobbly, the sculptor obviously taking liberties with nature's idea of beauty. More statues filled marble niches in the walls. His host had surely paid handsomely for the craftsmen needed to fashion both the decoration and the villa. "It doesn't bother you where the money came from?"

"I have long ago lost any semblance of conscience. And philosophizing will not make it any better. I did not steal the money or kill the victims."

"You just enjoyed the spoils."

Schüb stood impassive, as if considering the observation. A sad, remorseful mien swept across his face.

Bells clashed in the distance.

"Through the years, my son has said the same thing to me. I don't expect forgiveness or understanding, only that, before I die, I will try to make amends. You are right. I owe it to the victims, and it's time to pay that debt."

Lugano sat at the end of a deep bay framed by Mount Brè to the north and Mount San Salvatore to the south. The road into town wound through rugged Alpine scenery fringed with melancholy gray olive trees, white arcaded houses, and quaint inns, the lake cast in a cold leaden tint by light fading behind the peaks. Downtown was impressive with cypress, palm, and monkey puzzle trees lining arcades that hummed with a feverish pitch, the look more reminiscent of Southern California than southern Switzerland.

A driver deposited him and Schüb in front of a neoclassical building on busy Via Nassa. Only bars on the windows and a discreet bronze plaque—E. ORELLI & CIE, BANKIERS—announced the fact that the location was a bank.

"This is a private institution," Schüb said. "Consequently, they are not required to publish records or provide balance sheets. Even the local tax officials leave them alone."

Inside were roomfuls of period furniture and faded portraits illuminated by Bohemian chandeliers. Edouard Orelli himself was waiting for Schüb. He was a rosy, pleasant little man who reeked of cigars. He exchanged pleasantries with Schüb then led them downstairs, through a vault door, into an underground chamber. Orelli excused himself and Cotton followed Schüb down a brightly lit corridor lined with stainless-steel doors.

"Edouard has been most helpful through the years. He has set up investment trusts, purchased securities, offered tax advice." They reached one of the steel doors, and Schüb punched in a numerical code.

The lock clicked open.

Schüb pushed open the door. "And he obtained gold bullion."

The windowless room was forty or so feet square, its gray tile floor nearly obscured by stacks of gold bars, ten on each side, stacked high, at least a dozen piles in all. Cotton stepped close and examined one of the pallets. "There must be several hundred million dollars' worth of bullion here."

"A fraction over a billion actually."

"This is Hitler's Bounty?"

"What is left of it. Of course, I have multiplied the principal with wise investments."

He'd never seen so much gold.

"The Orellis are quite astute in the bullion trade. It is one of the hallmarks of the Lugano banks. Gold is truly forever. Hard to err with it."

He lifted one of the bars. Maybe thirty or so pounds, he estimated. He studied the top, half expecting to see a swastika etched into the surface. But there was nothing save for a notation on a purity rating of 999.9.

"The encounter in South America from a few years ago," he said. "With two American agents. Jonathan Wyatt and Christopher Combs. There was a report of pallets of gold."

"All fake," Schüb said. "We manufactured the scene. I orchestrated things from here, with Ada's help there. Only a few bars of that gold were real. We created the rest from tungsten. It's a common practice, and easy to do. We went to a lot of trouble in that encounter. The Americans had ventured far too close. I even had fake graves staged with sarcophagi, patterning them from the real ones you saw yesterday. After, everything was removed and we burned the house down so there'd be no remnants to find. A local man, a former SS officer, played me. He killed one of the Americans. Christopher Combs. The other, Jonathan Wyatt, became the messenger whom we ultimately discredited."

"A lot of the information I've heard and seen here was similar there, too."

Schüb nodded. "I provided all of that to Ada. Wyatt was shown some of my letters. Forgeries from the originals. He was also told and shown information I knew on Bormann. Similar to what you've been privy to read and hear. I thought the truth far easier to use than a lie. But they were told a slightly different story. In that version, Gerhard Schüb was the son of Hitler. Of course, Isabel's murder during that operation was never anticipated. That was Theodor's addition to the plan."

"Ada hasn't forgotten that."

"I know. All has been quiet since then. Until now. This was her opportunity, and I did nothing to dissuade her. Sadly, for Theodor, violence is the way to every end." Schüb paused a moment, grabbing a breath. "He and I were still on good terms then. After that things changed, and I decided it was time for me to die."

The room went silent for a moment.

"Bormann possessed a great hatred for the follies of man," Schüb said. "All who knew him were aware of that fact. No tolerance for frailty or passion, no mercy for evil, no pity for those who'd done him harm. He wished his enemies to hell, and put them there in his heart. He was, quite simply, a man of wrath. Theodor is exactly the same."

"Yet you served Bormann until he died."

Schüb took a disconsolate stroll around the stacks of gold bars, eyeing the gleaming metal in the cool white glow of the overhead fluorescent fixtures. "I served him. I even profited from him. All of this gold was re-smelted from its original shape and source, stamped with prewar markings to disguise its origins. But who knows what evil brought it here. I am now prepared to do what has to be done to right at least some of those wrongs."

"What do you propose? We can't prove anything. We have no bodies for DNA testing. Only this gold and your word."

"That is not true."

Now he was interested. "I'm listening."

Schüb motioned to a corner of the vault. Cotton's attention had been on the obvious and he'd failed to notice a wooden crate against the far wall. He followed Schüb around the stacks and glanced inside.

"I told you that toward the end of his life Bormann and Theodor communicated more frequently. To facilitate those encounters, Bormann started writing down his thoughts. He did this while serving Hitler also. He was obsessive about note-taking. *The savior of the administrator,* he would say. He created meticulous journals, textbooks he called them, for Theodor to study. We even used a set of forgeries in Chile with Combs and Wyatt. They'd been prepared a few years before to thwart another pair of nosy eyes and ears. Being forgeries came with the ability of allowing them to be discovered, which would totally discredit anyone who tried to claim them as real."

"Provided the forgers remained silent."

"None lived to an old age."

He got the message. "I take back what I said about you in Africa. You're not strange. You're dangerous."

"I was taught by one of the most ruthless men in the world, and I learned many things from him."

That he could believe.

"After Bormann died," Schüb said, "I gave many of the originals to Theodor, but kept a sizable number for myself. Also, the Widow maintained private diaries that she gave me for safekeeping. They tell her story far better than I ever could. But as I said, she knew nothing of her children. Her thoughts are of Hitler, Bormann, and what fate had prescribed for her. Bormann's journals, though, are far more extensive."

Cotton glanced into the open crate and saw that there were a number of leather-bound notebooks of varying shapes, sizes, and colors, all in remarkably good condition.

"I stored them carefully. They have been here for decades. I assure you, each is authentic and can sustain any test an expert cares to impose. Verified handwriting samples of Bormann and Braun would be easy to obtain for comparison, and the paper and ink are of the period."

He lifted out one of the books and parted the cover, studying the heavy, clearly male handwriting. He read some of the first entry. Bormann was lamenting about Khrushchev and how communism could never succeed. "This was written in the 1950s?"

"Not at all. Bormann penned most of these in the 1970s. His diction and syntax only create the illusion they were written contemporaneously. Remember, Bormann dealt in the realm of fantasy. He was a butcher and a murderer who thought himself brilliant, and he made himself so through hindsight."

"Which made Pohl believe he was a genius."

"Something like that. I read these journals with amusement. More of Bormann's pedantic personality."

He tossed the book back into the crate. "So they're historically useless. Am I, too, being manipulated?"

"The time for lies is over," Schüb said. "I brought you here to see this. You're the first person ever so privileged. I also want you to read one passage from the journals."

The old man reached down and removed another of the notebooks.

"More fiction?" he asked.

"No. This is real. I remember purchasing this notebook on one of my monthly trips to Johannesburg. I was to always buy half a dozen, never similar, and never at the same location. I found this one at a bookstore, near the post office, in the winter of 1956. It has rested here, on top, for a long time." Schüb handed him the volume. "The relevant part is marked."

He accepted the book and carefully opened to the page indicated. The leather binding cracked from the strain. More of the same male handwriting filled the sheet.

He read.

"I watched Bormann write those words myself," Schüb said.

He kept reading. His gaze halted, reversed itself, then scanned the lines again. He looked up in amazement.

"This can't be."

"As I said, this is the time for truth. Not only can it be, it is."

CHAPTER SIXTY-TWO

MUNICH, GERMANY
8:30 P.M.

MARIE TRIED HARD TO CONCENTRATE ON THE OPERA. SHE WAS
sitting in the Residenz Theater, the quadrangular hall a rococo gem
lined with gilded colonnades and elaborate loges that ran from floor to
ceiling. Mozart himself once commanded this stage, which for centuries was the Bavarian king's court theater. Now it was owned by the
state. Tonight's performance was a black-tie affair involving some of the
wealthiest people in southern Germany. The mood was high and festive,
the event an annual spectacular. With the national elections upcoming
she and Theodor Pohl had been invited and both were in attendance,
one of the few joint appearances they would make until their debates.
But the gala was billed as a night for charity without politics.

Which was fine by her.

Tonight was definitely not going to be about politics.

The music rose and fell with bursts of melody, sinking into hushed
chords before pealing forth in basso profundo. The opera was in three
acts, each more profound than the other. The symbolism was evident,
and she almost smiled at the choice of performance. A wicked countess
and her niece, who both wore silk shawls, the niece casting hers away—
in essence throwing off the yoke of aristocracy, becoming, as the lyrics
noted, an honest burgher maiden once again.

Interesting.

And prophetic.

She glanced across the darkened theater toward Pohl. He sat in a similar red velvet chair, both of them on the same level, with the same view. On the wall to Pohl's right loomed a sculpted Virgin standing on the moon, beneath which was a half-faced devil appearing in great discomfiture. At the moment she felt like that devil, her position equally as oppressed. Her opponent sat straight and still, his attention on the stage. She wondered what he was thinking. Nothing she'd read or been told about him indicated any great love for the arts. She doubted if he even understood the performance.

She glanced around the darkened hall.

Strange, but she did not feel drawn to any of the wealthy patrons. She felt a greater kinship to the panting old ladies with bows in their hair who ran the garderobe, and the frock-coated pensioners who held the key to the loge, and the younger gentlemen, dressed in tails, who'd shown them to their seats, and, even more so, to the dear hausfraus who cared for the patrons as if they were intimate friends. They were the backbone of Germany. The men and women who toiled to sustain a grand culture.

And she must never forget them.

On one count Pohl was right. None of those people bore any direct responsibility for what happened from 1933 to 1945. That was the folly of another generation, and too few of them remained to really matter any longer. What the people in the hall and the rest in Germany bore was the burden of assuring that nothing like that ever happened again. And the man sitting across the hall from her, still staring down at the stage, was a direct link to that awful past.

He must be stopped.

Tonight.

As soon as the final curtain fell.

Marie entered the banqueting hall located adjacent to the theater. A food table lined one wall, the serving plates heaped with pork, beef, smoked salmon, and salad. Though hungry, she avoided the crowded line and drifted toward one of her aides. The young man was instantly attentive, and she told him what she wanted him to do. He nodded and dissolved into the crowd of patrons surrounding her. She was told earlier that the press would be barred from the event, allowing for a more relaxed atmosphere, and that fact had sparked her thinking.

The aide returned a moment later and whispered in her ear. "Herr Pohl says he will be glad to speak with you in private."

She waited a few moments to give Pohl time to leave, then excused herself and climbed a set of marble stairs to the third floor where the room she'd requested was located. It was a holding spot for the performers before they went onstage.

She stepped inside.

Theodor Pohl turned to greet her. "I was surprised by your request, but intrigued enough to agree."

She closed the door.

Strange, she thought. The two of them were engaged in one of the hottest political battles in recent German history, almost daily launching volleys of volatile rhetoric back and forth, yet they hardly knew each other. Her contact with Pohl prior to the campaign was little beyond a few light conversations at social gatherings. Theirs was a relationship born of differing philosophies, their contrasts too great for them ever to be anything but opposites.

"Herr Pohl, I thought it best we talk."

"I gathered. What is so critical?"

"I am aware of your parentage."

He shrugged. "My mother and father were quite known in Hesse."

"I do not mean the Pohls. I am referring to your natural father, Martin Bormann, and your natural mother, Eva Braun."

He chuckled. "Have you been drinking?"

She ignored the question. "I recently was sent some information. Of course, you know this already, since it came from you."

"This is quite fascinating. Do continue."

"You were born in the Orange Free State, South Africa, one of two twin boys. Eva Braun, your mother, died at childbirth. You were given to the Pohls for adoption. Your brother stayed with Bormann until 1955, when he was killed in a fall from a horse. It was then that Bormann, your natural father, reentered your life, where he stayed until he died in 1981."

Pohl moved toward a small velvet sofa and took a seat. "I take back what I said earlier about your imagination. You are truly talented."

She'd expected bravado, so his comment meant nothing. "When I received the information detailing your relationship with Bormann and Braun, at first I believed it to be a hoax, but I have come to learn what all of it truly was." She paused. "Bait. For me to go look and destroy myself."

"And how did you come to that conclusion?"

She stepped toward the door and opened it.

Cassiopeia Vitt and Jan Bruin entered.

She closed the door and introduced them. "Herr Bruin's father is a man named Gerhard Schüb, whom I am told you know quite well."

"And who told you that?"

"Herr Schüb himself. He did not die two years ago. He is still alive." She watched closely for any reaction. Surely seeing Vitt was a jolt—she was supposed to have been blown up—but the combination of Jan Bruin and Gerhard Schüb, both still breathing, too, had to be disconcerting.

But Pohl maintained a stiff façade.

He was good, she'd give him that.

"We've never met," Bruin said. "But I was told a great deal about you from my father. I did meet your associate. Herr Engle. He came to kill me but, as you can see, was unsuccessful."

"I have no idea what you are talking about," Pohl declared in a low, solemn tone.

"Josef Engle is employed by you," Cassiopeia said. "He killed four people in Chile that we know about. He most likely killed a woman here in Germany named Hanna Cress. What do they call you in private? The Kaiser. Before she died, Hanna Cress uttered that word."

"I am curious, how do you intend to prove any of this? I will gladly submit to any test you care to run. Blood. DNA. Whatever you suggest."

"Which is kind of you," Marie said. "Considering that the graves of Braun, Bormann, and your brother are empty. There is nothing to compare your DNA with, or at least nothing that could provide a conclusive verification. Isn't that convenient."

"You located graves?"

"We did," Cassiopeia said. "The tombs are empty. But you already knew that."

Pohl did not answer. Instead he faced Marie. "I invite you to make this public. Please. It is precisely what the people need to hear. You have tried in vain to brand me a dangerous fanatic. Let the nation see that you are a deranged conspiratorialist."

"So you can steer the press toward the current investigation of my family concerns? You wanted us to find those financial records. You made sure we found them. But you never factored in that Schüb was still alive. You used his name in your contacts to me to give credence to your bait. But it's all turned around on you now."

"Assuming any of that is true, what do you intend to do?"

"I intend to do nothing," she flatly said.

"Then what is the point of this?"

"Simply to let you know what I know. All of us in this room know it is true. I will leave what happens next to you. Whatever that might be, it will be mutually assured destruction. You and I, and our parties, will go down together. Neither of us will be the next chancellor. Neither of us will even be in office."

A moment of strained silence passed between them.

"I assume this Gerhard Schüb is nearby to verify what you say?" Pohl asked.

"Close by, in fact. He's with Cotton Malone, whom your associate also failed to kill."

Pohl shook his head. "Another ancient Nazi trying to make a name for himself. Pathetic."

He stepped toward the door. "I'm leaving now."

"One thing, Herr Pohl," Marie said.

Pohl stopped at the door and turned back.

"Did I say Gerhard Schüb was a Nazi? I only mentioned he was a man you know. What gave you the impression of something otherwise?"

She couldn't resist.

Pohl stood impassive.

"Lügen haben kurze beine," she said in a quiet tone.

Lies have short legs.

Pohl left the room.

CHAPTER
SIXTY-THREE

MARIE STEPPED OUT INTO THE COOL NIGHT.

Nearly two hours had passed since her talk with Pohl. After, she'd noticed that if the Hessian was flustered he concealed his annoyance behind a remarkably pleasant façade. He'd worked the reception with determination, smiling, talking, and posing for pictures with one patron after another. She, too, had moved from person to person, fraternizing with the tenacity of a party leader determined to win.

Their paths never crossed, which was fine.

Enough had been said.

Pohl had left a few minutes before her, quickly climbing into a late-model Mercedes, ignoring the press. She noticed that Cassiopeia Vitt paid close attention, hoping perhaps Josef Engle would be in the car, but no one was inside except an anonymous driver. Earlier, she'd dismissed her regular driver, and Jan Bruin now waited behind the wheel of a black BMW coupe. The rear passenger-side door was open, and she climbed into the backseat. Two security men were in a lead vehicle.

She'd not been able to dismiss them.

Her exit from the theater was illuminated by a strobe of photographic flash. Reporters and camerapeople had been kept behind a barricade on the sidewalk and were now taking advantage of their one photo opportunity. Several screamed questions, but she politely waved them off as she closed the BMW's rear door.

"Let's go," Vitt said from the front seat.

Bruin eased from the curb.

They were headed south, out of Munich, to the lake district and the Herzog ancestral *schlöss*.

"Do you think Herr Pohl took the bait?" Marie asked from the back-seat.

"He has no choice," Vitt said. "He can't take the chance that you might act, regardless of proof. He now knows he's vulnerable."

The idea had been to spook Pohl with what they knew, suggest that they knew even more, and make him aware that everyone he thought dead was alive. All to worry him. Playing off his irrational fears. Forcing, perhaps, a mistake.

"The first thing he will do is go after Engle," Bruin said. "His employee clearly lied about my demise. That he will not tolerate. It should create some chaos."

"He'll also want to know why Cotton and I are still around," Vitt said. "Pohl will be angry, but he still needs Engle. Now more than ever."

"We are collectively targets now," Marie muttered.

"Quite correct," Bruin said. "He has the age-old dilemma every despot faces of too many targets. He will have to choose his battles."

They left the lights and traffic of Munich for the darkness of a two-lane highway that steadily rose into the Alpine foothills, following the security men in front.

"Has anything been heard from Herr Malone?" she asked.

"Not a word," Vitt answered.

Marie knew that Schüb had wanted Malone to go with him to Switzerland. There was something important there, something the old man wanted to share. So the continued silence was indeed troubling.

"My father is a secretive person," Bruin said. "I only learned the truth about his life when I was nearly thirty years old. He was trained to keep things close to himself."

"My father was the same," she said.

She thought about her dear papa. Born into an ancient aristocratic family of reactionary politicians, passionate in their beliefs, yet practical in application. Her mother was the daughter of a mayor, the marriage arranged. True to his Herzog heritage, her father led the anti-Polish movement that swept through Germany in the early 1930s, eventually raising money from industrialists to combat the hated Weimar Republic. As Hitler came to power her father acquired control of a publicity firm and eventually sold news and editorial space to the National Socialists at bargain rates, aiding the rise of the brownshirts from terrorists to leaders. He then started a chain of newspapers and headed the German National People's Party that eventually aligned itself with the Nazis and helped secure the demise of the Weimar Republic. She recalled how her father had always remained proud of that accomplishment. He sired three children, two sons and a daughter. Both sons never saw the end of the war, one dying in Russia, the other in France. After peace, her father became one of the countless disappointed men who'd made Hitler what he was, but could never admit that mistake. He lost all his newspapers, but luckily his concrete plants, paper mills, and oil refinery were needed so his sins, if not forgiven, were certainly forgotten. But not by her.

It was the one division between them that never faded. Her father had been a Nazi. He believed in Hitler and never saw the error in his folly.

She saw it plainly.

"Frau Bundeskanzlerin."

Her mind snapped back. Cassiopeia Vitt was speaking to her.

"It is imperative that we increase security around you."

"I agree, but if Pohl plans to make a move he must not suspect that we anticipate any action. That new security should be covert."

Her thoughts returned to her father.

There'd been a scare, about a year before the plane crash. He became quite sick and she'd been summoned to the *schlöss,* arriving in the early evening and rushing to his room.

"Papa." She knelt beside the bed and took his hand.

The old man's eyes opened and a smile came to his parched lips. Perhaps there was still life left in him.

"I waited for you," he whispered.

"Don't talk foolish. It is never time to give up."

"Good. I want you to stay strong." The words came only upon his breath, and she had to strain to understand him.

"Papa, don't you want to live?"

His eyes glazed over with moisture, and the oily glare was disconcerting. What was he thinking?

He slowly shook his head.

"You want to die?"

"I died long ago."

"What do you mean?"

"My world died long ago, and I with it. You are all that remains."

She understood what he meant. Her brothers were killed in the war. Neither ever married. She was the lone Herzog survivor. She started to speak, to reassure him, but his grip on her hand relaxed and she watched as his chest fluttered.

The eyes suddenly went wide, blue dots staring off beyond her.

His mouth opened and he softly said, "Heil . . . Hitler."

Her spine tingled every time she thought of her father's vile words. She'd loved the man with all her heart, but simultaneously hated him for the worship of something so evil. Rarely had he ever uttered Hitler's name. His thoughts remained his own yet, facing death, he felt compelled to proclaim an allegiance.

No one other than she heard those words.

Not even her mother.

Thank goodness.

After he recovered she confronted him and he brushed it off as delirium from the illness. A side effect of the pain medication.

Maybe. Maybe not.

The Herzog family was literally wiped out during the war. Nearly all of her aunts, uncles, and cousins perished. There were so few left, besides some distant relations. With no children of her own the demise of the bloodline now seemed assured.

My world. It is gone. You are all that remains.

Decades after her father whispered that declaration, her world was not much better. Her parents were dead. Kurt a stranger. The nation was all that remained. Knowing now that Theodor Pohl was indeed the offspring of a monster brought a new resolution to her cause.

She was not afraid of dying.

Only of failing.

CHAPTER
SIXTY-FOUR

COTTON DIALED HIS PHONE. HE WAS IN HIS ROOM, ON THE SECOND floor of Schüb's villa. He'd delayed making the call, wanting to be sure, but eventually realized that was not going to be possible.

"This has gestated into something way beyond what was first involved," he said to Danny Daniels.

"Enlighten me."

He told him everything he knew so far, including what he'd learned in the vault a few hours earlier.

"Unbelievable," Danny declared when he finished.

"Don't I know."

"Is it reliable?"

"Hell, no. But everything inside me says it's true."

"Any suggestions?"

"I'm going to Germany," he said. "After that, we'll see. Let's take it a step at a time."

"I'm sure you realize that there are massive security concerns here. International implications," Danny said. "We need to contain this."

"That's like trying to contain a hurricane."

"Maybe so, but at the moment only you and that old man know. And you're the guy on the ground. So it's your call as to what to do."

He agreed. Still. "Mr. President—"

"I know. Next time I need a favor, don't call you."

He descended the stairs to the ground floor.

Schüb sat in a lofty reading room that faced the lake. Out of habit his gaze raked the shelves and he spotted a rare text of Seneca and a Virgil manuscript, both side by side with English classics on theology and law. Schüb was apparently either a discerning reader or an intense collector. The old man sat before a quiet fireplace with a marble hearth. A good-sized English mastiff napped at his feet.

He took a seat beside his host and said, "I spoke with my superior. He's left the matter to my discretion."

"Former president Daniels?"

"You are well informed."

"It's kept me alive a long time."

"How wide is your information network?"

"Enough for me to know what I need to know."

Might as well take advantage of that. "So who killed Hanna Cress in that police station?"

"That was Theodor. Or more precisely, the man who works for him, Josef Engle. When the chancellor had her arrested, my guess is it seemed like a way to add greater emphasis to the information he was peddling. Cress' task was surely to deliver those documents and spur the investigation along. Killing her just made it that more enticing. Ada was monitoring things closely in Chile. Pohl and Engle would have surely manipulated the investigator Eisenhuth sent. But when Danny Daniels came along and involved you and Fräulein Vitt, that offered an even better means of achieving their goal."

"Nice to be so appreciated. Unfortunately, that investigator gave his life."

"I know. It's awful."

An understatement.

"Ada told me what Theodor was doing, using my name with the

chancellor, tossing out bait. I was unsure how this was going to play out and, I must confess, I still am."

"Where did the documents come from on Bormann that were provided to the chancellor? I read them. Some carried the seal from the Soviet archives."

Schüb nodded. "I obtained them, and much more, a few years ago. I purchased a lot of original information from Moscow, once the Soviet archives became available, purging that repository. *Das Leck* was real. There really was a Soviet spy in the Führerbunker. Stalin knew everything that happened there. That's what made it easy for him to deceive the West that Hitler might still be alive. But some of what you read was prepared by me long ago, and given to Theodor. Accounts of my encounters with Bormann. I also provided him with some of the actual Soviet documents, back when we were on speaking terms."

"He never knew of Jan?"

Schüb shrugged. "I always maintained a distance between my two lives. He knew of him. That's all. Jan knew only what I told him, and though Theodor knew Jan existed, he cared only about himself. It was actually quite easy to keep them separate."

In the German's lap he noticed the photographs from the hacienda and the scrapbook, along with the letters Ada had provided. He'd given them to Schüb earlier, when they returned from the bank.

"Reminiscing?" he asked.

The old man nodded.

"Is that you in the picture?"

"It is, when I was young. I went to Chile with my mother and Ada after the war. I was barely twenty. Just a youth who showed promise. My father bought me the uniform. Many retained a hope that the fascist movement could be revived. But by 1950 that hope had evaporated into self-preservation. Hollywood and fiction writers like to proclaim that Nazis continued to exist, but the movement died, as they do, simply from a lack of leadership. You see, in this world there are captains and lieutenants. One leads, the other follows. Bormann thought himself a captain, but he was merely an okay lieutenant."

"History portrays him a bit differently."

Schüb chuckled. "I know, and it would be fascinating to see his reaction. Hitler called him his *most loyal party comrade* and supposedly said that he could not win the war without Bormann." The old man shook his head. "Just another example of Hitler's inability to understand people."

"You probably knew Bormann better than anyone who ever lived."

"That's true. He became a lifelong study of mine. Many never realized that he came to the Nazi Party late, only in 1926. So the *alte kampfler*, the old fighters, who'd been there since the beginning, ignored him. Of course, ignoring Martin Bormann is a fatal mistake. He worked better from the shadows. He was diligent, determined, organized, tactical, cunning, and possessed of an extraordinary memory. He was the one who turned Hitler's chaotic orders into coherent commands. As I said, he taught me many things. But three stuck with me. Always blame others. Leave no trail on anything you do. And help those who can either hurt or help you—the benefit is the same.

"In the end all he wanted was the money, which he completely controlled. Unfortunately for all of the others in South America, on the run and scared, Bormann held the only key to the bank. Eichmann tried to implicate him before the Israelis hung the bastard, but to no avail."

The old man was talking, finally. Filling in the gaps. And he needed that filler badly. "Why did Bormann want you?"

"He didn't. My father recommended me and I initially performed several minor tasks to his satisfaction. Thankfully, he was a man of needs. He understood how to placate those above him, while abusing those beneath. That was how he ingratiated himself to Hitler. So it was easy for someone like myself to make a similar impression. Of course, it helped that he was completely dependent on others. He could do little for himself, as it might risk exposure. Only I, and a few others, even knew he was alive. Eventually, only I remained."

The old man went silent, lifting his picture from over half a century earlier to his oily eyes. "Ada kept this photo a long time." Schüb shook his head. "She is a good sister. Sadly, she's never met Jan. I'd like to rectify that."

Schüb laid the photo back in his lap atop the letters he'd sent to his sister. He seemed to steel himself, duty taking hold of emotion.

"I have been following matters in Europe. The new right is gaining support by the day. Exactly as Bormann predicted."

He waited for the old man to explain.

"He made clear to me on many occasions Hitler's errors. He loved to tell me how Germany could have easily won the Russian campaign politically, while a military victory was impossible. The territory was simply too vast to adequately supply an army of the size needed to win. But the people there hated Stalin. Treated right, they would have welcomed the Germans as liberators and supplied an army to defeat the communists. Instead, Hitler murdered them by the thousands, and they came to hate Germans worse than Stalin. Foolishness, Bormann would say."

"Wasn't he in the chain of command for those decisions? As I recall, one of his duties was to supervise the local governors. The *Gauleiters*. They reported straight to Bormann."

"He would never admit any complicity. He said Hitler made all those decisions."

"That's crap."

"I agree. But I never argued, I simply listened. Both he and Hitler ordered millions to their deaths. And that is the true absurdity of their folly. There was no national interest that mandated the slaughtering of Jews, Romani, priests, Slavs, and the mentally ill. Hitler was not a conqueror, unlike Alexander or Napoleon. He was a mass murderer, and that was, without question, his greatest flaw."

"And Bormann had a better idea?"

"More a vision. He believed power could be both obtained, and maintained, through a careful attention to organization and detail. After all, he managed to do that with Hitler. His weapons were not guns or bombs. Only words. He butchered millions simply with memoranda. He adhered religiously to something Hitler once said. *The masses have little time to think. And how incredible is the willingness of modern man to believe.* Ultimately, he pressed that philosophy on to Theodor with an equal fervor."

"He was right. It's how every despot manages to obtain power."

"At present, in France, Italy, Austria, Belgium, Denmark, the Netherlands, Hungary, and even here, in Switzerland, the people are poised to shift toward the new right. These are not simply conservatives. These are ultra-radicals, and they are gaining power. I believe it is Theodor's desire to place Germany at the forefront of this revolution. He is the strongest of the contenders for immediate power and the only one, at the moment, on the verge of obtaining a national consensus. The idea is most certainly to affect the European Union parliamentary elections scheduled in a few months. That's where they want to gain real control. Bormann said many times that history never repeats itself through actual events. But there are parallels. I would agree, there is no indication Germany will regress to barbarism, but who would be foolish enough to believe that the Bormanns currently among us have no opportunity to flourish. Theodor could well be the catalyst that launches them all."

"But what can he do?"

"Anti-immigration is at the core of each of those nation's movements. As is anti-Semitism. I talked recently with a French associate. He told me the story of a local synagogue that burned, and how little was done by the authorities. Today's hatred has taken on a new form. The perpetrators of this new type of violence are either fascists or young Muslims, who see in the local Jews a way to avenge the supposed sins of Israel. In France, as in most of Europe, society has become compartmentalized, each group to his own. The new right exploits this reality and uses it to generate fear. Ironically, some Jews in France even support the new right since they believe the current French government has done little to help them, so they turn to an alternative. Anything. Which is both foolish and dangerous."

He was beginning to understand. "Similar to what Hitler did. Played off unemployment and the humiliation from World War One to coalesce the people behind him."

Schüb nodded. "The European new right of today will not preach violence or genocide. No, it will be opposed to both in every form, at least publicly. Privately? That's another matter. Instead, the policies advocated will be subtle, more mainstream. Things such as giving citizens priority for jobs over immigrants. Limiting public housing and health benefits to citizens only. Financing health care separately for foreigners so that citizens' taxes are not used. Abandoning the euro. Expanding the police. Building new prisons. Re-instituting the death penalty.

Rewriting textbooks to preserve a so-called national memory. Requiring everyone to participate in patriotic displays. Even establishing a national language and religion. These are the directions our new despots will head and the people will willingly follow because, after all, who could argue with any of those."

What Schüb was saying made sense.

"The recent decline of the European Union has helped these reactionaries. Each EU member nation has deep cultural roots with strong nationalism. And none of those include Islamic elements. On the contrary, European history is replete with instances when Islamic culture has been outright threatening. Spain and Portugal were occupied for centuries. Eastern Europe throughout history faced a constant threat from an Islamic invasion. So a unified, strong Islamic presence within Europe will never be allowed. And the new right uses a fear of that reemergence quite effectively."

"Bormann taught this to Pohl?"

"That and much more. Bormann was a brilliant strategist. He understood the art of mass manipulation. He also appreciated the role that timing plays in politics. In fact, as he many times said, timing was the most crucial element of all."

On that he could not argue.

"It's time we go to Germany," Schüb said. "We need to speak with Theodor and Marie Eisenhuth. But there is one more thing we must do first."

He stared at his host.

"There is a place. In the Austrian Alps, near the German border. A house once owned by Bormann, now titled in one of my aliases. We must stop there on the way."

"Are you going to tell me why?"

"I prefer to show you."

CHAPTER
SIXTY-FIVE

LÖWENBERG
TUESDAY, JUNE 18
10:00 A.M.

POHL EASED OPEN THE HEAVY OAK DOOR AND ENTERED THE CORNER
tower. Its outer walls faced southeast and dated from the 15th century.
Each of the four stories within the tower contained a room, the uppermost
chamber once the castle's armory. He'd arrived back home a few minutes
ago from his trip to Munich. He'd called ahead and arranged the meeting,
stopping only momentarily in his study before heading to the tower.

He climbed the spiral stairs, past archer slits, and entered the top-
floor room. He shut the door behind him and bolted the latch.

Josef Engle stood on the far side beside a Gothic fireplace. Weapons and armor no longer constituted the room's décor. Now the
half-timbered walls were bare, the space used mainly for storage. An
unearthly green light filtered in through dirty opaque frames. The air
was cool and laced with the pall of time and age. He crossed the gritty
flagstones, withdrew from his pocket the pistol he'd retrieved from his
desk, and pointed the barrel at Engle's head. "I need to know why I
should not shoot you dead."

"Because whatever transgression I have committed is minimal
compared with your need for my services." His associate showed no
emotion.

"You smug bastard. I told you to kill Vitt, Malone, and Jan Bruin.
Instead they are all alive and pursuing me."

"Vitt and her partner are dead. I was there when the Chilean fighter reported blowing up the house, with them inside."

The report came matter-of-factly and still with no concern. He kept the gun level, his finger on the trigger. "He was wrong."

"You have seen them?"

He caught the surprise in the question.

"Vitt and Bruin in the flesh. Tell me what happened with Jan Bruin. The truth."

"He was waiting for me. I did not agree with your decision to start with. In the end, my assessment was correct. Bruin anticipated our move and was ready. He should have been left alone. Instead we simply roused him from his self-imposed sleep."

"I don't need you questioning my orders."

"I'm not. Simply noting that the decision was misguided. Bruin specifically sent me back to report his death to you, so he would be left alone. Since I agreed with that course, I saw no reason not to comply."

"Bruin lied. He played you. He is here, in Germany. Which is precisely why I ordered you to kill him." He motioned with the gun. "You are not indispensable. There are many willing to perform your tasks."

"But none you could recruit, school, and train in the time allowed."

He lowered the weapon. Engle was right, he wasn't going to shoot him, no matter how much he might want to.

Not right now, at least.

"The deceit with regard to Bruin was unfortunate," Engle said, the tone conciliatory, "but I thought he sounded sincere. He had kept what he knew to himself for a long time. There was no reason to doubt that he would continue. Besides, he was waiting for me with an armed guard. I had little choice but to comply."

"You could have told me the truth."

"That is not what you wanted to hear."

He whirled the gun up and fired. The bullet raced past Engle's left ear and ricocheted off the coarse stone wall. Engle never moved and the man's frigid nerve chilled his own resolve.

"Everything I planned has failed. Vitt, Bruin, Malone, even the old man Schüb, are here."

He was not accustomed to being cornered and did not like the feeling.

"Schüb is alive? What has happened?"

He lowered the gun and told his associate of the confrontation at the Munich court theater. "Eisenhuth was probing to see how I would react. But I gave her little."

"She was baiting you for a response."

"She was telling me that we are at a stalemate where we can each destroy the other. But we're going to give her a response. Immediately. Before she has time to prepare."

"That is exactly what she wants you to do."

"Thanks to your mistakes, I don't have a choice anymore. It's either her or me. This is now a battle to the death. I assume you have people willing to handle the matter and shoulder the responsibility."

"Our Chinese allies are quite anxious to intercede. I told you that months ago. They detest Chancellor Eisenhuth. She routinely sides with the Americans against them, so they have repeatedly offered to assist."

China was Germany's largest trading partner. Nearly two hundred billion euros last year alone. Their relationship dated back to the first Sino-German treaty in 1861. High-level diplomatic missions were commonplace, as was mutual cooperation. But their relationship with Eisenhuth had become increasingly strained. So much that they'd reached out and privately urged a change in leadership, one they were willing to help make happen whether that be with money or with in-kind services. Pohl had dealt with Beijing countless times while in the Bundestag and always found them negotiable. But he'd resisted being beholden to them, settling instead on a grandiose scheme of using his South American connections to reveal the financial web that would ruin Eisenhuth.

The whole idea had seemed flawless.

Until last night.

Now he needed another path. "Can the Chinese effort be revived?"

Engle nodded. "It would be an easy matter."

"Do it. No delay. I want a quick strike."

"And what of Cassiopeia Vitt?"

"Eliminate her, too."

"And Jan Bruin?"

"The same."

"And Gerhard Schüb?"

He said nothing.

"And Cotton Malone?" Engle asked.

He understood. Too damn many killings. "All right, you made your point. Just Eisenhuth, for now. But the rest will have to be dealt with since they apparently are well informed, too. The critical thing is nothing gets traced back to us."

"This information coming to light would be a problem," Engle said. "Heirs of Bormann and Braun can be found. Bormann fathered many children, some of whom have children and grandchildren of their own. Braun's family lineage can also be delineated. DNA testing is possible."

"Not without my cooperation."

"That could prove difficult to refuse. I agree, it would be better to eventually eliminate all of the participants. But those actions must be well planned."

"Which is why I pay you large sums of money. Find a way."

Something Eisenhuth said last night kept ringing through his brain. *"We have the assistance of an American, Cotton Malone, who is working with Herr Schüb to secure some additional evidence."* And what had she said when asked of Schüb's whereabouts? *"Nearby."*

His mind raced.

He should have thought of it before. "We may have an easy opportunity to get Schüb and the American, Malone."

He thought back years ago to when Gerhard Schüb traveled north from South Africa. By the late 1970s the old German was making the journey every few months, always bringing notebooks full of wisdom. He'd even come to like the wiry Schüb. They would meet, not in Germany, but just over the border in the Upper Bavarian reaches of Austria, at an elegant country house situated in a beautiful mountain valley.

"Malone and Schüb might be in Austria," he declared.

"How can you be sure?"

"Just a feeling, but a good one I think."

"What do you want me to do?"

"Have our Chinese friends check it out and, if I'm right, handle them. Now."

CHAPTER SIXTY-SIX

SCHLÖSS HERZOG
11:00 A.M.

MARIE WAS SURPRISED THAT KURT HAD RETURNED HOME SO SOON. Usually after one of their tiffs he stayed away at least a week. This time he'd come back after only a few days. Perhaps their talk in Frankfurt the other night had some effect? She'd not heard a word from him since then, and his silence did not bode well. Though she should be preparing for the first debate with Pohl, reviewing reams of information her staff had assembled, her mind wandered. The tables were turned. Now Pohl was in jeopardy, too.

What would he do?

That was a question she needed answered. Unfortunately, she possessed precious little evidence other than what Gerhard Schüb had said and, as Pohl correctly noted, those statements came with an assortment of credibility problems. The BND inquiries about the tainted money had yet to become public. At the moment, though, she could not allow any of that to distract her. She needed to talk with Kurt. So she headed downstairs to find him immediately after the chambermaid informed her of his arrival.

He was in the Mirror Room, named appropriately for walls of baroque dotted with hundreds of mirrors, each casting fractured images at every conceivable angle. French doors and windows allowed the sun to play upon the reflections, the mirrors' beveled edges splashing spectrums of color. She'd never cared for the room as the distorted refractions were, if nothing else, distracting, more irrational than beautiful, fantastical as opposed to real. Her father loved it, and while he was alive its furnishings had been elaborate and many. But she kept the space empty. More a curiosity than a functional part of the house.

She entered from the hall onto a lively terrazzo floor, whose pattern only added more confusion to the overall illusion.

"I am surprised you are back," she said.

Kurt turned from one of the mirrors, an elegant one overlaid with a gilt trellis. He wore a three-button glen-plaid suit and Bally leather oxfords, a bit casual for his workday, which made her wonder where he'd been. "No sense fighting forever."

He could be like that afterward, seemingly never holding a grudge, or at least not allowing her to think that he did.

"What did you learn at the company?"

"Not a hello or a how are you? Just, *What did you learn?*" he said.

"I don't mean to be short, but I am anxious to know what, if anything, appears in our records. Surely you can understand that?"

"Using our current unit of currency and value, a little over 370 million euros were transferred into our accounts since 1965. The amounts came in varying portions, scattered over time. The BND spent two days at our Frankfurt headquarters scouring records. Nothing would have raised any suspicions on our part since, as I have said, thousands of these transfers occur each year from banks all over the globe."

"So Father would have known," she said, more to herself than Kurt.

"Without question. In fact, nearly half the money arrived from 1965 until 1972. As you recall, that was a time when the companies suffered from inflation and the communists. It wasn't until the early 1980s that things turned around."

She'd heard that advertisement before.

Supposedly, Kurt had slaved for nearly a decade to counter her father's protectionist policies. He would tell her how he consolidated and refinanced debt, renegotiated labor agreements, expanded markets, and basically saved them from the embarrassment of receivership. Erwin Brümmer never thought much of what Kurt may or may not have done. Most of the reversals, Brümmer explained, could be attributed to a skyrocketing economy that propelled West Germany into the industrial forefront. The Eisenhuth and Herzog entities were simply among the many conglomerates in the right place at the right time.

But she still wanted to know, "Did we benefit from the money?"

He nodded. "Those funds helped keep our concerns viable, functioning, and expanding."

"Did you know where the money came from?"

"What if I did?"

She did not like his hedging. "How could you possibly ask such a question? To use assets derived from that evil is unspeakable. Go to Dachau, as I just did, see the ovens. To think I may have benefited, in any way, from that is repugnant to everything I believe. I thought it was repugnant to everything you believed, too."

"And what is that supposed to mean?"

She repressed a shudder. "Damn you, Kurt. Did you know about the source of the funds?" Her words slipped out from between clenched teeth. "Stop the games."

"*Ja,* I did."

Had she heard right?

She stood impassive, considering the admission. "That's not what you told me in Frankfurt."

"I lied." He seemed not to care about the pain he was causing her.

Tears welled at the rims of her eyes. She fought the urge to cry. She must be strong, but everything she'd ever feared about Kurt seemed now confirmed. "What are you saying?" she asked, holding her emotions in check.

Kurt came close. "I am saying the obvious. The money was offered and I accepted it."

"Who offered it?"

"That will hurt the most."

She waited for him to explain.

"Your father."

"What do you mean?" Her impassioned plea for understanding broke through a haze of shock.

"In the years before his death, he and I had many conversations. He told me of the funds, their source, and how to obtain them. I will say that I resisted the urge for a time, but finally succumbed. The money ultimately proved quite useful. Spent properly, the return has been substantial."

The words were steady, neutral, detached. No remorse. No guilt.

"My father knew all this?"

"Marie, your father was a Nazi. You may choose to deny the fact, ignore the obvious, but your father loved Adolf Hitler."

Her right hand swept up and slapped him across the face.

An almost unconscious reaction.

Kurt did not react to the assault.

He simply stepped back and rubbed his cheek. "Intense emotion. Violence. So you are human, after all."

She resented his analysis. Beads of sweat dotted her forehead. She'd not thought herself capable, either. "My father was a good man. His political beliefs may have been unorthodox, but he was no Nazi murderer."

Her nerves throbbed with excitement.

"So the fact he did not actually kill anyone makes him different? Do you really believe that? He agreed with everything Hitler advocated. He hated Jews and communists and Americans. He raised millions for the National Socialists and actively aided their cause. He willingly utilized slave labor. No, he did not actually kill anyone, he just made it easier for Hitler, Bormann, Himmler, and the rest to do it, all the while profiting from *their* effort."

She was not going to listen to him anymore. She turned and headed for the door. Kurt lunged forward, grabbed her arm, and spun her around. "You are not going to walk away from me. Not this time."

"Let go of me." It was a weak command, especially with the clear menace in his eyes.

"I am sick and tired of you parading around in your self-righteous role as our savior. You are so quick to tell everyone else what is right. Are you capable of making the same judgments relative to yourself?"

"I have done nothing wrong."

"How about your father? Can you judge him as harshly as you judge Theodor Pohl?"

"My father was harmless."

But the words felt bitter on her tongue.

"Really? All those Jews who died in the camps might take issue with that. Men like your father put Nazis in charge, and then worked to keep them in power."

"You are a despicable bastard. The sight of you makes me sick."

He wrenched her closer to one of the mirrors. Her reflection stared back, visible in other mirrors across the room, moving at odd angles. "Look at your face, Marie. The people will tolerate much from their leaders. They'll forgive theft, incompetence, sexual indiscretions. But there are two things they will not forgive. Arrogance and hypocrisy. You, my dear, will be perceived as suffering from both. No one will tolerate your sermons when your father was the guiltiest of all. It is not me, Marie, but you who will be the one to explain."

She freed herself from his grip and whirled around to face him. "Whatever you think is right, Kurt. Do it. You and Pohl both. Do it. I'm ready."

"You might be ready, Marie. But is your political party? Your supporters? You will cost them all."

She let the bait fly past her, resisting the urge to square off with him once again. Nothing would be gained.

So she stormed from the room.

CHAPTER
SIXTY-SEVEN

COTTON SLOWED THE MERCEDES AS HE AND SCHÜB ROUNDED A sharp bend. The highway traced gentle diminishing arcs across the upper meadowlands between Alpine parapets, descending as rapidly as it had climbed a few minutes earlier, on its way down into a broad valley cut between steep slopes. Groves of poplar and blue fir embroidered a path up the jagged slopes, all without the usual ski chutes, setting a scene of both solitude and solace. The upper peaks, hooded by sullen clouds, were enameled with snow, and he realized it would be only a few more months before the icing spread down into the valley.

A light rain smeared the windshield and he flipped on the wipers. Schüb sat in the passenger seat and pointed off to the east, into the valley, where through the mist a farmhouse came into view.

Schüb had explained on the trip north from Switzerland that the house was built just after World War I by a German Jew who'd been enamored with the projecting roofs, stone and mortar, and walls of wood and shingle found in Black Forest farms. So he'd erected a replica in the Austrian Alps. The Nazis eventually seized the land and occupied the premises throughout the war. When it was finally returned to the family in the early 1950s, they could not afford the upkeep so the estate was sold. Bormann recalled the locale from the war and thought it perfect, so he authorized the purchase and vested title in one of Schüb's many aliases.

"The Austrians ask few questions. Like the Swiss. They are quite easy to deal with," Schüb said.

He followed the road as it flattened into the valley, turning off onto a rocky lane that wound through dense trees, the day's shadows lengthening. They passed through a couple of Disney-cute Tyrolean villages, each a cluster of snowy plaster and ancient timbers. Finally their destination drew closer, and he saw that all of the house's shutters were closed. Fallen leaves and limbs dotted the space between the house and stands of fir and pine.

Nothing about the place signaled occupancy.

"It has been a while since anyone was here," Schüb said. "I have a caretaker who lives in Salzburg. He comes occasionally to check on things."

They stepped out of the car into the rain.

Schüb led the way to the front door.

The building seemed about three thousand square feet spread over three floors. There was electricity, for which he was grateful, since the rain and lateness of the day cast everything in a murky gloom. Schüb switched on the lights to reveal rooms of warm, traditional furniture.

"I see the caretaker has made sure everything stays clean," Schüb said.

"You came here a lot?"

"Four to five times a year. This is where Theodor and I would meet. We spent many hours here together."

He followed Schüb upstairs.

Under a high-pitched roof, along with chairs and a small sofa covered in a quaint embroidery, were kilim rugs, an Indian sitar, and what appeared to be ostrich eggs arranged in a woven basket.

"Most of these things I brought from Africa. Gifts from Bormann to his son. They made for good decoration." Schüb stepped to the window and gazed out into a fading, wet afternoon. "We would many times sit here. I would tell Theodor of Bormann, and he would read the latest notebook. I actually liked the boy in his younger days. He was handsome and strong. A lot like his mother. She was always there, in his eyes and mouth." Schüb turned from the window. "Do you know of the *heimliche Kaiser*?"

"The secret emperor?" He shook his head. "I don't know what that is."

He listened as Schüb spoke of 1189 and Barbarossa, one of the early Holy Roman Emperors, who created a German imperial grandeur that challenged all of Christendom. Unfortunately, his dream went unfulfilled as he died on the way to the Crusades. Ever since, legend had proclaimed that Barbarossa still breathed, asleep inside the womb of a mountain, waiting to be woken to wrench his homeland from defeat and lead Germany again to glory.

"It was no accident that Hitler named the Russian invasion Operation Barbarossa," Schüb said. "He was quite familiar with the *heimliche Kaiser*. Like the Nazis, he used legends to raise hopes. It is so sad how we Germans lose sight of political reality in the face of wistful dreams and romantic notions."

He'd read that same conclusion from many a historian.

"Bormann played off this fallacy," Schüb said. "He would write to Theodor about how to use folk-power. It was supposedly the task of the *heimliche Kaiser* to remove all vestiges of Western civilization and bring health to the German people. Hitler tried to do that and failed. He was the false *heimliche Kaiser,* Bormann would say." Schüb shook his head. "Myths have always been intoxicating for Germans. We never seemed to realize that they are merely invitations to doom."

"Could Pohl understand that?"

"Heavens, no. He loved the concept. Bormann said he would, and on that he was right. Legends kept the boy's interest."

"Did you ever try and tell him the truth about Bormann?"

"Twice. Both efforts failed. Theodor adored him. Looked up to him. Which is perplexing, since the man never contributed a single thing to the Nazi Party. He was simply a navigator. For him, there were those to dominate and those to fear. Deeds were far more important than ideas." The old man's eyes went cold. "Bormann's father-in-law said it best, after the war. *'He simply could not stand the thin air at the pinnacle of power. It drove him insane.'* I did tell the boy about his mother, though."

"You may know her better than anybody, too."

"Hitler mistreated her. He would say that an intelligent man should possess only a stupid woman, so she could never influence his decisions. But she still loved him. God knows why, but she truly loved Hitler. The only reason she fled the bunker and aligned with Bormann was because her husband told her to. She was a caring person who wished ill on no one, though she was surrounded by monsters." Schüb pointed to a colorful chest against the far wall. "Like the furniture in this room. Pretty to be seen, never to be heard, and powerless to affect anything."

"When did you realize you loved her?"

He was wondering if his hunch was correct.

"I have often considered that question. I was so young then. She was a beautiful woman. I was lonely, in a strange country."

He studied the old man. Twelve years as a field agent had taught him many things that years of retirement had not erased. One in particular was knowing when somebody had something to say.

"Tell me what it is you brought me here to learn."

CHAPTER
SIXTY-EIGHT

SCHÜB LAY NAKED NEXT TO EVA BRAUN, SATISFIED AFTER HE SPENT HIMSELF *inside her for a second time. Outside, rain continued to pour from the African sky with the intensity of a waterfall.*

"I'm so grateful you are here," *she whispered in his ear, cuddling close.*

"And I for you."

"Is Martin still due back tomorrow?"

"He was delayed at the mines in Kimberley."

"That means his latest concubine wanted another night with him."

He smiled. She knew Bormann well. But then she should, after six years together. "I do not get involved in his affairs."

She giggled. "Oh, Gerhard. You truly are a loyal servant. Martin chose well when he selected you. He does not realize that fact, but he chose well."

"I do as he asks, nothing more."

"Does he ask you to bed me?"

"That was my choice."

"He does not think me worthy of sex. He comes only sparingly. When it suits him."

The thought turned his stomach, but he said nothing. He couldn't. What he was doing was wrong. He'd known that from the first time a year ago, and each time thereafter he told himself there would be no more.

But he always returned.

Maybe Bormann knew. Probably not, though.

*He was fanatical about his things, and Eva Braun was his most prized posses-
sion. They were careful, coming together only when Bormann was far away. Thankfully, only the three of them lived on the farm, and the help was not allowed to stay
past dark.*

Another of Bormann's many rules.

*They lay still. He liked being naked in bed while it rained. Many times he'd lain in
his own bed and listened to the night, wondering if she was with Bormann.*

"Be grateful he stays away," he finally said.

"I am."

"He is not to be angered. There is a great fire inside him."

"He is a fool who would have been nothing, except for my Adolf."

*She always referred to Hitler by his first name. Whether that was her habit while the
Führer was in her life, he never asked. He wanted to know nothing of her other lovers.*

"Bormann is a determined man. Do not dismiss him easily."

"I despise him," she said. "I am here because where else am I to go?"

"We are all in that situation."

*"You can never go back to Chile," she declared, as if reading his mind. "Just as I
can never go back to Germany. We are both prisoners, history our keeper, in a strange
perverse way."*

She nestled tight and wrapped her legs around his. "I am glad to have you."

*He felt the same. Though Braun was older by eleven years she always allowed him
to take charge. It was what she needed. Physically she was a grown woman, emotionally
she was still an adolescent. Dependency was her greatest flaw, but it was also what had
brought them together.*

The rain continued to assault the tin roof.

Against his better judgment, he started responding to her presence.

She seemed to sense his anticipation.

"Good, Gerhard. I, too, want you."

COTTON LISTENED AS SCHÜB FINISHED TELLING HIM ABOUT HIS
relationship with Eva Braun, recalling how the old man's voice had

cracked a few days ago when he'd related the story of her death, how Bormann paid her corpse no mind, concentrating on the two infants and trying to decide on which boy to keep.

"That's why you buried her with such pomp," he said, understanding finally.

"My way of honoring her. She was my *häschen*."

His bunny.

"We needed each other."

"How long did the relationship last?"

"For the last two years of her life."

"Bormann never knew?"

"If he did, he never mentioned a word to me. In fact, after her death he never spoke of her again. She was nothing to him. Just a tool. Used, then discarded. The truth was so hard for him. He many times would say truth is only needed when *sufficient reasons make it necessary*." Schüb paused, a smile on his lips. "She loved to mock him. He was a short man, and conscious of the fact. She was taller, so he would never stand right beside her. But she would maneuver close, especially when others were around. She could be quite a devil. Loved to dance. Smoked with a fervor. And high-heeled shoes, my how they brought her joy. I brought her a pair back once from Johannesburg."

"Is this why we are here?"

Schüb seemed to return from the past and, in apparent answer to the question, brushed past him and descended the stairs. On the ground floor he followed the old man to the kitchen, and a pine cupboard, its shelves lined with pewter cups and dishes.

"We did little cooking here, but I would occasionally bake bread," Schüb said.

The old man reached into the cupboard.

A click permeated the silence and the shelves started to rotate, the entire assembly apparently set onto a center post.

"The previous owner added this modification. I am told he hid family valuables here as war approached. Unfortunately, they were found."

Schüb reached inside the dark space and yanked the chain for a bare bulb. The room beyond was little more than a closet, the width of the cupboard, about four feet deep, its back wall wooden shelves from ceiling to floor.

All of which were empty.

"Oh, dear," Schüb said.

Cotton waited for an explanation.

"I stored the Widow's diaries here. It was my desire to one day share them with Theodor. I thought perhaps he would want to know his mother. She wrote a great deal down. Loving thoughts. Her feelings. A boy should know those things about his mother."

"When was the last time you were here?"

"Four years ago."

"Who else knew of this room?"

"Only Theodor."

"Seems he now knows all about his mother."

"He does not know everything."

Schüb switched off the light and replaced the cupboard. "I have not been entirely truthful with you, Herr Malone."

"You want to tell me what I think I already know."

"I am Theodor Pohl's father."

"Any doubt?"

"None."

"Braun knew?"

Schüb nodded. "It is the only reason she carried the baby to term. There was no way she would have birthed Bormann's child. Of course, she possessed no idea of twins, and in those days there was no way to know if she was carrying two infants. Twins are prevalent in my family."

"It must have hurt a great deal to give that infant away to the Pohls."

"More than I ever realized, until the moment it happened. I watched as a woman I loved died a painful death, then I was forced to endure Bormann's choices. After, I had to hand my son over to strangers. It was nearly unbearable. Then, even worse, I watched him be cruel to my other son. Then I buried that boy."

"But what choices did you have?"

"That is the most painful part of all. I possessed none. By my own choosing. And I have lived with those regrets all my life."

"Pohl does not know anything?"

"I never found the right moment."

He realized that everything had now changed. "I think the moment to tell him has come."

"I agree."

CHAPTER SIXTY-NINE

CASSIOPEIA DID NOT LIKE THE SITUATION. THE CROWD OUTSIDE the cathedral was multiplying, all waiting for Marie Eisenhuth, whose appearance would begin in a little over half an hour. Inside wasn't much better, as the cathedral's staff and a variety of priests and nuns milled about, preparing the interior. This campaign stop had been scheduled for weeks, one of the few swings Eisenhuth would make through central Germany, much of which was staunchly conservative and once part of East Germany. As she studied the faces surrounding her, there seemed a lot of intensity and anticipation, which unfortunately only increased her anxiety.

Prior to her main speech Eisenhuth and the press were to be given a tour of the cathedral's grand interior. A way, Cassiopeia was told, for the popular lord mayor to be seen with Eisenhuth since he had agreed to publicly endorse her candidacy later, during the evening's festivities. Just one big media show, Cassiopeia had concluded, but also the first inviting opportunity for Theodor Pohl.

One he might accept.

They'd intentionally baited him.

Backed him into a corner.

Hoping to force his hand.

This was her first visit to Hildesheim. Earlier, she'd surveyed the narrow streets and concluded that the Lower Saxony town was little more than a sprawling outdoor museum of timbered medieval buildings. On the walk from the hotel, she'd marveled at the painted façades with finely sculptured friezes and quaint inscriptions bearing ancient dates of construction. The cathedral was also impressive, though not at the same magnitude as the nearby Church of St. Michael, where Eisenhuth was scheduled to appear tomorrow.

The local officials had been adamant that the cathedral remain open during both the press tour and the speech. Eisenhuth concurred, not wanting to restrict the people from their own church or alert the press about any security concerns. Cassiopeia had cautioned that the situation could easily spiral out of control, not voicing what was clearly understood: that Theodor Pohl was out there, possibly waiting to strike. So Eisenhuth had agreed to one concession—a protective vest, which she now wore beneath a maroon business suit.

It would have been better to set up a checkpoint at the main entrance and search everyone who came inside, but Eisenhuth had absolutely refused. So Cassiopeia had settled for discreet surveillance from a group of local plainclothes police, now ringing the vast interior.

She casually moved through the edge of the crowd as people filled the pews and milled in the transepts on either side of the long nave. The cathedral was a cadre of niches and shadows with towering columns rising throughout, all of which could provide excellent cover for any assailant. Eisenhuth and the press remained in the cloister, being shown the thousand-year-old rosebush, a local oddity of some renown. Cassiopeia was in radio contact with the other police, a tiny fob in her left ear, a microphone clipped inside her coat. She'd told everyone to keep chatter to a minimum. Each was armed and ready. She was the floater, drifting around, assessing threats, making decisions. Her presence had not been appreciated by the security forces. But Eisenhuth had issued orders that everyone was to cooperate and Cassiopeia could come and go as she pleased.

At the far end of the nave a commotion grabbed her attention.

Bright lights and cameras signaled that Eisenhuth was making her way into the nave. A murmur started to rise in the few hundred people present as the press eased toward the altar, followed by the candidate.

Cassiopeia's gaze drifted toward the main entrance, where more people moved inside. At the holy water font many stopped to make the sign of the cross. Trying to determine if there was any threat seemed an impossibility. And would any challenge be so obvious?

No, it wouldn't.

Eisenhuth made her way to the raised altar. The press knelt in front of the first pew so the people already seated could see. Someone was clipping a wireless microphone to the chancellor's jacket. She apparently was going to say a few words. This was not on the itinerary, which was all the better since unpredictability was their best weapon.

"If I may have your attention," Eisenhuth said. Her voice echoed throughout the church thanks to speakers high in the ceiling.

Conversation began to recede.

"I thank each of you for coming tonight. I will be speaking outside shortly, but I wanted to say a few words to those of you here inside."

Cassiopeia shifted her position, moving down the center aisle, closer to the altar, weaving around people who stood listening. Luckily, the way was not jammed and movement was easy. She cursed herself for allowing any of this to happen. It was foolishness to think security could be provided in a place this porous. And would Pohl really try to kill the chancellor of Germany? Conspiracies of that magnitude never succeeded. The act would be rash. Overkill, actually. But from her one encounter, Pohl appeared to be a man capable of anything, especially considering that his father was Martin Bormann.

"This cathedral is inspiring," Eisenhuth was saying. "As is your town. Your lord mayor told me of the bombs, and the destruction they caused in the last war. Yet the resurrection of this community is evidence of your resilience, and that is what makes us all German."

Applause erupted in seeming agreement with the patriotic observation.

Many of the priests and nuns had stopped their work and were focusing on Eisenhuth. Cassiopeia's attention alternated between the acolytes and the crowd. She pushed through the last of the onlookers and emerged at the velvet ropes that held everyone back from the altar beyond. No other police were near, so she ducked beneath the thick strand of velvet stretched across the center aisle and headed toward the shadows to the side. Two uniformed security men flanked either side of the altar and spotted her, but did not move from their post.

Eisenhuth was still speaking.

People continued to mill back and forth from the rear of the cathedral. Their footsteps echoed as background to the chancellor's voice. She caught sight of a man who quickly brushed past the holy water font. He was short, fair skinned, with reddish-blond hair. His face stayed frozen in a solemnity that, for an instant, bothered her. She moved closer to the altar, weaving around those who stood listening. To her right she caught sight of Red Hair. He was also edging his way forward through the sparser crowds in the south transept.

Then he stopped.

Standing like everyone else.

Listening.

Doing nothing.

Another man aroused her curiosity. Clearly Middle Eastern, probably Turkish. More light applause erupted. She kept her attention on the Turk. The man's right hand was in his pant pocket, which seemed odd, his left arm at his side. She did not like the look in his anxious eyes. She debated alerting the others, but decided to wait a moment longer.

"I have a target," a male voice said in her left ear. "Woman. Agitated. Making comments."

"Where?" she whispered.

"North transept, forward, near the altar."

She turned and focused, first spotting her agent, then the woman. She was mid-thirties. Dark hair. Rough face. Who appeared angry.

The woman started to scream. "You will be our ruin."

The outburst was directed at Eisenhuth, who turned her attention toward the heckler.

"You are plunging us into anarchy."

Two security men quickly blocked the woman's path. They seemed to have the situation in hand so she turned back and saw that the Turk was gone. Her gaze raked the crowd, but found nothing. The woman at the front was still yelling. Two agents pinned her arms and began to drag her from the cathedral. Cassiopeia spotted the Turk, emerging from a crowd near the altar.

She pushed forward.

"A man. To the right of the altar. Turkish. I don't like the look of him," she said into the microphone.

She hoped someone was closer since she was still fifteen meters away with a throng of people in between. The crowd was lighter in the transepts, which must have been how the Turk was able to move forward so quickly.

Pushing through the last of the onlookers, she emerged at the velvet ropes that blocked access to the altar. The Turk was still to her right, but had stopped his advance. She spotted no other agents near him. She laid her right hand on the butt of her automatic in its side holster. She came to within three meters of the Turk when a woman approached him and intertwined her arm with his. She kissed him on the cheek and there was clear surprise on his face, then recognition and a smile as the two started to chat, clearly glad to see each other. They then turned and walked, arm in arm, back toward the main entrance.

"False alarm," she said into the mike.

Eisenhuth started speaking again.

Then something new caught her eye. One of the priests. Fair haired. Light skinned. Clean shaven. Edging his way past the others. Slow. Deliberate. His eyes locked on Eisenhuth at the podium. None of the other priests were jockeying for a better position. All the rest were standing still, focused on the speaker. Not this guy. He kept moving closer. Steady. Determined.

Suddenly he shoved people aside, several to the ground, and rushed into the open space between the altar and the pews. He leaped the velvet ropes into a no-man's-land that would be defended at all costs. It was the one place inside the cathedral that Cassiopeia felt reasonably safe protecting, the crowd to three sides, Eisenhuth to the other.

The priest rushed forward, pulling open his cassock, exposing a bare chest wrapped with packs of plastic explosives, nylon bags of shrapnel on top, ready to explode outward and kill anyone within thirty meters or more. He continued his advance, his right hand rising to a short length of wire dangling from the body pack.

The detonator.

Cassiopeia plunged her hand beneath her coat and found the gun.

He was now within ten meters of Eisenhuth, who'd stopped talking and was focused on the approach of her assailant. One of the guards at the altar started toward the man, while the other lunged for the chancellor.

But neither of them would make it, she concluded.

She freed her weapon from its holster and steadied herself to fire. The priest's hand gripped the detonator wire. She aimed, but realized the bullet would arrive too late. Both she, Eisenhuth, and a good portion of the crowd would be dead before the suicide bomber could be incapacitated.

Then the man's head erupted, his face transformed into a mass of red jelly. One moment his scalp was intact, the next the skin split like a melon and disintegrated in an eruption of blood, bone, and brains. Momentum caused his body to pitch forward, both hands instinctively reaching out, but his frame simply went limp, then slunk to the floor as a sheet might find the ground in a wind. There was a moment of what she thought was utter silence, then the cathedral's interior was flooded with a mélange of screams and shouts. She rushed forward and pointed her gun at the lifeless body.

"Get her out of here," she yelled to the security men, who whisked Eisenhuth from the altar as panic sent the crowd fleeing for the doors at the far end.

She knelt beside the corpse and heaved a sigh of relief. Camera flashes erupted in a blast of nearly blinding light. She stepped to the side and focused her gaze to the back of the church and up fifteen meters. Standing before a stone balustrade, backdropped by the sparkling copper torrents of organ pipes, stood Jan Bruin, rifle in hand.

"Nice shot," she said into the microphone.

The burly South African tipped the barrel of the gun in her direction, signifying his acknowledgment of the compliment.

"Sadly, though," Bruin said in her ear, "we will learn nothing from that unfortunate fool."

CHAPTER SEVENTY

COTTON LISTENED TO THE WIND AND RAIN. THE SUN WAS GONE, the valley cast in near-total darkness. He stood outside the farmhouse, under the covered entrance, and studied the woods beyond, probing for what he might have missed. He could remember times in many a locale when he'd sensed something long before anything ever happened. He once tried to identify what in his brain gave rise to that apprehension, but there was no answer. His mind simply was able to assimilate his surroundings and, more often than not, determine that things were not as they appeared.

Like now.

He listened as the storm caressed the valley. The wind hummed and the rain lashed the ground. Not savage or destructive, just a steady drizzle disturbed only by a stiff breeze. Trees bristled and announced their presence in every direction. Only the rectangular slab of amber light cast out from the open front door pierced the blackness. Schüb had told him that he owned most of the valley and that there were no other inhabitants for several kilometers, another reason why Bormann chose the location.

"We need to be going," he said to Schüb as he stepped back inside.

The old man was switching off lights.

He really should call Cassiopeia and tell her of Schüb's confession of fatherhood and what else he'd learned in Lugano. But that would have to wait until a face-to-face discussion.

"Have you decided where?" he asked.

"To Hesse. Theodor lives there. I was told yesterday that he is in residence until tomorrow."

"How do you think he'll react to learning you're his father?"

Schüb shook his head. "He worshiped Bormann. So he will deny it, but thankfully there are ways of proving parentage today. There is no doubt in my mind. Evi was certain. I would assume no one cares that I might be his father. But Evi, as his mother, that could still be a problem for him."

He heard again the intimate name. *Evi.*

Schüb seemed to like its use.

"I will make right what has, for so long, been wrong."

He could see that the old German was serious. A lifetime of tough choices had seemingly come down to the next twenty-four hours.

"Do you have a child?" Schüb asked.

"A son."

"Are you proud of him?"

"More than I can say. He's quite levelheaded. More so than me at times. I never really knew my own father. He was killed when I was ten. I don't want my son to go through that."

He didn't really know why he voiced that concern. Maybe it was that unsettled feeling still swirling inside him.

"Good sons are precious things," Schüb said. "My Jan is a joy. But Theodor. That one is a devil. He seems to be my penance for a life of doing as I pleased."

He asked, "What would have happened if Eva Braun had lived past the birth?"

"We would have continued, as before. Both of us trapped, yet neither with the courage to walk away. It is strange how youth invigorates us with energy, but denies us the wisdom to make the right choices. I failed to make my share, Herr Malone. I am sure in your life you have made choices. Some good, others bad."

That was true, but he couldn't decide if the good ones outweighed the bad. At least he was alive, living in Europe, doing something he'd always wanted to do. And in love, too. That mattered. Then he realized he was currently in a secluded Alpine valley, with a dangerous, unpredictable man who could derail the entire German electoral process. Perhaps even rattle the European Union itself. Which brought back that unsettled feeling.

"We need to go," he said again.

Schüb reached for the last lamp and was about to extinguish the bulb when, through the open front door, two headlights in the distance came alive in the darkness and a vehicle sped toward the farmhouse.

"Kill the light," he said as he slammed the front door shut.

Outside, he heard the engine growing louder.

He stared out the window.

The headlights weren't stopping.

They were coming straight at the house.

He lunged toward Schüb and swept the old man off his feet, the two of them propelled into the room beyond. They slammed into the plank floor just as the front wall imploded from the impact of the vehicle. The farmhouse walls were apparently well constructed and the inside partition between the rooms held the upper floors from collapsing.

"You all right?" he whispered.

Schüb stirred beneath him. "My old bones are pretty tough."

He motioned toward the rear and the kitchen. "Head forward. Keep down. Stay quiet."

Schüb was indeed remarkably agile for someone in his nineties. The old man managed to come to his feet, crouch down, and make it to the kitchen. The front part of the house was demolished. Sounds could be heard outside. Cotton remained still and listened through the rain.

Voices.

Two different men.

He found his gun and pointed to Schüb, indicating that he should retreat farther into the kitchen. Neither of the attackers said another word. Which made it hard to pinpoint their location, and the wind further masked their intrusion. He slipped out an opening in the wall into the rain and saw one of the assailants toting an automatic rifle. Perhaps they thought the frontal assault with the car had taken care of the problem. A good conclusion, actually.

He gave a few short bursts of a whistle.

The Old Spice jingle.

The shadow whirled but never got around.

He shot him in the legs.

Which dropped the guy to the wet ground. Shooting him in the chest might not be effective since these people came prepared and Kevlar vests could have been part of that preparation. The man writhed in pain but managed to bring the rifle around and ready himself for a burst of rounds.

Not tonight.

Cotton shot him in the head.

Which ended the problem.

But he'd definitely alerted the other intruder.

He slipped back close to the wrecked house and called out in German, "I have him." Hoping the ruse would work.

He heard movement from around the corner and readied himself for a shot. But something nestled close to the back of his skull. Hard. Unsettling.

The barrel of a gun.

Three men?

So much for staying ahead of them.

"Drop the weapon," a male voice said in English.

Another rifle-toting assailant appeared ahead of him from the other side of the house.

"I said drop the weapon."

He held on to the gun. The barrel stayed to his head from behind and the other guy, with an automatic rifle, kept approaching.

This was going to be tricky.

Rain continued to fall and the wind howled down through the mountains.

He stayed calm and still.

Patient until—

He ducked to avoid the gun to his scalp and rammed his left elbow into the man's ribs. At the same time his right hand swung around and fired at the man in front of him, who tumbled backward from a round to the chest. The assailant behind him recovered from the blow, but his awkward stance and loss of breath rendered him momentarily vulnerable.

A blast exploded in the night.

And the man collapsed to the soaked ground.

A dark form materialized through the rain.

Schüb.

With a shotgun.

Which came up, level, and fired again.

He whirled.

The man behind him had tried to stand, but Schüb ended that attempt.

The old man lowered the rifle.

"I have long kept guns here. Thankfully, whoever pilfered the diaries left them. It appears Theodor has deduced that I am not dead, and that I came here. He's the only one who knows of this place, besides me."

He checked all three corpses. White males. Middle-aged. No identification. Dead. They stepped back into the house, out of the rain.

Schüb set the shotgun aside.

Cotton found his cell phone.

"We need to get out of here. And fast."

CHAPTER SEVENTY-ONE

MARIE SAT CALMLY IN THE CHAIR. THE PUBLIC FUROR OVER WHAT happened in the cathedral a few hours ago had yet to subside. Never had a suicide bomber been filmed in the act, but her assassination attempt had been captured on video in its entirety. Every German station, along with all of the cable news stations from around the world, had repeatedly broadcast the dramatic footage for the past few hours. The pundits had all weighed in with a multitude of opinions as to who, what, and why. A police sniper had been credited with the kill, but she knew who to thank.

She was alone in her hotel room.

Cassiopeia Vitt had demanded that she be ensconced there, with security outside, until the full extent of the threat could be assessed. Deciding she'd pushed Vitt enough for the day, she'd offered no resistance. Her press secretary was clamoring that she speak with reporters. There were questions, and her answers would reassure the nation that she was okay. All of her aides were quite excited. Nothing better to endear a candidate with the people than for her life to be openly threatened. For them, this was an opportunity that must be exploited.

And she agreed.

But for a different reason.

She'd seen her assailant as he rushed toward her.

Fair skinned, light haired—Aryan.

She was certain that a background investigation would reveal that he was no priest. Instead he probably possessed new-right connections and radical politics. It would be easy to link him with radical conservatives, then them with Pohl, then Pohl with Bormann, and finally Bormann to Hitler. Perhaps the failed assassination would be enough to alert the comatose German majority to the lingering evil that surrounded them. After all, the would-be assassin was no foreigner. They were not rid of fanaticism. In fact, the malady still existed, currently manifested in Theodor Pohl. Yet there was still the problem of the money her father and husband had accepted. What had Kurt said earlier in the Mirror Room? *Your father was a Nazi. You may choose to deny the fact, ignore the obvious, but your father loved Adolf Hitler.*

He was right.

Her father and husband had knowingly profited from the Third Reich. She could not deny that fact, and no one would ever believe that she was unaware of anything until today.

And that sad realization seethed inside her.

Like a virus, the legacy of Hitler and his promised Thousand-Year Reich still coursed through Germany's veins. Ridding the nation of that infection seemed impossible. Her personal efforts at a cure, through sixteen years in office, might end over the next few days. The press would brand her a hypocrite and her message would thereafter fall on deaf ears.

Damn him. Damn Hitler.

Damn them all.

She stood from a table where her staff earlier had laid out a map of Germany. They had been planning the next few days' events, deciding on the quickest route from town to town.

She stared down at her homeland.

Hildesheim was located only a few kilometers from the northeast corner of the neighboring state of Hesse. Löwenberg, Pohl's fortress home, sat just over the border. Her finger traced the highway route, and she estimated the driving time to be less than an hour.

There was no choice. She had to act.

Besides, what did she have to lose that was not already lost?

Her career was over.

She stepped to the door and told her security man that she needed a car brought to the rear of the hotel immediately. She did not want to alert the press or her staff.

"Are you leaving?" the man asked.

"That's not your concern. Just arrange the car."

CASSIOPEIA JOGGED UP THE STAIRS TWO AT A TIME TOWARD THE hotel's third floor. One of the agents stationed downstairs had alerted her that Eisenhuth wanted a car brought to a rear entrance. The two security guards remained positioned outside the chancellor's room, and both indicated that she was still inside, readying herself to leave.

Cassiopeia entered the room without knocking.

"You're slow," Eisenhuth said, stepping from the bathroom. "I told them not to tell you, but I assumed the instruction would be ignored."

The older woman wore a pair of light trousers and a black turtleneck shirt. "Where are you going?"

"To see Theodor Pohl."

"That's insane."

"Probably. But since I most likely will not be in charge of this country past tomorrow, I'm going anyway."

"What could possibly be gained? The man just attempted to have you killed."

"What's he going to do? Kill me in his own home? I don't think so. He has a serious political problem, too."

"This is foolishness. Would there not be political repercussions if the press learned of your visit?"

The older woman's face hardened. "Those money transfers to my father's company will end my career, regardless of Pohl's parentage. I'm sick to death of political repercussions. This I'm doing for me."

"I'm going with you."

"It's not your fight," Eisenhuth said.

"Maybe not, but I doubt those men outside are going to allow you to go alone."

The chancellor shrugged. "I know. I only ask that you stay out of my way once we're there."

POHL SWITCHED OFF THE TELEVISION. OVER THE PAST COUPLE OF hours he'd watched the news reports in earnest. Marie Eisenhuth was apparently safe in Hildesheim, the suicide bomber dead, a full investigation under way.

He checked his watch. Nearly 11:00 P.M.

He'd issued a statement over an hour ago condemning the attack and professing his relief that the chancellor was unharmed. He decried the sad state of affairs when violence seemed the answer to everything, calling on the German people to act decisively in the coming election and send a message to terrorists. All in all an effective spin on a pathetic situation.

But what happened?

Engle had assured him the Chinese wanted to help, reiterating to them privately that his new government would pursue a more cooperative policy. But the assassin had not been Middle Eastern, or even foreign, as he'd expected. Instead the man was clearly German, and that presented a dire problem. Surely an investigation would reveal some connection with the new right. Cities, towns, and villages were filled with thousands of similarly angry young men. To some their radical ideas were popular, but they frightened many others. He worried that he could become involved by association, since he'd yet to openly denounce any of the extremist organizations. He couldn't—they formed a large part of his support. He might actually be forced to take a stance that could alienate his political base, and no amount of spin by his consultants could unring that bell.

He shook his head.

What a truly horrible situation.

How had his position deteriorated to this? Two months ago he was riding high. Just a few days ago, after Eisenhuth's Dachau fiasco, his poll numbers were climbing. Now everything seemed in jeopardy.

The door to the room opened and Josef Engle entered.

"What in God's name happened?" he asked his associate, trying to remain calm.

Engle sat in the chair across from him. "Apparently the Chinese used the opportunity we gave them to take down both you and Eisenhuth. I can only assume because of our reluctance to initially recruit their support, they made a better deal with one of the other parties. With both you and the chancellor crippled, a third option now might seem more attractive to the electorate. I've just learned that the assassin was a member of the Conservative Aryan Party."

He winced at the mention. Definitely domestic. And a problem. The group had been linked to several unsolved bombings. "I thought the Chinese wanted a friend in the German government?"

"They do. Just not you or her. They have apparently decided to turn elsewhere."

He shook his head. "And you suspected none of that when you made arrangements with them?"

"They seemed quite enthusiastic to help. How was I to know they were lying."

"You don't get it, do you? That dead bastard lying at the foot of the altar in Hildesheim is not an immigrant. He's a German."

"It was you who ordered an immediate move. I would have waited. Speed lacks careful thought and generates too much risk. There was no time to ferret out any deception from the Chinese."

"I should have shot you yesterday."

Engle said nothing, and his silence was irritating.

"Tomorrow, I'll attack her with the money from Hitler's Bounty, but that won't be enough to counter the sympathy. Attacking her further might even spur more popular sentiment her way. She could spin the money transfers as a fake plot from the right. More of their attacks on her, combined with the assassination attempt. The Chinese may not have wanted her to keep the chancellorship, but they may have just

THE KAISER'S WEB | 367

handed it to her. What about Austria? Were Schüb and the American there? Are they dead?"

"I have received no report."

He canted forward in the chair. "What does that mean?"

"It means that I have heard nothing."

He forced himself to breathe deeply, controlling his rage. Anger was not going to be productive.

The house phone on the far table interrupted the silence.

Engle stepped over and answered, speaking in a hushed tone. His associate hung up and said, "Kurt Eisenhuth is downstairs."

He shook his head. "Just what I need."

"What do you want me to do?"

An idea formed in his head. It came quick and made immediate sense. He faced Engle.

"Go get the fool."

CHAPTER
SEVENTY-TWO

COTTON SHIFTED IN THE SEAT AND TAPPED THE HELICOPTER PILOT on the shoulder. They were somewhere over southeastern Germany vectoring northwest toward Theodor Pohl's Hessian castle.

"Patch him through," he said into the headset.

Danny Daniels was on the radio with a direct feed.

He glanced at his watch: 11:20 P.M.

From his call nearly two hours ago, Danny had arranged for the Austrian Air Force to dispatch a chopper and transport them wherever they wanted to go. They'd had little time to talk, other than to make the arrangements, and he knew Daniels would now want details.

"Cotton, tell me why it was necessary I piss off a multitude of people at NATO to make this flight happen," Danny said through the hiss in his ears.

"That parentage we thought was there is not. Schüb is the father, not the other man." He had to watch his words even though they were on a scrambled channel. There were two Austrian flight officers in the compartment, along with Schüb, and though the rotors were loud and the officers wore no headsets, they could hear him as he spoke into the microphone around his neck.

"That's great, but that other aspect, the one you reported earlier, is still there?"

"It is."

"Events are happening in Germany," Danny said. "There was an attempt on Eisenhuth's life this evening at Hildesheim cathedral. Tell Herr Schüb that his son, Jan, is an excellent shot."

"Is she all right?"

"Perfectly. But she's presently on the way to Pohl's castle."

That shocked him. "Why?"

"She wants to confront him."

"That's foolishness."

"In more ways than one. Just get there. Cassiopeia is with her. They are probably about half an hour from arriving."

"We're forty-five minutes away. This is getting way out of hand."

"Tell me about it. But you're the man on the scene, so handle it."

"I'm retired."

"Aren't we all."

And the line went dead.

Pohl's gaze focused on the door as Kurt Eisenhuth entered the study. He immediately noticed a strange fire in the man's eyes. Unusual for someone who lacked any semblance of a backbone.

"You did it, didn't you?" Kurt said, his voice raised. "You are the one who tried to kill Marie."

He saw no reason to deny anything. "Unfortunately, the attempt failed."

Kurt's right hand came out of his coat pocket holding a small Sig Sauer automatic pistol.

The short barrel was leveled straight at him.

"You intend to shoot me?" Pohl asked, with no fear.

"I should do this nation a favor and end you here and now."

Two hours ago he'd waved off an offer for added security. The last thing he needed was inquisitive guards watching his every move. So he'd politely refused, assuring the justice ministry that he would shore up his own private security. Of course, there was no real need to do that, though now, staring at the gun pointed at him, he wished he'd at least added one extra man to check on visitors. But something told him the benign fool standing across the room was no threat. More like a big dog who bolted from the stoop, growling, teeth bared, yet always stopped at the curb, never venturing into the street, where the possibility of failure became all too real.

"Then, by all means," he said, "pull the trigger and reelect your inept wife leader of Germany."

"I never agreed for her to be harmed."

"No, you simply allowed me to ruin her. Provided, of course, that you were not implicated." He was taunting the older man, but he thought he knew him well enough to understand his weaknesses. "When are you going to accept reality? I am all that we have left. Kill me, and it dies a second time."

The gun hand started to shake. He nearly smiled.

He'd struck the precise nerve.

"Sometimes casualties are needed," he said.

"Not her," Kurt declared.

He sensed it almost immediately. Years of reading the faces of friends and foes had taught him the signals. Less a look than a feel. Even those schooled in concealing their emotions betrayed the signs. The flutter of an eyelid. A gentle crease in a brow. The quiver of lips. The signs varied from person to person, but there was always at least one.

Like here.

Which said that Kurt Eisenhuth knew more than he was saying.

He cursed himself for underestimating this man. He should have realized much sooner but, after all, he'd never taken this fool all that seriously.

He stepped to where Kurt stood. The Sig Sauer stayed level. He stopped with its barrel centimeters from his chest. "You know, don't you?"

The man's eyes glazed over with a shine like marzipan gave to pastry, and the growing mist answered his inquiry.

Kurt nodded.

"That's good," he said. "I'm glad."

He reached out and gripped the gun, ever so gently releasing it from Kurt's grip.

Tears pronounced defeat.

He slipped the gun into his back pocket. "Come with me, Kurt. There is something, I believe, you now need to see."

He led the way down the winding staircase into the underground rooms. Kurt followed. At the bottom he flicked on the light switch.

"My God," his guest whispered, catching sight of the initial items in the collection.

A colorful Sturmbannfahne stood to the right. The banner was a red ground, with a large black swastika set on a white circular field. In the upper right corner, embroidered in silver thread, was the number 14, representing the 14th SS Signals Battalion of Vienna.

He noticed Kurt's interest.

"I acquired it from an Austrian veteran who possessed the good sense to carefully pack the cloth away."

"It is immaculate, as if it were sewn yesterday."

"Which is why it is displayed here, at the beginning. I have many Sturmbannfahne, but few in such exceptional condition." He motioned ahead. "Come, I have more to show you."

He led his guest past the array of artifacts. Uniforms, helmets, hats, insignia, weapons, posters, badges, medals, toys, porcelain, glassware. All from the so-called Thousand-Year Reich. There were also a few exhibits. One caught Kurt's attention, and he halted to study the clothed table and white painted chairs.

"It is from Berchtesgaden. An original from one of the lodges that housed the generals and party officials when Hitler was in residence. The terraces were filled with these tables. One of the locals managed to secrete it away before the Americans burned everything."

On top of the white cloth rested a place setting for four that included crystal goblets, sterling silverware bearing a tiny swastika, and cups and bowls, all of white china with a delicate rose design.

"Can't you just imagine the generals sitting around, enjoying soup and wine, perhaps a plate of pastries, some bread, discussing the war, waiting to be called before their Führer."

He watched as Kurt continued to stare at the table and chairs.

"I never realized the depth of your devotion," Kurt finally said.

He laughed. "Devotion? I have none."

"But all this. Why have these things, if not for devotion?"

"My dear Kurt. People collect for a variety of reasons. Some for the value of the items. Others for personal obsession. Some merely for the joy it brings. None of those apply to me. I actually abhor the Third Reich. It is a lesson in failure. One I do not plan to repeat."

He stepped to a pedestal that displayed a camouflage drill tunic. The pea-patterned cloth was decked out in the shoulder straps of an *Obersturmführer*. More awards were pinned to the breast pocket above a ribbon bar. A black-and-silver Knight's Cross hung around the neck. "The man who would have worn this uniform would have looked quite strange. Look at it. Camouflage fatigues adorned with ribbons and medals. Only an arrogant Nazi would be proud of such a display. They were truly odd people. We have no room for them in the new Germany."

"Yet you collect their symbols."

"To remind me of inadequacy. That's why I collected all this." He motioned ahead. "We have farther to go."

Down the tiled corridor he walked, Kurt following behind. He turned his head to see his guest stop and gaze at more of the displays, fingering the scratchy cloth of the uniforms, gently brushing the waxed bill of the caps, carefully caressing the porcelain, clearly in awe.

Their walk ended at the wooden door.

Kurt came to a stop. "What is in there?"

"Open and see."

Kurt stepped forward and pulled on the iron handle.

The plank door opened without a sound.

The room beyond was spacious and backlit from wall sconces. The far walls were lined with glass-fronted cases, each one illuminated by a ceiling-mounted floodlight. All of the oak shelves behind the glass teemed with odd-shaped volumes packed tight in long rows. The spines glowed in the light with a variety of color. But what dominated the room were the three sarcophagi in the center, each flooded in a pool of blue-white light. The exteriors were all of marble, one gray, the other pink, both similar in size, and one, much smaller, in a combination of taupe and gray.

Kurt entered the chamber and stepped immediately to the tombs. "Who are they?"

"My mother, father, and brother."

Kurt faced him. "Why keep them here?"

"Because they are not safe anyplace else."

"Your mother and father were not people of ill repute. What places their graves in danger?"

"My father was Martin Bormann. My mother was Eva Braun." He spoke the words with pride, so rarely had he ever been given the privilege of stating that declaration.

Kurt Eisenhuth stared at him in amazement. "You speak nonsense."

"Do I?" He stepped toward the shelves. "The words contained in these diaries do not speak nonsense. They were written by my mother and father, in their own hands." He stopped at the shelves. "They tell the story of their lives, from after the war. Their words have taught me so much."

Kurt said nothing.

"I am on the verge of accomplishing what my father and his contemporaries could not. Leaders are poised all across the European continent ready to spring forward. The electorate merely requires a spark, and Germany will be that spark. My election will signal the charge. It will be a new-right revolution. Europe will reclaim itself from all those who have tried to dilute us. When the effort ends, the liberals and moderates will be no more, and the new unified Europe will be strong and glorious."

He stepped close to Kurt.

"Now I ask you. Please, tell me all that you know."

CHAPTER
SEVENTY-THREE

CASSIOPEIA SPOTTED THE CASTLE, ITS DIRTY GRAY WALLS SPLASHED with a sodium-vapor glow, the spectacle matted by a velvet sky. Löwenberg was impressive. The citadel stood in clear defiance to the surrounding lowland, once surely the home of regional barons, now the bastion of a man linked with an unspeakable past.

Marie had remained silent on the drive from Hildesheim. She'd left the minister alone with her thoughts, wondering just exactly what was going to happen once they were face-to-face with Pohl. Surely he wasn't going to confess to any assassination attempt. In fact, just them coming here would raise far more questions than answers. But the chancellor was not to be dissuaded, wanting to speak with Pohl tonight, so that was precisely what they would do.

She wound the car up the road toward a gate in the wall curtain. A solitary guard stood outside the entrance dressed in a peacoat.

She eased forward and stopped.

"We are here to see Herr Pohl," she told the guard.

"It is after midnight."

"He called for us. This is the chancellor of Germany. Surely you recognize her."

The man glanced in through the open driver's-side window, and it was clear he knew the face.

"Herr Pohl telephoned earlier and requested we come. He is waiting for us," Marie said in a polite voice.

The man hesitated an instant before waving them through.

Worked every time. Speak clear, act authoritative, accept no rebuke, and most people backed down. Especially when you had the head of the country in the car.

She motored through the gate and entered a spacious inner courtyard that seemed to serve as a parking lot. Stone walls for the various buildings enclosed its perimeter. Some of the mullioned windows glowed with light, but most loomed dark and silent. She took in the height and depth of the courtyard, studying her surroundings, preparing herself for anything, then parked off to one side between a Volvo coupe and a Mercedes van.

They stepped out into a warm, clear night.

"That lighted entrance, there, seems the way in," she said, pointing to an illuminated archway.

They started across the cobbles, passing other dark cars. Near the archway, Marie suddenly stopped.

"What is it?" Cassiopeia asked.

The minister's gaze was on a BMW, its shiny exterior reflecting the glow from the nearby entrance. Marie stepped close to the car. She then rounded the trunk and approached the driver's-side door. She glanced in through the window and studied a sticker affixed to the front windshield.

"This is my husband's car. The sticker is a company identification. It is his personal vehicle."

There was amazement in her voice.

"What is it doing here?" she asked.

"Not it," Marie said. "What is *he* doing here?"

Shock filled the older woman's face, the look one of utter betrayal. But Cassiopeia was wondering the same thing.

What *was* Kurt Eisenhuth doing here?

Resolve came into Marie's eyes. Then the older woman marched to the door and, without knocking or otherwise announcing her presence, opened the latch.

They both stepped inside.

ENGLE STOOD BESIDE THE WINDOW ON THE SECOND FLOOR. HE'D watched as Marie Eisenhuth and Cassiopeia Vitt drove into the courtyard, then proceeded to the only lit door. He'd noticed the chancellor's examination of the BMW and concluded that she now realized her husband was inside the castle. He'd also watched earlier as Pohl led Kurt Eisenhuth down into the subterranean chamber. That was unusual, as his employer held that particular secret quite close.

The chancellor's presence here was puzzling.

Whatever Pohl had in mind, events were definitely unfolding.

He walked over to the bed, reached for the phone on the nightstand, and punched in the intercom code.

THE SHARP RING OF THE PHONE ACROSS THE UNDERGROUND chamber cut Pohl's concentration like a cleaver.

"Wait," he said, raising a hand to Kurt.

He marched to the wall unit and yanked off the receiver.

"You have more guests," Engle said.

He listened as his acolyte reported what was happening above. In-credible. The chancellor herself had come. He glanced across at the figure of Kurt Eisenhuth. Perhaps there was still a way to flush his op-ponent from the race and save his own chances. He turned away from Kurt and faced the wall.

"Send her down below," he whispered.

"What about Cassiopeia Vitt?"

"Amuse her."

"Understood."

He hung up the phone, returned to his guest, and said, "Please, go on."

ENGLE LEFT THE BEDCHAMBER AND PROCEEDED QUIETLY THROUGH the upper corridors. He stopped just short of the open balustrade and carefully peered down to the foyer below. Cassiopeia Vitt and Marie Eisenhuth stood looking about, admiring the opulence. The stewards were all gone for the night. Pohl had planned to retire early, supposedly upset over the news of Eisenhuth's death. His employees would later make excellent witnesses to an earlier scene of sadness and concern, shock and dismay.

But that had not happened.

He stepped to the open railing and said, *"Guten nacht."*

Both of the women's heads angled upward.

"Who are you?" the chancellor asked.

"Josef Engle," Cassiopeia answered.

"At your service," he said.

"Where is Herr Pohl?" Eisenhuth asked.

"Follow the corridor ahead into the master bedchamber. There is an open door there to a stairway. He is at the bottom."

"Is my husband there, too?"

"He is."

Eisenhuth pointed upward and faced Vitt. "That man is a murderer. Apprehend him."

And the chancellor marched off.

CASSIOPEIA STARED UP AT ENGLE. "ADA TOLD ME TO KILL YOU."

The man chuckled. "I'm sure she did. After all, as the chancellor noted, I did kill her friend."

Her hand reached for the weapon at her hip. Engle's right hand, which had been below the stone balustrade, out of view, came up holding a gun. She freed her weapon and pivoted right, hitting the hard floor, momentarily shielded from a direct line of fire. She rolled, swung the weapon around with both hands, and aimed high.

Engle was gone.

CHAPTER
SEVENTY-FOUR

COTTON SURVEYED LÖWENBERG FROM THE AIR AS THE CHOPPER
lost altitude and swooped close. There was an assortment of buildings, several once surely residences, keeps, chapels, stewards' quarters,
a bailey, a coach house, and a kitchen, the walls probably erected by a
succession of owners who apparently possessed the time and resources.
Mullioned, dormer, and graceful oriel windows were plentiful. Arc
lights cast the stone walls with a mellow, defiant medieval beauty.

He noticed cars parked inside a broad, stone-paved courtyard, perhaps once, centuries ago, a retainer's village that had clustered to the
castle like a coral growth, its occupants secure with the protection thick
stone walls then provided. He saw no one other than a lone guard at the
entrance to the courtyard.

He motioned down.

"Land on the road, outside the walls," he said in the microphone
around his head.

The pilot started his approach. Schüb was sitting beside him, but the
old man wore no communications equipment.

"The chancellor and Cassiopeia have to be inside by now," he said to
Schüb over the noise.

"I must deal with Theodor in my own way."

He wanted to know, "What do you have in mind?"

"That is between me and him."

He decided not to press. Decades of bad decisions had led the old warrior sitting beside him to this onerous place in central Germany. Actions the madman Martin Bormann conceived to save his own miserable hide had brought about the birth of a son and a movement that reality could never reconcile with rationality. Perhaps Schüb was right. Pohl was best left to his father.

The chopper touched down.

He led the way out, squinting against the blast of the rotors as the helicopter rose, leaving them in silence as it disappeared off to the east.

They approached the lone guard who stood before a pillared gateway.

"We're here to see Herr Pohl," he said in German. "We are with the chancellor's office."

"Nothing was said about others arriving by air."

The man was armed with a side pistol, as were both he and Schüb.

"Just an oversight. As you saw, we arrived by military transport. We were flown directly here per the chancellor's orders."

"I need to check."

He did not want to announce his presence, so as the guard turned toward a small booth where a phone awaited he wrenched the man back and slugged him hard across the left jaw.

The man's body went down to the cold pavement.

"That was rude," Schüb said.

"But necessary."

He motioned forward.

"Shall we?"

CASSIOPEIA RUSHED DOWN THE CORRIDOR TOWARD AN ENTRANCE at the far end. The space beyond loomed dim. Josef Engle was leading her. No doubt. But there was no other course.

She had to follow.

She stopped outside the doorway.

No lights burned on the other side.

She made a point never to rush into a dark room. So she quickly slipped past the doorway and entered what was once a grand knights' hall, adorned with colonnades that rose along all four sides. A procession of colorful banners draped down from above. The largest, illuminated by the weak light of sporadic incandescent fixtures, was the symbol for the former German empire—a black, red, and gold banner emblazoned with an eagle. Glass-walled display cases stood in rows down two sides, each containing a suit of armor. The room was clearly a place of splendor, where barons once impressed visitors and confirmed their imperial authority. Pohl was apparently enamored by such displays.

But she should not be surprised.

Her gaze probed the darkness, up and down, into each of the arches.

She stood just beyond a stab of light from the corridor, at the end of one of the archways. Was Engle here, on the ground floor? Or was he above, in one of the galleries, looking down? Was he right? Left? Or on the cavernous room's other side?

A gun fired and a bullet careened off the stone floor to her right. She dove left, seeking cover behind one of the tall display cases.

"You might find the task of capturing me more difficult than you think," Engle said.

COTTON NOTICED THAT THE ONLY DOOR LEADING FROM THE courtyard was partially open. He'd already felt the hood of a light-colored Mercedes coupe and determined that its engine remained warm. Probably the vehicle Cassiopeia and Marie Eisenhuth had arrived in. Schüb walked ahead of him, also apparently aware that the door leading inside was cracked open. The old man marched straight to the lit portico and entered the castle.

He followed Schüb inside.

A gunshot came from somewhere within.

Off to the left and above. His eyes locked on the second-floor balcony and a thick stone balustrade.

"I am going this way," Schüb said, and the old man slowly walked ahead toward a wide corridor.

"I'm headed there," he said, pointing up the staircase.

CHAPTER
SEVENTY-FIVE

MARIE FOUND POHL'S BEDCHAMBER. NORMALLY SHE WOULD never have ventured into such a private place, but her husband was here and she desperately needed to know why.

She entered the room and immediately noticed the enormous bed with bulbous Jacobean legs. Above its head hung a massive oil painting that depicted the Archangel Michael with his sword directing anxious wayfarers toward heaven. The symbolism was not lost on her. Pohl apparently liked angels, as a brace of flying nymphs, carved in wood, held aloft lamps that lined the walls.

Then she noticed the panel.

On the far side, in an alcove that jutted off the main room.

A slab of stone hinged open.

What had Engle said?

"Follow the corridor into the master bedchamber. There is an open door there."

She walked over, stepped inside, and saw stone stairs lined with a carpet runner that wound down in a tight circle.

"He is at the bottom."

She slowly descended and finished standing on a polished-slate floor, staring at a Nazi banner. Her attention drifted ahead and she spied more memorabilia, each object displayed with care, as if in a museum. She entered the macabre world, her mind reeling at the spectacle. Memories from her childhood flashed vivid. Photographs of her father wearing armbands adorned with a swastika, a jacket she'd once seen in his closet, similar to ones on display before her. A gorget, bandolier, and gauntlets, all familiar and, most disturbing, a porcelain basset hound puppy, similar to one she recalled being in her father's house for many years, innocuously displayed on a shelf in his study. She later learned how those sculptures were fashioned at Allach, near Munich, by prisoners from Dachau.

She stopped and stared at the shiny white dog.

Tears welled in her eyes.

Her father. That poor misguided fool. She'd loved him for his tenderness, yet hated him for his politics. Thankfully, he never forced his beliefs onto her, and rarely did he even speak of the subject, but the words he'd spoken when he thought death was near—*Heil Hitler*—verified all that she'd long suspected about his values.

Voices broke the silence.

Whispers.

Like the gentle rustle of paper.

She crept forward, her pace as if walking on shards of glass. Her stomach tumbled with anxiety and she swiped the moisture from her eyes. She rounded a corner, and an open door appeared at the far end of the path.

More voices.

Kurt's and Pohl's.

Her legs were numb, her hands clammy. An unsettling fear gripped her entire body, similar to the day when she buried her parents.

She walked on without a sound to a doorway, then stopped short.

And listened as Kurt spoke.

BORMANN WATCHED AS EVA BRAUN WRITHED AND SCREAMED IN *agony. The bitch was fighting the birth, though the midwife had cautioned her to relax. Her legs stiffened as another contraction racked her abdomen. She'd been nothing but*

difficult for the past few months. Pregnancy was not a condition she seemed to enjoy. But their constant movement had likewise complicated things.

They'd teamed up finally in Barcelona.

He'd come from the north, through Denmark and the Netherlands. She arrived from the south, starting in Switzerland and moving by rail into Italy, then across France. The Barcelona house had been used during the war and remained a secure location. Not taking any chances, he'd moved them farther into Spain, to an anonymous spot that he chose. The Führer was dead. He was in charge now.

And things were going to be different.

Braun screamed again.

He was tired of listening to her weakness. Women were so inept. Which was precisely why no fighting force in the world utilized them for anything beyond menial tasks. They were good for only one thing and that was precisely what Eva Braun was presently trying to perform.

Childbirth.

Braun screamed again.

"When will this end?" he asked the midwife. She was a Spaniard who thankfully spoke German.

"The baby is coming now."

He stood behind the woman, whose head was plunged between Braun's spread legs, each ankle tied to a post of the bed. Braun's legs pulled on the bindings, but the thick posts held firm.

"Hurry it," he said.

"Talk to God about that," the midwife said, never turning her head from Braun's writhing pelvis.

Another scream pierced the room. Thankfully, the farmhouse was isolated.

The midwife reached out as Braun gritted her teeth. "Now. Push with all you can muster."

Braun's head came up from the bed. For a moment Bormann's gaze locked with hers. Interesting. No fear. Instead he sensed resolution. Then why temper that virtue with a submission to pain? He wanted to tell her to shut up and finish, but it seemed that the end was at hand. Braun's teeth were clenched tight, her face contorted, all her focus seemingly on expelling the baby from her womb.

"Sí. Sí," the midwife said.

Braun pushed even harder. Her breaths came short and shallow. Sweat glazed her brow. The woman grappled between Braun's legs and he watched as a head became visible, then shoulders, arms, chest, and finally legs as the fetus emerged.

"What is the sex?" he asked.

The midwife ignored him. Her attention remained on the infant that was now cradled in her arms, the umbilical cord tracing a path back inside the womb. Braun had relaxed on the bed and appeared unconscious.

He could not see the baby clearly, so he moved closer.

"The sex. Tell me," he demanded.

"A girl."

Had he heard right? "Truly?"

"You sound amazed."

He recovered his emotions. No one must know what he thought. "I only speak of the joy she will bring to the mother."

"It is good to have a daughter."

The midwife turned her attention back to Braun as the afterbirth was expelled.

He stepped away and considered reality.

Hitler's daughter.

He recalled what his once Supreme Leader had told him after Braun had revealed in the Führerbunker that she was pregnant. There'd been no anger and no joy. Just a placid acceptance of another disappointment. But Hitler had wanted the baby to survive, harboring a dream of his issue one day resurrecting the movement. So he released Bormann from his duty to die and instructed him to ensure that both Braun and the baby survived. He'd accepted the charge only as a way of finally ridding himself of the yoke of death that remaining in Berlin would entail. He'd not wanted to stay in the first place and had urged Hitler to flee south to the Alps and the Redoubt.

But the fanatical idiot had refused.

Insanity.

Hitler actually thought that he could rally enough military might to thwart both the American and the Russian armies advancing across Germany.

He glanced down and noticed that the midwife had tied the umbilical cord and cut the tissue away from the baby. The infant started to cry, and the woman swiped the tiny face with a wet rag.

"She is a beauty," the midwife said.

"No flaws?"

"None I can see. She is perfect."

Not what he wanted to hear, but at least the child was female.

"Give her to me."

The woman laid the screaming baby in his arms. Sparse wisps of black hair matted the scalp. The mouth was open as the baby shrieked her presence to the world. He wondered what Adolf Hitler would have thought to be here, holding his daughter, admiring what he and Eva Braun had conceived. Most likely the placid fool would have felt nothing, merely congratulating Braun on doing her duty and producing another loyal citizen of the Reich. Would it have mattered that the baby was not male? Surely, but he doubted that there would have been any more attempts. Hitler had always been drawn to children, but only because they represented the perfect frame for his perfect image to society. Hard to argue with a leader who surrounded himself with innocence. Now, staring down at the daughter Hitler would never know, he was more convinced than ever as to what needed to be done.

He laid the baby on the edge of the bed, beside a still-unconscious Eva Braun. He removed the Luger he'd carried since leaving the Führerbunker and fired one bullet into the midwife's skull.

The woman's body slammed to the floor.

Eva Braun never moved.

Exhaustion had claimed her.

She would be told that the baby died at birth and the midwife was killed for incompetence. There would be no argument from her. Why should there be? They were now bound together. Their lives forever intertwined.

And that was fine.

She wasn't altogether unpleasant, and his ability to enjoy outside female companionship in the years ahead was, at best, limited. He must be careful. He'd watched how women could undo a man. That was not going to happen to him. Eva Braun would do as she was told or he'd plant a bullet in her skull, too.

He lifted the infant from the bed and walked from the room. Outside, in the shade of a porch that jutted from the front of the farmhouse, sat a man.

He handed him the baby. "Raise her as your own."

The man's eyes were misty with pride. "She is his?"

"Absolutely."

"I heard a shot."

"The midwife's duty."

The man seemed to understand. "There can be no witnesses."

"Just you and me, old friend."

"I will raise her well."

"It is of no matter to me any longer. I was to do as I have done, then leave it to you."

That was a lie. He was supposed to raise the child himself. But he possessed other ideas, ones that did not involve Adolf Hitler. He should have simply killed the infant. That would have ended any future problems. But nothing would be gained by that. Let the girl live. No one would ever know her parentage.

The man rose from his chair.

"Live long, old friend," he told him.

"You too."

As his visitor headed for a car parked under the shade of sprawling elm, he called out, "What will you name her?"

Albert Herzog turned back.

"She will be Marie, after my great-grandmother."

"Who told you?" Pohl asked.

He'd listened to Kurt Eisenhuth recount what he knew and had added some of the missing pieces to form a complete picture of what happened in northern Spain in January 1946.

"Albert related everything to me before he died," Kurt said.

"The old man kept his secret well."

"He considered it an honor to raise Hitler's daughter."

"And you, is it an honor to be married to her?"

"It is. She has been a good wife." Kurt's face softened. "She seems to have inherited her mother's temperament. But she became a leader thanks to her natural father."

"Do not despair," Pohl said. "I will lead this nation with all the strength required."

Kurt motioned to the tombs. "Why are they here?"

"To remind us."

A puzzled look came to Kurt Eisenhuth's face. "Of what?"

MARIE STOOD FROZEN. HER HUSBAND'S WORDS, COMBINED WITH Pohl's interjections, had made clear the unthinkable.

The unfathomable.

She was the daughter of Adolf Hitler and Eva Braun.

She stared down at her hands and arms, her chest and legs. Was every fiber of her being genetically linked to an unspeakable evil? Her entire adult life had been spent repudiating what the Third Reich stood for. She'd never said anything but the worst about Hitler and every single one of his henchmen. Her political philosophy abhorred all that had been National Socialism. Where some in the country preached the good in Nazism while rejecting the bad, she despised it all and made no secret of her complete revulsion. That was why it had been easy for her to appear at Dachau. So what if the truth angered voters. They needed to hear it and, more important, they needed to never forget.

But now.

Albert Herzog was not her natural father. She was adopted. Or more accurately, she was abandoned.

Given away.

She willed her feet to move, trying to muster enough courage to step forward. She needed to confront the two men in the other room. Her muscles seemed atrophied with anxiety from her husband's stunning admission.

Another step toward the doorway.

She must be strong. Show no weakness.

A few more steps.

She entered.

Kurt stood in the center of the windowless space, his back to her, beside three raised marble tombs. Pohl was across on the far side, facing her, before lighted shelves brimming with leather-bound books.

Pohl saw her immediately.

Try as she might, her face betrayed the fact that she'd heard every word.

"Ah, finally," Pohl said. "You are here."

Kurt whirled around and muttered, "Oh, my God."

Pohl seemed pleased with himself. "Do come in, Frau Bundeskanzlerin. After all, you and I are family, and it is past time you paid respects to our mother."

CHAPTER
SEVENTY-SIX

CASSIOPEIA HUDDLED ON THE FLOOR BESIDE THE DISPLAY CASE. She harbored no illusions that she was safe. Apparently Engle wanted her precisely where she now found herself. She still gripped her gun, but it was of little use since Engle commanded the high ground. She'd managed to see the barrel flash in the darkness, which confirmed that he stood in a darkened gallery above her, possessed of a clear view of the entire hall.

"Come and get me," Engle said.

The bastard seemed to be everywhere thanks to the lousy acoustics.

"I plan to," she called out.

Engle laughed. "I like you, Fräulein."

COTTON HEARD THE SHOT AND DREW OUT THE AUTOMATIC PISTOL he'd taken from the assailant in Austria. He then approached an open doorway, listening as Cassiopeia and another man spoke, their voices hollow in what was apparently a cavernous space. The corridor he was traversing was well lit, and its yellow light spilled on into the semi-darkness beyond the entrance. He did not want to announce his presence, so he stopped and used a tall cabinet full of swords for cover as he assessed the situation.

The far side of the corridor was cast in shadow as the nearest incandescent fixture burned ten feet back from where he stood. A couple of Claude Lorrain and Lucas Cranach canvases dotted the stone wall leading into the room beyond, their images blackened in the dim illumination.

He stepped across the corridor to the far side. Nothing betrayed his movement. He hugged the wall and eased past the paintings. He was now wedged in a corner directly adjacent to the doorway. Through the darkness he saw Cassiopeia, huddled beside one of several tall glass cases, each displaying suits of armor. She saw him, too, and used hand signals to alert him that trouble lurked above. He glanced upward and caught movement in the upper gallery.

Josef Engle?

Who else?

He decided to not announce his presence and signaled he was going up. She nodded her understanding. That was one of the things he really respected about her. No nonsense. Cool under pressure. Team player.

He slipped inside and moved toward a staircase to his right that led up to the second floor. He stayed close to the wall and made his way toward the first step.

Niches were everywhere.

Dark voids where trouble could lurk.

ENGLE POSSESSED ALL THE ADVANTAGE. HE TOWERED OVER CASsiopeia Vitt, and his view of the hall was unobstructed. Only the lower galleries remained shielded, but the staff was down for the night and would not return until morning so he should not be disturbed. He knew every square centimeter of the hall below, and he could maneuver Vitt at will.

Which was fine. That was the whole idea.

To amuse her.

Keep her occupied so his employer could accomplish whatever it was he had in mind. But the chancellor had changed things with the order to *"apprehend him,"* and apparently Vitt was taking the command to heart. He'd chosen the knights' hall specifically for its darkness and spaciousness. He stood in the recesses of the upper gallery, near the far end of the displays below, and wondered about the whole endeavor.

Marie Eisenhuth, here, in Löwenberg, was never in the plan.

But he had to trust that Pohl knew what he was doing.

And considering his failures of late, he decided to do his part.

He crept down the gallery, staying a couple of meters back from the balustrade, and selected a new vantage point.

Below was quiet. That was okay.

Passing the time was the whole idea.

CASSIOPEIA KNEW THE BASTARD WAS ABOVE HER. SHE FELT LIKE A rat in a maze with nowhere to go. But she had to give Cotton time to get into position. She had no intention, though, of crouching behind a glass case waiting for Engle to make a move. What was he going to do, shoot her? With the chancellor of Germany here? Hardly. How would Pohl ever explain her death? He couldn't. No. She was being played. Apparently her presence was not required wherever Pohl and Kurt Eisenhuth were located.

But she agreed with the chancellor.

Engle needed to be dealt with.

Might as well challenge him now and see just how far this game was going to go. So she pivoted back on her butt, still gripping the gun in one hand, and rolled to her right, firing once up into the upper gallery, which allowed her the moment needed to roll farther toward the next display case.

ENGLE SAW VITT MOVE IN THE DARKNESS, THEN A MUZZLE FLASH as she fired a round upward. Thankfully, he was nowhere near where she'd aimed.

So he returned fire.

Obliterating the glass in the case behind which she lurked.

CASSIOPEIA KNEW SHE WOULD HAVE ONLY AN INSTANT THANKS TO the momentary confusion she'd surely generated in Engle.

And he did not disappoint.

The glass case beside her shattered.

A bit too close for comfort.

So she sprang to her feet and plunged into the darkness that draped the base of the hall's towering walls. She was about ten meters from the nearest arch that led out into the first-floor gallery. Her eyes probed the darkness above, trying to see where Engle might be. The first gun flash had come from across the hall. If Engle was still there he would have a clear angle for more shots.

Then it occurred to her.

Engle had moved.

She angled her head upward. The wall stones progressively darkened as they rose past the second floor to the coffered ceiling.

He was there.

Right above her.

In the gallery.

COTTON CRESTED THE TOP OF THE STAIRS AND STARED AHEAD. Glass tinkled to the floor below as another shot was fired. On the way up he'd caught sight of Cassiopeia rolling out from behind the case and moving into the blackness. She was diverting attention. Keeping Engle busy. Allowing him time to get close.

Before him, more niches lined the outer wall of the gallery, each one a black hole. Ahead was equally stark. His eyes were still adjusting, but he was able to catch movement on the opposite side of the hall. He used the darkness surrounding him and crept forward, turning left at one end and traversing the short side toward the remaining long side, where Engle was apparently positioned. He stopped beside one of the supporting arches, peered around the edge, and realized that Engle was now directly above where Cassiopeia had last been seen. While Engle's attention was on Cassiopeia, he inched forward. For a moment he had a spark of déjà vu to a few years ago and another German castle where he'd been in a similar situation. That day he'd had some help. Not now. He was on his own, and the woman he loved was in trouble.

"Engle," Cassiopeia called out, her voice echoing. "It's all over."

"I don't see it that way."

"The election is finished for both candidates. That means you're finished, too."

Across the darkened hall, into the far gallery he spied Engle, who stayed in the shadows behind one of the arches, preventing a clear shot.

"You're not leaving here," Cassiopeia said.

"On the contrary, Fräulein, it is you who will not be going anywhere."

Engle came into view as he approached the upper balustrade and swung his gun up, then pointed straight downward to where Cassiopeia waited.

Cotton fired his weapon.

The round found Engle's chest and sent the German back from the railing. He finished the job and fired again. Engle's body teetered, then thudded to the floor.

Cassiopeia came into view below. "I was hoping you had a shot."

He lowered the gun. "Me too."

"The chancellor is roaming around this castle somewhere," she said. "As is Gerhard Schüb."

"I think we should find them both."

CHAPTER
SEVENTY-SEVEN

MARIE ABSORBED THE AMAZING SIGHT BEFORE HER. FROM A macabre underground museum of Nazi memorabilia, she'd entered what appeared to be a funerary chamber. And what had Pohl said? *"Do come in. After all, you and I are family and it is past time you paid respects to our mother."* Kurt was staring at her in disbelief—surely she was the last person he'd expected to see. She ignored his presence and continued to absorb the sight of the three tombs.

"The one to your left contains the mortal remains of your mother," Pohl said. "Eva Anna Paula Braun Hitler Bormann. She birthed me, as well. Though, as you seem to now know, our fathers were different."

She faced Kurt and asked, "Papa told you all of what you just spoke of?"

"You heard?"

"Every word."

He hesitated a moment before nodding. "You are the daughter of the Führer. Hitler's issue. His legacy. There is no question."

Enough pride came in the statement to make her stomach queasy. She heard again what her father said on his deathbed. *"My world died long ago, and I with it. You are all that remains."*

She knew now what he meant.

"Hitler wrote in his will," Pohl said, "*I die with a happy heart aware that there will spring up the seed of a radiant renaissance of the National Socialist movement.* You were the seed of which he spoke."

The thought made her sick.

"You were ready to attack me for my parentage," Pohl said. "Will you be equally as stern on yourself? Do the people deserve to know of *your* mother and father?"

"I don't know, Theodor, perhaps we should explore that more fully."

The voice came from behind her.

She turned to see a wizened old man standing in the doorway. His face carried a sad, remorseful mien, though the eyes—black dots in an oily sea—burned with life. She knew instantly who he must be.

Gerhard Schüb.

The old man entered.

She turned back and saw that Pohl was appraising his new guest with a look that combined curiosity and apprehension.

"It seems another corpse has risen from the dead," Pohl finally said. "You died two years ago."

"A necessary tactic to avoid your scrutiny. I could tell, then, that you were planning something. So I decided to fade away, where I could observe without your watchful eye."

"You know me well."

"Too well, I am afraid."

She watched the two men, who seemed to be ignoring everyone and everything around them, their focus on each other. The intensity was obvious, things only understood between them, as with she and Kurt.

"What are you doing here?" Pohl asked.

"I came to see you. A visit. Like we had so many times in the past."

Schüb studied the room's adornments, ending his perusal at the tombs. "So this is where you brought them. And the purpose?"

"They did not deserve an anonymous grave in Africa. They are my family."

Schüb stepped to the smaller of the large sarcophagi. Eva Braun's. "She would be appalled."

"That is your opinion."

"Did you know her? Did you ever speak with her? How could you possibly understand what would have pleased her?" The old man pointed. "You know nothing, Theodor."

Pohl's arm swept the air back toward the glass-fronted shelves. "I know what these say. Her words. Her thoughts. They are clear. I. Know. Her."

"No, they are far from her thoughts."

Pohl seemed not to hear. "She told me everything about her, in her own hand. And about my father."

"She told you nothing," Schüb spat out. "She simply told you what she wanted you to know. And I assure you, it was precious little."

Pohl did not react to the rebuke. Instead, he said, "I remember our talks. You spoke of her with pride. You, too, told me many things about her *and* him."

"I, too, told you only what I wanted you to know."

Pohl stormed across the room toward Schüb. The old man stood his ground as the younger man came close. "I ask you again, what are you doing here?"

"I came to tell you something."

"Then say it and leave."

"I have followed you closely through the years. Over the past few days I have learned even more. Quite a web you conceived." Schüb faced the chancellor. "It was Theodor who sent that information to you under my name. He thought me dead so it seemed a safe tactic. He knew that your morals and values would compel you to investigate. Which is what he wanted. Of course, the idea was for you to discover the money, not his or your parentage. My sister, Ada, changed his plan and led Fräulein Vitt and Herr Malone to Africa and me." Schüb threw Pohl a calculating look. "I was told you received the news of my death with great joy."

Pohl snickered. "Do not believe all that you hear."

"On that we agree. I followed your political rise, and wondered when you would finally emerge. I was well aware of the money transfers to the Eisenhuth and Herzog concerns. Bormann approved those, while in life. I authorized many myself, after he was gone." Schüb clasped his hands behind his back. "Frau Bundeskanzlerin, everything was a ruse. All to be taken out of context by you. There never were any pictures of Eva Braun with her children. Nor were there images of Bormann with them. The Chilean deputy minister of investigations, the one who started the investigation into you, was on Theodor's payroll. But he became a problem and did not live to enjoy whatever fruits were promised him. Martin Bormann liked to say that to win a war, don't attack the army, or the enemy's cities, or supply lines, or armament. To truly win a war, attack the enemy's plan. That's what Theodor did. To win the election, he diverted you on a chase that would lead to your own downfall. He made, though, two mistakes. The first was killing a dear friend of my sister's a few years ago. The second was forgetting about me."

She listened as the words came in a clipped, guttural voice. The corners of the old man's mouth drew down as he pointed at Pohl and said, "Isabel's death was a miscalculation on your part. A bad one."

Pohl said nothing. But there was clear anxiety. It was interesting for her to watch as *his* whole world also crumbled around him.

"And there is one more thing," Schüb said. "I am your father."

Pohl stared with an expression that seemed to grip Schüb like a hook. Then angry laughter seeped from clenched lips. "I certainly hope not."

Schüb seemed to ignore the insult. "Eva Braun despised Bormann. She stayed with him simply out of necessity. She sought comfort, and found it, with persons other than him. Toward the end of her life, that comfort was sought with me."

Pohl's face turned bland as he listened.

"She only carried the babies to term because she knew they were mine, not Bormann's. She told me immediately after she became pregnant. There was no doubt. I only stayed with the bastard, after she died, because of your brother. He was my son and I owed it to him to protect him from that monster. Unfortunately, I did not do a good job and he died anyway. Then I was forced to deal with you."

Schüb pointed at the smaller tomb.

"That child was a darling. He did not deserve to die so young. But there is something I never told you. At birth, when Bormann saw there were twins, he made a decision. I always told you that was because of the times, and caring for two infants in Africa would have been difficult. He told you that himself. But what he failed to mention was that he *kept* one. The other he *discarded*."

"I was sent to Germany to be raised a German. That's what both you and he said."

"Another lie told to a child not to hurt his feelings. You were the one he did not want. Until, of course, your brother died."

"You are a liar," Pohl declared. "A total and complete liar."

"I wish that I were. But there are tests today that can confirm our DNA link without question. In the beginning, when you were younger, I came to actually like you. But as you became more like Bormann, I grew to detest the sight of you. You were, what, thirty when he died? A grown man who'd become him. Sadly, though I wish with all my heart it were not true, you are my issue, not his."

Pohl seemed to be searching for the right words with which to respond. Schüb did not give him a chance to reply and turned toward her.

"And you, my dear, you have perhaps the worst fate of all. Where this wretched soul"—he motioned to Pohl—"has been granted a political reprieve regarding his father, you have the unenviable distinction of being the daughter of perhaps one of the most horrible human beings ever to live."

A wave of vertigo swept through her as his words took hold and the reality again rushed past.

"Those same DNA tests can confirm that connection, too. I am truly sorry because, from everything I have read, you seem to be a decent person, with a good heart, who has led this nation admirably." His voice was heavy with emotion. "Unfortunately, that will matter not. Your genes will doom you to eternal persecution."

Her mind was a numbed blur of anguish. She knew that what Gerhard Schüb had just said was true. The man she thought her father had deceived her. The man she thought she'd loved as her husband, at least once a long time ago, had also deceived her. Even fate itself seemed to have abandoned her.

She was the daughter of Adolf Hitler.

Pohl had gone strangely silent. He stood near the largest of the sarcophagi, the one that held Bormann.

"You should not have deceived me, old man," Pohl finally said, in nearly a whisper.

"Why not? Your entire life has been a lie. Nothing about you is true. You are pure fiction."

She heard footsteps and turned to see Cassiopeia Vitt and Cotton Malone enter the chamber. Both carried guns.

Marie asked Cassiopeia, "What happened?"

"Engle is dead."

"Good," Schüb said. "He killed Isabel. Ada will be pleased." The German motioned toward Pohl. "Meet the man who has been leading you around the world. Thankfully, you were able to leap a step ahead and discover the truth without him ever knowing."

Marie noticed something in Malone's eyes that years of judging other people's reactions had taught her. "You know about me, don't you?"

Malone nodded. "In a Swiss vault, I read a journal entry penned by Bormann that confirms how Eva Braun made her way from Germany to Spain. Then how you were given to Albert Herzog after your birth. Combined with Schüb's firsthand knowledge, I would say there is no doubt. You are Hitler's daughter."

Cassiopeia stared at her with astonishment. "That's what all this was about?"

"Apparently everyone knew," Marie said, "but me."

Malone stepped forward. "The question now seems to be, what's to be done?"

"It is quite simple," Schüb said as he reached beneath his coat and produced a pistol. The old man aimed directly at Pohl, who stood three meters away, and fired three times. The bullets sent Pohl staggering back toward the journals. With each exit wound, the glass that fronted the shelves shattered. Schüb leveled the gun again and sent two more bullets into his son's skull. Pohl said nothing, the attack coming too quick for him to react, and his eyes went blank as the life left him. His legs then gave way and his body crumpled to the floor, ending atop shards of bloody glass.

No one moved.

Schüb tossed the gun to the floor. "I have ended the problem that I helped start. There will be no more resurrections."

CHAPTER
SEVENTY-EIGHT

COTTON STARED AT SCHÜB. HE'D JUST WITNESSED A MURDER THAT ordinarily would have repulsed him, but he was glad.

"No more resurrections."

Schüb was right.

It needed to end, and death was the only way to ensure that result. Though not linked genetically, Pohl, like Bormann, possessed a survival instinct that, above all, dominated his every thought. True, the world had changed, but in many ways it remained the same as eighty-five years ago. Hate still existed. Bigotry could be manipulated. The masses were gullible. But at least one master of political misdirection was no longer a problem.

"We need to leave," Cassiopeia finally said to Marie.

Schüb stepped from the chamber, back out into the gallery beyond. Kurt Eisenhuth moved toward his wife and reached for her arm.

She jerked away.

"Stay away from me," she said. "Don't ever touch me again. Is that clear?" Kurt started to say something, but she waved him off. "Leave. Now."

Her commands seemed more like pleading.

Seemingly resigned to his fate, Kurt Eisenhuth walked away. Only he, Cassiopeia, and the chancellor were left in the chamber.

"I wish to be alone," Marie said.

"We need to go," Cassiopeia said again.

Marie shook her head. "Your duties are over. I no longer require your services. Please express my thanks to Danny for all his help."

"There will be repercussions from what has happened," Cassiopeia said.

"I am sure there will. They do not concern me."

Her comment was colored by sadness and regret.

Cotton was beginning to understand. "It's over for you, too."

Her hands gripped the marble of Eva Braun's tomb in a tight embrace. "It is. I am the daughter of Adolf Hitler. Do you know how many would relish that fact? I would be their idol to worship. Those who stupidly believe that he was some sort of great statesman. And believe me, there are a sizable lot of Germans who quietly think just that." She surveyed them with an insolent look. "Even you two. When you look at me, you think of him, don't you?"

He could not lie. "I do. But I also see you, and I think of what you represent. You are quite different from him."

"Unfortunately, few will make that distinction. I will forever be *his* daughter. The product of him and Eva Braun, the disgusting whore who resides right here, beneath this marble. And make no mistake, that was what she was. A whore, pure and simple. She profited from the blood of millions, all the while professing love for the maniac who engineered it all. I have no desire to harbor her genes, either."

"What do you plan to do?" Cassiopeia asked. "Resign from the race. Walk away?"

Marie stepped across the chamber and found the gun Gerhard Schüb had tossed away. She lifted it from the floor. "I intend to do as Herr Schüb has just done and end the problem."

Cassiopeia seemed astonished. "You can't be serious?"

"I am quite serious. Sadly, my father was a Nazi. I've denied that fact all my life. But that's what he was. For him to raise Adolf Hitler's daughter would have been regarded, by him, as a great honor. And that disgusts me."

Cotton watched the chancellor's face, which was a shifting kaleidoscope of intense emotion. There comes a time when everything must end. His military career. Government service. Marriage. Life in Georgia. All those moments came for him. Now the woman standing before him, the leader of eighty-three million Germans, was making a choice of her own, one with far more at stake.

But a choice nonetheless.

He stepped close and reached for the gun. His eyes told her that he wasn't going to stop her. In fact, he wanted to help. She handed him the weapon. He popped the magazine and noted it was empty.

Schüb had used all of the rounds.

He handed her his gun.

"*Bitte,* Herr Malone. Hopefully, history will treat me kindly."

"I have no doubt."

She threw him a weak smile. "That is most kind." Then she let out a long breath and seemed to steel herself, her former defiance shifting into resolve. "Now if you could leave me. I need to do this in my own way. Alone."

He turned and headed for the door, motioning for Cassiopeia to come. She did not argue. There was no point.

They left and he gently eased the wooden door closed.

Schüb and Kurt Eisenhuth were waiting at the opposite end of the twisting gallery, where the spiral staircase started up through rock. Each withdrawn into their separate contemplations.

"Where is Marie?" Kurt asked.

"She is tending to some business," he told him.

"What kind of business could she have in there?"

"The kind that should have been handled long ago," Schüb said.

The old man apparently knew what was happening.

"Ironic, really," Schüb said. "When I concocted a scenario a few years ago to divert some prying eyes, I envisioned a similar ending. It just wasn't consummated then. All an act. A show. But now—"

A shot thudded, like a balloon popping beneath a blanket.

"What was that?" Kurt wanted to know.

Cotton envisioned the scene in the chamber beyond, the despair of acknowledgment welling up inside him. Marie Eisenhuth had done exactly as her natural father. She'd ended her life with her own hand. The difference, though, between the two was startling. Where Hitler died a coward to avoid the repercussions from the misery he'd wrought, the daughter took her life in an act of bravery. Normally suicide would be deemed a weakness, the result of a sick mind or an abandoned heart. Here it was the only logical means to stop something that had been started long ago.

Everything had a conclusion.

National Socialism. Fanatical politics. Campaigns. Careers.

Life, itself.

So he replied to Kurt Eisenhuth's inquiry—*What was that?*—with the truth.

"Das ende," he whispered.

The end.

CHAPTER SEVENTY-NINE

Cotton stepped from the car.

It had been two weeks since Marie Eisenhuth's death. To the south, visible miles away, the jagged peak of the Zugspitze stabbed an azure sky. Müncher Haus at the top of the mountain was indistinguishable from the snow-clad granite folds. He was at the far end of a valley, north of Garmisch, in a cemetery beside Kloster Egern abbey. There weren't many graves, only those for the solitary monks who'd died in service to their church, and a few choice spots for those who'd been especially generous to the Benedictines.

Like the Herzogs.

Albert Herzog, his wife, and his adopted daughter were now all there.

Deep in the Bavarian soil.

He stuffed his hands into his coat pockets and started to walk through the graves, following a path that wound its way up a modest incline. Cassiopeia walked beside him. The state funeral had been attended by dignitaries from around the world. The nation had mourned *Oma* with a genuine sense of loss. The actual interment had been here, in a simple ceremony. There'd been no way to disguise any of what happened, not with both candidates for the German chancellorship dead, one murdered, the other dead by her own hand.

So the world had been told the truth.

No detail was omitted.

All of Bormann's and Braun's journals were released for inspection, the underground chamber at Löwenberg opened for photographers, the Swiss vaults exposed, the gold confiscated. DNA testing had confirmed all of the parentages. Schüb had made available all of the funds he still controlled, including the gold, which totaled into the billions of euros. Danny Daniels had appeared before the press and told the entire story. The credibility of a former president of the United States only added to its validity. Judging from the initial reaction, history was perhaps going to be kind to Marie Eisenhuth. She was being labeled a victim, unaware her entire life of the genes that dwelled inside her. Innocent of profiting off Nazi plunder. All regretted that she chose to die, but understood given the circumstances.

They approached the grave, the replaced earth dark, as if moist, a simple granite marker noting Marie Eisenhuth's full name and a simple epitaph in German. OMA, LEADER OF GERMANY FOR 16 YEARS.

They stood in silence and absorbed the moment.

"It's a shame," Cassiopeia said.

He agreed, but had to add, "Unfortunately, the stain of the past was too indelible."

"She did not deserve that fate."

No, she had not. A life of reason, ideals, and purpose had shifted in the blink of an eye into vengeance, fanaticism, and destiny. He thought of Voltaire's words. *Often the prudent, far from making their destinies, succumb to them. It is destiny which makes them prudent.*

Gerhard Schüb had once again disappeared. No mention was made that he'd killed Theodor Pohl. That had been deemed best since what to do with him might have proven vexing. He wasn't exactly a war criminal, but he wasn't a bystander, either. He'd killed Pohl in cold blood. But a trial would only aggravate an already open sore. So they'd concocted a lie that Josef Engle murdered Pohl, Cotton killed Engle, and Marie Eisenhuth killed herself. Better to leave her death a suicide, as it cemented the already growing sentiment that she carried no blame for anything. Kurt Eisenhuth, though a witness to it all, had remained silent and pledged that he always would. He mourned his wife and regretted his mistakes, preferring now simply to be left alone.

Danny Daniels had been most appreciative, thanking them repeatedly and assuring them both that he owed them.

Big time.

That he did.

Of course, they could have walked away at any moment, but neither one of them had. It wasn't their nature. And as much as he hated the risks, he loved the challenge and, secretly, he'd been grateful for the opportunity to play the game one more time. Stephanie Nelle once told him, *Even if you're down you can recover, as long as you're in the game.*

Damn right.

One thing was certain, though.

Everything ended with Marie Eisenhuth's death.

Time had finally cleansed the world of all the demented souls Germany had spawned during the 1930s and '40s. Those original participants were all dead. The legacy disgraced. The last vestige of some grandiose scheme now lying in the grave before him.

He thought back to 1933.

A Sunday in August when the German people were asked to elect a new leader. As in every election since, including the one that was now stalled, the voting was preceded by a cacophony of rhetoric, the tone then urging everyone to elect Adolf Hitler. What was lost from Hitler's victory that Sunday, what history notes only in footnotes, was that four million Germans said *nein.* He marveled at the courage it took for those four million, doubtful of their future and afraid of retribution, to vote no.

Yet they had.

"Time to go," he said.

He turned and started back to the car.

Cassiopeia walked beside him.

She looked lovely, her dark hair pulled back. He hadn't liked her when they first met, her haughty allure too much trouble for a man his age. But he'd come to know that she was a good woman. Being with her was a pleasure. Thankfully, she wasn't the type who required constant stroking.

Neither was he, for that matter.

They made it back to the car, and he took in the scene from the precipice. Mountains ringed the horizon to the south. Pinewoods framed spent fields, and a lake shimmered in the bright sun. The air was clean and fresh, as if nature were signaling that all of the maladies from the past were gone and a new day had arrived. In a few months winter would blanket everything with snow, then spring would remove the white shroud allowing, once again, the sun to work its magic.

A cycle.

As clear there as in politics.

Good, then bad, then good, then more bad, more good.

He remembered telling Stephanie when he retired that he was fed up with the nonsense. A change in habits must surely lead to a change of thoughts. There had to be a calmer place. She'd smiled at his naïveté and promptly explained that so long as the earth was inhabited by people, there would be no calm place. The game was the same everywhere: Only the players changed, not the rules, not the stakes, not the risks—only the players.

And again she was right.

He reached for the door handle and opened Cassiopeia's door.

Before she climbed inside, he drew her close. She laid her hands against his chest, sliding them upward around his neck, placing her face in the hollow of his shoulder.

Which felt really good.

In her ear, he whispered, "I love you."

WRITER'S NOTE

This book took advantage of the many trips Elizabeth and I have made to Germany, Austria, and Switzerland. I did not travel to Chile or South Africa. One day we'll make it there, but others I know did visit both and I was able to learn a great deal from them. Overall, though, the various locales in the novel—Cologne, the Chilean lake district, Santiago, Hesse, Bremen, the Free State, Worms, Munich, Frankfurt, and Lugano—are faithfully represented. Astute readers will notice a similarity between this novel and *The Devil's Gold,* a novella I published in 2011. That story was then intended as a lead-in to my novel *The Jefferson Key,* introducing the character Jonathan Wyatt. But I always planned for that novella to serve a double duty, becoming a prequel to another tale entirely.

That story is this one.

Time now to separate fact from fiction.

The swastika described in chapter 6 is based on one that existed in a remote pine forest of northeastern Germany, the trees planted sometime around 1938. Eventually they matured and each autumn revealed themselves in a distinct shape, only from the air, in multicolor. They were first noticed in 1992 and eventually destroyed in 2000.

All of the details regarding German elections (chapters 12 and 35) are accurate. Their political system is quite different from that in the United States.

The plane crash described in chapter 38 happened, just not on June 14, but on September 8, 1974, a direct result of a terrorist's bomb.

The book *Five Love Languages* exists (chapter 13). Written by Gary Chapman, it was first published in 1992 and became a #1 *New York Times* hit. It remains popular, still appearing, from time to time, on the best-seller lists (Elizabeth and I have also taken the quiz at the end, with results similar to those of Cotton and Cassiopeia).

Dachau is located just north of Munich and was Hitler's first concentration camp. All of the information detailed in chapter 21, including the newspaper accounts, the support local Germans showed for the camp, the contempt some of them showed for the prisoners, and the books denying the Holocaust are real.

The various letters from the Orange Free State depicting life there in the 1940s and '50s were taken from actual accounts (chapters 29, 33, and 39).

The tale of what happened inside the Führerbunker (chapter 8) is based on historical record. It's important to note that we will never know exactly what happened there. All of the eyewitnesses later contradicted one another, and many later totally recanted their statements. The most definitive source, Hugh Trevor-Roper's *Last Days of Hitler* (1947), is flawed. Roper relied heavily on war reports filed by British, American, and Canadian intelligence officers. He never interviewed anyone who'd actually been in the bunker, save for a few German detainees in American custody, who had every reason to lie. He also had no access to the Soviet archives, which only became available after 1991. Subsequent investigations have shown that much of what Trevor-Roper reported may not be correct.

Did Hitler die in the bunker?

Some say no.

I went with yes for this novel. But the addition of a blue dress that was wet, then dry, is purely my invention (chapter 8). The presence of *das Leck,* a Soviet spy supposedly inside the bunker, has been postulated by historians for decades (chapter 64). I decided to agree with them. It would certainly explain how Stalin knew for certain that Hitler was dead.

The Russians were indeed the first to take the Führerbunker in May 1945. They supposedly found the charred bodies of Hitler and Eva Braun buried in the Chancellery courtyard. Hitler's dentist, Hugo Blaschke, a dental assistant named Käthe Heusermann, and a dental technician named Fritz Echtmann confirmed that the teeth belonged to Hitler and Braun. But that's all according to the Soviets. No documents or other physical evidence to support that conclusion has survived. The Soviets then secretly buried the remains in Magdeburg, East Germany, along with the bodies of Joseph and Magda Goebbels and their six children. Twenty-five years later, on April 4, 1970, a KGB team exhumed five wooden boxes from the site. Those were then burned and crushed, after which the ashes were thrown into the Biederitz River.

Why was this necessary?

No one knows.

What is known is that Stalin continually misled the West, asserting that Hitler had escaped and was on the run. That fear kept everyone off guard. We also know that the FBI and the fledgling American intelligence agencies of the time actively searched for Hitler across the globe. In 2000 a skull fragment (chapter 10), supposedly belonging to Hitler, surfaced in Moscow. But DNA testing in 2009 revealed that it was from a woman, not a man. Could it have been Eva Braun? Not likely, since there is no evidence that she was shot in the head and the skull possessed a clear bullet hole. So to this day there is no definitive evidence that Hitler or Braun died on April 30, 1945. An excellent book on this entire subject is *Grey Wolf* by Simon Dunstan and Gerrard Williams.

The presence of Nazi memorabilia both in South America and inside Theodor Pohl's castle is nothing unusual (chapters 22 and 72). A great deal of it still exists. As do collectors. In June 2017 a cache of seventy-five rare Nazi mementos was found within a secret room in a Buenos Aires suburb (chapter 19). The find included a memorial dagger, a framed medallion emblazoned with Hitler in bas-relief, commemorative statues, medals, awards, concentration camp products (chapter 75), photographs, and an impressive bust of the Führer himself. Part of the collection also included a pair of head calipers, its handle bejeweled with a black-on-white swastika, used in the determination of so-called Aryan skull shapes.

Martin Bormann remains a mystery. All of the background on him detailed in the novel is true (chapters 9, 10, 20, and 64), as is the label of the Brown Eminence (chapter 25). He definitely fled the Führerbunker after Hitler's suicide. One account says he was killed in Berlin, his body lost in the rubble, eventually unearthed in 1972 (chapter 10). He was legally declared dead in 1973 with the qualification that his death *had not been completely established* (chapter 19). DNA testing on the remains that were found happened in 1998. Supposedly the tests confirmed that they were Bormann. But all of that was during the early days of DNA analysis when the science was young and, strangely, the bones were destroyed in 1999, the ashes scattered in the Baltic Sea (chapter 10), preventing any subsequent retesting.

Bormann and Eva Braun's escape from the Führerbunker (chapters 20 and 54) is wholly my invention. The Bormann sightings noted in chapter 19 are based on actual accounts. In fact, those incidents became commonplace in the 1950s and '60s. Whether Martin Bormann survived the war is still a matter of debate. But undeniably, he did control the Nazi purse strings. He also engineered Project Land of Fire and Project Eagle Flight (chapters 10, 26, and 54), along with managing Hitler's Bounty, more formally called the Fund of German Business (chapter 22). Contributions to that were the price corporations paid for the ability to profit from the Third Reich. So much money was accumulated that, by 1945, Hitler was the richest man in Europe. Many German corporations reaped huge rewards from supplying the German war effort. Some even employed slave labor, and an astonishing number of those corporations survive today. In addition, many foreign entities routinely did business with the Third Reich. For example, during the war Sweden sold Germany iron ore and ball bearings, all paid for in gold or Swiss francs. Switzerland became a conduit for money laundering, its privacy laws and numbered accounts Hitler's salvation. Incredibly, even American entities and banks traded with Germany, right up until 1942 when Congress finally outlawed it.

The meeting in France on August 10, 1944, between Bormann's representative and German businessmen happened (chapter 26). Afterward, massive amounts of cash, precious metals, gems, patents, and other assets were funneled from Germany to South America. Bormann created nearly a thousand foreign companies, most in neutral countries like Portugal, Spain, Sweden, Turkey, and Switzerland. Over a hundred were in Argentina alone. All were used to both launder and harbor assets. Germans themselves also fled across the Atlantic to South America, both during and after the war, many settling in Argentina and Chile (chapter 27). Today nearly four million of the forty-five million people in Argentina have a German origin.

Lago Girasol (chapter 33) is my invention, but there are many lakes like it in southern Chile. The house described in chapter 34 is also fictional, but it is based on the Inalco residence located near the town of San Carlos de Bariloche in Argentina. This is a ten-bedroom mansion near the Chilean border, on a lake, hidden from view by two small islands that each contain guard towers.

Doesn't sound like your typical vacation home.

Patagonia has long been a German refuge. Thousands immigrated there in the early part of the 20th century. About one and a half times the size of Texas, bordered on one side by the Andes and on the other the South Atlantic, by 1939 sixty thousand Germans lived there. Nazi Party membership files captured after the war showed a hundred thousand members in Argentina alone. The southern tip of Patagonia is called Tierra del Fuego, Spanish for "land of fire." So it was no coincidence that Bormann named his plan to launder money and assets out of Germany, Project Land of Fire. The idea was to create a secret, self-contained refuge in an out-of-the-way place. Bormann wanted no repeat of 1929, when Germany was pillaged and decimated. He wanted all of the wealth safeguarded. It helped that Juan Perón rose to power in Argentina during the early 1940s, as Perón was friendly toward the Germans. By 1942 every nation in North and South America had severed relations with Japan, Germany, and Italy, except Chile and Argentina (though Argentina, at least on paper, finally did in 1944).

The town of San Carlos de Bariloche became the center of their safe haven. To this day the whole place oozes an Alpine look and feel. We know that after 1945 several war criminals called it home, and a persistent rumor is that Hitler and Eva Braun escaped to there, too, living for a while in the Inalco residence.

Is that possible?

We'll never know.

Eva Braun is another mysterious character—Hitler's mistress who eventually, for a few hours, became his wife. All of her background in the story, including the nickname Evi, is real (chapters 20 and 27). She was a mere footnote to the history around her, but still a key player in an evil game. She detested Bormann and liked to make fun of him behind his back (chapter 54). She never birthed any children, though. But even in the face of the approaching Russian army, she did willingly return to Berlin on April 15, 1945. Why? No one knows. And whether she survived the war will forever remain an unanswered question.

This novel deals with the rise of the new right across Europe. It's a troubling issue, one that continues to escalate (chapter 64). Incidents of violence and how local courts and law enforcement turn a blind eye (chapter 18) are not fiction. Anger toward Jews and immigrants is steadily increasing (chapter 57). Nationalistic parties across the Continent are gaining more and more followers.

Why is this happening?

A number of factors are contributing.

The greatest mass movement of humanity since the beginning of the 20th century, refugees from Eastern Europe, Turkey, Africa, and the Middle East, has placed an enormous strain on resources. A decade of little to no European economic growth has only added to the frustration, as has the failure of the old social welfare state. A generation of strong leaders are aging and dying off, their places taken by less competent populists who have a growing disillusionment with the European Union. They argue that the EU is no longer a place of peace, prosperity, cooperation, and harmony.

And many are agreeing.

Which has made it easy to spur the rise of nationalism.

Compounding this is widespread voter apathy and an inherent inability of government to counter extremism.

So instead of fading away, fanatics prosper.

Sadly, memories of World War II, the Holocaust, and the gulags fade by the day. New-right leaders promise a return to the strong welfare state of the past, but with the caveat that it be ethnically and racially bound. They spew forth a range of patriarchal, racist, and homophobic ideas, each made more palatable by wrapping those concepts in racial purity and national honor.

And they are winning elections.

Even more important, they are framing issues.

And the old wisdom is correct.

He who frames an issue, wins that issue more often than not.

Sadly, what Hitler said so long ago still rings true today.

> *The masses have little time to think.*
> *And how incredible is the willingness of modern man to believe.*